MW01125444

"In a city that demands nu
precision. Each character's
each one as complex and r

— Aaron Foley, Chief Storyteller, City of Detroit and author, *How to Live in Detroit Without Being a Jackass*

"Cinematic, lyrical, and unflinchingly raw, *Awaiting Identification* is both a love letter to Detroit and a cautionary tale. If you're looking for a fresh new voice in fiction, R.J. Fox is the real deal."

— Camille Pagán, bestselling author of *Life and Other Near-Death Experiences*

"*Awaiting Identification* opens on Devil's Night . . . and why not? This book isn't waiting on anyone. It races forward, driven by attitude and suspense. Here is a world fully formed, a novel that puts you deep inside its characters as they confront Detroit in all its perverse, gritty glory."

— Scott Lasser, author, *Say Nice Things About Detroit*

"At first, reading R.J. Fox's *Awaiting Identification*, I had intimations of Elmore Leonard meets Donald Goines. But that impression was fleeting and soon I was caught in Fox's own unique lyrical style and a scenario that keeps you engrossed. Seeping between his lines as well as background to his ensemble of doomed characters is Detroit's industrial pulse, which Fox expresses with a profound intimacy. Throughout *Awaiting Identification* there is a cinematic quality that is enhanced by fresh, spiky dialogue and literary cachet."

— Herb Boyd, author of *Black Detroit: A People's History of Self-Determination*

"R.J. Fox is a writer of great talent and skill. In *Awaiting Identification*, he carefully guides his readers through the mean streets and back alleys of contemporary Detroit. The reader is brought along on an urban mystery into the 'heart of darkness.' A rich and suspenseful narrative that will keep the reader anxiously turning each page. Fox is a wonderful writer who truly knows Detroit and how to tell a damn fine tale."

— M. L. Liebler, award-winning Detroit-based poet and editor

"R.J. Fox is a master of dialogue—a sharpshooter who sends out blasts of words that never miss the mark. *Awaiting Identification* hits readers with the sights, sounds and smells of Detroit as five lost souls travel its streets in search of human connection. It is loud, bold and insightful— everything you want in a story that stays with you even after you have torn yourself away."

— Karen Dybis, author, *The Witch of Delray*

"A triumph! *Awaiting Identification* is the keen-for-a-brawl bastard child of *Last Exit to Brooklyn*. Superbly crafted characters and a fetid Detroit I could sniff from the page."

— Ian Thornton, author, *The Great & Calamitous Tale of Johan Thoms*

"Fox weaves together five gritty tales of love, loss, despair, and hope—all set to a throbbing Detroit underground techno beat. As the characters cross paths, you get the sense that there is something more at play here and what lies beneath the underground is not all that it seems. Fox paints a picture with words so vivid, you feel the cold and weary bleakness of the night and the warm glow of the approaching dawn."

— Sean Deason, Matrix Records, Detroit

"1990s Detroit was a forgotten city, with a forgotten history, and forgotten people. In *Awaiting Identification*, R.J. Fox masterfully imagines five of those Detroiters, creating in stark, gut-punch prose, the stories that give them life. *Awaiting Identification* weaves the desperation and decimation of the city with the funk, resilience, and hard-luck histories of its too-often ignored inhabitants."

— Lori Tucker-Sullivan, Detroit-based essayist

"R.J. Fox has composed a cinematic ode to the gritty streets of Detroit, while seamlessly weaving together the doomed journeys of an entire cast of downtrodden characters. At once, Fox proves he is deeply in tune with the chaos and the glory of the Motor City, and that he is decidedly adept at tying together delightfully loose strands of character until they culminate in a unified package that is both haunting and powerful."

— Frank Morelli, author, *No Sad Songs*

"Fox deftly intertwines stories of the tumultuous last hours of several desperate Detroiters. Though from the start he makes no secret of their deaths on Devil's Night, he makes their harrowing journeys through the city streets fascinating and their unwillingness to abandon hope compelling. Fox also makes the Detroit of another era into a lively, struggling character in its own right."

— John G. Rodwan, Jr., co-author, *Detroit Is: An Essay in Photographs*

"This fast-paced, enervating novel, pays homage to Detroit, while telling the stories of characters who long to rise from the ashes of their own lives, some with more success than others; all with moments of much-needed hope and redemption."

— Kelly Fordon, author, *Garden for the Blind*

AWAITING

IDENTIFICATION

Published by Fish Out of Water Books, Ann Arbor, MI, USA.

www.fowbooks.com

© 2018 by R.J. Fox.

ISBN: 978-0-9899087-6-4

Library of Congress Control Number: 2018930204

Pop culture · coming of age · culture shock · going against the grain ·
adversity · triumph · extraordinary lives · ordinary lives ·
non-fiction - creative non-fiction - realistic fiction.

Michigan via Manchester, England.

We are all fish out of water.

We publish non-fiction, creative non-fiction, and realistic fiction.

For further information, visit www.fowbooks.com.

Cover design by J. Caleb Clark; www.jcalebdesign.com.

AWAITING

IDENTIFICATION

R.J. Fox

Fish Out of Water Books

www.fowbooks.com

For Lillian and Bobby.
Never stop dreaming.

~Introit ~

"Speramus Meliora: Resurget Cineribus."
"We Hope for Better Days: It Shall Rise from Its Ashes"

— City of Detroit motto, created after a fire destroyed
most of the city on June 11, 1805.

~Requiem Aeternam~

October 31, 1999
Halloween

Wayne County Medical Examiner's Office: Detroit, MI

Jane Doe: "NYC Girl." A badly bruised and bloodied female. Late-20's. Pregnant. "I Love NYC" medallion. Severe head trauma. Multiple fractures. Laceration on left hand.

John Doe #1: "Leaf Man." Bloated. Mid-20's male with a gunshot wound to the chest. Marijuana leaf ring on right ring finger.

John Doe #2: "R.I.P." Late-30's male. Obese. Barely decipherable "R.I.P." tattoo etched on left bicep.

John Doe #3: "Zealot." A mid-40's male. Thin. Pale. Multiple stab wounds to the chest. A cross-shaped scar across his torso.

John Doe #4: "Cat Man." Late-50's male. Scraggly, peppered beard. No obvious sign of physical trauma. Smile etched onto face.

The Night Before — Devil's Night

NYC GIRL

1

NYC Girl stepped off the now vacant bus that had been her prison for the past twenty hours.

"You take care out there, okay?" the driver said, a split second before she turned her ankle on the broken concrete.

Welcome home.

As she surveyed her surroundings, Detroit felt almost as unfamiliar as the numerous boondock stops throughout Pennsylvania and Ohio that she had passed through in and out of consciousness.

She bent down to rub her ankle, grabbed her suitcase, and glanced around the empty bus terminal as though she were expecting a welcoming committee. But despite her brief self-delusion, NYC Girl understood one simple truth: nobody was expecting her.

I'm a ghost

In fact, not a single soul even knew she had returned home from her seven-year Big Apple experiment. At one point, she would have preferred it this way. But not now. Not even close. And what did "home" even mean now?

Seven — fucking — years.

Seven years of rejections and wrong turns.

So fitting that it all began with a nasty argument between a daughter and her coked-up mother over dirty dishes, followed by a broken mirror while frantically packing for a fresh start, on the heels of a vanished "mercy" scholarship for graduating from the school of hard knocks. Despite her flaws and the endless roadblocks, she somehow managed to keep her grades up. Before she simply threw it all away.

Life had been a conveyor belt of bad luck ever since. There wasn't a day that had gone by when she didn't replay that scene in her head. If only she had tried to be the better person and just washed the fucking dishes.

Would her life have turned out differently? Or, was that simply just the straw that broke the camel's back? After all, the dam of built-up resentment can only hold water for so long before it bursts.

And rather than picking up the pieces and trying to make things right, she did the "easier" thing.

She fled.

Her homecoming felt like self-surrender. But it was time.

Time to make things right. A return to starting position. Sometimes a fresh start means returning back to where you started, before you begin anew.

How in the hell had it been seven years?

She wanted to believe that her luck was about to turn, but she knew better. Her whole life was a shattered mirror. Fractured shards of glass interlaced with sharp, invisible slivers.

But that certainly wasn't going to stop her from trying to sweep up the mess. She was never one to quit, and she sure as hell wasn't going to start now. On the other hand, it would have been the logical thing to do.

Now that she had found the guts to return home, she wished she had a better idea as to where her life was headed.

For the majority of her ride aboard the sweatbox of a Greyhound bus, she was convinced that she had it all figured out. But by the time the bus had entered the Detroit city limits, her thoughts had begun to waver. One thing was clear: she needed food and shelter.

But when your only option isn't really an option . . .

NYC Girl was getting ahead of herself. What she needed more than anything was rest. But where?

I just have to get through the night.

And then, maybe, just maybe, she would finally see things more clearly.

Without doubt, she would need a concrete plan beyond tonight. She had to find work. She would rather die of starvation than turn another trick for a lukewarm meal and bed.

She smelled fire in the distance and was struck by how oddly comforting it felt.

Home sweet home.

And then she remembered the date: October 30.

Devil's Night.

Detroit's unofficial holiday.

This time on the cusp of a new millennium.

Though she no longer believed in God, she had no doubt that these were end times.

Her childhood was apparently alive and well, despite a recent citywide counter-initiative known as Angels' Night, aimed to thwart an epidemic of Devil's Night arson, of which once upon a time she had been a willing participant. Or was it guilt by association?

Let the motherfucker burn.

But then where would she go?

She needed a restroom. Again. A natural, irritating side effect of the unwanted, bastard parasite she was carrying. Adorned in knock-off gray and pink-trimmed workout clothes, she dragged her rolling suitcase and headed inside the Greyhound building—which appeared to function more like a halfway house. It smelled of piss, shit, and vomit.

If any of the few, scattered bums happened to look up from their own misery, they would have seen someone who—in a different lifetime— could have been a model, a dancer, or a Broadway star. It wouldn't have been a stretch. After all, that *was* her plan. But in NYC Girl's dark, lonely corner of the universe, the spotlight only shone on the unpolished poles of seedy strip clubs.

She made her way toward the restroom door.

Locked.

Seriously?

She approached a ticket clerk, who was asleep with her head propped up by an ashy, callused hand.

"Excuse me…" she began, startling the clerk awake.

NYC Girl was equally jarred by the sound of her own voice.

When had she last spoken?

"I need to use the restroom."

"It's locked," the clerk said with a disdainful yawn.

"Well, can it be *un*locked?"

"No."

What the fuck?

All she wanted was a toilet—and preferably one that wasn't coated in disease. Goddamn fucking drug dealers and rapists. They ruin everything.

She would have to wait. As she headed toward the exit, she passed a man jacking off in an empty row of chairs.

This was her welcome committee.

Fuck this place.

She headed outside onto the broken, familiar streets of her youth.

From a distance, one might assume that a beautiful city filled with promise was on the horizon. Detroit always looked best from afar.

It was all one, grand illusion. Once upon a time, she thought she could find her utopia in New York. Never has she been more wrong.

Rainbow smoke billowed out of smokestacks above dirty, stained civilization, in tandem with scattered, half-lit skyscrapers aglow like orange embers in the night—anchored by the massive, not-quite-as-promised Renaissance Center. She was waiting for her own, personal renaissance.

Waiting to mend the broken pieces of her life.

A phoenix of the night in a world afire.

She boarded a city bus en route to the only home she knew prior to New York. She took her usual seat at the back of the bus and immediately felt something squishy beneath her foot.

A used condom.

She nudged it loose with the broken heel of her sidewalk-ravaged shoe and shoved it until it was hidden beneath her seat.

Her preference for the back row was a safety measure—to be able to see everyone ahead of her, rather than wonder who might be lurking behind.

NYC Girl struggled to wrap her head around the fact that she was back in the place she vowed to turn her back on forever when she charged out of her house, suitcase in hand, toward a smoke and mirror-coated dream that had quickly turned into a nightmare.

And now. Back to the place where her dream was first born.

Once upon a time, a little girl with big dreams danced in a pink tutu. If only she could go back in time and beg herself to give it all up before it was too late, before the damage was done.

If only . . .

Maybe then, she could have avoided boarding a bus that was in even worse condition than the one from which she had just escaped, headed to southwest Detroit.

At least this ride would be shorter.

NYC Girl noticed a few scattered construction cranes rising above the city skyline. She never remembered seeing a single crane during her childhood. They resembled the skeletal remains of dinosaurs, shrouded in smoke, juxtaposed against rows of abandoned buildings—tombstones of a bygone era.

An echo of an ancient civilization.

What could they possibly be building?

Yet, the nostalgic factor made the decay strangely comforting.

She realized that less than an hour ago, she was riding on this same stretch of road aboard the Greyhound bus, heading in the opposite direction.

Her life was an endless loop.

She clutched her faux gold and ruby-encrusted "I Love NYC" medallion with one hand and, with the other, her lower abdomen, where a new life grew—just like her mother almost thirty years prior.

The rotting apple doesn't fall far from the rotting family tree.

A tree that her mother gave two shits about, evident in an abundance of ways. After all, if you don't give a shit about your own offspring, why would you give two shits about the ancestors that came before?

For instance, even though her *abuela* had raised her mother to speak Spanish, her mother—despite NYC girl's pleading—had been too lazy or too strung out to teach her daughter any part of her heritage.

Most kids could give two shits about their heritage. And most parents practically have to force it upon their children. But not NYC Girl. She *wanted* to learn. To keep the past alive, before it could be erased from history altogether. Her mother, however, all but erased herself. It was up to NYC Girl to somehow find a way to carry the torch. To keep the past alive. Before it was fully erased. Before it became a ghost. Or nothing at all.

Meanwhile, NYC Girl was following the footsteps of her mother. But for all the wrong reasons. Just like her mother's situation, the father was a roulette wheel of possibilities.

The motherfucking circle of life.

The only evidence as to the identity of NYC Girl's own father could be found in her dark caramel complexion, several shades darker than her mother's Mexican DNA.

However, unlike her mother, NYC Girl refused to bring a child into a world of suffering. *That* would be the immoral choice.

Yet, she couldn't help but waver over what she had earlier considered a slam-dunk decision. Then again, is there such a thing when it comes to a matter such as this? She had thought so back in New York. But the closer she got to home, the murkier everything became. And whom better for a girl to discuss such matters than with her own mother?

The closer she drew toward her destination, the further her mind drifted from the certainty of her decision. The bottom line was, going home meant facing her greatest fear: *her mother.*

But who the fuck was she fooling? Even if she wanted advice from her mother, would she be available? And even if she were available, what kind of advice could she expect to find from someone who had been through countless abortions herself?

She had no choice but to make this decision on her own.

NYC Girl had not attempted to contact her mother during her seven-year exile. In fact, she had vowed never to talk to her again — just as she had vowed never to return to Detroit.

But if anybody knew anything about empty promises, it was her.

Had her mother tried to look for her? NYC Girl certainly didn't leave an address. Besides, there were so many, it wouldn't have made a difference. But in all likelihood, her mother never gave a shit.

Which was worse?

Every time she convinced herself that making amends was the right thing to do, she talked herself out of it. Partially out of stubbornness. But mostly out of fear.

But deep, deep down, no matter how hard she tried, she just couldn't shake the instinctual bond that could only exist between mother and daughter.

What hurt the most was the fact that her mother had so quickly severed the cord.

Though NYC Girl pretended not to care, she did wonder from time to time if her mother ever felt the remnants of their spiritual synapses.

Like a phantom limb.

NYC Girl could justify a child cutting ties with a parent—but not the other way around. Though it made leaving so much easier, it was this bond that had indirectly led to her slow, full-blown implosion.

Would her mother want to take her back? Did she even *want* her mother to take her back? Her biggest fear was being turned away at the doorstep. This led to the onset of a panic attack settling into every fiber of her being. To calm herself, she just had to remind herself that she didn't *have* to go through with it. She could choose to continue. Or she could choose to simply get the hell out.

The world was her motherfucking oyster.

But she wasn't fooling herself. She was only choking on its pearl.

She had returned to the rotten corpse of her childhood home; not because she wanted to, but because she felt like it was the *only* thing to do.

But was it?

She realized that a major reason for her apprehension stemmed from the fact that as long as she did not contact her mother, she could continue to perpetuate the illusion in her mother's mind that she was fine, thus proving her mother—and in some way, herself—wrong.

Besides, how does one tell their estranged mother news such as this?

"Hola mamá. No lo vas a creer. Vas a ser abuela! And no, I don't have a fucking clue as to who the father is. Just like you, right, mamá?!"

Her bus passed the hollowed-out ruins of the former Michigan Central Station, which stood tall like a gateway into hell. A land-dwelling, urban Titanic.

A lump formed in her throat as she passed beneath a railroad overpass onto the edge of Mexicantown. She knew she was getting closer to home—not just by sight, but by *smell.*

The bus finally reached her destination—Delray—which, like much of the city, had seen better days, but refused to go down without a fight.

Essentially isolated from other parts of Detroit, and in many ways a no-go area, Delray felt like a ghost town within a ghost town. Much of its population had moved out once big industry and a giant wastewater plant moved in, but a small number of residents showed their true grit by refusing to budge, still living amid squalor and the industrialization that had replaced people with belching smokestacks and an omnipresent stench.

Around the time NYC Girl had left town, you were more likely to encounter gang patrol than police patrol. Of course, NYC Girl had first-hand experience. It was almost impossible for a neighborhood kid to avoid it. Fuck a gang member and you're fucked for life.

But in this moment, there were no signs of human life, aside from the distant, haunting cries of trains, accompanied by the diesel driven rumble of semi trucks, rattling as they hit pothole after pothole. It all felt strangely comforting. It was the sound of *home*. And it was music to her ears.

Maybe things *were* better? Maybe *nobody* was left?

Looming in the distance along West Jefferson, she could see the industrial behemoth of Zug Island, a man-made island floating in the middle of the Detroit River.

A dystopian habitrail.

Zug Island's black towers resembled an enormous, scrambled pipe organ topped with orange and green flames, accompanied by a techno cacophony of clicks, clanks, bleeps and bloops of whirligigs, gremlins and what-not overlooking an industrial wasteland devoid of human existence.

A couple of blocks down Dearborn Street, in the heart of an old Hungarian enclave, NYC Girl plopped down on a graffiti-laden bench to pop the loose heel back into her shoe, chipping one of the long nails that she kept both for aesthetic and self-defense purposes.

At that moment, an all-too-recognizable refrain rang out behind her.

"Excuse me! Excuuuuse me!"

She immediately got up and walked on, not even bothering to turn around.

"I don't mean no harm," the voice continued, working off a familiar script as he closed in. "But I'm hungry. I'm homeless. Please, can you spare a little change to help a brother out?"

NYC Girl quickened her pace, certain that surrender was imminent. But he continued to nip at her heels. At least *he* wasn't giving up on her.

She could hear loose change in a cup. From the sound of it, it was very likely that he had more change on him than she did.

"Hey, sweetheart!"

She detested being called that—*by anyone*. He was lucky that she was too exhausted to let him have it.

"I got something for you, ma'am."

Please don't let it be his dick.

It wasn't. It was a tiny, paper American flag, hoisted on a toothpick, held by a homeless man with a slight limp who bore an uncanny resemblance to Redd Foxx.

Despite a constant twitch, he seemed harmless enough. She was smart enough to know that the moment she laid a finger on his flag, payment would be expected, a rule she understood all too well.

She tried to ignore him, but he waved the flag in her face, trying to force surrender. She bit her tongue to suppress her growing rage.

"Please, sweetheart. Help a vet," he begged, in an obvious ruse to fill a prescription from Dr. Smirnoff, Hennessey, or Colt.

She remained silent and held her ground.

"Well, have a nice evening, ma'am, and God Bless!" he said, waving his flag in self-surrender.

As he limped and twitched away, she realized she had more in common with him than she wanted to admit. Only, he had found a way to make money.

She had no place to call home . . . so, by definition, was homeless.

And all before the age of thirty.

At least she still had her faculties intact.

Or did she?

She had never been more in doubt of her own sanity.

As she continued to watch the drifter fade into the distance, she felt an unfamiliar twinge of compassion. She chalked it up to exhaustion.

She *used* to feel sorry for people like him—no matter how many shits life took on her. Now, having pity on them would mean feeling sorry for herself—which she absolutely refused.

She now realized that the embers of empathy still burned deep inside. It reminded her that she still had a soul—or, at least, the charred remnants of one.

The remnants that mattered most.

Her only belongings were jammed into her tattered, secondhand rolling suitcase with a busted wheel that trailed behind her on the crumbling concrete of Vernor.

She wished that desperation wasn't a factor in her decision to return home. Even though she felt it was the right thing to do, she still wasn't fully convinced it was what she *wanted* to do.

No matter how things had transpired with her mother, she tried to take solace in the fact that coming home was a *giant* first step.

But in what direction?

She was in the heart of one of the most dangerous and most polluted zipcodes in the nation. However, it was so deserted, it was difficult to imagine anything left for criminals to pillage or plunder. She probably had a better chance of being attacked by wild dogs than being mugged. From as far back as she could remember, this stretch always consisted of an endless slideshow of abandonment and decay.

Now, it somehow seemed worse.

How was that even possible?

When the pimps and hos have to go, a neighborhood reaches a new low.

So many places from her past had simply vanished, replaced by vast expanses of unkempt land. What remained were burned out homes and empty lots, morphed into urban prairies fecund with trash. Existing structures adorned with graffiti and broken windows reflected the broken tenements.

And there didn't appear to be a soul in sight.

As she finally reached her old neighborhood, the lump in her throat felt as though it would explode, as she passed by abandoned houses that were once *homes* she knew so well. Some ceased to exist at all. It would come as no surprise if some of the vacated houses were in better condition than the inhabited ones.

Nobody was around to do further damage.

NYC Girl turned down her street, pausing in front of the one lone bright spot on the block, illuminated like an urban Thomas Kinkade painting. This was the residence of Mrs. Harris, the grandmother everyone wanted, or—in NYC Girl's case—the surrogate mother she desperately needed. As long as Mrs. Harris was still alive, so was the neighborhood. Even criminals knew better than to prey on Mrs. Harris. Break into any other house and they might get away with it. But break into Mrs. Harris's home? No way. Not without retribution. NYC Girl lost count of how many times her own childhood home had been robbed.

Seeing Mrs. Harris's habitat still in such pristine, immaculate condition could only mean one thing: Mrs. Harris was still alive and well.

And the day she goes, so goes the city.

Some could argue that the city had already gone a long time ago. If so, then Mrs. Harris had outlived them all.

Mrs. Harris was truly a guardian angel. And not just to NYC Girl, but to the entire neighborhood. She longed for the fresh-baked cookies and milk after school, often followed by a warm, tasty meal, contrasting with the expired, processed food from her *real* life. She used to pretend that Mrs. Harris *was* her actual mother. However, it wasn't long before reality erased any remnants of the fantasy life she longed to one day have for herself.

More important than her cookies was the fact that Mrs. Harris not only helped a young girl realize that the way she was treated at home wasn't right, but she taught NYC Girl how to keep her head up high as she waited for brighter days ahead.

The latter was key.

"And as God as my witness," Mrs. Harris proclaimed during one of her annual outings to Boblo Island. "Those days will come, child. Those days will come."

As much as Mrs. Harris disapproved of NYC Girl's mother, she never once badmouthed her.

"She's sick, dear," Mrs. Harris said. "And needs help she can't afford. She doesn't mean to do what she does."

For the first time, NYC Girl understood. This was no small feat, considering NYC Girl's disdain toward her mother began before kindergarten. It doesn't take a child long to discover what love is—and isn't.

And the gap between the two couldn't be wider.

Incidentally, there was only one person on the planet who ever took issue with Mrs. Harris: NYC Girl's mother. This stemmed from an argument that was sparked when the former attempted an intervention with the latter, after eleven-year-old NYC Girl came over with yet another black eye.

"For the love of Jesus Christ, and for the sake of your only child, get your damn shit together, woman."

It was the only time NYC Girl had heard Mrs. Harris swear. Chances are, it was the only time she swore, *period*.

When NYC Girl's mother reared back to slap Mrs. Harris in retaliation, she slipped and tumbled on the porch. Weak and feeble Mrs. Harris rushed to help NYC Girl's mother to her feet and cradled her like a child, repeating over and over, "God is listening, honey child. God is listening."

For once, NYC Girl felt something she never thought she would ever feel for her mother: *pity*. And it was no surprise that Mrs. Harris had something to do with it.

She continued to stare at Mrs. Harris's house, overcome with bittersweet feelings of nostalgia and regret. She had never said goodbye to Mrs. Harris—the person she would most miss—before she skipped town; the guardian angel who actually encouraged her to follow her dreams when nobody else cared—which at times, included herself. She learned early on that it's difficult to follow your dreams when you're too busy chasing after your next meal.

Mrs. Harris taught her to keep an eye on both.

At the time, she couldn't bear the thought of saying goodbye because deep down, she knew that she would probably never see Mrs. Harris again. Now, due to circumstances fucked up beyond belief, she was being given a second chance, though she dreaded admitting defeat to the one person who believed in her more than anyone else; more than she ever believed in herself. NYC Girl couldn't help but feel that in letting herself down, she was really letting Mrs. Harris down.

As she passed Mrs. Harris's house, she noticed a broken mailbox, hanging lopsided by a rusted thread. Though not unusual in this town, the Mrs. Harris she knew would never stand for something to remain broken for so long. She would have found a way to fix it.

And usually with her own hands.

How long had it been broken? Hopefully not long. She would make an effort to fix it. But when?

NYC Girl finally reached her mother's modest single story ranch. It was shrouded in darkness. It had fallen into such disrepair she wondered if her mother still lived there, or whether she was even still alive for that matter.

Overcome with trepidation, she held a hand over her swollen belly, as though expecting to find an answer there.

She attempted to move toward the weed-covered sidewalk that lead to the front door of her former life, but she felt as though her feet were encased in concrete. She peered toward the window to see if her mother was inside, but giant ghetto palms obstructed her view. She had travelled more than six-hundred miles to get here and now she was unable to take ten more steps to reach the front door.

Fuck it. Maybe it was simply time to leave everything buried in the past. But did burying the past mean going in, or avoiding it all together?

Like sewage water under a rotting bridge.

Once upon a time, she would pray during moments like this. Now, she knew better. The way she saw it, prayer was no different than talking to herself; it was not only a sign of being crazy, it simply expended unnecessary energy.

NYC Girl felt her body pull away from the house, as though she were a marionette, toward the warm illumination of Mrs. Harris's domicile. For a brief moment, she considered seeking refuge there, but she refused to beg. Those days were behind her—or so she hoped. She also realized that doing so would probably mean never going home. Then again, maybe this *was* her home. She finally made up her mind: she would return *after* she got her feet back on the ground. When she had both the upper hand and the ability to hold her head up high. First to make peace. And then to *find* it, rather than crawling back on her hands and knees—to give Mrs. Harris any reason for further concern. And she absolutely refused to give her mother any reason to have the upper hand. That would be the greatest act of desperation of all. Furthermore, the last thing she could stomach was another "I told you so," at least not until she had something resembling a plan.

She realized these thoughts were probably all an attempt to justify her apprehension.

To somehow seek an easy way out.

But since when is *anything* easy?

Certainly not in this life.

As she began to walk away from her childhood home, she caught herself off guard when she realized how much part of her *wanted* to be seen. She imagined her mother watching her only child turn her back on her one more time, after waiting so long for her to return home.

Minute by minute.

Hour by hour.

Day by day.

Week by week.

Month by month.

Year by year.

She still couldn't shake the feeling that her mother didn't care at all. *Or couldn't.* But deep down, she knew better. That beneath the drugs, and abuse, and neglect her mother *did* care. Despite the rage and hatred bubbling at the surface, it was because of this deeper understanding that NYC Girl continued to imagine this same woman—hobbling from a body ravaged with crack, and a life of slipping through cracks—walking into her daughter's bedroom, untouched since she left seven years earlier. She envisioned her mother picking up the framed picture of her when she was six, in her ballet costume, and staring through the dusty glass, wishing that she could go back in time and make everything right.

As she passed Mrs. Harris's house, she took note of the broken mailbox. And in its demise, she saw unexpected hope. That despite being broken, things *can* be fixed. As she rounded the corner, she encountered a tiny break on the horizon of gray clouds up ahead, as though the sun wanted to catch one last glimpse of the dying city before it turned in for the night, even as the moon suddenly revealed itself from behind a cloud as if to remind the sun of its place. Surreal rays suddenly made of a mix of moonlight and sunlight burst through, shining upon the city, like some sort of blessing from a heaven she didn't believe in. As she looked around at the density of ashen desert, the sudden presence of otherworldly light seemed to defy all logic, giving her a respite from despair.

Another cruel illusion of hope?

As quickly as it came, the sun and the beams of light were swallowed up by the same clouds that momentarily parted for this glimpse of temporary beauty.

She knew right in that moment where she was heading: *downtown*. Where there was life. And anything was possible.

She would never forget this moment.

She saw it as a sign.

But of what?

She had no clue, but took comfort in it nonetheless until a red-tinted cloud formation formed what to her looked like a dwarf.

One thing came immediately to mind. An old Detroit legend Mrs. Harris taught her.

Nain Rouge. Red Dwarf.

A mythical legend that is known as the cause for all of the problems that plague the city.

And then, just as quickly as it had appeared, it was gone.

2

As dusk folded into night, downtown loomed through a heavy fog as NYC Girl dragged her broken suitcase, which made a rhythmic *clunk-clunk* sound that reminded her of the techno rhythm of Detroit's factories.

For the first time in ages, she felt a tinge of steely determination, evaporating the clouds of doubt plaguing her since she first made the decision to return home.

She took a short bus ride over to Mexicantown, getting off on Vernor, dotted with Mexican restaurants and littered with fast food joints, barbershops, gas stations, auto repair shops, storefront churches, thrift shops, Cash-4-Gold emporiums, beauty parlors, and nail salons, with names such as Sis'ta Sa'lon, Nailz 'n Such, and Bongz & Thongz.

Ahead of her was the neon glow of Mo's Fuel Palace—her former hangout spot—where she and her friends could be themselves: raw, uncensored, and unrated. When she was sixteen, she served a brief stint as a cashier, eventually tripling her earnings by turning tricks in the restroom, which ultimately paved the way for her current predicament.

She entered and was instantly greeted by a familiar face shelving liquor behind the bullet-proof glass-enclosed counter: Mo Jr., the owner's son—put to work at a young age to run the store while his father had his way with hookers in the backroom, herself included, or frequented the neighborhood strip club. Unlike Mo Sr., NYC Girl didn't have to blow Mo Jr. for cash. She did it for free.

"Holy shit, am I seeing a fucking ghost?!" Mo asked.

"Yeah, something like that," NYC Girl replied, dreading any obligation to provide details.

Mo came out from behind the wall of bulletproof glass and gave her an enormous hug. Though NYC Girl wasn't "huggy" by nature, this was far better than the physical attention she was accustomed to. And to her surprise, it felt good.

"I kept looking out for you on TV! And now you're back!"

She was already forced to admit defeat. And though she once craved entertainment headlines, she realized that the headlines she once sought were more likely to have been traded for the crime beat.

"Yeah, well, you wasted your time," she replied.

"Maybe you should have tried Hollywood instead?"

"I wanted to be on stage. Not screen," NYC Girl snapped.

"So what brings you back?"

"Still trying to figure that out. You hiring?"

"Wish we were. Barely staying afloat as it is."

"I understand," she said.

One down . . .

"Can I use the restroom?" she asked, hoping to at least accomplish an even more immediate goal.

Mo headed back to the counter and slipped a key through the rotating door on the counter.

"You know where it is."

She grabbed the key, still attached to the same late 80's Winston-Salem keychain from her high school days, and, dragging her suitcase, headed toward the restroom in the rear of the building. She could already smell its putrid, yet oddly nostalgic, stench.

She pushed the key into the graffiti-littered door, but the lock was broken.

Great. Just make it easier for them.

"Well it's not rape if she's a hooker, right?" she had once overheard.

Someone had actually uttered these very words. At the time, to her own dismay, she didn't challenge the jerk; didn't do anything about it. *But why not?*

Did Mo know the lock was broken? If so, why hand over the key?

She hesitated, then entered anyway.

The first thing she noticed was that the door to the stall was now completely missing. Piss and shit were smeared over the toilet seat.

She tried to keep things in perspective.

Better to piss on a dirty toilet than to be bent over one.

The only roll of toilet paper was half submerged in the bowl, which contained a mixed stew of shit, piss, tampons, and condoms. The leftover shredded remnants of what was once a bar of soap sat on the sink, next to a rusted-out cloth towel dispenser, from which hung the torn, yellowed remnants of what once passed for a towel.

If Detroit is the armpit of America, this restroom is the armpit of Detroit.

She squatted over the toilet, still managing to graze the cracked lid, distracting herself by reading juxtaposed graffiti, splattered with caked feces and other human waste. One scrawled quote was untouched by excrement:

"They have seen her nakedness: yea, she sigheth, and turneth
backward. Her filthiness is in her skirts." Lam. 1:8-9

Unable to wipe herself, she headed to the rusty sink, then decided that *not* washing her hands there was the more sanitary choice. Anxious for a fresh change of clothes, she opened her suitcase and removed a skirt and halter-top. Sure, it was cold, but that wasn't going to stop her from looking good. Besides, she had a job to do: *finding a job*.

Once dressed, she pulled out a make-up bag, and fumbled to add a layer of pretty over her damaged interior.

She looked at herself in the cracked mirror.

Still look damn good!

Despite it all, the one thing she never lost confidence in was how fucking hot she was. She knew it. And men knew it. By that token, it was also her downfall. Before she headed out, she turned to glance at the fractured reflection of her hot ass and put her jacket back on.

She hadn't looked—nor felt—this good in weeks. It was amazing what a little makeup could do.

Even if nobody else gave a fuck.

Back inside the gas station, NYC Girl set the keys on the front counter.

"Wow!" Mo said.

"You sure you're not hiring?"

"Trust me, I *really* wish we were."

"So when was the last time you cleaned that shithole?"

Mo shrugged with a smirk. The fact that he didn't seem to give a shit came as no surprise.

NYC Girl searched the aisles for a snack. She settled for a granola bar. While Mo's back was turned stocking shelves, she debated over whether she should steal it, before she remembered the promise she made to herself before she left New York: she was *never* going to steal again.

Easier said than done.

"How long you in town?" Mo asked. "Maybe we could meet up for a drink once you get settled?"

"Time will tell," NYC Girl replied. "And, yeah, a drink would be nice."

But she didn't mean it.

Now that she was back home, part of her preferred to start over with a blank slate, rather than dredge up the ghosts of her past—even if that meant starting with a primer made from arsenic and shit.

As far as drinking was concerned, she knew she technically shouldn't drink in her condition, but also knew it didn't really matter. Even though her mind was *almost* made up regarding her condition, she couldn't help but feel a twinge of guilt whenever she drank. Perhaps there was a motherly instinct buried somewhere deep inside her after all. Or, maybe she knew deep down that there was still that one percent chance she would keep it. Maybe coming home would somehow alter her view?

"How's your dad?" NYC Girl asked, attempting to change the subject. By the same token, she really couldn't give two shits about the motherfucker.

Mo pointed upward, to a heaven she didn't believe in.

"Oh."

"Yeah. Robbed. And shot. Right where you're standing."

NYC Girl looked down, half-expecting to see a bloodstain; not feeling a twinge of sympathy for the dead fuck.

"I'm sorry," she said. But really she wasn't. She'd be kidding herself if she didn't fantasize about killing the fucking asshole herself.

"His legacy lives on," Mo said, surveying his inherited Fuel Palace with pride.

As NYC Girl continued to mull over her beverage options, she caught Mo's reflection in the door, staring at her ass from behind the register.

Like father, like son.

She whipped around, catching him off guard. He pretended to be looking over an invoice. She brushed it off and grabbed a bottle of non-fat milk and headed back to the counter. He rang her up.

She dug through her purse until she managed to find a couple of crumpled dollar bills. Her wallet had been stolen months earlier, her knife even more recently. The sad truth was if she could only afford to replace one, she'd probably have more use for the latter. At some point, she would need an ID, although in this town, nobody usually gave a fuck.

She scrambled for loose change to make up the difference.

"Shit. I don't have enough," NYC Girl said, needing to keep enough for bus fare downtown. "Just the milk, I guess."

"No worries, it's on me," Mo said. "Like old times."

"These ain't old times no more."

"Ain't no problem."

"Well, I ain't here for charity."

She put down enough for the milk, leaving the granola bar behind.

"It's not charity," Mo insisted. "Just trying to help a friend."

Had he offered to give it to her free from the get-go, she would have been more inclined to take it. But now, the whole transaction just reeked of desperation.

NYC Girl grabbed her milk and turned toward the door.

"Bye, Mo."

"Nice seein' you. Take care out there."

As she made her way out the door, he added, "Don't be a stranger."

But NYC Girl headed out into the night without a response. She looked back once, but Mo had resumed shelving liquor, as though she had never been there at all.

Like a fucking ghost.

She gulped down her milk like a hungry baby on a tit. She already regretted that she hadn't accepted Mo's offer of the granola bar, considering she hadn't had an actual meal in over twenty-four hours—which was half the amount of time since her last full night's sleep. She would have to find a way to sleep and eat eventually.

If not, then nothing else mattered.

It wasn't too long ago that she would have gladly given a lap dance in exchange for a bag of chips, or a hand job in exchange for a warm meal and bed. Pride could only outlast hunger pangs for so long. But she wouldn't go back—*couldn't* go back.

She would find a way. She always did.

But how? And when?

She realized that despite all the uncertainty, she did at least have some semblance of a game plan; and, so far, she was sticking to it:

Step 1: Come home.

Step 2: Find a job.

Step 3: Make things right with mamá.

It all made sense when she first mapped out her plan two weeks earlier, lying in a bed belonging to some corporate fuck whose face she never even saw outside of a thrusting blur.

And thus far:

Step 1: √

Step 2:

Step 3:

Though only a baby step, NYC Girl felt emboldened by progress and hopped on yet another bus downtown—an illusion of perpetual momentum.

She disembarked at another old haunt—the Cass Corridor, infamous for its abundance of prostitutes and drug dealers. There was never a job shortage there.

While stepping off a curb to cross the street, she landed on a smashed, rotting jack-o-lantern, just as a shiny Lexus pulled up alongside the curb.

Here we go again.

"Hey, baby," a well-dressed businessman yelled out, either with the knowledge no one else was around, or not caring if there was. "You workin'?"

NYC Girl flipped him off and kept walking.

Fucking suburban prick.

"C'mon, baby. Don't play me like that. Hop in. How much you askin'?"

She continued to ignore him, but he was relentless. He slowly crept alongside her, waving a hundred dollar bill out the window.

Real fucking smart!

She hoped a carjacking wasn't far behind.

"C'mon, baby, you know you want it!"

Once upon a time, she'd be lying if she said she wasn't tempted. But now—even in her current state of desperation—she would give it more time before going down that path again. She had to prove to herself that those days were behind her . . . for one night at least.

After wordlessly riding alongside NYC Girl for a good two full blocks, the businessman slammed on the gas and drove off.

"Fucking whore!" he shouted.

He would have no shortage of other options.

Despite her mounting, desparate pangs, she took comfort that her pride—though recently reduced to a low simmer—was still intact, hanging ever-so-slightly by a thread.

3

NYC Girl arrived at the Fort/Cass People Mover station. Built in the 80's as an effort to inject new life into a city already on life support, the People Mover amounted to a glorified model train that took a three-mile loop around downtown, offering unprecedented views of abandoned skyscrapers and other various degrees of urban blight. Dubbed the "train to nowhere," the unmanned vessel was usually bereft of passengers. No other major U.S. city provided so many opportunities to feel like the planet's lone survivor of the apocalypse. There was a certain, calm beauty to it. It was one of the few things about Detroit that NYC Girl truly missed.

She entered the stairwell, which smelled of piss and weed. When she reached the top landing, she took a quick look-around to make sure no one was lurking in the shadows, and then leaped over the turnstile. She realized she had broken her vow. But then again, she had *never* paid to ride the train.

Why start now?

If she were arrested, at least she'd get a warm meal and bed out of it.

Desperate times.

She reached the platform, greeted only by a cold wind whistling through the station. As she waited, elevated above the city, she sipped on what was left of her milk. Her hunger pangs intensified in the indifferent silence.

Finally, the low rumble of the People Mover growled, unseen, until its headlights appeared like the glowing eyes of a phantom panther, as it eventually morphed into the empty train that came to a screeching halt in front of her.

The doors slid open and NYC Girl climbed aboard. She took a seat in a corner of the car, certain that she had the whole train to herself, which made her feel both safe and unsafe. As the doors slid shut and the train rumbled on its lonely way, NYC Girl heard a wet, productive cough, kitty-corner on the opposite end of the train.

She looked up and made eye contact with what appeared to be yet another homeless man.

Motherfucker! I'm like a vagrant magnet.

How had she not noticed him?

Was *he* a ghost?

He wore a tattered green military jacket and sweatpants, Velcro-strapped black shoes, topped off with a knit cap with more holes than fabric. A rusty shopping cart filled with trash sat by his side.

A classic Detroit beggar.

Though he didn't ask her for a single thing, she knew it was only a matter of time. Then again, considering her current state of affairs, she knew that she shouldn't be so judgmental. She was well aware that it was only a matter of time before she would be mistaken for a beggar. She wasn't at that point yet. But in order to avoid getting there, the tide would have to turn. *Soon.*

There was something familiar about him, but she just couldn't put her finger on it. Whether she knew him or not, she did know that it would only take a few seconds before he attempted to communicate with her.

Despite his appearance, her fellow passenger's countenance did not suggest despair. In fact, he appeared jovial. Though he appeared on the surface to be in his late-sixties, it was quite possible that he was younger.

"How you doing tonight, ma'am?" the beggar finally burst out with great enthusiasm.

NYC Girl closed her eyes, hoping that when she opened them again, he would be gone. She tried to snooze, but a sudden rustle of paper piqued annoyed curiosity. She opened her eyes and watched as the beggar folded the paper into *something.* She couldn't look away.

The man dug through his cart with determination until he found exactly what he was looking for—a seemingly insignificant piece of trash that he wove in with the original piece.

The train made a couple of stops at empty stations, its doors opening like curtains revealing the proscenium of an empty stage.

At one of the stops, NYC Girl was startled by the bronze statue of a man reading a newspaper, which—for a split second—she mistook for an actual person, just as she had the last time she had been on the People Mover.

The beggar chuckled.

"It's okay, ma'am. He scares me every now and again too. But he's harmless."

The station was otherwise deserted. The doors closed and the train continued its looped journey into the night.

NYC Girl noticed that the beggar had finished his trash sculpture, which he inspected with an equal measure of pride and wonderment. He then stood up and, with a slight limp, slowly made his way over toward NYC Girl. She rolled her eyes, hoping, maybe, that he would notice. If he *did* notice, it didn't seem to faze him.

Better to be trapped in here with this bum, than a rapist. Unless, of course, the bum was a rapist.

She knew better than to assume good intentions from anyone.

"How you doin' tonight, ma'am?" the man repeated.

NYC Girl turned away, but it was no use. He either ignored her cues all together, or lacked the ability to interpret them. Yet, she couldn't help but find him compelling and, dare she admit it, *safe*.

Careful now.

Perhaps sensing that NYC Girl's guard was down, the beggar plopped himself down right next to her, forcing her to shift away from him. She caught a faint whiff of mildew and dirt, as though he had just dug himself out of a grave. He offered her his sculpted trash—which he had expertly formed into the shape and colors of a rose.

"I ain't got no money," NYC Girl warned, assuming he was just a variation on the patriotic beggar with a flag. "As in *no* money. So save yourself the trouble."

He continued to hold the flower out to her.

"Oh, I don't want no money, ma'am. I just want you to have this," he said, as he pushed it closer to her. She took it with the hope that in exchange, he would leave her alone. But she knew she wouldn't be so lucky.

She cringed as one of his grimy fingers touched her hand.

"I made it especially for you," he beamed.

"Thank you," she said, reaching for it, fully aware of her lack of sincerity. By the same token, she struggled to keep her icy demeanor from melting on the inside. She was surprised she actually took it.

"You like cats?" the man asked.

Initially, she assumed this was the non-sequitur rambling of a mad man, but when he opened up his coat's torn front pocket to reveal a cute, scruffy kitten, she was pleasantly surprised that this wasn't the case. The kitten let out a small peep, which reminded her of an abandoned kitten she had found in an alley when she was five years old. She snuck it home and kept it hidden in her bedroom for two weeks before her mother found it and forced her to put it back on the street. Two days later, she had found it dead on the side of the road, a few feet away from where she left it.

And then her mother beat her for crying about it.

"Gotta keep her safe from the Devil tonight," the beggar rambled. "Gotta keep her safe." He repeated this refrain as he petted his kitten and looked out the window, seemingly in a trance. NYC Girl glanced down at the kitten, which was now asleep, hanging halfway out of his pocket. She made accidental eye contact, then closed her eyes and took a sip of her milk.

"Can I have some milk?" the man asked. "For my cat."

There were only a couple of sips left and since she knew it was for his kitten—rather than him—she had no problem giving it up. She handed it over, this time, careful to avoid any physical contact.

As the train approached yet another empty station, the man carefully poured some milk into the bottle cap, somehow managing not to spill a single drop as he set it on the floor. He gently removed the kitten from his pocket and set her down, where she promptly lapped it up.

"That's my girl," he smiled as he let out a warm chuckle that quickly morphed into a coughing fit. He hacked up a wad of phlegm, but rather than spitting it out, as NYC Girl expected, he politely swallowed it.

"Excuse me," the man said. She sensed his embarrassment and felt unexpected sympathy toward him.

What the fuck is wrong with me?

The train slowed to another stop. The door opened and a tall, dark, handsome man, dressed in black pants and a shiny black dress shirt, stepped on. He looked as though he had just arrived from the future. Most likely an artist. Maybe gay? A gay artist from the future?

He carried a cup of coffee or tea, and pulled a rolling suitcase in much better condition than NYC Girl's—at least until the train doors slammed shut on it.

"Son of a bitch!" he yelled, as he struggled to yank his case on board. He sat across from NYC Girl, down a few seats. The gay vibe he gave on initial impression quickly dissipated. NYC Girl realized she was only making this wild assumption because he wasn't dressed like a thug. Like her other fellow passenger, this man seemed to give off an aura of trust. Once again, she knew from experience not to be so gullible.

She noticed a gold, marijuana leaf ring on his right ring finger, then looked up, making brief eye contact. He nodded at her in a calm, friendly manner. She nodded back with no hint of friendliness.

"How you doin' tonight, sir?" the beggar directed toward the new passenger, who flashed a wave and smile. The beggar then scooped his kitten back up and placed it gently back into his coat pocket.

"Do you like cats?" he asked the man, before he began working on another paper sculpture.

NYC Girl sneaked a glance at the artist, just as he transferred a couple of vials out of his coat pocket and into a small compartment in his suitcase, which she noticed was filled with vinyl records.

A drug dealing DJ. Of course.

Her view was suddenly obscured by the beggar, who presented his latest creation to the not-gay-from-the-future-drug-dealing DJ: a perfectly formed treble clef.

The DJ seemed genuinely pleased.

The beggar wasted no time starting his next masterpiece.

"One man's trash . . ." the DJ said. He then turned toward NYC Girl.

"I think you're on the wrong train."

NYC Girl looked up, confused. He nodded toward her suitcase.

"Story of my life," she said nonchalantly.

"A train to nowhere?"

"Something like that."

She felt safe enough to close her eyes for a few seconds, before opening them back up to stare at her own reflection, along with the void outside the window.

She felt the gaze of four eyes on her and closed her eyes again. She was in no mood to converse with any fellow passenger. And she was certainly in no mood to fake it.

"Seriously, where you headin'?" the DJ asked.

"I'm going to heaven," the beggar interjected. The DJ laughed. A kind laugh that caught her off guard—not the laugh itself, but how quickly she concluded that this stranger wasn't a threat. NYC Girl almost *never* let her guard down. And in the rare instance that she did, it was never this quick. And certainly not in the absence of liquor and drugs.

Had this drug-dealing DJ from the future cast some kind of spell on her?

"So, you gonna answer my question?" the DJ asked her, unknowingly backing her into a corner, and triggering her natural instinct to fire a warning shot.

"First, what makes it your business and, second, why you gotta give a shit?"

"I don't. But there ain't no one else on this train to talk to, other than Picasso and his pussy over here."

NYC Girl suppressed the urge to smile, then added, "It's a long story."

"It's a long ride. I don't mind," the DJ replied.

She hesitated, before deciding that it wouldn't hurt to talk about it, despite knowing full well of the risk of opening up to someone—especially a complete stranger.

"Long story, short: went to New York with a big stupid dream, failed miserably, proved everyone right, got knocked up, and now I'm back home to try to make amends with my mother. There. Happy now?"

"Actually, no," the DJ replied. "Sounds pretty fucked up."

"Yeah, well, again . . . story of my life."

"It don't have to be."

"Do you charge hourly for your services?" NYC Girl quipped.

"No. Do you?"

"Fuck you and your new age bullshit! Who the fuck you think you is, Aristotle?"

He didn't deserve it. And she certainly didn't deserve what she got in return, either. But being a bitch was her usual line of defense. She would defend the rugged turf that was her life. Or, die trying.

"First of all, my name ain't Aristotle," he began with a sly grin. "I think you're confused. Secondly, I sincerely appreciate the offer."

"You got some big balls. You know that?"

"Yeah. So I've been told."

What a dick!

"So as I was sayin', if you constantly expect bad things to happen to you, they will."

He doesn't possibly believe this Hallmark shit he's spinning, does he?

"Here's how it is," she retorted. "Shit keeps happening to me. So as a result, I expect shit to keep happening to me."

"That so?"

"Hey. You don't know shit about me."

"You're right. So I'm going to need a few details if I'm going to be able to help you."

"But I ain't asking for your fucking help."

"Just tryin' to have a conversation," the DJ replied, holding his arms up in mock surrender.

NYC Girl rolled her eyes.

But the DJ was relentless.

"So are you going to . . ."

"Off it?"

"Or, keep it?"

"The fuck's it to you?"

"To me, nothing. But to you, a lot. So you won't."

"Excuse me?" she said, equally pissed and confused.

"I said you won't go through with it."

"Who the fuck you think you is?"

"Does it matter who I think I am?"

"Look, if I could, I'd do it right here, right now."

"Then what are you waiting for?"

"Tomorrow."

"Tomorrow don't always come," he smirked.

"Then what the fuck difference would it make? And nice use of clichés, asshole! You get that shit from some Deepak Chopra day-by-day calendar?"

"Naw. I'm my own self-help guru. And, honestly, I get my philosophy from Tupac."

NYC Girl dismissed him, before turning away and closing her eyes. The thing was, he was right. Tomorrow *didn't* always come. Sometimes, she wished it wouldn't. Yet somehow, for her, it did keep coming back, like some villain in a horror movie. And she kept battling through each day only to live to battle another.

Beneath her anger, she sensed the realization that it felt good to actually have a meaningful conversation. And with that thought in mind, she felt herself drifting off to sleep. As she did, her purse slid off her lap and onto the ground, its contents spilling, snapping her awake.

"Fuck!" NYC Girl exclaimed, scrambling to pick up the items. The DJ rushed to help. As he picked up her lighter, she snatched it from him.

"I got it," NYC Girl snapped, but the DJ stubbornly continued to gather her stuff.

"Hey! I *said* I got it! I don't need or *want* your help . . . or company!"

"I just wanna . . ."

And then she finally boiled over in anger.

"Look! Let me say this to you in a language you can understand. Leave-me-the-fuck-alone! Does that translate, *asshole*?"

Judging from his expression, *it did*.

If there was one constant to NYC Girl's personality, it was that she never felt comfortable receiving help from *anyone*—especially the "kindness of strangers." Accepting help equaled weakness. And in her experience, help usually had strings attached. Or, a dick.

Besides, she wasn't looking for a superhero. She'd prefer to save herself. To be her own hero.

An old-fashioned rotary phone rang, piercing the silence like a sharp blade. The DJ answered his cell, talking in hushed, hurried tones. His attempt at coded language did nothing to conceal the fact that a drug deal was taking place.

Meanwhile, the train continued to plow through the night, casting its shadow on lonely, desolate streets before it would come to a stop at one empty station after another.

As the train squealed into Greektown, NYC Girl and the DJ stood up in unison. Both grabbed their suitcases.

He certainly doesn't look like a predator.

Experience taught her to know better, yet there was a part of her that still wanted to be followed. The part of her that had a habit of consistently letting her down.

As she waited for the doors to open, she looked down below at the semi-bustling streets of Greektown—a thriving nightlife district; a shimmering, urban mirage. Though only a handful of blocks, it was one of the few areas in the city where suburbanites felt safe.

Disneyland Detroit.

"You be careful now," the beggar said as his two fellow passengers headed out separate doors. "God bless."

"You too, dude," the DJ said, tossing a wink at NYC Girl.

"Your cup!" the beggar said, pointing to the DJ's coffee cup on the floor of the train as the doors slid shut.

"Have a nice night," the DJ said to NYC Girl.

NYC Girl followed him at a comfortable distance, until she caught up to him at the elevator, where they waited for the door to open in what felt like eternal silence. When it finally opened, the DJ motioned for NYC Girl to enter first. She hesitated for a second, then entered.

What a convenient way to get cornered.

Yet, when it was clear to her that he was making an effort to leave as much space as possible, she felt an odd, comforting relief.

When they reached street level, she motioned for him to go ahead of her this time.

"Thanks," he said with his signature smile.

"Yeah," she said, dropping the word from her lips in mechanical obligation.

And with that, the DJ headed off in one direction; NYC Girl in the other.

4

NYC Girl made her way toward an old, familiar haunt: Steve's Place. She was relieved to see that it was still open. But who knew if old man Steve was still alive? Then again, if Mrs. Harris was, then there was no reason Steve shouldn't be, either. And the fact that the bar appeared open told her all she needed to know. Deep down, she knew that once Steve was gone, so would go his beloved bar.

She paused to take notice of some graffiti painted on a nearby building:

"THOU HAST UTTERLY REJECTED US; THOU ART
VERY WROTH AGAINST US." LAMENTATIONS 5:22

Finally, something from the Bible to agree with!

She entered the surreal dive—her last *real* job before she had found more lucrative, less legitimate ways to make money.

A scratchy recording of Billie Holiday's melancholy "Solitude" poured out of an ancient jukebox that sat in front of the dusty window, as cobwebbed Christmas lights flickered on and off without regard for the rhythm of the music.

There was a unique, timeless quality to the old joint that appeared to show no regard to the outside world.

To NYC Girl, it was a sanctuary.

She situated herself on a rusty barstool. No bartender in sight. This, in its own unique way, signified that Steve was indeed alive and well, most likely upstairs in his living quarters. Whether his wife, Sophia, was still alive remained to be seen.

Everyone's gotta go eventually.

Greek immigrants who traveled halfway around the world fifty years prior to start life anew in Detroit's Greektown, Steve and Sophia had not left the premises of the bar they owned, operated, and lived above since the seventies.

The American Dream.

For the time being, the joint was empty, save for a lone customer sitting at the far corner of the bar—an ancient-looking man wearing a framed, 8 x 10 photo around his neck like a medallion. The black and white photo was that of a beautiful woman, taken in perhaps the 1930s or 40s. His wife? Mother?

He stared into the bottom of an empty class.

The only other person in the bar was a blues musician, whom NYC Girl recognized, snoring away in a booth, using his guitar case as a pillow. It was "Travelin' Blues."

And then it hit her—how she knew the beggar from the train. He used to live here. In a booth. How did she not realize that sooner?

The song came to an end and NYC Girl sat in silence, listening only to the snores of the bluesman.

Though the kitchen had been shut down by the health department years ago, an old plastic menu featuring long-defunct menu options, now missing several letters, hung behind the bar.

Mon: Ro st B ef/Chi k n Noo le

Tu s: Ro st Chi ken/Na y B an

We : Me balls & Spa.

Thur: Sh rt Rib / t Pea

Fri. Fi h & Chi s/Cl am Ch wde

NYC Girl remembered how hungry she felt.

She then heard shuffling footsteps from above, followed by a slow descent down an unseen staircase. After what felt like an eternity, a door at the back of the bar opened and out of the darkness appeared Steve himself, hunched over from a lifetime of weariness. He appeared more gaunt than she remembered, but his jovial spirit appeared to be intact. As he drew closer, his feet never once left the ground, but instead, he shuffled along the faded black and red tiled floor, worn and beaten by time itself.

It was clear that Steve didn't recognize NYC Girl. His vision was bad seven years earlier. Surely, it had only gotten worse.

"What would you like to drink?" he asked in his heavy Greek accent, still not realizing who it was.

"Hi, Steve," NYC Girl replied with a smile on her face.

Steve looked up and warm recognition filled his face. He threw his hands up in the air in jubilation and made his way around the bar, as fast as his withered body would allow, to give her a big hug.

"My sweetheart! Where have you been?"

NYC Girl didn't answer, but Steve was too busy giving her an enormous hug and a kiss on each cheek. When he finally withdrew, he held up a finger, adding, "one minute!"

As he shuffled over toward the jukebox, the bar hummed with the sound of a dying radiator and the buzz of shoddy electrical work. Although the radiator sounded broken, it was now generating perhaps too much heat after a slow start.

Steve deliberately punched in his selection before making his slow journey back to the bar. His song choice sent her into a state of nostalgic paralysis.

Stevie Wonder's "You Are the Sunshine of My Life."

He still remembered, after all these years.

"I play your favorite song, yes?"

NYC Girl nodded, fighting to hold back tears.

"Yes. Thank you."

The song was deeply embedded in her DNA and her soul. It was the song that Mrs. Harris would sing to her when she was a little girl.

Her *de facto* lullaby.

A song that meant happiness, safety, and above all else—*love.*

When she was five, Mrs. Harris had taught her how to play it on the piano. For a high school dance recital, she had selected it for her solo. It was also the impetus for her decision to return home, when it suddenly came on over the PA in a dimly-lit laundromat in New York City. *A ghost song*, triggering a reaction very similar to the one she was having now. Only, even stronger. She now realized that coming home was less about her mother and more about Mrs. Harris. It was a reminder of everything Mrs. Harris was. And everything her mother wasn't.

But, as hard as she tried to deny it, her mother, as Stevie sang, truly did forever stay in her heart. And if anyone could help her summon the courage to make amends, it would be Mrs. Harris. When she first left for New York, she assumed she would never see her mother again. Now, she was being granted a rare second chance.

"What have you done with life?" Steve asked in his heavy Greek accent.

"I ask myself that question every day, Steve," NYC Girl chuckled.

"You not come here in long time. You okay? You sick?"

"I'm fine, Steve."

Steve smiled.

"What can I get you?" Steve asked. He proceeded to adjust the collar of his plaid shirt, buttoned to the very top. It was faded and torn, neatly tucked into his pants, which were pulled up high above his twisted, thin waist. His peppered hair was neatly combed with grease.

"Oh, Steve, I'm broke."

"On the house," Steve insisted. "Long Island?"

"You remember!"

NYC Girl had never met anyone who so genuinely loved giving.

Steve smiled and got to work. Long Islands had become her drink of choice at around the age of thirteen and Steve made the best, possibly due in part to the fact that he didn't follow any particular recipe. They always did the trick—which, in turn, helped her turn tricks—after which she would then drink more, in order to forget.

She immediately regretted her order, but said nothing.

Perhaps, if she played her cards right, alcohol would take care of her current "problem" without having to step foot into a clinic.

During the short silence between songs, Travelin' Blues's snores deepened, only to be drowned out by Steve's signature tune: "Sweet Dreams (Are Made of This)" by the Eurythmics. Steve smiled and nodded along to the music.

With trembling hands and a nodding head, Steve set the drink down on the blue laminate, faux-wood bar, which was peeling off in every possible direction, its edges accentuated with green, tattered, and torn vinyl padding. He then poured out two customary shots of peach schnapps. One for her. One for himself. Another Steve's Place tradition.

"To old times," Steve said, raising his glass with a shaking hand.

NYC Girl held up her glass, reluctantly echoing "To old times."

She didn't exactly yearn for old times, but took solace in such good company, downing her shot, before taking a long, healthy sip of her Long Island.

"It is okay?" Steve asked.

"Still the best. Not only in Detroit. But anywhere. Better even than New York."

Steve beamed with pride.

"So that's where you been? New York?"

"For a while, yes. So . . . you looking for any help, Steve?" she inquired, hesitantly.

Steve took a look around at the all-but-empty bar, mournfully shaking his head.

"Yeah, figured as much."

Steve simply shrugged. She sensed he wanted to say more, but didn't know how to sufficiently express himself. Despite the language barrier, Steve was as good a listener as Mrs. Harris.

"How about you check Saint Andrew's next door, yes?"

"That's my next stop."

The man with the frame around his neck began to sob.

"Every night," Steve said, rolling his eyes.

Things could always be worse.

NYC Girl sipped the remainder of her drink.

As Steve's theme song came to an end, NYC Girl heard more footsteps, shuffling from up above.

She was alive!

Steve could barely contain himself, like someone waiting to be reunited with a loved one he hadn't seen in ages.

Oh, to want someone . . . or be wanted by someone like that.

After what felt like an eternity, the door opened and a ghostly, catatonic woman appeared in a red and white polka-dotted nightgown, a beacon of light standing in the shadows of the back hallway. She began her long, slow shuffle toward the bar.

"My Sophia," Steve announced with pride and a love so deep, it inspired a strange sense of envy in NYC Girl.

Sophia shuffled, zombie-like, across the floor from the back of the bar, her lifeless eyes zeroed in on her husband, as though nothing else in the world existed. Steve smiled, waiting patiently at the end of the bar. When she finally reached him, Steve helped her into a tattered chair that was padded with an enormous pillow, and retrieved a can of Vernor's ginger ale from behind the bar. He popped the top and handed it to her. Sophia reached for the can and took a long, slow sip, her gaze never leaving her husband.

To be that goddamn in love.

Steve took another stroll toward the jukebox, this time with an extra spring in his step. He carefully made another selection.

As Steve made his way back toward Sophia, Nat King Cole's "Stardust" kicked on. The old lovers reached out for one another, despite the distance between them. Sophia's eyes were now overflowing with life.

When Steve finally reached her, he took her by the hand and helped her up before they danced to the melancholy melody. NYC Girl watched in awe as the couple radiated a lifetime of shared love, happiness, tears, and loss. The rest of the world no longer mattered—or perhaps it simply never existed at all.

Finally, something beautiful.

At the key change, Steve dipped Sophia back with sudden grace and agility. Sophia buried her face into Steve's shoulder as he held her, as though fighting off the reality that the song was beginning to fade—like everything else in life. Knowing this, they did not let go of one another until the echo of the very last note.

Steve kissed Sophia's hand and then watched as she slowly shuffled back to the door from which she came, out of the light, into shadow, and then back into darkness, until all that remained were the sound of her footsteps slowly ascending the stairs.

"My Sophia," Steve beamed with pride.

"Another shot?" Steve asked.

"No, thanks," NYC Girl said.

"Come on! One more!" Steve insisted. "On me."

He poured her another shot of schnapps.

"To love . . . and life," Steve exclaimed.

Though she knew that she shouldn't, she downed it anyway.

"Thanks, Steve. So great to see you. And Sophia," NYC Girl said, as she stood up from her stool and grabbed her suitcase. She stumbled from the unexpected buzz. Her empty stomach certainly wasn't helping matters.

"Come back soon."

"Always."

NYC Girl paused at the jukebox and made a selection: Billie Holiday's "I'll be Seeing You."

The old man with the frame around his neck began to weep.

She headed out the door, the old man's sobs ringing in her head long after the door had closed behind her.

Out here, in the real world, time kept on ticking.

5

Through the hazy buzz of liquor and nostalgia, NYC Girl made her way over toward the legendary Saint Andrew's Hall, where until recently, a white, wannabe rapper named Marshall Mathers distributed free demo tapes to customers waiting in line outside and performed epic rap battles in the club's basement, the "Shelter."

Tonight was a special Saturday edition of the weekly "Three Floors of Fun" (aka "Three Floors of Drugs," "Three Floors of Skanks," and "Three Floors of Fucks"). As she approached the club, NYC Girl noticed a cryptic message spray painted on a nearby wall:

DON'T CRY FOR US. CRY FOR THEM.

Standing against that very wall was an eerie-looking, pale, emaciated man in his early forties, dressed in black. She didn't have to rely on her sixth sense to get the heebie-jeebies from this guy. As she passed by him, she kept her head down, avoiding eye contact, but could still feel his icy gaze upon her.

As she reached Saint Andrew's, she climbed the steps leading to the front entrance, which always reminded her of the apartment building on *Sesame Street*. All that was missing was Oscar's garbage can, though there was certainly no shortage of trash.

A handsome, middle-aged, light-skinned black man in a tailored pin-striped suit and drenched in cologne hurried out the door, nearly knocking NYC Girl down.

As though she were not there at all.

When she reached the top of the steps, she noticed fliers posted on each side of the door:

INTRODUCING DJ ANONYMOUS
LIVE SET
HALLOWEEN EVE
DEVIL'S & ANGEL'S NIGHT

"Help you?" asked a booming voice. She was caught totally off guard. How did she not notice the sudden emergence of a bouncer as large as this man?!

"You hiring by any chance?"

"What kind of work?"

NYC Girl couldn't help but wonder if he recognized her from when she had "worked" these very streets. Then again, he likely would have been too young.

"Bartender. Coat check chick. Whatever."

"No clue," the bouncer said, amid the chaos of pre-show set-up.

"Can I speak to somebody who has one?"

"Hey. Look. I got a job to do."

"And I'm tryin' to get a job to do. So can I talk to someone who can help me?"

"You might wanna try back tomorrow."

"Ain't there someone I could talk to before the doors open?" NYC Girl asked, adding a sarcastic, candy-coated, "pretty please?"

Sensing her desperation—or perhaps giving in to her flirtation—the bouncer pulled open the door.

"The person you need to talk to is Elijah. He'll be in and out throughout the night. Your best bet is to wait for him upstairs. There's couches. Bar's open. I'll let him know, okay?"

She would wait. What else was she going to do?

At least, she would be warm.

Hungry. But warm.

She stepped forward to enter, but was halted once again by the bouncer, who patted her down, giving way too much attention to areas he didn't need to.

Same old song and dance.

"You're going to have to leave your suitcase with me."

"Seriously?"

The look on his face gave her no choice but to hand it over.

"We'll keep it safe and sound."

As though that were possible here.

NYC Girl entered and was immediately greeted by the old, familiar stench of stale pot, sweat, and beer. As she walked up a small flight of steps past the coat check to the foyer, she felt a sudden urge to leave, but chalked it up to fatigue and paranoia.

She entered the dimly-illuminated foyer—the central terminus to all "Three Floors of Fun." Straight ahead was the main floor—a converted gymnasium—which still had the houselights on as a crew scrambled to make final preparations. Seeing the club empty and illuminated felt like fucking with the lights on. The hardwood floor was warped and burned from years of abuse. Surrounding the perimeter of the floor was a balcony that had been blocked off years earlier for "security concerns." Patrons simply found other dark corners where they could fuck.

As NYC Girl began to ascend the stairwell leading to the third-floor Burns Room, someone came racing down. A man. Once again, NYC Girl found herself narrowly avoiding a collision.

"Excuse me," the man said.

Recognition.

"You gotta be fucking kidding me," NYC Girl said.

"You followin' me?" the DJ from the train quipped.

"Yeah. You wish," she said, not skipping a beat.

"Maybe," the DJ replied, sheepishly, adding, "after you."

She slid past him on her way up.

"I'll be right back. Don't miss me too much."

He disappeared down the stairs.

She hurried to the top, but something was amiss: she was smiling.

NYC Girl entered the empty ballroom and sat on a tattered, sunken couch in an adjacent corner. *This* was the most comfortable she had felt in at least forty-eight hours.

She could still feel the lingering effects of the Long Island and craved nourishment. She took a look around the room. Exactly as she remembered, including the mangled chandelier that still hung crooked from the ceiling. She was surprised that it hadn't collapsed. A small stage was wedged into the corner, flanked by speakers, stacked floor to ceiling.

She felt herself begin to doze off just as the DJ returned, an extension cord in one hand and a bottle of water in the other. He hopped onto the stage, surging with energy. He winked at NYC Girl who tossed an icy nod back at him—a defense mechanism to conceal her interest.

"So, are you Mr. Anonymous?" NYC Girl asked the DJ, as he tweaked the controls on the mixing board.

"Shhh. Don't tell anyone," he teased.

"Figured you weren't a *real* musician."

He rolled his eyes.

"Whatever. And for the record, I'm also a saxophonist. Alto."

A defensive vulnerability she hadn't noticed until that moment.

"Had a regular gig at the Soup Kitchen Saloon until it closed."

"Ain't never heard of it."

"You're kidding, right?"

She smiled.

He leaped off the stage to shut the house lights off.

"So what about you?"

"What about me what?"

"What's your special talent?"

"I'm a dancer."

"I'm sure you are," he said, with raised eyebrow.

"Fuck you."

Nigga's already got me pegged.

"I told you," NYC Girl continued. "My business is my own."

"Okay, okay. Fair enough," the DJ said, as he dropped the needle in full swagger mode, opening with what sounded like some sort of dark opera, backed with electronic beats.

As much as he annoyed her on the surface, it felt good to receive attention that wasn't physical. She watched with utter fascination as he spun a web of musical mastery. When he caught her gaze, she snapped out of her trance and turned toward the window to look at the small line of people that was forming outside. She surveyed a diverse crowd of techno freaks and hip hoppers dressed in Halloween costumes, ranging from old school to new school. In many cases, it was difficult to distinguish between costumes and "individual expression." It was equally difficult to ascertain *Matrix* costumes from standard club gear.

When she turned back around, she noticed the DJ's eyes were closed, lost in his "art," so she closed hers, joining him on his sonic voyage. As the music coursed through her veins, it felt, again, as though he had put a spell on her.

An aural roofie. *Stay alert!*

She snapped her eyes open and gazed down onto the street below. The line had grown with club goers. Promoters passed out flyers.

NYC Girl spotted the pale man she had encountered earlier approach the line. His face seemed to glow like a orb of white light. Was he in costume? It was possible. There was something about the way he had looked at her that made her feel very uneasy.

The pale man began to pass out some sort of flyer. He certainly didn't look like a musician or promoter of an after-hours party. Her guess was that the only thing he was there to promote was the preparation of an *afterlife*—specifically what would happen if these ecstasy-laced debauchers didn't change their ways.

She came across lunatics like this almost as frequently as the crazy cat man on the train. Only "holy" men like this were crazier. Sick fucks who secretly got off on the "heathens" they were trying to convert.

In fact, many had been her freakiest "clients."

As expected, nobody in line appeared to give two shits as to what the pale man had to say. A few taunted him, but he appeared non-plussed— fully focused on getting his pamphlet into as many hands as possible. A man disguised as the devil ripped one of the flyers to shreds, before tossing the pieces back into the pale man's face.

Unfazed, the pale man looked up, appearing to make direct eye contact with NYC Girl. His eyes seemed to penetrate her like laser beams. Startled and unsettled, she quickly turned away and returned her focus to the DJ, who quickly looked down at his turntables. He had been totally checking her out. And she was okay with that.

NYC Girl turned her attention back toward the window. Down below, the pale man continued to force his flyers on disinterested clubbers. Across the street, she spotted the beggar from the train making his way through a parking lot in the shadow of the Renaissance Center, his shopping cart in tow.

The beggar stopped at the curb to peer inside his jacket.

Presumably at his cat?

Distracted, he began to cross the street and was almost immediately plowed down by a black Cadillac. Unshaken, the beggar made his merry way toward the line of clubbers. He immediately tried to strike up a conversation with anyone in sight, but, just like the pale man, he was mostly ignored.

NYC Girl's Long Island buzz was finally wearing off, replaced by complete and utter exhaustion. There was nothing she wanted more than a warm meal, followed by a warm bed—a dangerous combination of desperation.

Question marks wrapped around her entire being like a suffocating cloak. Though the night was still young, she felt familiar pains of anxiety creeping in. In fact, she felt them the moment she had crossed into the Detroit city limits. What had started out as a steady simmer now threatened to boil over, threatening to overwhelm her.

One thing remained clear: she needed both rest and nourishment. And there were no viable options. A one-night stand was a last resort, but also a very realistic one.

The DJ changed one of the records to create an electro-gospel sound. She wasn't certain, but she thought she recognized the melody as one of the ones Mrs. Harris used to hum to herself while whipping up something in the kitchen.

A sign, perhaps?

If she believed in that sort of thing.

Where the hell was this Elijah guy?

NYC Girl closed her eyes and tried to clear her mind with deep, meditative breaths, which provided momentary relief. Once she reopened her eyes, she knew that the anxiety would immediately return.

From across the room, the DJ smiled at her.

To her own surprise, she smiled back.

I could totally marry this guy.

What the fuck?!

She chalked her momentary lapse of judgment to exhaustion.

First off, she wasn't one to act on impulse. At least, not anymore.

Furthermore, not only had she made a vow to never get married, she never even fantasized about marriage as a little girl. She was way too independent for co-dependence.

To shake off these thoughts, she looked out the window. The line was beginning its slow funnel into the club. Very soon, she would have company. Meanwhile the beggar continued his attempts to strike up conversation with anyone within earshot and seemed to be failing miserably.

NYC Girl looked for the pale man, but he was nowhere to be seen.

Did he leave?

She would have to stay vigilant. Another reason to stay awake. She wished people would begin filling the empty room. She no longer wanted to be alone and missed the feeling of safety she had felt at Steve's Place.

At least the DJ was there. But he had a job to do. At that precise moment, he flashed her a knowing glance that seemed to suggest: *I have your back.*

She was smitten. She *never* got smitten.

Temporarily relieved, she sank back into the couch, with one eye on the room's entranceway, just in case.

Meanwhile, the DJ slapped another record on the turntable, before he sprung off the stage.

She hoped he was heading her way, but he headed straight downstairs.

Now she was completely alone.

6

Just as NYC Girl dreaded, the pale man appeared at the top of the steps.

A Halloween phantom.

He floated past NYC Girl, over toward a tattered corner armchair. As he sat down and closed his eyes, his translucent face appeared to shine like the moon. His twisted lips appeared to be chanting. Perhaps in prayer?

Although he was a good fifteen feet away, the pale man's physical manifestation felt like a boa constrictor wrapped around her soul. NYC Girl moved over a few inches to further the distance between them, but this did little to calm her nerves. What she really had to do was get the fuck out of there.

Like fucking now!

But, at that moment, her DJ in shining armor reappeared, easing the boa's grip by half. He leaped back on-stage, dug another record out of his crate, placed it on the turntable, then winked at NYC Girl; a vinyl-coated dedication just for her.

She watched him take notice of the pale man, but he showed no sign of concern. Though a bouncer stood near the stairwell, his only duty seemed to consist of flirting with any female within earshot.

A small group of costumed clubbers entered, in the center of which was a tramp-stamped pixie chick wielding a glow stick that she twirled around as she made her way toward the dance floor. Now it was a party and to prove it, the DJ kicked the beats into a higher gear.

The raw, throbbing, industrial pulse of Detroit.

As the pale man appeared to pray with more fervor, NYC Girl found herself, once again, becoming lost in the music, transfixed by pixie's laser light show. After a few minutes, she turned around and refocused her gaze out of the window. The line was now wrapped around the building and down the alley that ran alongside it. She watched as the beggar from the train was chased away by a bouncer with a broom.

How long would it be before she received such treatment? Not that she wasn't already receiving enough unwanted attention. She certainly wasn't deprived of abuse. It was always lurking around the corner.

NYC Girl was suddenly taken aback by someone grinding her from behind. She turned around to face a cowboy and realized that she was the choice cut of beef in the biggest meat market in town. Though she showed no initial interest, some gentle coaxing helped her slip back into the old routine.

Her instinct was simply to go along with it. It was a stress relief diversion—if only for a couple of minutes.

Old habits . . .

They seemed harmless enough, although she had certainly made that mistake before.

Fucking suburbanites.

A 1950's-era milkman next to them lit a joint and joined in from the front, offering her a hit. She took a couple of drags, coughing momentarily, before her body, mind, and soul remembered how much she loved this shit.

As the milkman and the cowboy led NYC Girl out toward the center of the dance floor, she caught the judgmental gaze of the pale man who apperared to have emerged from his holy trance.

The milkman took a hit off the joint, then offered her another hit. She gladly took it as the two men grinded harder against her body. She could feel the cowboy's massive, swollen cock rubbed against her and was surprised by how good it felt. She noticed she had caught the DJ's gaze, then looked away in shame. Sandwiched between the rapt attention of the two men, she couldn't help but feel she was somehow betraying the DJ.

But why did she give a shit?

She couldn't explain it.

Yet, cloaked in her old, familiar habits, she let herself slide down against the milkman, feeling his entire length. As he kissed the side of her neck, she imagined he was the DJ. And imagined his fingers on her like a record on a turntable.

She could tell that the DJ was watching her with, what she assumed to be, judgmental envy. Suddenly, the music took on a more melancholy tone, as though the DJ was communicating directly to her.

She extricated herself from the cowboy and milkman, and retreated back to the couch. They tried to coax her back to the dance floor, before giving up and heading off to their next conquest. NYC Girl's ability to ward off men was *almost* as impressive as her ability to attract them.

The DJ seemed to smile in approval, while the pale man stared in silent judgment.

The pale man stood up.

Don't you fucking dare come near me, you fucking freak.

NYC Girl tensed with fear as he drew closer, before he glided past her and headed toward the stairs. Before he descended, he turned around and glared at her with a stare that seemed to glow red.

Meanwhile, the DJ continued to check her out. She reciprocated. Despite the hordes of writhing dancers and swirling glow sticks that obscured their sightlines, when they locked eyes—brief though it was—nothing else existed. Nothing else mattered. Though the weed probably had something to do with it, she was shocked at how suddenly content she felt with *everything*.

She knew from experience that this feeling wouldn't last.

Nothing good ever did.

7

Sure enough, NYC Girl's momentary happiness evaporated, once the pale man returned a couple of minutes later. He sat his emaciated frame on the opposite end of her couch, absorbing every last particle of positive energy from her body and soul. A waitress, carrying a tray filled with a rainbow assortment of shots, approached.

"Care for a shot?"

The pale man gave her an icy glare.

She turned her attention toward NYC Girl.

"Naw, I'm good," NYC Girl said.

Just as the shot girl turned around to leave, a booming voice came out of nowhere:

"Yo! Gimme two of them. One for her. One for me."

NYC Girl turned around and realized the voice was coming from the suave-looking man who had almost knocked her over when she was walking up the steps to the club entrance.

"Thanks, but I'm good," NYC Girl said.

"I don't like drinking alone," the man countered.

"Then don't drink."

The man smiled, without the sincerity of the DJ, and took two shots off the tray.

"I said I'm fine," NYC Girl insisted.

"This seat taken?" the man asked.

"Something tells me it wouldn't matter if it was."

Though she wasn't thrilled, at least he would be a buffer between herself and the pale man.

The man sat down and offered his hand.

"Elijah."

"*The* Elijah?" NYC Girl asked.

How did she not assume so from the start?

How fucking high am I?

"The one and only," Elijah said with a smug grin and a handshake that lasted longer than necessary.

Elijah handed one of the shot glasses to NYC Girl and raised his glass. NYC Girl clinked it. They drank. It certainly wasn't her first interview to start off with a shot. And probably not the last. Rarely did these jobs ever end well. She already had that old familiar feeling that landing the job would mean having no choice but to surrender to this man completely. She had to be careful—but could she afford to be?

She could feel the DJ's protective eye—and the pale man's judgmental one—on her.

"So, I hear you're looking for work?" Elijah said, officially kicking off the interview.

"You hiring?" NYC Girl asked.

She hoped she didn't come across as too desperate.

"Perhaps," he said with the appearance of a Cheshire cat. "I'm gonna go out on a limb and assume you turned down that shot because you were broke?"

"Maybe I just like saving my hard-earned cash," NYC Girl said, trying desperately not to lose her upper hand.

She refused to grant him further opportunity to penetrate her armored exterior, but sensed that he could see right through her as he tossed another half-sinister, half-seductive smile her way.

"Look, I'm not here to mess around. I just want a job. Shot girl, bartender, anything, don't matter."

She immediately regretted that she didn't stop at bartender.

"How about a real drink," he asked.

"Is this a *real* interview?"

"It is. But is this not a bar?"

She looked toward the DJ for comfort, but he was too distracted by his turntables to notice.

"Red or white?" Elijah said, as he rose to his feet.

"Red," NYC Girl said.

Wine? Classy motherfucker.

Wine was her weakness, more so than any liquor. Wine usually made her drunker faster, as though her body was not wired to handle such alcoholic sophistication.

"Wise choice," Elijah said, before walking away and down the stairs.

NYC Girl knew she should have left right there and then.

But once again, she handed over the reins to desperation.

Resigned to her all-too-familiar fate, she threw her back against the couch and closed her eyes, wishing the rest of the world would just get sucked into the same black hole as her own life.

For the first time since her return, she began to feel regret at having left New York City. As bad as it was, there were more options there. There were more options *anywhere*. Sure, there's no place like home, but that's not always a good thing.

So why the fuck am I here?!

NYC Girl tried to conjure the clarity she had felt that day in that laundromat when "You Are the Sunshine of My Life" was playing over the speaker system and she had made up her mind to return home, but she was far too stoned and intoxicated.

Old habits die hard. Or do they ever fucking die at all?

She did remember that she had ultimately decided that the comfort of the "known"—no matter how bleak—often outweighed any positive "unknowns."

But now, she wasn't so sure.

She looked back at the DJ, hoping that he could somehow give her some sort of sign. He popped a pill into his mouth and winked at her.

She closed her eyes and allowed his music to wash over her, like a drug, until she felt somebody's presence. It was Elijah, holding two glasses of wine. He handed her the red. He kept the white. And within arm's length of both of them was the pale man, who must have slipped closer to her when her eyes were closed.

Elijah sat down next to her, his leg pressed against hers. Though it was true that the pale man left little room for him, there was certainly enough real estate left for him to at least leave *some* space.

She leaned away from him, hoping it wasn't too obvious.

"Too close for comfort?" Elijah asked.

"Just tryin' to keep it professional," she replied, realizing this could possibly hurt her chances.

"The wine should help," he said, his glass raised for another toast.

Damn, this motherfucker likes to toast.

"To the future," Elijah began. "And all its endless potential."

Seriously?!

They clinked their glasses, and sipped their wine. In one smooth motion, Elijah put a firm bicep around her, but she grabbed it and placed it back where it came from.

"The interview?" NYC Girl said, less out of a desire for professionalism and more out of desperate necessity. If there wasn't a job to be had, then she didn't want to waste more time than she had to on this prick.

"Of course," he said, showing no sign that he was offended by her denial.

"So, tell me what makes you qualified to work here?"

"Qualifications. Umm, let's see. Worked across the street at Steve's Place. Three years. Worked in bars all over New York for seven."

"What kinda work?" Elijah asked.

"Let's just say I wasn't bartending."

Elijah perked up.

What are you saying? Shut the fuck up!

"Bouncing?"

"Something like that."

The Cheshire Cat reappeared.

She looked around. The room was closing in on her as it reached full capacity.

"So what kind of work do you got?"

"So you're definitely interested?"

"I mean, I wouldn't be here if I wasn't. Ain't exactly a lot of people hiring these days."

"One just has to know where to look," Elijah added.

"But it also depends on the nature of the work."

"I may have a few things suited for someone with your . . . skill set."

NYC Girl slugged down her wine. Way too fast.

Need to be careful.

"Want another?"

Without giving it a thought, she responded: "Yes."

Self-destruct mode activated.

"Be right back," Elijah said, patting NYC Girl's head like his little pet, before heading downstairs. She felt woozy, but not in a typical wine and weed way. And she could no longer feel her legs. She rubbed her forehead and closed her eyes.

And then she felt a cold breath on her neck.

"Are you aware you're in danger?"

She looked up through blurred vision. The pale man was hovering right beside her. He had managed to slide over undetected, like the phantom she suspected he was.

"From what?" NYC Girl said through slurred speech.

"From sin," he hissed.

"And you know this how?"

"Every week, it's someone different. And they never come back."

"The fuck you talking about?" she barked.

"I think you know the answer to that question."

"You do, huh?" Perhaps he was on to something.

"Let me ask you something," the pale man continued. "Do you have God in your heart?"

She laughed. He recoiled back, as though she had spat acid at him.

"Look, if you wanna help people find religion, this ain't the place."

"You're right," he countered. "Which is why if you fail to heed my word, you will pay the price."

"Is that a threat?" she asked.

"It's a promise."

"Fuck off!"

"And that's precisely your problem," the pale man said.

"I *said* get the fuck outta my face, asshole!"

"So be it," the pale man said, as Elijah reemerged, looming over both

NYC Girl and the pale man.

"In God's name, I go," the pale man said in surrender.

"You got a problem, nigga?"

"The problem is you . . . *nigger.*"

"Who the fuck you think you talking to, *freak*?"

The pale man disregarded Elijah and turned his attention back to NYC Girl.

"Remember, if you fail to take heed of my advice, you face certain death. This I promise you."

"You face certain death if you don't get your sorry old cracker ass outta here, you clown-faced motherfucker!" Elijah shouted over the DJ's thunder.

Elijah set the drinks down and lunged at the pale man. But the pale man was too quick, and instead pushed Elijah, who toppled backwards. The pale man then darted toward the stairwell. Elijah followed.

NYC Girl continued to slip into a void, hypnotized by the DJ's beats and enveloped by the fog from a smoke machine. She felt oblivious to reality, until the fog cleared to reveal a glimpse of the DJ, whose stare penetrated her soul like a laser beam.

"You hangin' in there?" asked a disembodied voice belonging to Elijah.

She turned around, feeling as though she were submerged in water. She nodded, but it didn't feel like her head. In fact, she no longer felt connected to her body at all. She felt as though she were watching herself.

An old familiar feeling.

She was a puppet.

"Sent Pastor Fuckface's ass to the promised land," Elijah said.

NYC Girl nodded, completely oblivious as to what Elijah was saying.

He pointed to her untouched wine glass.

"I'm good," she barely managed to mumble.

"I bet you are, baby," Elijah said. "I bet you are. Hey, come with me."

He offered a hand. She took it and he helped her to her feet. She struggled to keep her balance, but Elijah put an arm around her waist and helped guide her toward the stairwell.

A devil in knight's clothing.

As they reached the lobby at the bottom of the steps, Elijah led NYC Girl through the crowd and past the coat check.

"My suitcase . . ." she mumbled, as the sound of a gunshot, followed by loud commotion erupted from above.

"Wait here," Elijah told NYC Girl, helping her sit down on a church pew against a wall. He headed upstairs and she drifted off into a dream state.

He returned and led her outside, where cool, crisp autumn air filled their lungs, not that she had any awareness to any form of reality.

She could no longer recall her own name.

Church bells struck midnight at St. Mary's Cathedral, in perfect sync with DJ Anonymous' hammering beats, which throbbed and pulsated into the night.

Meanwhile, Elijah continued to prop her up.

A marionette.

To the casual observer, NYC Girl appeared no different than any other highly intoxicated person stumbling out of a club.

By some devilish miracle, Elijah managed to keep her up on her feet as he helped her walk. It was certainly no easy task.

Within a few minutes, they reached the parking garage—converted from the abandoned Michigan Theater. The arched proscenium above the stage was still relatively intact, worn thin and ravaged by brutal Michigan winters and neglect. Tattered curtains wafted in the theater balcony.

Elijah led NYC Girl to his shiny black Suburban, which was parked on a nearly empty floor. He opened the door for her and—ever the consummate gentleman—helped her into the passenger seat, and strapped her in like a child.

And then the world went black.

8

NYC Girl woke to an overplayed rerun; spread eagle, still dressed, minus her panties, her blouse pulled up over her breasts, on a filthy, moldy mattress. Her limbs felt like jelly.

The moon and stars shone through a rotted ceiling, from which the remnants of a broken chandelier dangled precariously.

Where the fuck am I?

The mattress was a deserted island in the middle of a floor. Everything else came in and out of her consciousness in fragments.

Deteriorating hardwood.

Scattered crack pipes and empty liquor bottles.

Rusty needles.

Weather-damaged walls adorned with graffiti.

She had been in dozens of places just like it—both in Detroit and New York. Usually, with a client. But not always as a victim. In this town, there was certainly no shortage of free fuck space. Sometimes they took her to a place like this. Sometimes she took them. Sometimes she came alone, seeking shelter for the night. Or to hide—from authorities, boyfriends, pimps, and johns. On more than one occasion, she ran away from home, from any combination of her mother's drug binges, random fucks, or abusive hand.

And look at her now!

The circle of motherfucking life.

And then. A familiar face.

Elijah.

Pants down. Massive cock at eye level. Erect, but floppy. The massive ones are always the floppiest.

He didn't seem to notice that she was awake.

She thought about screaming, realizing that this was likely to only set him off.

Nobody would be around to hear her screams anyway.

If a rape victim screams in the woods . . .

But then what?

"What the fuck are you doing awake?" he said, more panicked than angry that she had snapped back to consciousness.

She didn't respond. She was too busy drumming up a plan.

This time, she was going to do something about it. *But how?*

She would figure it out. If nothing else in her life was going to change, she was going to do everything in her power to ensure that this is the one thing that would.

And if she were going to die, it would be on her terms. Furthermore, despite her intentions, she refused to let this predator hurt the life growing inside her.

It was the first time she had felt protective of her unborn child.

"You may be awake," Elijah threatened. "But you sure as shit ain't getting away. And if you fucking tell anyone about what happened tonight, I *will* personally hunt you down and rip out your fucking guts. And as an added incentive . . ."

He removed a $100 bill and waved it in front of her face.

This motherfucker.

And then she spotted her golden ticket.

Elijah's 9 mm.

Lying right there on the edge of the mattress, within reach.

Stupid asshole.

Elijah turned around to set the money down.

"I'll leave this right here for you to take when you finish your job."

With Elijah's back still turned, NYC Girl somehow summoned the motor skills needed to grab the gun. When he turned back around, she took shaky aim at his one-eyed monster

It was no longer a person she was confronting, but rather the embodiment of every dick forced into her.

How the fuck can any man be aroused in a situation and in surroundings such as this? Sick fucks, all 'dem.

To NYC Girl, this was one of life's greatest mysteries. And Elijah was certainly no exception.

This time, she had one in her crosshairs. But rather than responding in horror, he simply laughed.

The goddamn motherfucker laughed. He refused to take her seriously.

But NYC Girl, in turn, refused to back down.

She held all the cards.

"Put your goddamn hands up in the air, you miserable motherfucker," NYC Girl demanded, struggling to keep the gun aimed at his cock. It wasn't that the gun was heavy. It was just that her faculties were still adjusting.

Somehow, the bastard remained erect as he threw his hands up in the air. Not in surrender. But in *mock* surrender.

And then—BANG!

Right through the palm of his hand!

Blood splattered onto NYC Girl's face.

Time stood still as they both attempted to process what had just happened.

Having never fired a gun before, NYC Girl couldn't believe her luck.

Once the immediate shock passed, Elijah screamed out:

"Motherfucker!!"

She continued to aim the gun, this time squarely at his chest.

His dick finally went limp, retreating back into the depths of hell from which it came.

"You goddamn crazy ass bitch!" he shrieked in a high pitch wail.

"Put your hands behind your head, asshole," she continued.

Elijah complied, moaning in pain, as blood dripped from his wounded palm and onto the bed.

"Please," he cried, "before you do something you regret."

NYC Girl continued to aim. Only now, her aim was steady.

"Get dressed," she ordered. "Then get the fuck outta here."

Elijah, moaning in pain, pulled his pants back on, and backed toward the door.

And then, he was gone.

And then there was silence.

NYC Girl would live to see another day.

But she had to remain vigilant. In case he came back.

As she slowly began to process the magnitude of what had happened, her entire nervous system quivered. For the first time in her life, she had not only fired a gun, but she had actually shot someone.

Someone who *deserved* to be shot.

There were no regrets. No fear.

Just an overwhelming sense of unfiltered courage.

NYC Girl attempted to stand, but her legs still didn't feel like her own. She desperately summoned her deep reserves of strength. But felt stuck.

At that moment, the smell of smoke filled her nostrils. It was strong. At first, she assumed that it was coming from somewhere down the street. But no. It was coming from *inside*. She needed to get out. *Fast.*

But her legs refused to budge.

As smoke began to drift into the room, she finally mustered the strength to stand up on legs made of Jell-O. She collapsed while attempting to take her first step, landing on top of the filthy mattress, next to a pool of fresh blood.

His? Or hers?

She kept her balance on her second attempt. She spotted her discarded panties, but felt too weak to pick them up. Pain enveloped every square inch of her body, inside and out.

She spotted the $100 bill and stared at it. She wanted to leave it on principle, but money was money, and money was one thing she needed more than anything. She picked it up and shoved it into her pocket, along with Elijah's gun, before she fumbled around the room until she found the doorway through smoke that grew thicker by the second. Her foot landed on a liquor bottle, almost causing her to fall back, but she managed to stay on her feet this time.

A small victory.

She finally found the exit and staggered her way down rotted stairs into the foyer, now completely engulfed with flames.

A piece of plaster from the ceiling fell, barely missing her.

This is not how I fucking die.

She turned back upstairs, thinking she had no choice but to jump. Even if it meant breaking a leg. Or, two. It beat the alternative. And though there was a part of her that invited death, she didn't wish to die this way.

Frantic, she looked around for her best exit option. No matter what, she would have to deal with a twenty-foot drop into flaming foliage. Just when she thought she had no other choice, she discovered the *one* window with no burning bushes below. It was also the only window not already broken, which presented a new challenge.

She spotted a brick lying on the floor, which probably *entered* the house through another window, and used it to smash this one. She looked down below to make sure it was safe enough to survive. There was only one way to find out.

She lifted one wobbly leg over the splintered, rotting window-frame until she was straddled over the window ledge, slicing her left hand on a remaining shard of glass. If she pushed off the ledge hard enough, she might be able to clear the shrubs all together and land on the weed-strewn lawn.

If she were lucky.

She turned back around to look down the hall. The fire had now reached the staircase. A wave of intense heat surged down the hallway.

Now was the time.

She lifted her other leg over the ledge, and lept.

She managed to barely clear the bushes and landed with a thud on the damp ground, knocking the wind out of her. She was pretty sure she had both cracked a rib and sprained an ankle. Curled up in a ball, she gasped for air, and cradled her belly.

Blood dripped down her arm from her lacerated hand.

She spotted Elijah's $100 bill on the ground, but as she reached for it, a gust of wind blew it away. She mustered the strength to pull herself up and limp toward it, but it landed in a burning bush.

As she collapsed back down, she tried to maintain some semblance of perspective: she was alive, but deep down, she knew she would be better off dead.

But she wasn't.

It was time to move on.

She slowly sat up and struggled to regain her breath. A large crash emanated from inside—presumably the staircase.

She grabbed the gun and limped across the street toward an empty lot. She couldn't help but feel that Elijah was lurking somewhere in the shadows.

There was always someone lurking in the shadows of her life.

She noticed a trail of blood. Hers? Elijah's? Was he waiting for her to emerge so he could finish what he started? Surely, he set the fire, right? At least she had a gun this time.

Although relieved that she had managed to maim the bastard so she could escape, she wished that she had shot his motherfucking dick off so he could never rape again.

Better yet, if only she shot him dead.

She was alive. And that's what mattered most.

But was it?

As she reached the lot, she realized that she couldn't go any further. She felt woozy and leaned against a hollowed-out tree. She clutched her ribs and gazed over at the mansion, now fully engulfed in flames.

Whether or not Elijah was still around remained to be seen.

How could *nobody else* be around?

Then again, that's exactly who she was: a *nobody*, surrounded by the condemned, Victorian mansions of Brush Park that once were home to the city's greatest somebodies: auto barons, doctors, and lawyers. It was now almost a completely abandoned, ramshackle haven for pushers, prostitutes, and the homeless.

Prime real estate for predators like Elijah.

Even if she were to encounter someone, it was unlikely to be anyone she could trust.

The blaze intensified against the dead black of night. As she stared into the flames, she couldn't help but feel she had somehow cheated death and that everything from her past was now burning inside that manor. But she knew better. The future would more than likely be no different than the past.

Something fell out of her pocket. She looked down. It was the beggar's origami rose sculpture. She reached for it and held it tightly against her heaving chest.

In that moment, there was nothing more important in the world.

And that's when she realized that her NYC medallion was missing.

Her most prized possession.

Gone. Consumed by flames.

She stared at the gun, sensing an easy way out.

She raised it to her head and held it there for several seconds, before lowering it.

As much as she welcomed death, it was not going to be at the hands of that motherfucker's gun.

9

Pressing her bleeding hand tightly against her body, NYC Girl limped down the middle of the abandoned street, surrounded by abandoned homes filled with the ghosts of abandoned dreams.

With the flames at her back, she was the nomadic queen of an urban desert, the sparkling lights of downtown a mirage.

Steam rose from sewers like smoke serpents.

At first, she doubted whether she would have the strength and stamina to make it one block, let alone several. But like a wounded animal that stays alive only because it knows of no other option, she trudged onward. But after three blocks, the pain in her ankle became unbearable. She wondered if it was broken. The cracked rib was bearable in contrast. Despite the pain, she knew she couldn't afford to stay inert. She had to keep moving.

And then, for the first time since the moment she decided to leave New York: *perfect clarity.*

It was time to go home.

She just had to get there first.

No. Not like this.

So where?

No fucking clue.

She couldn't make a decision with a clear mind, let alone after everything that had happened.

And then she remembered her suitcase.

Fuck!

No way she was going back to Saint Andrew's Hall tonight. She would come back for it tomorrow, hoping they would hold on to it for at least one day.

A wild peacock wandered in the middle of the street, before it disappeared into a patch of weeds against the background of a cat screaming in agonized heat. A persistent squeak echoed in the empty night, like a dying rodent. As the sound drew closer, she realized that it was too mechanical to be a living being. And then she had her answer, as a shopping cart rounded the corner across the street, pushed by an all-too-familiar figure.

At first, the beggar didn't seem to notice her, as though she were a ghost. But when he finally did, he flashed his pure and infectious grin.

"Hey! I remember you!" he exclaimed, shattering the silence. "From the train. How you doin', ma'am?"

For an instant, the world was once again full of color.

NYC Girl smiled back, stunned that she still had the wherewithal.

"You have yourself a good night!" the beggar shouted. "And sweet dreams!"

"You, too," NYC Girl replied.

And with that, he was, once again, gone. At this rate, she knew it was only a matter of time before she would see him again.

His presence reminded her that there were still echoes of kindness in this world.

Where was he going? Did he even know? Or, were they both simply two lost, wandering souls?

As the squeaks from the beggar's cart faded into the night, she found herself overcome with uncharacteristic compassion for her star-crossed acquaintance.

She suddenly wanted to *know* him.

At one point, he was new at the homeless game, too. She wanted to ask him: at what point does a temporary situation become permanent?

Somehow, he had found a way to survive. She needed to know how.

As NYC Girl limped across an overpass, she felt a sharp pain inside her gut. She buckled over and took deep breaths, but the pain intensified, before it finally subsided.

She returned her focus to her missing medallion.

A purchase made on the day she arrived in New York.

A symbol of her new life.

She spent more than she had any business spending, but in that moment, she was more confident than ever that her financial woes were finally going to be a thing of the past. And the medallion instantly became a tangible representation of her bright future.

Now that the future she envisioned was gone, it made perfect sense that her medallion would go with it. She was overcome with a sudden wave of nausea. She bent over and dry-heaved, and then vomited, filling a jagged, concrete crevice before she fell to the ground and began to sob.

Yet again, spread eagle to this fucked up thing called life. She couldn't remember the last time she cried this hard. Her ribs roared with pain.

After a few minutes, she regained some semblance of composure and hauled her body another couple of blocks, heading east on Jefferson Avenue, which ran parallel to the Detroit River. At least some semblance of human existence existed here: a steady parade of ghetto cruisers and pumping deep bass.

She passed by one of Detroit's most famous landmarks—the infamous Joe Louis fist, gifted to the city by *Sports Illustrated*. The perfect symbol of both a beat-up city and a city that refuses to go down without a fight. The only thing missing was an extended middle finger. Also in view was the Spirit of Detroit statue, mocking and taunting her

As she edged her way out of downtown, she figured it was only a matter of time before someone harassed her. But for once, nobody did.

She was already a ghost.

She trudged block after deserted block with no destination in mind until she finally reached the MacArthur Bridge, which connected the mainland to Belle Isle—the fabled island "playground" of her youth, smack dab between the U.S. to the north and Detroit's utopian neighbor to the south: Canada.

She stopped at the midway point of the bridge and stared down into the dark, swirling water.

She pulled out Elijah's gun and examined it, before tossing it into the river, as a leftover tear rolled down her cheek and joined an entire river made of tears.

She looked up, in search of answers that would never come.

A single raindrop landed on her arm.

She climbed the railing, fighting against the searing pain, and lowered herself toward the water.

It was the only thing that made sense.

She was going to end both her own misery and her unborn child's misery before it ever had a chance to know what misery was.

Two for the price of one.

Until tonight, she never thought herself capable of this.

She always feared death more than life.

Until now.

Why couldn't she have just died in that fire?

That was the *real* fucking tragedy.

The wind kicked up, as though offering a helping hand.

And then it began to pour—tears from heaven in a world gone to hell.

LEAF MAN

1

The glazed, beady eyes of a stuffed teddy bear stared up at Leaf Man as he hurried down the street, a battered, rolling suitcase trailing behind him like a lost puppy.

The stench of smoke assaulted his nostrils. And then he remembered.

Goddamn fucking Devil's Night.

He raised the volume on his Discman. A demo mix of his favorite new track—DJ Rolando's "The Knights of the Jaguar"—got his adrenaline pumping, instantly making him feel invincible, a reminder that as long as he continued to play his cards right, he would one day be up there with the DJs he had kept close tabs on since the 80's, when his dream was born.

Though it saddened him to see so much abandonment enveloping him, he found beauty in the squalor. In fact, the industrial blight inspired his creativity as much as did any of his musical heroes. More significantly, where most saw a city on its death bed, Leaf Man saw a blank canvas.

As Leaf Man stood upon the precipice of a new millennium, he imagined himself front and center.

A rebirth.

For himself.

And for the city he loved.

A city that had made an indelible mark on the world.

Only to be shunned, spit upon, kicked, and burned.

And left for dead.

A city finally ready for a true Renaissance.

Rising from the ashes.

A phoenix emerging in the form of his dream.

A couple of blocks from his destination, the wheel of his case became lodged in a crack, almost pulling his arm out of the socket. After a brief struggle, he wiggled the wheel free and continued on his way until he reached a dilapidated ranch, which one could easily assume was uninhabited, as suggested by its shattered windows and rusted bars.

Leaf Man knew otherwise.

Not only did he know *exactly* who lived there, but he had timed his arrival for when he knew no one was home—not by choice, but by court mandate.

He headed toward the back door, past a pile of putrid trash bags. The corroded handlebars of a child's tricycle poked through overgrown weeds.

Leaf Man removed two-hundred dollars from his wallet and slipped the money inside a box of chocolates from his suitcase. He sidestepped the rotted wooden step that led to the door and placed the box inside the torn screen door.

He walked away, saddened that he couldn't deliver the gifts by hand and fully cognizant of the fact that the intended recipient—his three-year-old son, Marcus—might never even get it.

Leaf Man's desire to once again see the joy on his son's face was the driving force behind everything he did. He was confident that day was only just around the corner.

Just have to make it through the night.

Of course, he knew that one slip up would mean losing *everything*, which is why this final deal couldn't be over soon enough.

He wanted to make headlines someday.

But for the right reasons.

He arrived at an empty bus stop, en route to soon becoming free from his self-made prison. Leaf Man was never one to place blame on others for his situation, or for the choices he made. Blaming himself meant that *he alone* was in control.

As the minutes rolled by, his hopes for a bus diminished. He knew one was *supposed* to arrive, but he also knew better. If he were lucky, he might find a cab, but he probably had a better chance at catching a bus. He could possibly reach his destination faster if he walked.

He would give it ten more minutes. Nine minutes later, he was on a bus. As the bus rumbled over streets strewn with potholes, he twirled his lucky ring on his right ring finger—gold, with an embossed marijuana leaf on it. As he thought about Marcus, pangs of panic settled in.

Every day that he couldn't see his son was a day he would never have back. Now that he was a father, Leaf Man had become fully aware of the importance of each and every day. His precious little boy was the only reason he was saying goodbye to the only life he had known for the last decade.

After several years dealing marijuana and, for a short time, heroin, he had turned his focus to the illegal distribution of *legal* prescription drugs and medical marijuana. In his mind, the pharmaceutical companies were the real criminals. Not him.

Robin Hood of the hood.

But none of this meant shit in the eyes of the law. As far as child custody law was concerned, it didn't matter if the drugs he sold were legal or not. Sure, he had the financial means to support his child, but he had to find a legal way for it to count in the court of law.

Despite his illicit trade, Leaf Man took pride in his strong sense of ethics. His clients knew this. He saw himself as no different than any start-up entrepreneur with legit business dealings. But it was no longer about his clients. It was all about Marcus.

In Leaf Man's line of work, he couldn't fear death. What he did fear, however, was leaving his child without a father. In many ways, that was already the case. But he had done everything he could within his legal limits. And he was trying everything he could to do even more.

Though the danger factor had diminished, the downside to his decision to point his moral compass toward pharmaceuticals was a steep drop in available cash flow. He still managed to turn a profit and—most importantly—could live without the guilt and fear of a harsher penalty if the time ever arrived for a long-delayed comeuppance. He could also sleep better at night in the knowledge that the prescription drugs helped keep his clients alive, unlike heroin. As for the ones who *were* dying, he could at least make their death more tolerable.

To ease his anxiety, Leaf Man pulled a tattered copy of Dreiser's *An American Tragedy* out from his case. He could always depend on boring literature to settle his nerves. The struggle and determination to get through *Moby-Dick* had required Captain Ahab-like dedication. Though he had been laboring through Dreiser for months, he wasn't going to give up on it. He regarded the reading of "boring," classic literature as the literary equivalent of green vegetables. In fact, the only classic he truly enjoyed was Ralph Ellison's *Invisible Man*.

At that moment, however, he just couldn't seem to focus. The magnitude of this night weighed on him like an anchor as he struggled to stay afloat. He looked up from his book as the bus rolled past his grandmother's old neighborhood in the Brightmoor district (aka "Blight More"), where, once upon a time, he knew true happiness. Going home to one's roots was bittersweet in ordinary circumstances. Returning after years of blight and neglect was downright tragic.

"Detroit turned out to be heaven, but it also turned out to be hell."

Marvin Gaye, one of his heroes, knew what was up.

In fact, most of the neighborhood was not only gone, but had since been returned to nature; the wilderness rapidly reclaiming what had been lost.

The vast majority of the businesses that lined the edges of the old neighborhood had long been boarded up, including the toy store his grandmother used to take him to every Sunday after church. Though the church was now a burned out shell, at least the embers of his faith that were fostered there were still burning.

Ten minutes later, Leaf Man disembarked at the intersection of 7 Mile and Greenfield. On the horizon, he noticed a tiny break in the clouds up ahead, as though the sun wanted to catch one last glimpse of the dying city before it turned in for the night. But looking around at the density of gray desert, the dual emergence of both the sun and the moon painted an otherworldly sky that seemed to defy all logic.

A glimmer of hope?

Leaf Man took this as a sign that better days lay ahead.

But as quickly as they appeared, the sun and the moon were swallowed up by the same clouds that had momentarily parted for this glimpse of temporary beauty.

He would never forget it.

And then a red-tinted cloud formation formed what looked, to him, like a dwarf.

One thing came immediately to mind.

Nain Rouge.

An old legend his grandmother had taught him.

His former DJ moniker.

2

Leaf Man walked a couple of blocks until he reached his "legitimate" employer, the Ma & Pa Pharmacy—an unknowing accomplice to his illegitimate one. In a few short hours, he would begin his new, legit job.

And if everything went according to plan, this would be the only job he needed.

The Ma & Pa Pharmacy was a bygone from another era—one of the few that hadn't been eradicated by the national, corporate chains. Unlike in most cases, it wasn't so much a matter of time; it was more a matter of nobody else *wanting* to set up shop in this particular location.

Leaf Man entered to the sound of a laughing Halloween skeleton, and was greeted by a familiar voice behind the counter.

"Well, well, well. Look what the cat dragged in," the elderly pharmacist exclaimed.

"What's up, Doc?"

"How many times do I have to tell you that I'm no doctor," the pharmacist sighed.

Leaf Man simply shrugged.

"So what brings you in here on a day off?"

"Just making sure I'm on the schedule for tomorrow. And while I'm here, pick up my dead presidents."

"You always work Sundays. Why would this one be any different?"

Leaf Man sensed a degree of skepticism.

"Just double checking. It's gonna be a late night tonight, so if I ain't on the schedule for some reason, I'd hate to be comin' in for nothing."

"You couldn't have called?" the pharmacist continued.

"Yeah, well, I was in the neighborhood . . . and, well, I figured you could use the company, you know."

"Well, it does get lonely in here, that's for sure. Want me to take you off the schedule?"

"No! No. I need the money."

"I'm sure there's nothing our customers want more than someone with little sleep filling their prescriptions."

"No worries. I'll be fully caffeinated and ready to go."

"Trembling hands caused by over-caffeination, in combo with lack of sleep, is also low on any customer's wish list."

"Have I ever let you down?" Leaf Man asked.

The pharmacist looked away, sighed, and changed the subject.

"So. You got big plans tonight?"

"Gotta work," Leaf Man replied.

"What? I don't pay you enough?"

"I landed me a gig. A *big-time* gig!"

"What kind of gig?"

"DJ."

"Like a mix master? Wooka-wicky?" the pharmacist said, pretending to scratch invisible turntables.

Leaf Man chuckled. "You know it!"

"I know *of* it."

"You should come down, Doc. Tonight. Saint Andrew's."

The old man laughed and peered over his glasses. "You know, I might have a pill for delusional thinking. If I can find some back here, they're all yours."

"I'm serious, Doc!"

"Let's just say the last time I went to a club, they had a separate section for folks like us. And they also used all live instruments."

"Well, then come see how things have changed."

"Maybe next time. I better get your dead presidents before they start to rot."

The pharmacist disappeared into an office tucked away in the back of the store. This was Leaf Man's cue. He grabbed some empty bottles from his suitcase and filled them with stock from the shelves. Efficiency was key and he had mastered that long ago. He hadn't been caught yet and he intended for tonight to be nothing short of business as usual.

Normally, he had numerous prescriptions to fill.

But tonight, he had just one.

His final curtain call.

Just as he managed to stuff the bottles into his coat pocket, the pharmacist stepped out of his office with a wad of cash and handed it to him. Leaf Man didn't even bother to count it.

"Gotta roll," Leaf Man said. "Can't keep my fans waiting!"

"You mean the ladies?"

"Now you're talking, Doc!"

"Break a leg!"

"And I'll know exactly where to come for painkillers afterward!"

"I'm sure," the pharmacist said with a wink.

Does he know?

Leaf Man could never quite figure out if the pharmacist was clueless, or whether he simply turned a blind eye. He leaned more toward the latter. The old man was way too smart. But if so, why so generous?

As Leaf Man turned to leave, he was almost knocked down by a large beast of a man, who huffed and puffed his way in like the Tasmanian Devil.

A powder keg ready to explode.

Leaf Man lingered for a while, just in case he needed to have the old man's back. The beast glared at Leaf Man in a manner that suggested that he better get the fuck out of the way.

"So what is it today?" the pharmacist asked.

The man was in no mood for idle chit-chat. He slammed a wrinkled piece of paper on the counter with a meaty hand. The initials "R.I.P." were etched onto his massive left bicep.

The pharmacist studied the prescription.

"Not even gonna ask."

"How much?" the beast demanded.

"You looking to kill pain, or a person?"

"Come on, man. You know who it's for. And he's getting worse every second you're wasting!"

"I can't just keep giving this stuff out willy-nilly. I can lose everything if someone thinks my client is the new Dr. Jack."

Leaf Man's ears perked up at the desperate man's plea. His natural instinct. It was how he had amassed most of his clients.

Desperation. The name of the game.

The man's demeanor softened for a second, before he realized that Leaf Man was eavesdropping.

"The fuck you looking at?!"

Leaf Man held up his hands in peaceful surrender.

"No need to give my man a hard time," the pharmacist said. "Ain't his fault."

"Come on man," the beast continued. "You want my father's death on your hands? You know him. You're his friend!"

Leaf Man sensed the old man not only *wanted* to help, but had helped countless times before.

"I'm begging you," the beast continued.

Leaf Man knew he could get the man what he needed, but fought off the urge to help.

When he promised himself a clean break, he meant a *clean* break.

"Look. If you're asking for miracles, this ain't the place," the pharmacist said.

"I ain't asking for no miracles. I just need a little goddamn fucking help."

"Listen. This ain't a charity I'm running here," the pharmacist said. "It's a *business*. Now, I've stuck my neck out for you and your father before—Lord knows how many times—but I just can't keep doing this. Take a look around, man. Times are tough. And they ain't gettin' any better. And if I keep sticking my neck out for you, pretty soon, I'm going to be the one asking *you* for favors."

Infuriated, the man grabbed his prescription slip, crumpled it into a ball, turned, and charged out the door, which he slammed with enough force to knock a few bottles off the shelf.

The laughing skeleton echoed in response.

"Sometimes, I feel like I'm running a goddam soup kitchen," the pharmacist said to Leaf Man.

"Maybe you should consider expanding your business?"

The pharmacist rolled his eyes.

"Alright, Doc. I'm out," Leaf Man said.

"See you at the break of dawn."

Outside, Leaf Man looked around for the man. At first, he thought he was gone, but then he spotted him slouched against the wall, hands over his face.

"Hey," Leaf Man said. He looked around to make sure no one else was around.

"Get the fuck outta here, asshole!"

"What if I told you I can hook you up for half the market price?"

"The fuck you know about what I need?" the man demanded.

"I know enough. And can probably help."

"Shit. Whatever," the man replied, his voice rife with doubt.

"You want my help or not?"

"Why should I trust you?"

"Why should I trust *you*?"

"Look. I don't have no fucking time to waste!"

"It won't be a waste. I promise you. Can you meet me outside the Boat Club on Belle Isle at 3:30?"

"You can't get it no sooner?"

"Not before 3:30."

"Why the fuck should I trust you?"

"How desperate are you?"

"Desperate as fuck."

"Can you pay?"

The man nodded. "Yeah."

"Then it looks like we're both just gonna have to put faith in each other."

Leaf Man offered his hand. The man reluctantly offered his bear paw of a hand and shook it.

"Looks like today is your lucky day," Leaf Man said. "Let me have your number so I can call you when I have confirmation."

"I don't have a phone."

"Then I'll see you over there."

"If you're fucking with me . . ."

"Right back at ya, man!"

Leaf Man walked away.

What-the-fuck-did-I-just-do?

The stage had been perfectly set for his first legit DJ gig, to follow immediately on the heels of his final deal.

And just like that, he had fucked it all up, again.

Old habits . . .

Leaf Man quickened his pace. The sooner he could get to work, the sooner he could get his mind off . . . *everything.* His music was the only way to do that.

He reached his bus stop and glanced at his watch.

Still ahead of schedule. Barely.

As he waited for his bus, he looked up and noticed that the gray skies had darkened against the backdrop of a setting sun and gathering clouds.

Would he ever escape his past? Or, was this so-called bright future just a mirage?

He had his doubts. Pangs of panic began to course through his entire being. He reminded himself that he didn't have to go through with it. But would there be payback? His unexpected, "accidental" client certainly seemed like the type who was quite familiar with retribution. So which scenario posed the greater risk?

The last thing he wanted was to wind up dead on the doorstep of his dream just as he was finally about to go completely clean.

Nor, did he want to go into hiding just when he was making a name for himself.

He was also not one to go back on his word.

I never should have opened my goddamn mouth. Too late now.

The bus arrived and he boarded the empty vessel—en route to his now *second-to-last* deal. He pulled out his phone and dialed the supplier he only knew as "the Canadian."

"Got an order for you," Leaf Man said.

"Thought you quit," said a hushed voice.

"Yeah, I thought so, too."

"Knew it wouldn't last."

"I'm still out of the game after tonight. Just something came up."

"Old habits die hard, eh?"

"Trust me," Leaf Man pleaded with confidence. "It's a one-time thing. Then I'm out like a light."

"To make it clear, you got a lot of nerve quitting on me. In fact, you're lucky I let you off the hook as it is. You got even bigger balls for crawling back."

"Believe me. This wasn't part of my plan."

"Thing is, I'm already in town. A bit short notice, ain't it?"

"If you can't swing it, I'd understand," Leaf Man said.

"Tell you what. If pulling this favor can convince you to stay on board, then I'll get it done."

"Sorry. Ain't gonna happen."

"The night's still young. So, I'm going to bank on the hope you'll change your mind. What you need?"

3

As Leaf Man climbed off the bus on Vernor, the words of the Canadian echoed through his head.

Old habits die hard, eh?

I'm going to bank on the hope you will change your mind.

What if he was right?

Fuck that.

It's my life.

I call the shots.

He put on his headphones and blasted Bowie's "Sound and Vision," a quick pick-me up as he made his way down Livernois and through yet another neighborhood dotted with more empty lots than homes. The homes that were still standing were burned out beyond repair, defiant shells of buildings, daring to be torn down, cocky in their confidence that it would probably never happen.

It begged the question: *is a neighborhood still a neighborhood when there are no neighbors?*

Stevie Wonder's "Sir Duke" was up next.

And, suddenly, he never felt more at home.

This particular tract of land at least had a pulse, faint as it were. And that pulse belonged to Mrs. Harris, his favorite and most tenured client. Though he wouldn't miss much about his soon-to-be-former life, he would certainly miss her. Mrs. Harris always felt more like family and it was only fitting that she was *supposed* to be his curtain call.

Leaf Man approached Mrs. Harris's well-manicured sidewalk, which seemed even more immaculate against the backdrop of its tumbledown surroundings. When he reached her warmly-lit porch, he noticed one blemish he promised to tend to: her broken mailbox, still lying propped up against her porch as it had been for months. He wouldn't have time to fix it tonight, but at least he would have an excuse to visit again—not as her dealer, but as her friend. It saddened him that nobody else had taken the time to fix it. It was even sadder that he was probably the only one who would.

He gave three hard knocks. He knew the door would be unlocked and that he would be expected to come in, but he didn't like to go in unannounced. It was no secret that Mrs. Harris kept a loaded 9 mm in her end table—a gift he had given her in response to her request. And it was also no secret that she had successfully used it to ward off intruders on a couple of occasions. He didn't want to become an accidental third victim.

Though she was expecting him, it appeared to Leaf Man that Mrs. Harris was beginning to lose some of her marbles. He didn't know what to expect anymore.

Leaf Man knocked one more time, but Mrs. Harris didn't answer. He entered with caution and walked past a long, doily-draped table, lined with framed portraits of the disappearing act known as her family. Though still alive, they all might as well have been ghosts.

When Leaf Man reached the end of the hallway, he saw a familiar sight: Mrs. Harris sitting in the ragged, vintage orange and brown recliner she affectionately referred to as "the best seat in the house."

In fact, Mrs. Harris's entire home was a time capsule hearkening back to the city's hey-day.

Before everything became lost.

Despite the immaculate exterior of her home, the interior was a lot more "lived-in." It was cluttered, but not like that of a hoarder, but rather, in a warm and inviting sense.

"Throwing away old newspapers is like throwing away history," she always said, with no evident awareness of modern media.

This same philosophy clearly applied to *everything* else in her house. In fact, Mrs. Harris had lived in this house for over sixty years, along with her husband who had passed away four years earlier. When they bought the house, the neighborhood was still fairly new.

Before it all changed. Before big industry had moved in and before everything became coated with a strange, colorful dust that many believed to be a cause for the upsurge in cancer diagnoses among Delray's residents.

Though Leaf Man found it hard to believe, Mrs. Harris told him frequently that he was her favorite visitor. And it wasn't a stretch to say that the feeling was mutual. She reminded him of his own grandmother, who raised him until she passed away when he was seventeen. Fortunately, by that point, she had taught him everything he needed to know about being a gentleman, with old-fashioned decency and respect.

With Mrs. Harris, it felt like he was making up for lost time, which was perhaps the main reason he dreaded telling her that he could no longer be her personal pharmacist.

"Is that the gigolo I ordered?" Mrs. Harris asked in a creaky, dry voice when she heard his footsteps.

"You wish," Leaf Man said, laughing, somewhat taken aback by her uncharacteristic, ribald greeting.

"So when you gonna start locking your door, Mrs. Harris?"

"The day I leave for heaven," she responded, in the dry humor he was more accustomed to. Despite her frail frame and sunken face, her spirit shone brightly.

"So how you doin', Mrs. H?" Leaf Man asked.

Before he had even finished his question, he already knew the answer. Although Mrs. Harris has been losing weight for some time, the change was now becoming increasingly obvious. Mrs. Harris was looking more like a living skeleton with each passing day.

"Still vertical," she sighed. "Still living. Just ain't livin' too well."

"Well, hopefully I can help with that."

"Just having you visit me is all the medicine I need, sugar."

Though she lived alone, she did have a son, a daughter, and five grandchildren, all living in the metro area. But in their minds, Detroit might as well have been on the other side of the world. While she remained in the family home, the rest of her family fled for a comfortable suburban existence the first chance they got.

Like so many others in post-rebellion Detroit, her family fled north of 8 Mile. As Mrs. Harris's family proved, it wasn't just "white flight" that contributed to population loss. It was a matter of who could afford it. Despite constant pressure from her family to join them across the 8 Mile divide—especially after yet another break-in—Mrs. Harris stood steadfast.

Over time, once the excuses had run out, her family simply stopped coming to visit.

"The only way I'm leaving my home is in a box," she would insist, along with "my next home is in the promised land."

Next to Mrs. Harris on a cluttered end table was an empty, stained, plastic camping mug—the only cup she used—and from what Leaf man ascertained, the only one she owned. The only thing she drank out of it was water. No juice. No tea. No coffee. And certainly no alcohol. Never a drop in her life.

"Let me get you some more water," Leaf Man insisted.

"My feet still work, honey."

"And so do mine, Mrs. Harris," Leaf Man said, taking the cup over to her cluttered kitchen, where a week's worth of dishes lay piled up in the sink. He would wash them, as he always did.

He turned on the tap. Rust-tinged water spurted out, so he waited several seconds until it became a light yellow, which was about as clear as it got. He filled up the cup, and brought it to Mrs Harris.

"Thank you, honey," she said. She took an extra-long sip. He wondered how long it had been empty—and how long she had been thirsty.

"We gotta do something 'bout those pipes," he said.

"Son, I've drank that water for over sixty years. Ain't no reason to change the recipe now."

"Is it possible it's getting worse?"

Mrs. Harris shrugged him off.

"I'll be right back."

Leaf Man headed back to the kitchen to wash the dishes. Despite the time crunch, he was still in pretty good shape. He couldn't help but wonder who would clean the dishes when he was gone.

"Glad to see you're eating again," he said, taking note of the dirty dishes.

"Don't bother with them dishes, honey," Mrs. Harris said from the other room. He ignored her plea.

He left the dishes in the rack to drip dry, and then made his way back to the living room. He paused to examine Mrs. Harris's wedding portrait, which hung next to a picture of a little girl in a ballet costume. She appeared so vibrant—*so alive*—in contrast to the withered old soul whose emaciated frame barely dented the cushion of her recliner. But she still had that same spark in her eyes.

Leaf Man sat down on the sofa, adjacent to the recliner. It was time to get down to business. He removed a prescription bottle and a single blue pill. Mrs. Harris took it from him, popped it into her mouth and, with a trembling hand, took a large sip of water, nearly choking on it. Leaf Man had to tilt the mug upward to prevent her from spilling the water on her lap.

"Easy there, Mrs. Harris."

She laughed, triggering yet another cough.

"Now don't forget, Mrs. Harris. Three times a day, okay?"

"Haven't forgotten once."

"And don't take it on an empty stomach. Take it with your meals. You remember what happened last time, right?"

She shook her head, confused. It wasn't like her to forget details such as these.

"And avoid operating any heavy machinery. Or driving."

"The only machine I'll be operating is this old, knock-off La-Z-Boy."

Leaf Man laughed.

"Why do you insist on telling me all of this every time?" she asked.

"Protocol, Mrs. H. I'm a professional."

Mrs. Harris reached deep into her bra and removed a couple of twenty-dollar bills. Leaf Man was totally caught off guard.

"Here you go, sugar," she said.

"Naw, this one's on me," Leaf Man said.

"Stop talking like a fool," she said.

"Consider it my goodbye gift."

No turning back now.

Mrs. Harris's joyful demeanor sunk.

"Oh, Lord. My time is up isn't it? And you're really the Grim Reaper in sheep's clothing coming to reap your just reward."

He couldn't tell if she was serious.

"You know damn well that you're going to outlive all of us, Mrs. Harris."

"Dear Lord, I certainly hope not. Now, tell me, son, what's this goodbye business all about?"

"Before I explain, please, put that money away."

She stuffed the money back down her shirt. He expected more resistance.

"It's time to finally go after what I've been chasing my whole life."

"Music?"

Leaf Man nodded.

"Praise the Lord! About damn time!"

When her joy quickly morphed into concern, he knew exactly what she was thinking.

"And don't worry. I already lined somebody up for you next month and beyond. He's good. You'll like him."

"Nobody can replace you," she said. "But I understand. Best get out while you still can. I'm happy for you."

"Thank you, Mrs. Harris. Can I get you anything before I go?"

"Son, what I need, you wouldn't want to give an old lady like me."

Leaf Man was thrown for another loop.

"Easy now, Mrs. Harris," he said with a nervous chuckle.

She had never flirted with him before.

"Don't mean I won't be back," Leaf Man assured her.

"Thank you. You're one of the good ones, son. Lord knows you're a dying breed."

"For the sake of the planet, I hope not," Leaf Man said. "On both counts."

"You are. And you know it."

"Take care of yourself," Leaf Man said. "And remember, you were always my favorite customer. And not just because of all the business you brought me."

"Whatever you do, don't look back. Unlike me, you're still writing your prologue. I'm finishing up my epilogue."

"Like I said, you're gonna live forever, Mrs. Harris."

"*Shiiit*," Mrs. Harris said. "Come give me a hug, you son of a bitch."

Until tonight, swearing—like flirting—was simply not in her character. Mrs. Harris was a genuine Christian in all the right ways—his type of Christian. She even went so far as to watch church on TV when she could no longer leave her house. In fact, it was her stubborn insistence to go to church that led to an unfortunate slip off her icy porch. Fortunately, she suffered only a few scrapes and bruises, but she knew right then that God was telling her that the time had come to become an armchair Christian.

Leaf Man wondered if she'd ever leave her house again, especially with another long Michigan winter looming. He would see to it that he would take her for a stroll every now and then.

As they continued to hug, he tried to push back the tears swelling in his eyes, but it was no use.

"You take care, Mrs. Harris."

"It has been a true pleasure knowing you, you hear me now?" Mrs. Harris said, through tears of her own.

"Hey, come on, Mrs. H. Enough of that. I'm gonna be back. I promise. Somebody gotta fix your mailbox. In fact, I'll be back in a couple of days.

And if you ever need me for anything else, you got my number. You take care, okay, Mrs. Harris."

"Don't you worry about me, son. God bless you. God bless."

And with that, Leaf Man headed out into the cold, dark night, his back illuminated by the warm glow emanating from Mrs. Harris' home—like the dying embers of a fire set ages ago.

4

Leaving the warmth of Mrs. Harris's home made the outside world seem even colder and emptier. Despite what he said, for the first time since Mrs. Harris became his client, Leaf Man no longer got the sense that she would be around forever. Then again, his uneasiness was probably just compounded by the fact that what should have been his final deal wasn't.

Just have to get through this one night.

A night that had barely just begun.

After a short bus ride, Leaf Man arrived at his renovated loft on Woodward Avenue, a turn-of-the-century edifice itself that had just re-opened two months prior to his arrival after decades of neglect and decay—one of many derelict buildings that had been spared the wrecking ball.

An hour from now, he would be spinning his magic. His big moment. But first, he had to get ready.

When he reached his fifth-floor abode, he threw on a pair of sleek black pants and a shiny, silver button-down shirt.

A techno-noir disciple of the future.

He realized he had around twenty minutes or so to spare, so he dropped a needle on Coltrane's *A Love Supreme*—the calm before the storm before he blew the roof off of Saint Andrew's Hall.

He poured himself some stale coffee—he hated waste—then sat in his grandfather's old, wooden rocking chair to delve into more Dreiser. Beneath him was the same deteriorating cushion that his grandfather had sat on for most of his adult life. Though Leaf Man often thought about replacing it, this nostalgic heirloom had more value than comfort and support.

As forward thinking as he was, Leaf Man considered the past to be the fuel that propels the future. And as of tonight, he felt as though he had finally reached the doorstep to his own future: a gig at the legendary Saint Andrew's Hall, a long-deferred pipe dream that had spent years adrift in a swampy no man's land.

His elusive white whale.

Every square inch of Leaf Man's loft was a shrine and testament to his dream, starting with the alto sax resting nobly on a stand in one corner, artfully against exposed brick.

His mother's sax.

His most prized possession.

He planned to someday fuse it into his electronica. Now that he had finally "made it," it was up to him to defy expectations of what a DJ could be. He had full faith that there was no music on earth that couldn't be fed through his turntables and mixed to create sonic experiences never before heard, nor felt, to traverse and transcend all genres of music and thereby creating his very own while pushing the boundaries of techno into unexplored dimensions.

Leaf Man's obsession with music began from the time he was in utero, when he would dance around the womb to his mother's constant mix of Motown, soul, and jazz.

Although his mother had died in childbirth, the music she embedded into his soul kept her close to him, along with a picture of her from high-school graduation, less than a year before he was born, that he kept taped inside the cover of his turntables. She would *always* be there for him, his musical soul and muse, and he felt both her presence and absence in equal measure.

Leaf Man's grandmother also did her part by telling him story after story about his mother, including the moment her water broke. If his mother had any flaws, his grandmother certainly didn't let on. If there was one single thing that made him feel his mother's presence more than anything, it was "I Hear a Symphony" by The Surpremes, which she had played and sung to him throughout her entire pregnancy. Sometimes, she simply hummed it. That song became part of his DNA. In essence, it was the only direct emotional link he felt to his mother.

Though times were often tough during his childhood, music was a constant in his grandmother's home, functioning as a much-needed elixir. After all, it was his grandmother who had instilled his mother's love for music to begin with. And as long as there was music, there was joy, even in the worst of times.

As his grandmother once told him, when you have music deep in your soul, there is even music in the silence.

Leaf Man knew how to dance before he could walk. His favorite toys were all musical instruments. And any toys that weren't instruments, he somehow fashioned into instruments. When he was two, his grandmother found him a Casio keyboard at a local thrift shop. By the time he was three, he had learned to play "Mary Had a Little Lamb" and "Twinkle, Twinkle Little Star." Though never short of playmates, he usually preferred to spend his free time with his instruments than with his friends.

Though money was tight, his grandmother did all that she could to foster Leaf Man's musical talents, which included piano lessons. His mother would have done the same. It was the best way to honor her legacy.

Leaf Man also learned at an early age that music transcended time, space, language, and cultural barriers. There was no such thing as old music, new music, white music, black music. It was all just music. The cure to all ills. The maker of peace. The ultimate love maker. And now that he had been granted a stage, it was his duty to make everyone else a convert.

Though he loved pretty much all music, he did have his favorites, his musical anchors, to which he would continuously return. In addition to techno, he was fixated with Motown, Miles, Coltrane, Bowie, Iggy Pop, Prince, The Eurythmics, Gary Numan, Kraftwerk, and, for the psychedelic element alone, Pink Floyd. He even had a soft spot for those blue-eyed soul muthas, Hall & Oates—for reasons that not even he could understand.

Leaf Man drew further inspiration from Manchester, England, which he viewed as Detroit's musical twin city. Like Detroit, Manchester was a northern industrial working-class city whose music—from the likes of Joy Division, New Order, and the ramshakle chaos of The Fall, to his favorite, A Guy Called Gerald—reflected the diversity and vibrancy of its citizens. His friend and mentor, Johannes, had introduced him to the rave music made famous through Manchester's fabled Haçienda nightclub, and although the Haçienda had long since closed, Leaf Man vowed to one day to make a pilgrimage, once he was able to land a world tour. And hopefully when it was all said and done, he himself would become synonymous with Atkins, May, and Saunderson. The Belleville Three had laid the foundation; Leaf Man planned to take it to the next level: the ultimate Detroit sound for the new millennium.

During his high school years, it was easy for Leaf Man to become lost in his dream as he began to spend almost every waking moment recording and making demos on a four-track home studio. He began to skip school with increasing frequency. The moment he put his headphones on, all of the hassles and nonsense of the outside world ceased to exist. Nothing could penetrate his sanctuary, well, other than his grandmother ordering him to the dinner table. Certainly not his classmates, despite having to endure taunts of listening to "dat cracka-ass shit." In fact, the more they got on him about it, the deeper he disappeared into sonic landscapes, made by his own hand, borrowed from others, or that blurred the lines between the two.

Yet again, as future-thinking as he was, Leaf Man believed that the future arrived on the ghosts of the past, so it came as no surprise that following a recent Motown phase, he set his sights on gospel. It wasn't that he was feeling particularly religious; perhaps just a tad more *spiritual*?

After all, music was his church.

In fact, if anything, he owed this gospel phase to Moby's recently-released "Play" album, a fusion of techno and gospel music. Moby was his current muse. And of course, Moby himself was a disciple of the Detroit sound.

There was nothing Leaf Man loved more than unearthing layers of creativity he otherwise never would have tapped into. And he only had to please an audience of one: *himself*. That was the key to success as far as he was concerned. He also wasn't afraid of failure. It worked like muscle memory. Being an innovator meant fucking up more often than those who remained in their comfort zone. He had stalwart faith that as long as he did not deviate from his mission, he would eventually end up where he needed to be. And then an audience would follow—once they caught up with him. Just like they eventually caught up to Johannes.

Leaf Man had met his mentor, Johannes, at Saint Andrew's Hall as a naive sixteen-year-old with a huge dream and no idea what to do with it. Johannes had moved to Detroit from Berlin and was one of the resident DJs at Saint Andrew's. Leaf Man was eager to learn from the European techno master, and Johannes took Leaf Man under his wing.

Constantly hopped up on speed and ecstasy, the crazy-ass DJ would talk a mile a minute, name dropping bands like there was no tomorrow. He would foist mix tape after mix tape on Leaf Man—"you must listen here, ja!"—techno, classic rock, punk, new wave, classical, industrial bands with crazy unpronounceable names like Einstürzende Neubauten.

LEAF MAN : 79

At first, the names Johannes tossed at him were a blur. A disharmonious drone. However, over time, the music not only became familiar to him, he learned to mix his own blended concoctions into the pot. It was Johannes who introduced Leaf Man to fellow Michigander, Iggy Pop, who—like Leaf Man—was inspired by Detroit's noise and chaos, turning his memory of the titanic thud of the machine press at the Ford River Rouge Complex into his own industrial backbeat.

Though Leaf Man had discovered the Detroit techno scene on his own and knew it like the back of his hand, it was through Johannes that he had learned about Kraftwerk and Neu!—the forefathers of electronic music who created the music that essentially laid the groundwork for the birth of techno. Of course, Johannes arrived stateside already equipped with a sincere appreciation and knowledge of the first wave of Detroit techno royalty. Fast on their heels came the likes of Carl Craig, DJ Rolando, and Jeff "The Wizard" Mills.

Although Johannes returned to Berlin after his visa expired, Leaf Man had everything he needed to reach this exact moment in life—a moment into which he had poured every waking hour of the last ten years. Johannes had even given Leaf Man his first mixer, which was technically intended for "safekeeping" until he returned.

Leaf Man was still waiting. And still using that mixer, dreaming of the day it would be reunited with its original owner, either in Detroit or in Berlin.

The needle reached the end of the Coltrane record moments before he finished a chapter. He thought about switching records, but as every musician understood, sometimes silence was the best soundtrack.

This was one of those moments.

Leaf Man closed his eyes, and cleared his mind of everything until all that remained was *tonight*.

He twirled his leaf ring, which always helped put his mind at ease. Just as he began to feel the inner peace he needed to carry him through the night:

KNOCK!

KNOCK!

KNOCK!

Fuck.

He slid the peephole cover open, even though he already knew who it was: the friendly neighborhood junkie from across the street in need of a "cup of sugar." He wore a hoodie displaying the Olde-English "D"—a disgrace to the logo, but sadly, a fair representation of it these days.

"Out of business," Leaf Man said from behind the door.

"C'mon man!" said a voice on the other side of the door. "I know you got something for me. Please, one last time. For old time's sake."

"Show's over, man. Finito!"

"One last time, dude. I swear!"

"Gotta find someone else."

"Fuck that shit, nigger! I know you got something for me in there, so cut the bullshit!"

Leaf Man raced to an end-table, pulled out his 9 mm, and stormed back to open the door as far as the door chain would allow. He cocked his gun, and aimed it square at the junkie's face.

"What part of out of business don't you understand?"

The junkie backed away from the door, tripped, then scurried down the steps, muttering something along the lines of "go fuck yourself."

Gun still in hand, Leaf Man walked across the open space toward the large picture window of his downtown loft. The tail end of a sunset shrouded a dying city. He had already been through so much, yet night had barely fallen. He felt tired. Not a good sign, considering what lay ahead. Caffeine was certainly in his future.

Meanwhile, the junkie staggered into Leaf Man's view, rocking back and forth in the middle of the empty street, before wandering out of sight.

Leaf Man couldn't help but feel partially responsible for the deterioration of this man. Even though he would have found another dealer, Leaf Man wasn't willing to let himself off the hook. He was well aware of the fact that he had directly contributed to some of the problems that plagued the city. This would always be his cross to bear.

And his mission now was to dedicate his life to reversing the damage he had done, if only through his music.

He attempted to purge these thoughts temporarily as he gazed toward the Ambassador Bridge on the horizon, heading *south* to Canada. Detroit couldn't even keep its fucking geography straight.

When he finally shook the junkie's disruption, he stuffed his gun into a hidden compartment at the bottom of his traveling suitcase, where it joined forces with a Swiss Army knife, and his wallet. If somebody were going to steal his wallet, they would have to steal his whole fucking bag.

If it weren't for the fact he had one more deal, he probably would have left both at home. He wasn't proud of the fact that he owned a gun at all, but it was a necessary evil in his line of work. Though he never had to pull the trigger, he had come close on numerous occasions. And always in self-defense. He always figured that it was only a matter of time. Now that he was finally going clean, he was hopeful that those days were behind him.

Leaf Man headed over to a stack of neatly-labeled crates filled with records and selected several to load into his suitcase. He refused to go digital, though he knew it would make life so much easier. Vinyl was his medium. Like the masters that came before him.

He made sure to throw in his good luck charm—his mother's "I Hear a Symphony" album. More for sentimental reasons, than anything else.

His security blanket.

As he prepared to head out, he put on his headphones and cranked up Tchaikovsky's bombastic "Piano Concert No. 1 in B-Flat Minor." This song captured everything it meant to be on the precipice of a dream bigger than himself. *This* is what he lived for. It was his holy mission to make the whole world feel the same way.

He headed out, past the building's only elevator, which had been "out of service" since he moved in six months before. The stairwell smelled of piss and rot.

Outside, the final vestige of the sun was overshadowed by a sudden gathering of dark clouds in perfect harmony with his music. Leaf Man lowered the volume, as he kept his eye open for anyone suspicious, but only a cocktail of dead leaves and assorted trash accompanied him down the street, drawn to his body like magnets. With no signs of life, he quickened his pace. The emptier the streets, the more dangerous. He didn't fear people. He feared the empty spaces where people hid.

As Leaf Man turned a corner, a voice rang out behind him. He didn't even have to look up.

"C'mon, man. You can't just hang me out to dry. I got money."

"Find somewhere else to spend it," Leaf Man said, without looking back.

"Hey! I ain't taking no for an answer," the junkie said, right on his heels.

"I can't turn water into crack. Time to move on."

As Leaf Man continued walking, he heard a metallic spring and click behind him.

A switchblade.

In one swift moment, he spun around and put the junkie in a headlock. The junkie surrendered instantly without a fight and pocketed his knife. Leaf Man saw the eyes of a defeated man and released him.

The junkie then staggered about-face and ran off into the night, through the steam pouring out of manholes with missing covers like spirits escaping hell.

Re-energized with adrenaline, Leaf Man quickened his pace toward the nearest People Mover station. Despite the unexpected adrenaline rush, he knew it wouldn't last, so he stopped en route at a liquor shop to purchase a bottle of unsweetened iced-tea. His dedication to a clean life included the food and drink he put in his body, though he often fell short of his goal.

Leaf Man finally reached the edge of a mostly empty, half-lit downtown and headed toward the People Mover's Fort/Cass Station, where a small group loitered.

Just as he was about to enter, a voice shouted from behind him.

"Hey!"

Leaf Man ignored the call. Besides, he wasn't sure if he was being targeted specifically, or if the caller was just shouting out to anyone within earshot.

"Hey! You! I said hey! I'm homeless! Give me some goddamn money, motherfucker!"

Unfazed, Leaf Man entered the station.

Damn, they're getting more aggressive. Or, desperate?

He paid his fare and pushed through the turnstile.

The wind whistled with brisk indifference as he waited for the train. Five minutes later, it squealed into the station. As he attempted to enter, the doors slammed shut on his suitcase.

"Son of a bitch!" he said, as he pulled on his bag with all of his might before he finally managed to bust through. A homeless man chuckled in the corner of the train. Leaf Man brushed it off and sat down and took note of the only other passenger on board: an attractive female with a don't-fuck-with-me look on her face. A banged-up suitcase sat at her feet.

Leaf Man gave the girl a friendly nod. She glared back and looked away. He left what he assumed was a fair distance between them, but her obviously annoyed demeanor seemed to suggest otherwise.

As the train chugged along, he snuck a few furtive glances at the female passenger. She showed no interest. The homeless man, on the other hand . . .

"How you doin' tonight?" the man asked from his corner of the train.

Leaf Man nodded in a way that suggested "I am acknowledging your presence, but please take note that I would like you to leave me the fuck alone."

The homeless man smiled and waved with childlike enthusiasm. Leaf Man redirected his attention back toward the woman, who continued to avoid eye contact and stare out the window.

He transferred a couple of vials out of his coat pocket and into his suitcase.

Why the fuck do I still have this shit?

He would throw it out the first chance he got.

Normally, he wouldn't waste his time on someone not willing to waste time on him, but something about her was just—*different.*

"How you doin' tonight?" the homeless man repeated.

Leaf Man continued to ignore him.

"Do you like cats?" the homeless man asked out loud. When Leaf Man didn't respond, he proclaimed, "I like cats!" before rummaging through his cart.

Meanwhile, Leaf Man hoped to somehow draw the girl's attention, but instead, the homeless man drifted toward him and offered what appeared to be a wad of trash. Upon closer inspection, it was a perfectly formed treble clef.

"Wow! Impressive," Leaf Man said.

It truly was.

"I made it myself," the homeless man beamed like a toddler.

"I see that."

Leaf Man removed his wallet and pulled out a five-dollar bill.

"Here ya go, my man."

"No, thank you," the homeless man said. "I don't want no money."

He pushed the clef toward Leaf Man. "It's a gift."

"And so is this," Leaf Man said, waving the money.

"But I don't want it. It cost me nothing to make. It's like music."

"Right on, my man. Right on."

If anyone understood that he didn't need money to feel good about his art, it was Leaf Man. But payment certainly made everything sweeter.

A tiny squeak emitted from the homeless man's coat, from which he pulled out a dirty kitten for Leaf Man to see, using one hand to balance himself on a pole.

"You like cats?"

"Naw, man. Allergic."

The homeless man appeared taken aback.

"Yours is definitely cute, though," Leaf Man said, hoping to spare the man's feelings.

"She sure is," the homeless man said, stroking his kitten. "Is that cat nip?"

He pointed to Leaf Man's hand.

Say what?

"On your ring?" the man clarified.

"Yeah, kind of," Leaf Man said with a laugh.

As the homeless man headed back to his seat, Leaf Man looked over at the girl to gauge her reaction. Her face showed zero emotion.

"Made a new friend," Leaf Man said.

She ignored him, but Leaf Man could tell she was fighting back a smile.

Yes! He had an in! He could work with that.

Meanwhile, the homeless man dug through his cart again.

"One man's trash . . ." Leaf Man directed toward the woman.

She didn't even flinch.

He noticed her necklace, which he assumed was fool's gold, from which hung an equally faux-ruby "I Love NYC" heart medallion.

"I think you're on the wrong train," Leaf Man said, connecting the dots between the necklace and suitcase.

"Story of my life."

She closed her eyes. He got the hint, yet couldn't help but feel an unexpected impulse to save her.

But from what?

It dawned on him that it was the first time he had ever felt that way since . . . well, the first time since the last time he truly loved someone.

Before the overdose.

An accident.

He could have done more to stop it.

But didn't.

Why didn't he?

He was scared.

A weak excuse.

Was this his second chance?

Leaf Man shook these thoughts away and gazed out of the window as the train stopped at one empty station after another, casting its shadow on lonely streets, before rumbling past the glowing embers of the Renaissance Center, running concurrent with the Detroit River and through the rafters of Cobo Hall.

He glanced over at the homeless man, whose kitten was now lapping milk out of a bottle cap, before turning his attention back to his damsel in distress.

"So, seriously, where you heading?"

She opened her eyes for a moment, before closing them again.

"I'm going to heaven," the homeless man replied.

The girl wasn't quite so eager to respond.

"First, what makes it your business and, second, why do you give a shit?"

"Honestly, I don't. But there's no one else on this train to talk to, other than Picasso and his pussy over here."

The homeless man didn't even flinch. And though Leaf Man wasn't sure, it appeared she was again fighting the urge to smile.

"It's a long story," she finally said.

"It's a long ride," Leaf Man retorted. "I don't mind."

She hesitated, then recounted her journey into hell and back. He certainly didn't blame her for being so bitter—particularly toward men.

Shortly after their conversation, her purse slid off her lap and onto the ground. Its contents spilled out like intestines.

"Fuck me!" the girl shouted, as Leaf Man quickly rushed to her aid.

As he attempted help her, she snatched her lighter from his hand like an alligator after prey. After making it clear that she didn't want his help, he surrendered, backing away, his hands up in the air, into his seat.

Message received.

They continued their journey in silence, accompanied only by the whirring and buzzing of the electric motor pulling the driverless train through a bottomless night.

After a few minutes, Leaf Man's phone rang.

He checked the number.

"Hey."

"All set," the voice said on the other end. "Meet at the Belle Isle Boat House. 3:00 a.m. You got that?"

"Why there?"

"Hey! You want this to happen or not?"

He hesitated.

"Yes."

"You owe me . . ."

And then silence.

What did this last statement even mean? Nothing about this situation felt right. And he only had himself to blame. Why didn't he make a bigger push to change the locale?

As the train finally approached Greektown, Leaf Man stood up at the exact same time as the girl. They both grabbed their suitcases.

Great. She's gonna think I'm following her. And I'm sure she got mace. And a gun.

The train pulled to a squealing stop above the streets of Greektown. Though most of the Greek immigrants were long gone, their restaurants and bakeries remained.

"You be careful now," the homeless man said as his fellow travelers headed out separate doors. "God bless!"

"You too, dude," Leaf Man replied.

"Your cup!" the homeless man shouted as the doors slid shut.

Leaf Man made a conscious effort to keep a respectable distance behind her as they headed toward an elevator. They waited in silence for the door to open. He wanted to speak to her, but sensed she would much prefer he kept his mouth shut. He wished he had the homeless man's tenacity. Then again, he got the sense that it would make no difference. She clearly had no interest in him, so why antagonize her any further?

The elevator finally arrived. Leaf Man debated whether the "gentlemanly" thing for him to do would be to enter first so she wouldn't assume he was following her, or to let her enter in front of him. Decisions,

decisions. He banked on the latter. She hesitated for a beat before she headed in. He gave her as much space as possible.

Did she even notice?

He hoped so, but got the sense that there wasn't enough room in the world. When they reached the bottom floor, she gestured for him to leave first.

"Thanks," Leaf Man said.

"Yeah," she said as she nodded.

Progress.

And with that, Leaf Man headed off in one direction, the girl in the other.

5

Leaf Man made a beeline through a mostly empty parking lot across the street from Saint Andrew's Hall, where club bangers were in equal measure with homeless drifters and drug pushers. He passed a familiar face: a homeless man in a wheelchair with salt and pepper dreadlocks. Leaf Man nodded. The man nodded back, but he knew that the gesture was meaningless without the offer of money. Being homeless in Detroit was rough enough with legs.

He put a couple of dollars in the man's coin cup.

"God bless," the dreadlocked man said.

Leaf Man crossed over the street and approached the entrance to Saint Andrew's Hall.

The stairway to his dream.

Despite the pervasive nervousness that he felt throughout the day, he immediately felt an overwhelming rush of calm ease the flutterings of the butterflies swirling around his stomach. Leaf Man had long ago learned to channel his anxiety into his art. His confidence in his abilities put his mind at ease, but by the same token, he struggled to fully shake the reminder of what was at stake if he blew it.

Marcus. Custody.

Not to mention everything he had worked towards since he was a kid.

He took nothing for granted, realizing that a steady job wasn't a guarantee—but at least it gave him a shot. If getting his son back meant giving up on his dream, he would do so in a heartbeat. There was nothing else on earth that could do that. His priorities were crystal clear.

He looked at his watch. An hour before doors opened to the public. Too much time to kill, but plenty enough time for his confidence to wane.

He passed through an alley on the side of the club.

Graffiti scrawled on the club's bricked wall read:

DON'T CRY FOR US, CRY FOR THEM

Truer words had never been written.

When he reached the rear entrance to St Andrew's, he took a deep breath and grabbed the door handle.

Locked.

He knocked. Once. Twice. The door finally swung open. A beefed-up security guard greeted him with an indifferent nod.

"I'm the DJ."

The DJ equivalent of "I'm with the band."

He couldn't help but feel a little bit smug.

"Yeah, I know who you is," the bouncer said, halfway between condescension and simply not giving a shit. At least the bouncer knew who he was. That counted for something.

As he was patted down, he remembered his weapons stash, hidden away in a secret compartment. He banked on the fact a DJ wouldn't be under the same level of scrutiny as everyone else.

His assertion was right. He received only a light-pat down before being granted entry. He made his way up through the basement level, to the main floor and up toward the third floor, where he would reign supreme. Though the third floor certainly lacked the size and glitz of the main floor, his music would more than make up for that. At the center of the stage was a long, folding table covered by a black cloth, featuring two turntables and a mixer.

Of the three floors, the upper one was not only the most minimalist, but also the most avant-garde. This suited Leaf Man perfectly. The adventurous souls who wandered into this room were treated to a sonic adventure—the pulsating heart of Detroit techno. Its brain center. His turntable hypnosis had the ability to transport people to levels that were usually reserved for hallucinogens, which of course could take his art to otherworldly levels.

Though Leaf Man wouldn't pack the house like the main floor, he was confident the abundance of passion and appreciation for his sonic mastery would more than make up for it. His disciples would come for the music; not the meat. He preferred it that way. Art was his guiding light. Not hype. He took pride in being *underground*. Anything short of that would not be him.

He climbed onto the stage and opened up his suitcase, moving his fingers along the records, before he began setting up. As he made some adjustments on the mixer, a voice boomed behind him.

"The man of the hour!"

Startled, Leaf Man turned to see the floor manager, Elijah, adorned in a perfectly tailored suit and sporting a bullshit smile.

"Feelin' good?" Elijah asked.

"I'll feel better once I get those beats pumping."

"Until then, can I get you anything?"

"Naw, thanks, man. I'm good," Leaf Man insisted.

"Nervous?"

"Maybe a little," Leaf Man said, hoping he at least *appeared* calm. "But I feed on that."

"If your demo reel is any indication, you have nothing to worry about."

"I hope not."

"You're gonna own this place," Elijah assured him.

"Thanks. That's the plan."

"Speakin' of your demo, remember that producer from LA I told you about?"

"Yeah?"

"Well, he wants to work out a deal."

"No shit?!"

Leaf Man tried his best not to come across as too eager, lest he be perceived as desperate.

"He's supposed to pop in tonight. Not that I want to make you more nervous."

"Wow! Well, damn."

"Can't make any promises, but . . ."

"Ain't nothin' I can't handle, man. I'll be on top of my game one way or another."

"I'm sure you will be," Elijah assured him. "Tonight is going to be one for the ages, man. I can feel it."

"I appreciate this. I really do."

"I know a way you can return the favor," Elijah hinted, with no surprise to Leaf Man.

"You got any of that good shit on you? I just ran out. It's for medical purposes. For my knee."

"Aw, man, you know I'm done with that. Candy shop's closed. I got this now."

Leaf Man nodded toward his DJ setup.

"Bullshit!" Elijah said through a phony smile.

Elijah wasn't fucking around.

Why didn't he get rid of them earlier? He could have flushed them down the toilet before he left his loft. He could have flushed them down the toilet the moment he arrived here.

Why am I being so fucking clueless?

Though Leaf Man previously used the drug for his *own* recreation, it was highly probable that Elijah had other, more sinister intentions.

"Remember what I was just saying about that producer friend of mine?"

"C'mon, man," Leaf Man pleaded. "Don't play me like this."

"So you want me to tell him to go fuck himself?" Elijah threatened. "Is that what you're saying?"

Leaf Man surrendered and reached into an inner pocket inside his bag and removed the remaining stash, leaving behind a handful of his "in case of emergency" stash.

Leaf Man could have insisted he didn't have what Elijah was looking for, but he knew exactly why he didn't—despite being well aware that his product could be very dangerous in the wrong hands. What made him so sure he could trust that Elijah wouldn't also use it for sinister purposes? Of course, it wasn't lost on him that drugs were what ultimately led him to Elijah in the first place, and subsequently his dream gig. He couldn't escape from the shadow of his illicit trade.

A fucking parasite.

Like a dog chasing its own tail.

"Ha! I knew you'd come through," Elijah said with a smirk. "My knee thanks you." He winked, handing Leaf Man a fifty. Leaf Man snatched it, overridden with paranoid unease, distrust, and shame.

Ulysses S. Grant sneered at him with judgment.

"Burn this fucker down tonight," Elijah said with his stupid, bullshit smile, before he walked out of the room.

"Will do," Leaf Man said. What he really wanted to do was to punch that asshole in the face.

After a few more tweaks of his gear, he was just about ready, with fifteen minutes to spare, but he needed an extension cord. He headed down the dark stairwell and narrowly avoided colliding with someone heading up.

"Sorry, man" Leaf Man said.

"You gotta be fucking kidding me!" the woman responded the exact moment that he realized who it was.

Her!

"You following me?" he teased.

"You wish."

"Maybe." He nodded with a sheepish grin. He stepped aside for her to pass. She wasn't impressed.

"I'll be right back," he said as he rushed down the stairs. "Don't miss me too much."

"Take your time."

He skipped past several steps. Without doubt, her arrival had elevated his senses. She may have acted like a bitch toward him, but he just couldn't shake the feeling that she was—something.

Like a soul mate?

Da fuck?!

As he made his way to the bar, he forced himself to redirect his energy and focus on his music. He *had* to. He couldn't afford to be knocked askew by an irrational desire for a woman he didn't even know, especially one who clearly had no interest in him.

He entered the main floor and approached the bar. No bartender in sight. He looked toward the stage, where the headliner DJ was chilling with his crew and a gaggle of groupies. He felt a slight tinge of jealousy, but reminded himself that if that's what he truly wanted, he could make it happen. This put his mind at ease.

"What can I get you?"

A gorgeous bartender with a bare midriff and the bluest eyes he had ever seen stared directly at him.

"Got a spare extension cord by any chance?"

"Lemme check."

As she stepped out from behind the bar, Leaf Man surveyed the main floor. Up on stage, the DJ was sound checking mainstream hip hop.

No thanks.

The bartender returned with an extension cord.

"Will this work?" she said with a flirtatious smile.

"Perfect. Thanks."

"Can I get you anything else?"

"A bottle of water?"

"You're a DJ, right?" the bartender asked, retrieving his bottle.

"Yes," he said, "third floor," surprised that she knew this.

"On the house."

"Cool, thanks."

"Don't drink it all in one place."

"I'll try my best."

"Knock 'em dead."

"Not dead. But more alive than they ever felt before."

Leaf Man flashed the bartender a sly wink and a nod, then soared back upstairs, somehow still more intrigued by the girl from the train.

But why? He had no clue.

On the cusp of show time, he felt an unexpected surge of something he hadn't felt in a long time:

Freedom.

When he returned to the third floor, there she was. Alone on the couch. He wanted to approach her, but had to get to work. Besides, what difference would it make? She was a lost cause.

Yet, he couldn't stop thinking about her.

He hopped on stage, trying to clear his mind, and connected the extension cord. He pulled out a record, slapped it on the turntable, and dropped the needle.

"Confutatis" from Mozart's Requiem rang out.

A hard driving number set to heavy, pounding beats, flanked by the largest stack of speakers he ever had access to. It was how he planned to open every set.

After a full minute, he added a second layer of sound and snuck another glance in the direction of his lone audience member. She seemed to be nodding her head along to his beats.

Wishful thinking?

Maybe, but it gave him an unexpected, renewed sense of vigor.

After a couple of minutes, he transitioned out of Mozart and into a steady, scratchy, hypnotic beat, which served as the foundation upon which he would build subtle layers, barely noticeable on a conscious level. Subconsciously, however, it moved mountains.

With his turntables in a perfect, synchronous groove, Leaf Man headed over to one of the large windows overlooking the outside world. The line of costumed clubbers still wasn't moving. He wondered which ones would be under his spell by the end of the night. Somehow, this thought brought with it a fresh wave of anxiety.

To settle his nerves, he transported himself back into the bedroom of his childhood, which consisted of nothing but an old, tattered mattress in the middle of the floor. It was in this squalor that the seeds of his techno dream were cultivated on a hand-me-down Commodore 64, awaiting for this exact moment. He always thought of himself as a DJ. Now, others would finally have a chance to lay witness.

He could feel the girl's eyes on him. He turned, hoping to catch her off guard, but she averted her attention elsewhere.

Perhaps she was never staring at him at all.

He looked back down. The line was finally moving.

Showtime.

6

Leaf Man never felt more alive than when he was behind a turntable.

It was better than any high. Better than sex.

He added another layer to his mix to welcome the masses: a gospel track. A preacher behind the pulpit of his holy turntables, with his sonic sermon, ready for his parishioners.

A true techno maestro.

No matter how much Leaf Man tried to get his mind off the girl from the train, it was a futile effort. She would be his unknowing, one-night muse, fueling his art. On some level, he wanted to communicate this to her, but he knew it would make him sound like a crazed stalker.

He usually had no interest in women who had no interest in him.

Until tonight.

She had him hooked. He had never believed in love at first sight. But then, *what* was this? It wasn't the first time that he had fixated on an attractive female. But this was on a different level.

Why her? He realized he hadn't felt this way since the confused feelings he had toward Johannes. Though he was in denial then, there would later be no doubt in his mind.

Since then, he had pretty much sacrificed any semblance of a social life for the sake of his dream, sabotaging several meaningful relationships and leaving them in the dust. Usually, he was fine with being alone, but lately, he felt the tide beginning to turn.

He put another record on the turntable, tweaked his levels, and headed downstairs. When he reached the lobby, he was greeted by a blended cocktail of bass reverberating from all three floors in synchronous rhythm.

He poked his head toward the entrance, where security guards patted down the masses. A few began to head upstairs.

My disciples.

He headed toward a restroom and entered a stall, which was littered with graffiti and stickers that showcased a mish-mash collage of human indecency, creativity, and mystery, from floor to ceiling. For every cliché *"FOR A GOOD TIME CALL . . ."* there was a handful consisting of a deeper level of creative sophistication, including such literary gems as:

RACISTS CAN SUCK A BIG BLACK COCK

HUMP DA POLICE

I LOVE LABIAS. LEMME SUK ON YOURZ

THINGS DAT MAKE SENSE DON'T ALWAYS WORK. BUT IF SOMETHING WORKS, IT DON'T HAVE TO MAKE SENSE

R U HAPPY BEING SO IGNERANT? CUZ U IZ A DUM ASS

Just as he was finishing up, he noticed someone enter; a tall, thin, pale-faced figure in a black trench coat. The pale man approached the restroom's only sink.

Was he in costume? *The Matrix?* Unlikely. There was something *sinister* about him. Even more strange was the pale man's meticulous hand-washing technique, which was preceded by the rolling up of his black sleeves. He turned on the faucet and conducted a thorough handwashing unlike any Leaf Man had ever witnessed. The pale man's methodical, obsessive-compulsive hand scrubbing was accompanied by under-the-breath chants. Leaf Man couldn't tell if the man was speaking English, or in tongues, or, maybe, a combination of the two.

Leaf Man flushed the urinal with his foot, as the stranger continued the ritualized cleaning of his arms, with suds up to his elbows. He then waited patiently at the sink, before taking a not-so-subtle step closer. This did nothing to speed up the process, but it did give Leaf Man time to notice the raw, cross-shaped scars running up and down the inside of both of the pale man's arms.

Meanwhile, the pale man continued to mutter under his breath.

"I think they're clean, bro," Leaf Man said, losing patience.

"But is your soul?" the man hissed, locking Leaf Man's eyes in a vice grip.

What the fuck?!

"Judge not, lest thee be judged," Leaf Man responded, breaking the gaze.

"Who is judging who?" the pale man said, turning toward Leaf Man with a demonic glare.

Leaf Man bit his tongue. He had learned not to argue with crazy people—especially religious crazies. Nothing good could ever come out of it. It wasn't that he had a problem with religion. In fact, he was a semi-regular churchgoer. And God was *always* on his mind. However, when it came to the perversion of his faith, he had no tolerance. In fact, Leaf Man had spent most of his adult life proving to others that he wasn't *one of those.* If there was anything he learned, it was that trying to convert someone to your faith at a booze-and-drug-fueled club was like selling popsicles in a blizzard.

"Okay, look," Leaf Man began. "I appreciate the Bible study, but you're not the only one who wants clean hands, dawg. I got a job to do."

"Like corrupting souls?"

"Wow, man. Their souls are already corrupted. I'm just tryin' to provide them with an escape for a few hours."

The pale man ignored him, as he continued to rinse off his hands, before he began an equally thorough and ritualistic drying process, unfazed by the petri-dish of a communal cloth towel. When he was finally done, he rolled his sleeves back down and reached into his coat pocket to reveal a pamphlet. He offered it to Leaf Man, who reluctantly took it.

"Good luck getting out of this house of Sodom alive," the pale man said, before he exited.

"Why would I want to leave?" Leaf Man asked, unsure as to whether the pale man had heard him

Leaf Man could feel oxygen—which had been absorbed by the pale man's suffocating presence—return to the room. He looked down at the pamphlet, despite already having a pretty good idea as to what awaited him. Pamphlets like this passed out by people like that annoyed him, because he felt they did more harm than good for the religion they were proclaiming. It wasn't the message as much as the manner in which it was delivered.

For one thing, he believed that one's faith was personal business, and in turn, this meant keeping one's business to oneself. Tonight, he was in the kingdom of Dionysus, and Jesus was not on the guest list. Despite the "Saint" in its name, Saint Andrew's Hall was the last place where salvation could be obtained.

Music was where he found God.

And by extension, he believed so could others.

In fact, he honestly believed his music had a better chance to redeem souls than any pamphlet ever could. Not that it was his goal to help anyone "find" God. He just wanted people to feel good. And Saint Andrew's was a refuge for those who wanted to celebrate life and the rebirth of the city they loved, despite its myriad imperfections.

As Leaf Man headed back into the packed foyer, he looked up from the pamphlet and saw the pale man standing in quiet judgment against the wall, like a stone gargoyle. The chaos and constant movement swirling around him made his solemn, stationary presence even more disquieting.

The two men made brief eye contact. Leaf Man nodded at him in recognition, but the pale man held steadfast in his transcendent gaze of condemnation.

Yeah, well, fuck you too, man.

He stuffed the pamphlet into his pocket.

He certainly wasn't going to lose any sleep over this freak.

As Leaf Man was about to make his way back upstairs, the main stage emcee made an announcement. "We're on the cusp of a new millennium. As the clock strikes midnight on New Year's Eve, planes are gonna fall from the sky and all the computers in the world are gonna blow up! So let's make the most of the time we got left, you Detroit motherfuckers, shake off some of this pre-millennium tension, get fucked up, get fucked dowwwn . . . and party like it's motherfuckin' 1999!"

The assembled revelers went nuts as the sound of Prince came blasting out from the speakers.

At least he got something right.

Leaf Man smiled as he jogged back upstairs, where he hopped onto his own altar behind the turntables.

The girl from the train was gazing out the window.

At what? An escape?

Once again, Leaf Man felt an overwhelming desire to be her knight in shining armor. And nothing else. She was the sun to his universe.

It was time to change records.

At the change of the beat, she turned to look, catching Leaf Man's gaze—if only for a second. Was she relieved that he was back? Or was she simply reacting to the change of music?

Lost in the hypnotic web in which she ensnarled him, he was totally caught off guard at the sight of the pale man who was now seated in a tattered armchair in a dark corner, draped in shadow—a dark lord on a sinister throne.

Leaf Man noticed the girl's entire demeanor change with the pale man's arrival. At least they were on the same page about *something.* She glanced over toward an aloof security guard, who stood near the stairwell, flirting with a group of girls.

If only she knew I had her back.

The crowd on the third floor had swelled. He dug through his crate until he located another gospel album.

That Jesus freak oughta like this.

He slapped it on a turntable, found the right groove, and gazed out at his parishioners. A small opening in the crowd was just enough to give him a clear view of the train girl's beautiful, round ass as she stared out the window. He averted his eyes to pale man sitting to the right. Although Leaf Man couldn't be certain, the pale man also seemed to be staring at her ass.

Goddamn fucking hypocrite.

Two men pointed at her as though they were selecting a fine cut of meat in a butcher shop's window. One man was dressed like a cowboy; the other an old-school milkman.

Within seconds, she was sandwiched between the two men.

And she didn't appear to mind.

Jealousy instantly overshadowed his urge to protect.

But how could he be jealous over someone he didn't even know?

Meanwhile, as the girl began to grind her ass against the milkman, Leaf Man raised the levels on his gospel track and glanced over toward the pale man. The pale man's eyes were now closed and he appeared to be chanting to himself.

Leaf Man watched the girl accept a lit joint from the cowboy.

Dejected, he crouched behind the turntables and retrieved an "E" from deep within the interior pocket of his suitcase. He held the pill in the palm of his hand and examined it. A smiley face etched into the tablet stared back at him. It dared him to pop it. He tried to fight off the urge, but lost. He downed it with a giant swig of water. Another step backward, followed by an immediate rush of euphoria, as it raced through his body, dissolving into his bloodstream.

Time to join the party.

7

Leaf Man's senses were opened, his mind expanding into abstract thoughts that couldn't be translated or expressed in any conscious language. He had already passed through the gateway on a runaway train into another dimension. He could *feel* the whirring ceiling fans overhead, the oscillations melting into his music. Time ceased to exist. Light and sound waves vibrated in perfect unison. Their pulsating molecules revealed themselves to him, dancing in unison around the room, as he absorbed every sensation, on the cusp of infinity. Yet even in his drugged out state of mind, as master of the universe, there was still a part of him—his rational, *true* self—that knew that none of this shit was real.

Through an out-of-body haze, Leaf Man watched his muse take another hit off the joint from the cowboy, before she pulled herself away and disappeared into a haze of glow sticks, smoke, and an orgy of costumed freaks and ravers.

Suddenly, a pixie appeared before him with glow-sticks that swirled around in perfect synchronous rhythm to his turntable virtuosity, casting off iridescent shapes and patterns that heightened the hallucinogenic effect, capped off with perfectly-formed illuminated figure-eights. The pixie floated away, but in place of his muse was now an empty void.

Where did she go?

Awash in the ecstasy of his drug, Leaf Man kicked his artistry into a higher gear and whipped up creative nuances of which he never thought he was capable. As though on cue, the crowd began to leave the dance floor, revealing his muse, back on the couch and now surrounded by an angelic, golden glow. Her eyes met his, only this time, rather than looking away, she held his gaze, until a new swarm of revelers blocked their view once again.

Suddenly, the crowd of dancers floated off the ground, rising up in a cloud of brightly-colored smoke, leaving his muse in wide open view as the clubbers danced above their heads.

He had never experienced a high quite like this before and he wondered how long it would last.

Then, suddenly, Leaf Man found himself sitting on the couch in place of the girl from the train.

Standing in his place behind the decks was his former mentor, Johannes. As the two locked eyes, Leaf Man realized, in that otherwordly moment, how much he truly missed his friend.

How is it possible to miss someone that much and not even be aware of it?

Leaf Man was once again reminded of how special their bond was—no matter how confusing it felt at the time. Although some bonds can never be broken, they can certainly take on different forms.

Leaf Man finally understood what it was he had been seeking all along. And all it took was a happy pill and the incarnation of a new muse for him to finally realize it. One thing was clear: he never wanted to lose it again. Whatever "it" was.

Leaf Man's vision dissipated when both needles reached the end of their respective records, and the revelers floated back down to the dancefloor, snapping him out of his trance and, once again, back behind the controls.

In the ensuing silence, all eyes were now turned toward him—their musical messiah.

He quickly grabbed two albums out of his suitcase and swapped them out with the ones on his turntables.

Order was restored.

The only trace of the hallucination that remained was the aura that still surrounded his muse. He refocused his attention back to his primary goal:

to keep customers on the dance floor. His thoughts suddenly returned to Elijah's producer promise.

As the butterflies of panic returned, the aura around his muse dimmed.

Was the producer here? Had he witnessed this momentary lack of focus?

Leaf Man took a few deep breaths, and looked over at his muse, just as the pale man emerged out of the darkness and sat next to her.

And then the aura was gone.

The girl leaned her head back against the couch and Leaf Man wanted nothing more than to make the pale freak beside her disappear.

He adjusted his levels. When he looked again, Elijah was there, handing her a drink.

Now, he wasn't sure who he needed to protect her from more.

And then he remembered: the drugs he gave to Elijah.

"For my knee" my ass.

Why the fuck did I let him hoodwink me?

Because I had to protect my fucking dream.

Now what? He certainly wasn't in the right state of mind to make an informed decision about *anything*. But shouldn't he at least try? Shouldn't he warn her? Would she trust him? Should he confront Elijah? And jeopardize everything he worked so hard for? Should he call the police?

Yeah, right! Who the fuck am I kidding?

He had nobody to blame but himself.

Besides, what proof did he have? Elijah could just as well have consumed the pill himself.

But Leaf Man knew better.

Elijah whispered something into the girl's ear, and the manner in which she nodded left no doubt. Leaf Man watched as Elijah led his muse toward the stairwell. It felt like watching from the shoreline while someone was drowning and doing anything to prevent it.

Do something. For God's sake.

But he didn't.

History repeating itself.

Like a needle skipping on vinyl.

Leaf Man attempted to bury his guilt in the chemistry still flowing through his veins. As he spun himself into a trance, he looked back at the spot in which his muse had been sitting. It was now occupied by a couple making out. They were quickly eclipsed by the return of the glow stick pixie and her merry band of assorted fairies of light, casting distortions and shadows and odd patterns of double helixes and spider webs.

One particular glint caught his eye—like a moth drawn to flame. Upon closer inspection, he realized it was the NYC medallion, now worn by the pixie.

A coincidence? No fucking way.

The pixie thief continued twirling, spinning and crisscrossing her glow sticks in front of her face. When she finally pulled them away, she had somehow morphed into the likeness of his muse, who disappeared as soon as the pixie brought the glow sticks back up to her face. Shocked at the vibrancy of his hallucination, Leaf Man began to fret as to when the comedown would commence. He had a feeling it would be a while. In fact, he wondered how much further down the rabbit hole he was about to go.

And whether he would ever come back?

One thing was certain: in this very moment, he had reached an artistic peak he never knew possible. But was Elijah's producer friend even there to witness it?

And then it dawned on him. Would he be able to replicate this level of sonic mastery while sober?

Doubtful.

Frightening. Yet he never wanted this high to end.

Suddenly, a commotion broke out in the center of the dance floor. Within seconds, the room had exploded into chaos. A group of bouncers rushed in to break up the fight, but they were outnumbered. One of the bouncers tackled someone he presumed was a ringleader, jettisoning him into the tower of speakers, culminating in a loud crash that filled the whole room with screeching feedback.

A gunshot echoed throughout the room with a flash of light, as the suspects darted off down the steps, with the bouncers in hot pursuit.

The house lights came on. And the once vibrant, otherwordly space instantly took on the appearance of Detroit Receiving Hospital ER on a Saturday night. Muffled beats filtered up from the floors below.

His high now a sobered memory, Leaf Man surveyed the wreckage, which consisted of injured ravers, smashed speakers, dented turntables, and shards of splintered vinyl—many of which were rarities that could never be replaced. Frantically, he searched around for one record in particular: his mother's "I Hear a Symphony" album.

But it was nowhere in sight.

No fucking way! What the fuck was I thinking?

Elijah appeared, looking shocked, and shaking his head in disbelief. Leaf Man's muse was nowhere in sight.

"Guess I should have played something more chill," Leaf Man said, still scanning the floor for his cherished album.

"Looks like you brought the house down—literally," Elijah said, handing Leaf Man his payment.

"Oh, and my producer friend sends his regrets for not making it in tonight."

"Probably a good thing."

"True, true. Anyway, he wants to meet you next week before your set. Eight cool?"

Leaf Man beamed.

"Yeah, man. Absolutely! Cool, cool."

"Alright, my man. Tomorrow's another day. Try to get some rest."

Elijah patted him on the back.

"Gotta run. Got a hot date," Elijah added.

Fuck.

Leaf Man had one more chance to stop Elijah, but he simply lacked the strength and wherewithal at that point. He wanted nothing more than to go home and rest.

Miles to go before I sleep.

If he had stuck with his fucking game plan, that's exactly what he would have been doing.

His final deal now hung over him like a black cloud. He searched in vain for an exit strategy, but every road his mind went down headed to the same destination: the crown jewel of the Detroit River. Belle Isle.

He reminded himself that he *had* an exit strategy. But he blew it.

He finally convinced himself that this wasn't a setback, but rather a huge step forward into an ironclad future that could finally set sail. The ship, however, was the least of his concerns. It was the storm he couldn't control.

Meanwhile, he continued searching for his mother's precious album, continuing to salvage what he could of the rest of his records.

Where in the hell could it be?

And then he saw it; jutting out of the carnage, propped up against the stage.

He examined it: unscathed on the front. Relief. He flipped it over. A deep gouge cut across the vinyl on the flipside. He could live with that.

And then something else caught his eye.

The Holy Grail itself.

The glass slipper.

It was the girl's NYC medallion.

What goes around comes around!

The pixie girl must have dropped it during the commotion.

Leaf Man grasped the medallion in the palm of his hand and vowed to return it to its rightful owner. He slipped it into his shirt pocket.

He gathered his broken records and made a quick scan through the rubble to make sure he hadn't missed anything worth saving.

Then again, he already had everything he needed.

Filled with renewed purpose, he vowed to go to the ends of the earth to return the necklace to its rightful owner.

Prince Charming of Motown.

Leaf Man grabbed his suitcase and made his way toward the stairwell where he was greeted with nods of approval and appreciative slaps on the back by staff and a few remaining spectators. He descended down the dark stairwell, case in tow, and out into the light of the lobby, and, finally, out the front door and into a sea of flashing lights.

Parked outside the front entrance were three ambulances, surrounded by even more police cruisers. A clubber put up a stalwart fight with two police officers, but was quickly subdued and thrown into the back of a squad car along with another suspect. Leaf Man peered into the open ambulance, and noticed the glow stick pixie receiving treatment on her eye, her glow sticks still aglow.

Illuminated by the ambulance, he noticed a Biblical passage scrawled on a nearby wall, awash in red and blue:

"THOU HAST UTTERLY REJECTED US; THOU ART VERY WROTH AGAINST US." LAMENTATIONS 5:22

So we turn the other cheek and trudge onward.

Until it's too late.

It was time to put on his other hat—one last time.

8

With one hand clutching the NYC medallion inside his pocket, Leaf Man headed back toward Jefferson. The more he mulled over his gig, the more pissed he got at its premature climax. He was flying high and was denied the chance to climax with a bang. Instead, the bang of a thug stole his spotlight. Despite it all, he looked on the bright side.

He got bodies moving.

He impressed his boss.

He lined up a contact that could lead to national attention.

Most importantly, he stuck to his game plan while simultaneously reaching undiscovered creativity, unearthed from part of his soul he never knew existed.

It certainly could have been worse.

As he reached the platform, Leaf Man popped a coin into the turnstile and waited at the empty station. He looked down at the street below, hoping to locate his wayward muse.

One by one, the ambulances began to pull away from St. Andrew's, as more police cars arrived on the scene.

Just in case.

Down the street, Leaf Man watched a homeless man pester a hot dog vendor, as the familiar rusty squeal of the People Mover echoed in the distance.

Thank God.

Thirty seconds later, the empty train arrived.

He entered and situated himself in a corner. He threw his head back in exhaustion and carefully removed the medallion from his pocket.

Did she know it was missing?

And if not, how would she react when she realized it was gone?

Did she even give a shit?

He got the sense that she didn't really give a shit about much.

But what if this was her "I Hear a Symphony"?

No matter what, he was determined to get it back to her.

By any means necessary.

But how?

As the People Mover trundled along, Leaf Man propped his legs up on his suitcase, relieved that he now had a little extra time to spare, due to the premature end to his set. This would give him some time to unwind along the riverbank, and think about the future.

Meanwhile, he fought off an intense urge to sleep. He couldn't risk missing his stop, however he finally surrendered to the sandman between the sudden loud *dings* at every stop that woke him up. He forced himself to stay awake before he reached his destination.

With well over an hour to go before his meeting, an unexpected sense of calm followed him off the train, as the glowing embers of the Renaissance Center towered behind him like sentries protecting him on his long-awaited journey into tomorrow.

He grabbed a bus down Jefferson toward Belle Isle, past numerous empty storefronts, open liquor shops, and rundown warehouses. Despite the steady flow of traffic, he could see no visible signs of life, with the exception of scattered stray dogs roaming the streets.

When he reached his stop, he headed across the bridge to Belle Isle. As he looked out across the expansive river, he was instantly reminded of boat trips to long-shuttered Boblo Island with his grandmother. It seemed like yesterday.

As he reached the midway point, he spotted a figure standing against the railing. An old fisherman, perhaps? Nope.

His muse.

Impossible!

One of her legs dangled over the railing.

You gotta be fucking kidding me.

Leaf Man could feel his heart beating like a deep bass track.

He approached cautiously.

As he snuck up to within striking distance, the girl lifted her other leg over the railing, and stared into the abyss below.

Leaf Man reached into his pocket and removed the medallion.

This was his only chance.

NYC GIRL & LEAF MAN

"Lose something?"

Without looking, NYC Girl knew who it was. She continued to stare down into the black void below as she teetered over the railing.

In one swift motion, Leaf Man managed to leap and grab hold of NYC Girl by both wrists. Despite her immediate resistance, he wrestled her back over the railing, quickly wrapping his arms around her waist in a tight bear hug, as they both toppled backwards onto the concrete sidewalk.

The NYC medallion landed several feet away, but neither of them noticed.

NYC Girl landed softly on top of Leaf Man, unscathed, writhing to get loose, despite Leaf Man's secure grip. Leaf Man, on the other hand, endured the full consequence of gravity, landing with a heavy thud onto the cold, hard concrete. Despite a searing pain in his shoulder, he did not let up on his grip, sacrificing his body to serve as her own personal landing pad.

"Get off me, you fuckin' asshole motherfucker!" NYC Girl screamed, as she continued to do everything in her power to escape from his grip; kicking, scratching, punching, biting.

But Leaf Man continued to hold on.

"Help!" she screamed over and over, unwilling to accept that Leaf Man *was* the help.

She continued to bite and scratch until he had no choice but to surrender.

As he slowly loosened his grip, she elbowed him in the stomach and broke away. Breathless, she leaned against the railing over which she had just tried to plunge. Winded and bruised, Leaf Man sat with his back to the railing, careful to leave what he considered would be safe distance between them, as they both struggled to fully grasp the enormity of the moment.

"You okay?" Leaf Man finally asked.

She nodded, though this couldn't be further from the truth.

He noticed the medallion on the sidewalk, retrieved it, then collapsed back down next to NYC Girl.

"Found this," he said.

Without a word of thanks, NYC Girl simply snatched it out of his hand.

He furthered the distance between them.

After what felt like an eternity, NYC Girl finally spoke.

"What the fuck you want from me?"

"Nothing. I was intent on minding my own business."

"You followed me!"

"No, I did not! But when I saw you, what choice did I have?"

"My fuckin' hero."

"I'm nobody's hero," Leaf Man said.

"Then why you stalking me?" NYC Girl asked.

"You wish."

"Hey, you fucked up my night, motherfucker."

"You mean your plan to kill two birds with one stone?"

"You have no fucking right to . . ."

"Care?"

"Give a fuck."

Leaf Man shook his head in disbelief, and after a brief moment of silence, said "Why do you give a fuck if I give a fuck?"

"Cause I know what you doing."

"And just exactly what is it that you think I have to gain?"

"Same as what all fucking men want."

"Right. Oh, and speaking of which, I thought you left with Elijah. What happened?"

"I've no idea what happened to that creep. And what the hell does it got to do with you anyway? You always such a nosy motherfucker?"

"Depends."

"Just leave me the fuck alone!" NYC Girl screamed. "Get the fuck outta here! I'm the last person in the world you should be wasting your time on."

"Guess I better look for someone else," Leaf Man replied, pretending to search for someone else to talk to. "Damn. Looks like we truly are the last people on earth. Guess we better get used to each other."

"Stop being so fucking nice to me. You're creeping me the fuck out."

"I get it."

"Then leave the fuck outta here. Now! Go!"

"Okay, I will. And listen, I know you won't believe a word I am saying, but as God as my witness, I truly and honestly care about your well-being right now and trust me, this is not the place for a woman to be alone . . ."

"Oh, but since you the big man . . . ?"

"No. It ain't safe for me, either. Trust me, I wish I could be anywhere but here right now."

"Then why don't you get outta here and leave me the fuck alone?"

"Because I have a strong feeling that you didn't come all the way back from New York just to jump off a bridge. There are plenty of way more impressive bridges to plunge off in New York."

"Don't you fuckin' pretend you know shit about me. How the fuck is this any of your business?"

"Because once you get caught trying to off yourself, you lose that privilege."

"Stop trying to act like some kind of goddamn guardian angel. They don't exist. And the last thing I need is some motherfucking knight in shining armor."

Though she realized he had a point, she refused to accept it. At least, not outwardly.

"Don't you got more important things to do?" she asked. "We both know why you're here."

"Actually, I've been trying to figure that out," Leaf Man said, seething with sarcasm. "Maybe you can shed some light on the matter."

NYC Girl looked down at his ring.

"Guess you already got your mind made up 'bout me," Leaf Man said.

"Like you have about me?"

"Name one thing I said that wasn't true."

The straw that broke the camel's back.

With explosive might, NYC Girl charged at Leaf Man with everything her tiny, broken body could muster. Both were equally surprised.

All of her rage, pain, failure, and abandonment came gushing out as her fists pounded Leaf Man's chest and arms. He did everything he could to deflect the blows with minimal force.

And it goddamn fucking hurt.

But he continued to take it, *allowing* her pain to become his until her fury was drained and she crumpled into a ball on the damp ground.

As she lay there crying, Leaf Man retreated against the railing to regain his breath. Within arm's reach lay her medallion.

He snatched it off the ground and offered it back to her.

The very sight of it unleashed a further downpour of tears, from a hidden reservoir buried deep within the depths of her soul.

As her tears continued to cascade, she finally conceded, allowing Leaf Man to put the medallion around her neck, then surrendered into his arms, where she dissolved into a sobbing mess.

Two lost souls alone in a lost city.

Neither spoke.

As Leaf Man rocked NYC Girl in his arms like a child, her tears finally subsided.

A heavy wind blew in from the river.

He noticed that she was staring at his ring again.

His cue.

"I wear it as a reminder . . ." He paused. "A reminder of where I came from. Where I used to be. Where I'm going. And where I'll never go again. After tonight, it's coming off. For good."

"Why tonight?"

"Because for the first time, I finally have everything I need."

"Lemme guess. You found God."

"Never lost him. If anything, He lost me."

God was the last thing she wanted to discuss. How could something she didn't even believe in piss her off so goddamn much? She quickly turned the tables on him.

"And yet, you're here *why*?"

"Tonight is my close-out sale."

"Guess I was right about you after all."

If she was getting to him, he didn't show it.

"For one more night, yes. I technically shouldn't even be here at all."

"You and me both."

Leaf Man took out his wallet and opened it up to reveal a photo of a three-year-old boy.

NYC Girl stared intently at the photo, her face a mixture of awe and sadness.

She did not respond.

"This boy right here. *He* is the reason why the ring's coming off after tonight. For good."

She could not look away from the photo. It was like magnetic force.

And then she finally broke the spell. "I'm not capable of loving someone like that."

"Yeah? Well, I thought the same thing. And from the sound of it, you already know what kind of mother you *shouldn't* be. And you've been given the chance to prove it. But you got to first give yourself a chance."

"Stop with the goddamn sermon," she began. "I know what you trying to do. And it ain't working."

But was it?

"Hey, I hear ya. I also wanted to put an end to something I thought I never wanted. In fact, I begged my—whatever she was—to get rid of it. And I couldn't have been more wrong."

Though she appreciated his sentiment, she refused to let on. She had already shown enough weakness tonight.

"Nothing you can say can convince me to change my mind. A child don't deserve to be brought into this world by some whore mother like me. I know this from experience."

"Is that how you see yourself?"

"Ain't that how you see me?"

"No."

"And even so," Leaf Man continued, "your past ain't your future. It's up to you to decide what kind of mother you're gonna be."

"Hey, spare me the motivational bullshit, Oprah," she countered. "We are who we are. And I don't see what chance someone like me could provide for some kid."

"The chance to give someone the life you never had for yourself?"

"Yah, well, like I said, we is who we is."

"In the present, yeah. But the future gives us a chance to be who we wanna be. I'm proof of that."

"Oh yeah? And how exactly is that?" she asked.

"Well, for starters, I'm leaving the drug trade. That counts for something, right?"

"Yeah, whatever. If you say so," NYC Girl replied.

"There you go with the whole judgment thing again. You just can't help yourself."

"Okay. So why don't you tell me exactly how I'm supposed to think then."

"I wasn't peddling crack. I was peddling prescriptions."

"Getting people hooked on prescription drugs? How noble of you."

"Why don't you tell it to the old lady I was with tonight before my gig? Or dozens of others just like her. The sick. The elderly. Children. *Saving* lives. Not *taking* lives. But it still wasn't enough to win back my son. So I threw myself into my music. And it led me through the door of Saint Andrew's tonight. In less than an hour, I'll be completely legit for the first time in my life. And it's all because of my son." His eyes brimmed with tears. "It's *that* powerful."

"Yeah, well I'm glad to know that one of us got it all figured out," NYC Girl replied.

"It wasn't always this way."

"So, this was your first night on stage?"

"At Saint Andrew's, yeah."

"Well, you looked like someone who knew what he was doing."

"Everything I worked at for the past thirteen years of my life led to what you saw and heard tonight."

"How does it feel?"

"Greatest feeling in the world. Sometimes, you just have to trust that God will put us where we need to be."

She rolled her eyes.

"Yeah, I know, I know. It wasn't that long ago when I would have had the same reaction. I get it."

"I used to pray," NYC Girl began. "A lot. The last time I prayed was the night before I left for New York. But a girl can only take so many unanswered prayers before she is left with two conclusions: either God is dead, or he simply don't give a fuck."

"Which is worse?"

NYC Girl shrugged.

"So this dream of yours . . ." Leaf Man began.

"What about it?" NYC Girl asked.

"What happened to it?"

"Nothing. It died."

"You got it wrong," Leaf Man said, shaking his head. "We might be done with our dreams. But our dreams ain't ever done with us. If we ain't chasin' them, they gonna chase us. They *stay* with us. They become who we are. It's up to us to end up where we're supposed to be. It's never too late."

NYC Girl looked down at her swollen belly.

"It's too late."

"Following your dream will make you a good role model."

"Oh right. Because it's so fucking easy for a single mother."

"I didn't say it would be. But now that you've been given a second chance . . ."

"Bull. Fucking. Shit!"

Deep down, she knew he was right, but for her own protection, her defense shield was always up. Meanwhile, Leaf Man could feel himself falling deeper and deeper under her spell.

And when she saw the way he truly listened to her, she couldn't help but be drawn to him, making it harder to hide behind the shadow of her doubts.

"You came this far, right? You must have come home for *something*."

NYC Girl stared off into the distance, across the river, and did not reply.

"I think you know what you gotta do," Leaf Man said softly.

"Well, I can't. So that's that."

"You mean, you don't *want* to. Or, you're too *scared* to?"

"I tried."

"Couldn't don't mean can't. It just means you need to try again. And if not now . . . when?"

"I don't know if I could handle any more rejection."

"Then at least you tried. And you can keep on trying. "

NYC Girl continued to stare across the river.

Leaf Man continued. "At least you knew your mother. You don't know how goddamn lucky you are for that. My mother never even got to hold me. How unfair is that? The Lord took her away before she could hold her own, newborn child."

NYC Girl stared at him, searching for words that wouldn't come.

"Look, as long as you're alive, it ain't *never* too late. What matters right now is everything you do from this moment forward. All that matters from here on out is you, me, and tomorrow."

After a prolonged silence, NYC Girl uttered a simple, but sincere "Thank you."

Leaf Man wondered what this implied. Was she just thanking him for his unsolicited advice? Or, was she going to follow it?

He met her gaze and *this* time, she didn't look away.

"You know what time it is?" she asked

Leaf Man looked at his watch.

"2:15."

"It's past my bedtime."

Leaf Man laughed.

"Not that I want this day to ever end!" she said with a sarcastic smile.

A lone car crossed over the bridge and the illusion that they were the last two people on earth was shattered.

"I gotta get going," NYC Girl said.

"And where exactly do you intend to get going to?"

"Home."

Leaf Man stood and offered his hand to help NYC Girl up. She took it without hesitation. They walked toward the road. Hand in hand. He dragged his suitcase behind him with his free hand

"So it's all going to be okay, then, right?" NYC Girl said.

"You're going to be okay. I'm going to be okay. We both going to be okay."

"So, we supposed to wish upon a star or some bullshit?"

Leaf Man laughed. They both looked up into the starless sky. Even on a clear night, the stars were absent. Not even the city's lack of adequate street lighting made the stars any more noticeable.

"You know, the first time I saw a sky full of stars was when my bus to New York made a stop in the middle of nowhere."

"First time ever?"

NYC Girl nodded.

"Sad, ain't it?"

"I get it," Leaf Man replied.

After a brief pause, Leaf Man added, "so, which way you headed?"

"Southwest side."

"You shouldn't go alone."

"Never stopped me before."

"Let me at least walk you to the bus stop. It's dangerous out here."

They both chuckled.

"What about your *meeting*?" she asked with finger quotes.

"I'm early."

"Why so early?"

"So I could save your sorry punk ass."

"Yeah, sure."

"God puts us where we need to be."

Somehow, despite all her hardened, inner logic, she agreed.

They set off along Jefferson, cloaked in the comfortable shared silence of knowing that there was nothing left to be said.

For this night at least.

They had the whole future to resume their conversation.

The Renaissance Center loomed ahead.

Sparkling like stars.

Church bells signified 2:30 a.m. as they reached an empty bus stop on an equally empty street.

"So, I guess it's goodbye?" NYC Girl finally said, breaking the prolonged silence.

"Yeah. For now."

"For now," she echoed.

"Oh! Your number?" he added.

"I don't have a phone," NYC Girl said.

"Wow, you are in rough shape."

"You've noticed."

"Okay, then let's try this: what you doing Monday night?"

"My calendar—if I had one—is empty. So I can probably squeeze you in. What time?"

"Meet here at six? And maybe take you out for some dinner and jazz? You like jazz?"

"Yeah. Okay," NYC Girl replied.

"And if it turns out that you can't make it," Leaf Man added, "you know where to find me. Every Friday and Saturday night. For the foreseeable future, at least."

"And, hopefully, under better circumstances." NYC Girl added.

"Yeah, I promise."

"I'll hold you to that."

"Please . . . don't stand me up," Leaf Man begged.

The bus rumbled up before squealing to a halt.

"Oh, shit!" NYC Girl exclaimed.

"What's up?"

"I'm broke."

Leaf Man dug into his pocket and handed her enough for her fare.

"I'll pay you back," NYC Girl promised.

"I won't accept it."

"Thank you," NYC Girl said, before adding: "For everything."

"No. Thank *you*. For everything."

And with that, she climbed onto the bus, as the first raindrop fell.

As the doors began to close, they both called out in unison:

"What's your name?!"

But it was too late.

R . I . P .

1

R.I.P. saw smoke before fire. But as expected, no one else was around to notice.

He reached a deserted street off 7 Mile where flames poured out of an abandoned house.

The sun hadn't even set on Devil's Night.

Not that he gave a flying fuck.

After all, Devil's Night comes but once a year.

R.I.P.—who, as he liked to think, bore a close physical resemblance to his hero, Biggie Smalls—was certainly no stranger to Devil's Night. At one point, he participated out of peer pressure and the need for acceptance. But then he became addicted—a card-carrying arsonist—until he decided to give it up for good after *possibly* causing the death of an 18-month old girl five years prior. No one ever questioned him. And partially because he wasn't sure himself, he sure as fuck wasn't going to turn himself in.

By no means had he turned into a choirboy. He had merely stumbled upon another, far more lucrative activity to put food on the table.

Lately, however, food was the least of his concerns.

He eventually came to the conclusion that there was no money to be made in arson, anyway, unless it was for shady insurance purposes. But that option would involve actually owning property to burn down in the first place.

Though he missed the thrill of watching something set ablaze by his own hand, he needed money—but not for himself. In fact, he hardly spent a dime on his own wants and needs. Most of the money he "earned" went toward his father's medical expenses.

For the past couple of years, R.I.P. desperately needed money to keep his father alive. More recently, however, it had become more a matter of doing whatever it took to keep his father as comfortable as possible, for however long necessary. Despite the realization that he would be better off without his father, he knew he would miss having someone to care for. There was something uniquely special about feeling *needed*. Caring for his father gave him purpose, something he was scared to admit he would otherwise lack.

He was en route to his neighborhood pharmacy. As he reached into his pocket to grab yet another prescription, the paper sheet was swept away by the wind. R.I.P. chased it halfway down the block, before he finally caught up to it and pinned it to the damp concrete with his foot. He picked it up and wiped off as much of the mud as he could. He was completely winded. In fact, if his increased wheezing was any indication, he had never felt this out of shape—at least not since he decided at the age of fourteen to begin working out, to defend himself against bullies. And maybe, *just maybe*, pick up chicks.

It didn't help.

R.I.P. entered the sparse, bare-essentials pharmacy in a huff, almost knocking down another customer half his size. R.I.P. glared at the customer, even though he knew damn well that he was the one at fault.

"Well, look who the devil dragged in," the pharmacist said. "You look like you're about to drop dead of a heart attack. Should I call 911?"

R.I.P. was too focused on regaining his breath to respond.

"So what is it today?" the pharmacist asked.

R.I.P. slammed the wet, crumpled, mud-stained prescription down on the counter with his meaty hand.

The pharmacist took one look at the slimy slip.

"Not even gonna ask."

"How much?" R.I.P. interjected. He meant business.

As the pharmacist looked at the prescription, his eyes widened.

"You looking to kill pain, or a person?"

"Come on, man. You know who it's for. And he's getting worse every second you're wasting!"

"I can't just keep giving this stuff out willy-nilly. I can lose everything if someone thinks my client is the new Dr. Jack."

R.I.P. felt the gaze of the other customer in the room and turned toward him.

"The fuck you looking at?"

The man diverted his eyes away from R.I.P.

"No need to give my man a hard time," the pharmacist said. "Ain't his fault."

"C'mon, man," R.I.P. pleaded, hoping to guilt trip him into giving him what he needed. "You want my father's death on your hands? You know him. You're his friend!"

"Your pops is one of my favorite customers. Truth be told, he pretty much keeps me in business."

"Then why can't you do him a favor?"

"As opposed to all of the favors I've already done?"

"Then what's one more?"

"You know I would if I could. But without insurance, I can't help you with this one."

R.I.P. struggled to quell his rage.

"Look! I *need* to get that script filled. I know it's a lot, but that's exactly why I'm asking for a favor. I'm begging you, man."

He refused to give up.

"If you're asking for miracles, this ain't the place."

"I ain't asking for no fucking miracles. I just need a little fucking help."

"This ain't a charity I'm running here. It's a *business*. Now, I've stuck my neck out for both you and your father before—Lord knows how many times—but I just can't keep doing this. Take a look around, man. Times are tough. And they ain't getting better. And if I keep sticking my neck out, pretty soon, I'm going to be the one asking *you* for favors."

With the realization that he was wasting his time, R.I.P grabbed the prescription, crumpled it into a ball and charged out the door, slamming it behind him.

Feeling more hopeless than ever, he headed to one of the few payphones that hadn't been removed, stolen, scrapped, or vandalized beyond repair. Someday, he would be able to afford a phone of his own.

You're such a pathetic piece of shit.

He knew he shouldn't be so hard on himself.

But he was his own worst enemy.

R.I.P. dropped a few coins into the slot and dialed a number that was scribbled on the back of the prescription slip. He knew it was no use, but if by some divine fortune it worked, he would be able to get what he needed for his father on a moment's notice.

One ring . . . two rings . . . three rings.

Dial tone.

In a rage, he slammed the phone against the booth with enough force to snap the receiver in half.

R.I.P. slid against the wall, with his hands over his face. His entire body quaked.

"Hey," a voice said.

R.I.P. looked up, expecting to see a bum. It was the customer from the pharmacy.

Probably a faggot looking for a quick buck.

"Get the fuck outta here, asshole!" he said through tears.

"What if I told you I can hook you up for half the market price?"

"The fuck you know about what I need?" R.I.P. demanded.

"I know enough. And can probably help."

"Shit. Whatever," R.I.P. replied, his voice rife with doubt.

"You want my help or not?"

Though wary of the man's offer, he was finally convinced, if only out of desperation. He was more concerned about the fact that he wasn't sure if he could come through on the money end.

He reluctantly shook the man's hand and noticed a ring embossed with a marijuana leaf.

"I'll call you when I have confirmation," the man assured him.

"I don't have no phone."

"Then I'll see you over there."

"If you're fucking with me . . ."

"Hey! Same goes for you. But, you know what? Looks like today is your lucky day!" the man proclaimed with full confidence.

R.I.P. knew better. He didn't have lucky days. Though the man *seemed* legit, he wasn't convinced that this wasn't some kind of bullshit scam.

Regardless, it was time to check in on his father.

As he headed home, R.I.P. noticed that the gray skies had darkened, against the backdrop of a setting sun and gathering clouds. There was a tiny break on the horizon of gray clouds up ahead, as though the sun wanted to catch one last glimpse of the dying city before it turned in for the night, even as the moon suddenly revealed itself from behind a cloud as if to remind the sun of its place. Surreal rays made of a mix of moonlight and sunlight burst through an otherworldly horizon, shining upon the city. As he gazed at the ashen sky, this sudden presence of otherworldly light seemed to defy all logic, giving him a brief respite.

Fool's gold?

And then the rays of light were swallowed by the very clouds that had briefly parted to reveal the glorious, temporary beauty.

Suddenly, a red-tinted group of clouds formed what, to him, looked like a dwarf.

And one thing came immediately to mind:

Nain Rouge.

He once went to a Halloween party at Saint Andrew's dressed as that little red fucker.

And then, as quickly as it had appeared, it was gone, as a smoky dusk settled over the barren landscape.

2

R.I.P. turned down another street that any outside observer would assume was completely abandoned. It was the only place he had ever called home.

When he reached the end of his driveway, he retrieved a batch of mail from a budging mailbox. He labored up the crumbled, weed-filled walkway and entered the house. Once again, he had to catch his breath.

I really fucking need to get in shape.

R.I.P. tossed the mail down onto a table cluttered with junk mail, bills, and past due notices from assorted collection agencies.

The incessant sound of squawking parakeets emanated from somewhere within the depths of the hoarder's paradise he called home. In R.I.P.'s defense, there was little he could do about the mess. Every inch of space was covered in clutter. His father always stuck to the firm belief that there was *nothing* he wouldn't somehow need someday. Even ancient, faded, unread copies of the *Detroit News* and *Free Press*.

The familiar, muffled sound of a 70's sitcom through a closed door filled the house with the warm nostalgia of early childhood. Tonight was *Sanford & Son*, but on any given day, it could be *Good Times*, *The Jeffersons*, *Taxi*, *Three's Company*, or *Welcome Back, Kotter*. Not that the shows themselves mattered. His father slept through most of them.

There was no credible reason as to why R.I.P. couldn't tidy up the rest of the house without his father's knowledge. If only to honor his mother's legacy. She would never have stood for such a mess. His father was never the same after her passing. Not even close. He simply gave up, entering a rapid downhill slide into a ghostly realm of non-existence.

His mind—and body—simply closed up shop with nothing left to do but to wait for the Going Out of Business sale to end.

R.I.P. didn't have any such excuse. But where would he even begin? He was far too lazy to keep his own bedroom clean, let alone the rest of the house. He couldn't remember the last time he had made a bed.

Yet, his father somehow maintained a stubborn insistence that he would get well soon, no matter how many doctors told him otherwise. Although R.I.P.'s rational self knew otherwise, there was still a part of him that desperately wanted to believe his father, therefore making him a willing accomplice. The fact that his father was still alive was proof that it truly was mind over matter.

Quality of life was a whole other matter. The years piled on along with the trash, as father and son lived out their days in their derelict debris palace, where the cockroaches roamed and the mice and bacteria played.

R.I.P. walked past a littered den, where his father's dozen or so feathered fucking friends lived out *their* days.

Glorified goddamn rats with wings.

Splashes of vibrant color soaring above a sea of shit.

Weeks' worth of feces and seed casings littered the cage; the wooden perch entirely coated in dry bird shit. His father never would have forgiven him. It was bad enough he had to deal with his father's feces, never mind all of the bird crap. If it were up to R.I.P., he would have found the birds another home long ago. Or, better yet, simply set them free. Perhaps if they had lived in a warmer climate, he would have done. But a Detroit winter? They wouldn't stand a fucking chance. They certainly deserved better. Then again, so did his father.

They all deserved better.

Even if R.I.P. wanted to get rid of them, there was no way he could get away with it. His father's faculties were too good—especially his hearing. From sunrise to sundown, the little shits never shut the fuck up. At least the fuckers weren't breeding anymore. Perhaps they refused to fuck in such filth, which was probably the only upside to not cleaning the cage.

Population control.

"Can't stop nature from taking course," his father would say. "A bird's gotta fuck. Ain't no different than any man."

Or this gem: "I know why the caged bird sings . . . because it's getting a ton of tail feather."

Birds aside, R.I.P.'s mission was to honor his father's wishes—the most important of which was to keep him out of a nursing home, even though conditions in *any* nursing home would surely be an upgrade. But it was the principle that mattered, not that they could afford a nursing home anyway.

As R.I.P. headed down the hallway, he was convinced more than ever that the trash had somehow found a way to reproduce itself. He had to kick some of the junk out of the way to forge a temporary path, but it was no use. It simply folded back in on itself.

He entered his father's closet-sized bedroom. On the floor against the back wall lay a yellowed, moldy twin mattress, where his emaciated father lay sleeping; his mouth agape. One could easily have assumed he were already dead.

Alongside the mattress lay numerous empty prescription bottles; a crucifix hung on the wall above the mattress, minus the crucified Christ, which had fallen off who knew the fuck when.

"Only God knows where," his father once said.

R.I.P. knew better: there was no God. And if he were to someday discover that there *was* a God, he would tell him that he was full of shit.

Though his lack of faith allowed him to live without guilt, it did nothing to alleviate his fear of death. In fact, lately, he feared it more than ever.

R.I.P. watched his father sleep.

Why can't you just fucking die?

He hated himself for thinking this way, but his motives were as compassionate as they were selfish.

He spotted his father's faded Detroit Stars Negro League baseball cap sitting on top of the dresser. Despite the sea of trash that accompanied it, this hat was one of his father's most prized possessions.

And he would more than likely never wear it again.

Feeling the need to be useful, he took the bedpan into the bathroom, dumped it into the toilet and rinsed it out in the grimy tub before returning it to the bedroom. He picked up his father's half-empty drinking glass that was coated in dried saliva and rinsed it out in the bathroom, before filling it up with "fresh" rust-water. After setting the water down, he searched among the sea of prescription bottles.

We really need to get a fucking pillbox.

He searched for a random piece of paper, which was more difficult than he would have guessed. He finally weeded out a discarded prescription package, tore off a piece and wrote:

"TAKE YOUR GODDAMN FUCKING PILLS DAD!"

He punctuated the note with a smiley face and placed it next to the glass of water.

There were two likely outcomes: it wouldn't be noticed; or it would be ignored.

He then placed the pills on top of the paper and headed into the den to remove the birds' shit-encrusted food dish. He dumped the empty shells into a trash-strewn corner, before filling the dishes with fresh seed. He made the same mental note to buy a new bag of seed that he had made last week, and the week before that. Oblivious, the birds scampered off their perches with excitement, pecking at one another for prime position.

R.I.P. headed into the kitchen to refill their cesspool of a water dish in a sink overflowing with dirty dishes. A thick layer of grease and crud coated the countertops, which hadn't been cleaned in the twenty years since his mother passed away following her drawn-out battle with breast cancer. The condition of the house was both an affront to her legacy, as well as a physical manifestation of how much both men had depended on her.

R.I.P. had found his own way to honor his mother: with an inked tribute.

The tattoo was *his* most prized possession.

Instead of R.I.P., it could just as well have said "Mama's Boy," just like the taunts his classmates relentlessly threw at him. As much as it hurt, his classmates were right. He *was* a mama's boy. Just like being called "fatty" was true. He just didn't need a constant reminder. The Mama's Boy moniker hurt even more *after* his mother had passed away. This fact only served to intensify the taunts.

After placing the water dish back in the cage, R.I.P. grabbed a bag of stolen jewelry he had accumulated throughout the week, and a 9 mm out of a junk drawer, before he headed out to face the night, filling his overburdened lungs with crisp autumn air.

It was exactly what he needed to begin his long journey into the night.

3

Now that R.I.P knew how to achieve his goal, he just had to find the *means.*

Darkness enveloped the landscape. And so here he was, his sights set on Indian Village—one of the few upscale enclaves in town.

An oasis.

Or was it a mirage?

One thing was certain: R.I.P. needed to boost his cashflow. He had been down this road countless other times. But desperation knows no bounds.

Someday, he would find a legit job, but it was getting harder and harder to play by the rules. And if past history were any indication, once he found a job, he would be sure to find a way to lose it. Though he liked to play the victim, deep down he knew that he had no one to blame but himself.

He was lazy. And an asshole. The worst combination. He couldn't bring himself to bust his butt for minimum wage when he knew he could make more money in other, less legal, ways. And for so much less effort.

He turned onto Iroquois, then approached an immaculate Tudor Revival home, shrouded in darkness. This was by no means a random selection. Though lazy about most things, he took his criminal exploits very seriously. He noted on a previous scouting expedition that this particular house was consistently in darkness at night and that it lacked any kind of a security system. The mostly white neighborhood was growing too complacent to take precautionary measures.

After tonight, he was pretty certain that the owners would reconsider their home security strategy.

He confidently sauntered up the sidewalk, which cut through a perfectly manicured lawn and ascended the ten or so steps leading up to the porch. He moved neither too fast, nor to slow. Both extremes could arouse suspicion.

He knocked twice to make certain nobody was home, took a quick 360-degree surveillance as he slipped on some gloves, then casually walked over to the side of the house, which was surrounded by a wrought-iron fence. The gate was locked, so he climbed over the fence with the dexterity of a drunken elephant.

The second he landed, he was greeted by a German Shepherd.

The white man's pitbull.

R.I.P.'s knee-jerk reaction was a direct stomp to the dog's head. The dog yelped and dropped to the ground like a rock. It twitched slightly, then lay still. Another stomp in the skull for good measure, immediately triggering:

A playground.

A friendless eleven-year-old boy.

Face shoved into the ground by his daily dose of bullies.

As other classmates watch and laugh.

Or look on with indifference.

Where were the adults?

Did they really not notice?

Or, did they simply not give a shit?

How was this dog any different?

Desperation knows no bounds.

Had his bullies been desperate?

None of that mattered now.

What mattered was getting in and out of this house as quickly as possible.

Early on in his illustrious burglary career, R.I.P. would shoot dogs without reservation. However, doing so would give him no other choice but to flee the scene. Unlike other neighborhoods in the city, where gunshots are more common than chirping birds, a single gunshot in Indian Village wouldn't go unnoticed.

And why did he suddenly feel pity for this fucking dog?

Am I the dog?

R.I.P. checked his surroundings to make sure that his cover wasn't blown and headed toward the back door. He peered through a dark window, partially obscured by curtains, and then took one last look around before he took off his jacket, removed a MagLite from his pocket, and placed his jacket over a window. He gave it a couple of firm whacks and the glass broke. A neighbor's dog barked. R.I.P. froze for a moment, waiting for the barks to die down, before clearing away the remaining glass with his jacket and reaching in to open the door.

As he cautiously entered, something soft and rubbery squeaked beneath his foot. He aimed his flashlight at a dog's chew toy and was overcome with a brief, unexpected wave of guilt, but not enough to stop him from making his way through the house in search of loot.

R.I.P. darted the flashlight around and caught snippets of the tastefully-decorated house, rife with treasures. He headed into the master bedroom and quickly located a half-full jewelry box, a gold tie clip, $50 in cash, and what turned out to be a crusty dildo he initially mistook as a flashlight. He tossed everything into a large plastic bag.

Just as he turned to head out, he heard something shuffle in the hallway. R.I.P. froze in terror, as the sound drew closer. An image silhouetted by moonlight materialized in front of him—a man covered in blood, slithering down the hallway, leaving a bloody trail behind him. When the man finally reached the bedroom doorway, he slowly lifted his head up into the beam of R.I.P.'s flashlight to reveal a bludgeoned, misshapen face. This one was tough to process. R.I.P. had seen some crazy shit over the years, but this one took the whole motherfucking cake.

The man attempted to speak, but in place of words, came blood, erupting out of his mouth like hot lava. R.I.P. made a mad dash out of the bedroom, loot in hand. As he carefully stepped over the man, a bloody hand grabbed hold of his pant leg. He managed to wiggle himself from its grip, his heart pounding.

He rushed around a corner, only to trip over a large, unidentified mass on the floor. He dropped his flashlight in the process, which rolled until it landed with its beam shining directly into the face of a dead woman with a hole where her face should have been.

Behind him, the shuffles continued, growing louder as they drew near. R.I.P. looked up and could see the whites of the bludgeoned man's eyes. Unable to get to his feet, R.I.P. crab-walked backwards as fast as he could toward the door until he was able to scamper against a wall into an upright, standing position. He turned toward the front door, only to be greeted by a young boy—probably no older than twelve— pointing a .38 snub-nose at R.I.P.'s face. The boy's entire body trembled in fear; his eyes welled with tears.

"What did you . . . do?" the boy demanded, as his gun trembled in his hands.

"Me? I didn't do shi—" R.I.P. started, as the boy pulled the trigger. R.I.P. managed to dive out of the way as the gun went off, scrambled to his feet, and raced out of the front door.

He hightailed it down the street, looking back in time to see the man slither out of the house, before falling off the porch and into the shrubs below.

He headed around the block and hid behind a row of tall bushes panting and trying to regain his breath. He was too frightened and numb to make any sense of it all.

And then, suddenly, he felt as though he was eleven again.

Hiding behind bushes from his bullies.

Only now, he was the bully.

The circle of motherfucking life.

Once he was certain that all was clear, he ventured back out to face the world, which now seemed like an even darker place than ever before.

4

What R.I.P. wanted to do more than anything was climb into his bed, but instead found himself climbing aboard yet another empty bus headed downtown. He was sick to death of busses. But walking was becoming increasingly difficult. The one upside to being tired was that it calmed his nerves. But tired was the last thing he could afford to be.

He disembarked in the epicenter of desolation and headed up Brush Street, where there was at least *some* semblance of life. This awakened his senses, giving him a much-needed boost of energy.

R.I.P. honed in on a middle-aged couple that was heading his way. Their faces wore the customary suburban countenance of fear in a Gotham still in need of a superhero.

With no shortage of villains.

R.I.P. realized that he was likely the exact stereotype the couple thought he was. As much as he wished he could change this reality, he reminded himself that crimes were often committed for much more selfish reasons than his.

Or, so he thought.

At least he never had to resort to killing another man. Justifications such as these helped him sleep soundly at night.

He slipped into an alley and waited for the couple to approach—a monster lurking in a haunted house. He struggled to suppress his labored breathing.

As the couple darted past the alley, R.I.P. slipped out of the shadows and trailed behind. The woman turned around and gestured for her husband to quicken their pace.

Racist bitch.

R.I.P. took this as his cue. He had to strike before they got too far away.

"Excuse me."

The couple picked up the pace.

"Excuse me, sir? Ma'am?"

When he finally caught up to them, he grabbed the man by the shoulder.

"Excuse me, sir. You got a light?" R.I.P. asked as the couple turned around, probably in fear of becoming the exact type of headline they saw on the news every night as they lay in bed blanketed by their peaceful, suburban comfort.

"I'm sorry. We don't," the man said, his voice quivering.

R.I.P. spotted a gold necklace and crucifix around the woman's neck. And with one swift move, R.I.P. sucker punched the man square in the jaw. As the man dropped to the ground, the woman screamed in terror. In one quick swoop, R.I.P. put one hand over her mouth, put the index finger of his other hand to his lips as if to say "shhh," before tearing the gold chain off her neck, and yanking a gold watch off her wrist. He snatched her purse, at which point she let her diminutive frame go limp as though playing dead. She didn't put up a fight, nor did he expect her to. Confident that she would remain silent, R.I.P. slowly removed his hand from the woman's mouth, and placed her jewelry into his pocket. Her husband was out cold.

R.I.P. proceeded to rifle through the man's pockets until he retrieved a wallet, then bolted off into the night. He had a feeling it was the last night this couple would spend in Detroit. He was envious.

With adrenaline pumping through his veins, R.I.P. headed over to the People Mover's Cadillac Center station. As he climbed the stairs to the platform, struggling for breath with each step, he passed by a handsome, distinguished black man, talking on a phone:

"Of course it will work. When hasn't it? For starters, he's done after tonight, so it's not like we have to worry about losing a client. And since he's made it clear that he wants a clean break, if anything goes wrong, the last thing he's gonna want is any sort of retribution. And most importantly, he trusts us. I made his dream come true, remember? Nobody questions a dream maker. It's low-risk all the way. Now what time is your appointment?"

Detroit business as usual.

R.I.P. finally reached the top of the platform, struggled to climb over the turnstile, and collapsed onto a bench, barely able to catch his breath. At this rate, his father might outlive him. R.I.P. realized that he could probably walk to his destination faster than waiting for the People Mover.

But instead, he dozed off.

As the train's rusted rumble entered the station, R.I.P. awoke with a snap. Its screeching halt was like a slow, painful death. He felt as though he had been asleep for hours.

The doors slid open. R.I.P. took a step forward, accidentally kicking a balled-up piece of paper into the train. It landed at the foot of a bum sitting in the back.

R.I.P. plopped himself down as far from the bum as he could. He sensed he was being watched, but refused to take the bait.

"How you doing tonight?" the bum blurted out.

R.I.P. ignored him.

This motherfucker better stay the fuck away.

"Is this yours?" his fellow passenger asked.

R.I.P. looked up to see the bum holding up the trash he had kicked onto the train. He continued to ignore the bum and stared down at the train's dirty floor. He struggled to quell the growing rage within him by thinking positive thoughts, but it was a wasted effort.

There were no positives.

The bum waved the wad of trash in front of his face.

R.I.P. closed his eyes, as though doing so could magically make the bum disappear. He counted to ten under his breath, with his breaths growing more and more intense with each passing number until he exploded with bottled-up, volcanic rage.

"GET THE FUCK OUTTA MY FACE!"

The bum backed off and retreated into his corner of the train with his tail between his legs. Though he would never show it, he couldn't help but feel a little sorry for the little fucker.

Why did I have to be such an asshole about it?

Then again, that little fucker should mind his own fucking business.

Both men sat in silence until the next station. Uncharacteristic guilt still lingered. Once again, R.I.P. had become the thing he most detested: *a bully.* He wished he could stop, but like all history, he was on constant repeat.

As the doors opened, R.I.P. stormed off the train, down the stairwell and onto Michigan Avenue, which he saw as his yellow brick road that could take him all the way to Oz, aka Chicago.

All it would take was a bus ticket.

But as he stared westward down the empty avenue, R.I.P. realized he could never leave. As long as his father still had a pulse, he wouldn't even reach the city limits. The question was: would he have the balls to skip town once his father passed? As much as he wanted to think so, he had severe doubts.

Walking felt good. It relieved his stress. He was relieved that he hadn't resorted to violence with the bum on the train. Anger management was something he continued to work on. All he had to do was remind himself that one false move could land him in prison once again—or worse.

And then who would take care of his father?

He shuddered at the thought of his father starving to death in his own piss and excrement and left to rot among his debris, only to be discovered months later when one of his neighbors noticed the stench.

He tried to clear the thought from his mind, but it nagged at him.

R.I.P. finally reached Sam's Loans, aka Gold Cash Gold—a pawnshop down the street from Tiger Stadium which had recently closed its doors for good—another landmark left to rot.

He paused to look at the stadium's crumbling edifice. Even though he had never stepped foot inside, he certainly felt an emotional attachment to it. For years, he had begged his father to take him to a game. *One stinking game.* But his father never forgave history. The Tigers were the second to last team in the league to integrate (the Red Sox held out the longest). The older he got, the more R.I.P. understood his father's reluctance to attend a game, despite embracing black players like Lou Whitaker and Chet Lemon, who were at the center of the 1984 championship run. His father's personal favorite was Willie Horton, who took to the streets during the riots of '67, not to join the fight, but as a symbol of resistance and unity. The Tigers would go on to win a World Series the following season, which in no small part, helped heal the wounds left behind by the smoldering ashes of the previous summer. Truth be told, the city was never the same after that. For anyone.

Now that the stadium was closed forever, he regretted never catching a game there, particularly with his dad. It would have been a lasting memory. Father and son. Between the closure of Tiger Stadium and his father's failing health, it was certainly the end of an era.

R.I.P. reminded himself that now wasn't the time for nostalgia and entered Sam's. He was greeted by a gruff proprietor with a mixture of recognition and disdain.

"Almost closing time, Chief."

Without saying a word, R.I.P. dumped his accumulated loot onto the counter. He brought his hands down on the glass countertop in between a faded decal that read "DO NOT TOUCH GLASS." The "GL" was worn or, more likely, had been rubbed off.

The proprietor sorted through the goods. He inspected the watch and frowned at the broken clasp. Even though there was a strong likelihood that most of the shop's stock was stolen merchandise, R.I.P. figured that receiving the items was akin to seeing food alive before it's cooked and served.

The proprietor finished his cost analysis, opened the register, and pulled out two $100 bills and slapped them onto the counter.

"You gotta be fucking kidding me," R.I.P. fumed.

"Take it or leave it, boss. If you can't tell the difference between the real thing and this fake shit, you better find another line of work."

R.I.P. wasn't certain of the items' authenticity one way or another to put up an argument. Besides, the proprietor not only cut him many favors in the past, but consistently compensated better than any other shop in town. He knew it. And the proprietor knew it. So with that, he snatched the bills and turned around to leave.

As he was halfway out the door, the proprietor called out.

"Hey! You got a car?"

"What the fuck's it to you?" R.I.P. barked back.

"Do you have a car?"

"I can get one."

"That's not what I asked. *Do you have a car?*"

"I heard you. And I said, I can get one."

"I've got this friend who needs a little help tonight."

"How much?"

"How much help?" the man asked.

"No. How much cash?"

"A couple grand. Maybe three. You interested?"

"Yeah."

"Go to Saint Andrew's at ten," the man instructed. "Ask for the Grim Reaper."

"The Grim Reaper?" R.I.P. asked.

"Yeah. The Grim Reaper."

"What's he look like?"

"Are you fuckin' with me? He looks like the goddamn Grim Reaper! Death! Tell him Gabriel sent you."

"Man, this is some bullshit. What kind of crazy ass shit you gettin' me into this time?"

"You want the job or not?"

R.I.P. simply nodded, then walked out, noticing the cranes towering above the site of the Tigers' new ballpark silhouetted in the distance.

He needed a car.

Desperate times . . .

5

It had been less than a year since R.I.P. decided that his car-stealing days were over, following a botched robbery that left his best friend dead, an "associate" in a coma, and his own ass briefly in jail. The circumstances leading up to that most unfortunate incident, combined with the immediate aftermath, were enough to finally get R.I.P. to question the morality of what he was doing.

So, as surprised as he was to find himself getting back into the game, he was a master at moral justification.

My father needs medication.

And I need money to get the medication.

All I have to do is get through the night.

Just this one night.

Easier said than done.

He knew it would break his father's heart if he knew what his son had succumbed to.

Not to mention the dishonor to his mother.

And, of course, he would be lying to himself if he claimed that his actions were for philanthropic reasons only. Lately, however, that was very much the case.

R.I.P. surveyed the area for a target. It was less about the type of car and more about limiting exposure during the theft process. If stealing a rusted out Buick made more sense than a Lamborghini, then so be it. No matter which car he stole, he would be ditching it as soon as the job was done.

Though he would have preferred something less flashy, R.I.P. honed in on a shiny new Mercedes-Benz parked on an empty street in front of a broken meter.

Finders keepers.

What kind of dumbass motherfucker parks a car like that here, anyway?

Perhaps it was the couple he had already stolen from? Then again, they would have been long gone by now.

Or, were they taken to a hospital? Or, still talking to the police?

No time for second guessing.

R.I.P. located a small chunk of concrete from a pile of rubble that used to be a curb.

Sometimes, this town made the job too goddamn easy.

He looked around for witnesses, before smashing the window and entering his new ride. In a few swift motions, he removed the housing beneath the steering wheel with the greatest of ease and ripped out a braid of wires beneath the steering column.

The engine revved to life.

Still got it.

R.I.P. took one last look around, adjusted the mirrors and drove away from the curb, only to be greeted with the ding of the fuel indicator light. The gas gauge actually dipped below 'E.'

Probably another fucking suburbanite who was too afraid to fill up in the city, but didn't realize the car needed gas until they had already reached city limits.

Despite the underlying racism, he certainly couldn't blame the poor motherfucker. Not with motherfuckers like him roaming around.

R.I.P. headed off down the street in search of gas. The first station he passed was abandoned. Three blocks later, he found another one: Mo's Fuel Palace.

As he filled up a quarter tank, he noticed a car seat, various scattered toys, and a baby doll.

Fucking perfect.

He entered the station lobby, paid for his gas, a Faygo Rock & Rye, and a 100 Grand bar—after mulling over a healthier option for a quick second—before hopping back into the car and peeling out.

A yellow light loomed two hundred feet ahead.

He gunned it, then slammed the brakes. The last thing he needed to do was to get pulled over. Then again, he hadn't seen a single cop all night, nor heard a single siren. But it would be just his luck to have a cop pounce the one time he decided to blow a light.

As he waited for a green light, a blur of a white man in a black hoodie and matching ski mask appeared at his window, pointing a revolver. In a hushed, calm, yet threatening tone, he said "Get the fuck outta the car."

R.I.P. closed his eyes.

What next?

"C'mon, motherfucker!" the man said, becoming more agitated. "Move your punk ass. Now! Do it!"

Motherfucking cracker picked the wrong fucker to fuck with tonight.

R.I.P. swung the door open with one hand, slamming it into the would-be carjacker's kneecaps. The carjacker collapsed to the ground.

"Listen, motherfucker," R.I.P. said aiming his gun at the carjacker's temple. "This ain't my car no more than it's yours. But last time I checked, I'm the one in the driver's seat. Not you."

And with that, R.I.P. slammed the door shut and peeled out. He had dodged a bullet, but wondered if the safer choice would have been to just surrender the car. He could have just as easily found a new one.

But pride is blind.

R.I.P. drove through empty streets at the *exact* speed limit—as he knew from experience, going *under* the limit would likely arouse even more suspicion than going over—until he reached downtown.

He approached Saint Andrew's Hall—an old haunt that dated back to his teenage years where he had tried, unsuccessfully, to hook up with women, back when he had been 120 pounds lighter. R.I.P. learned early on that women aren't typically attracted to men whose tits are triple the size of their own. In fact, his inability to pick up women became the impetus he needed to shed his weight. But it made no difference. So, he ended up letting himself go, even further. Food was just as much of an anti-depressant as it was a leading cause.

An endless loop.

It had been three years since he last stepped foot inside the hallowed venue. More specifically, it had been three years since he had been thrown out and blacklisted from the joint.

Would they recognize him? He was about to find out.

As he scouted out his parking options, he noticed on a nearby wall:

DON'T CRY FOR US, CRY FOR THEM

Or, how about don't be a bitch and don't fucking cry at all.

R.I.P. had found that it was easier to hold everything in. It's how he had made it through most of his childhood, a defense mechanism that could be traced back to his elementary school playground.

Raised on a diet of fast food and loneliness, R.I.P. never stood much of a chance among his peers. He was an easy target because: (a) he was fat, and, more importantly; (b) his bullies knew that he wouldn't push back. Deemed too soft by the tough kids and too tough for the soft kids, he was in a catch-22 that made him invisible to almost everyone. So rather than try to do anything about it, he simply accepted his fate.

Several factors prevented R.I.P. from defending himself. Reason number one was fear of further retribution from his bullies. He was convinced that he would be bullied *less* if he didn't resist. However, he couldn't have been more wrong. However, another, and even more important, reason as to why he didn't fight back had to do with a promise he had made to his mother shortly before she passed: to follow in the footsteps of Martin Luther King Jr.—a message of peace and turning the other cheek.

Always do what's right.

And so he did. For a while at least. The main thing was to steer clear of the wrong crowd. Then again, even if he tried, the "wrong crowd" didn't exactly want to hang out with him. They were the ones beating him up on the playground. And in truth, that was pretty much his only social interaction.

Over time, however, he found it increasingly difficult to keep his promise, changing course from MLK and onto the path of Malcolm X, without really even considering the cause either man stood for.

Straying from the promise he made to his mother left him racked with guilt. But it was a vicious cycle he was unable to break.

Before he strayed, however, he routinely turned the other cheek, routinely returning home with black eyes and cracked ribs.

Perhaps if he had lost some weight? He would have stood a better chance of making it as an Olympic sprinter than having the discipline to lose weight. Besides, eating was his only solace. But once the last chip or cookie was gone, his solace turned to self-loathing, deserving of the ridicule and shame.

What might have helped at least a little would have been if some of his teachers had come to his aid to shelter him from the storm of his tormentors. But, most likely, they simply labeled him as the fat, lazy kid who didn't give a shit.

But he *did* give a shit. He was just too goddamned depressed to do anything about it. So with each passing year, he slipped further and further through the cracks.

And nobody offered a hand to pull him out.

Well, nobody apart from Mr. Vernor—his eighth-grade English teacher: the only teacher who had ever inspired R.I.P. to actually read a book—and enjoy it.

To Kill a Mockingbird.

Though he was able to scrape by with passing grades in all of his classes, this was the only class in four years of high school in which he had received a grade above a D.

71.6% to be exact.

This 71.6% had given him an unexpected level of confidence he had never felt before.

But just as Mr. Vernor had also taught him: "Nothing gold can stay."

The following semester, Mr. Vernor was discovered dead inside his car. A single gunshot to his head. No motive, nor arrest was ever made.

And after that, R.I.P. was never the same.

In fact, it was right around that time he decided to show his hand at what everyone had him pegged for anyway.

A thug.

With bottled up rage.

If you can't beat 'em . . .

And it worked. After he had teamed up with some new "associates," nobody fucked with him anymore. Because, as it turned out, most of his bullies were a bunch of punk-ass pussies who sang in the choir on Sundays on their mothers' laps.

It wasn't exactly R.I.P. they were afraid of. It was the people R.I.P. worked for. But he was okay with that. Because in exchange, he received protection.

And once he began working out, he at least *appeared* more menacing, until he realized that he was still a pussy—and then had simply let himself go again.

Thug on the outside, pussy on the inside.

Eventually, all storm clouds have to burst. But rather than raining tears, R.I.P. would erupt with thunder that rarely ended in his favor. As much as he wished he could get his anger under control, it was getting harder and harder. Tonight alone, he already come close to exploding several times: inside the pharmacy, the bum on the train, the dog, and the pawnshop. One thing after another, each episode pushing him closer to the edge.

Lost in thought, he almost failed to notice a shopping cart appear in front of his car. He slammed on his brakes, missing the cart's owner by mere inches.

The pedestrian buckled over into a coughing fit.

Once he had recovered, he looked up.

It was the bum from the train!

"I'm so sorry. I'm so sorry," the bum kept repeating.

Stupid fuck!

R.I.P. replied with a middle finger. The bum brushed it off, then turned around, retrieved his cart, and trudged onward.

Annoyed by the inconvenience, R.I.P. slammed on the gas and drove a few blocks before arriving at a former movie-theater-turned-parking garage. Though a bit of a hike, he, fortunately, had a few minutes to spare.

What better use of vacant real estate?

Detroit: the parking lot capital of the world!

After finally finding a spot on the 5th floor, R.I.P. placed his gun into the glove box and headed out in search of the Grim Reaper.

6

R.I.P. hurried down the street, chomping on his 100 Grand as if it were the last one on earth. He reached into his pocket, pulled out the stolen wallet and removed the cash. He tossed the wallet and candy wrapper into an overflowing trashcan and counted the cash as he continued on his way.

$28. *Motherfucker!*

R.I.P. shoved the money into his pocket. After all, if anyone should know why one should not walk around with a wad of cash in his hand, it was him.

Across the street, the bum sat on the curb, still coughing.

R.I.P. made a beeline across the street toward the club, where a long line wrapped around the building. He wasn't sure whether or not to wait in line, so he approached a bouncer standing along the curb in front of the line.

"Excuse me."

The bouncer ignored him.

"Excuse me!" R.I.P. said with more authority.

"Da fuck you want?!"

"I got a meeting with the, um . . . Grim Reaper."

The man studied R.I.P. with a scowl. Perhaps further elaboration was necessary. However, the bouncer seemed to understand and pointed to his comrade at the top of the steps:

"Let him in."

The bouncer turned toward R.I.P. with a nod: "Go ahead."

R.I.P. gave the bouncer a gracious nod and headed inside.

What the fuck am I getting myself into?

Perhaps he should have sought an alternate route. After all, it was probably in his best interest not to team up with a man disguised as death.

But he was desperate.

And this was his most desperate measure.

Upon entry, he was immediately frisked by security, before heading off in search of the Grim Reaper, amid a crowd of costumed freaks.

He poked his head into a dark office. Nobody. As he continued his wild goose chase into the basement—the Shelter—he couldn't help but wonder whether he was chasing shadows or, perhaps, on the ass end of some bad joke. Just as he was about to give up his search, he spotted his elusive phantom—sitting in a corner. Mask and all.

Salvation in the form of death itself.

R.I.P. approached. The man looked up, but did not remove his mask.

"I'm here for the job."

"What the fuck you talking about?"

"Heard you might have some work?"

"I think you got the wrong nigga."

"Ain't you the Grim Reaper?"

"I'm *a* Grim Reaper. But not the one you're looking for. So get the fuck out of my face, faggot."

"Suck my dick!" R.I.P. managed to fire back, leaving the scene before things could escalate. The last thing he needed was to start a fight.

Frustrated, he walked away. It was a fucking Halloween party and he was searching for a man dressed as death.

His confidence began to buckle as he suddenly questioned the validity of his plan.

Stop being a pussy and stick to the game plan.

But at what cost?

He located another Grim Reaper kitty corner to the first. Only this one wasn't wearing a mask. He was counting cash, surrounded by a couple of bouncers. This one *had* to be him.

He shoved aside all of his doubts to sum up the necessary courage for the task at hand and approached the second Grim Reaper with as much bravado he could muster.

"You *the* Grim Reaper?"

"What the fuck you think?" he replied, thumbing through a stack of cash, and without looking up.

"Gabriel sent me."

"You got a ride?" the Grim Reaper asked.

"Yeah. Of course."

The Grim Reaper scribbled an address and a rudimentary map on a napkin, before handing it to R.I.P., adding:

"Meet me here at one."

"What, is this a scavenger hunt or something? Can I get some more specifics?"

"You want this job or not?"

"Yeah."

"Then do what the fuck I'm sayin' and shut the fuck up. You understand?"

R.I.P. nodded, and walked away, realizing two things: this motherfucker meant business. And don't fuck with this motherfucker.

He glanced at his watch: 11:30 p.m.

With his attention diverted, R.I.P. collided into someone, causing an eruption of flying pamphlets.

Next thing he knew, he was staring into the red, club light-reflected eyes of a pale, gaunt mad man. The pale man stooped down to gather his pamphlets, which R.I.P. could tell were religious in nature. He pocketed one. Not for himself, but for his father. R.I.P. would have happily wiped his ass with it for all he cared.

R.I.P. left the club and headed back to the car. Maybe things *were* finally lining up in his favor?

Down the street, something caught his attention. A scene he knew all too well: a helpless soul being tortured by a bunch of skinny ass thugs. And then he recognized the victim: the bum from the train, the one he had almost mowed down.

On any other night, R.I.P. would have kept on walking. This would have been the last fucking thing he wanted to deal with.

But in this moment, he was watching his eleven-year-old self on the playground.

Once again he was Fat Fuck, Pig Man, Fat Albert, Black Jabba, Fattoush, Sumo, or any other number of cruel names. He had been offered candy wrappers and chip bags filled with trash, because he couldn't conceal his frequent food binges.

One day, a kid everyone called Fresh Mike—his name wasn't even Mike—invited R.I.P. over to hang with his posse. Surprised, but happy to actually get an invite to hang, R.I.P. cautiously made his way over. Fresh Mike offered him a bag of Better Made potato chips. He should have known better, especially since all eyes were on him, but he took the yellow bag.

"Go ahead and open it," Fresh Mike urged him.

R.I.P. hesitated.

"Open it!"

R.I.P.—now regretting his decision—slowly opened the bag.

A fresh pile of fucking dog shit.

R.I.P. recoiled and immediately dropped the bag to the ground as the entire playground erupted in laughter.

And then Fresh Mike—with the help of two henchman—dropped R.I.P. to the ground.

R.I.P.'s face landed an inch away from the dog shit.

"Hold him down!" Fresh Mike commanded to his cronies, who helped force R.I.P.'s face to hover an inch from the shit.

"Lick it," Fresh Mike insisted.

"No way," R.I.P. replied.

"Lick it. Before I make you eat it."

R.I.P. froze in terror.

"Do it!" Fresh Mike demanded, pointing to the turd pile.

R.I.P. continued to resist.

"I thought you'd eat anything!" Fresh Mike insisted as he placed his hand on the back of R.I.P.'s neck and shoved his face into the shit, smearing it every which way. The more R.I.P. tried to resist, the more it spread like butter on bread, until Fresh Mike finally relented:

"If you tell anybody . . ."

"I won't," R.I.P. said. And he didn't. The retribution would have been too much for him to bear. Instead, he ran straight inside into the restroom to wash the smeared shit off his face, then hid in a stall until it was time to return to class.

The shit wasn't even the worst part. It was the laughter, especially from the girls.

R.I.P. never fully recovered from that incident.

Why didn't anyone ever have my back?

Not in the hood, that's for damn sure.

Where were the goddamn superheroes?

As R.I.P. continued to watch the bum get shoved around by this new generation of Fresh Mikes, he realized that for once, *he* could finally be the hero he never had. But in order to do so, he would first have to climb out of the playground of his youth and take a stand.

Like a hurricane out of hell, R.I.P. unleashed his fury on the hapless cowards of his past with three meaty punches that knocked each one to the ground.

Only one tried to resist, so R.I.P. punched him again. The would-be bully lay motionless on the ground as the rest of his gang scurried off, leaving their fallen comrade like the pussies that they were.

R.I.P. briefly considered getting on his way, but then decided to offer a hand to help the bum back onto his feet.

And it felt fucking great.

If only for a moment.

"Thank you, sir! Thank you," the bum said, while struggling to catch his breath in between violent coughing jags.

"You okay?" R.I.P. asked.

"I am now. Thanks to you, my friend. I have been waiting for you."

Waiting for me to save him? What the fuck?!

The bum held out the wallet R.I.P. had stolen earlier.

"I believe this is yours."

R.I.P. now understood.

"What the fuck makes you think I want that?" R.I.P. said, immediately drawing the line in the sand between temporary hero and friend.

"I found it in the trash."

"Exactly."

Has this fool been waiting for me the whole time?

"I thought maybe it was an accident?"

R.I.P. couldn't help but laugh at the bum's childlike naiveté.

"You're one crazy ass motherfucker."

"Take it, please," the bum insisted.

"Naw, man, I'm good."

The bum opened it and revealed a perfectly-formed dollar sign made out of a 100 Grand bar, intertwined with the familiar yellow hue of a Better Made potato chip bag.

"It's money," the bum said, a childlike grin plastered on his face.

"Impressive," R.I.P. managed to say, awed by the coincidence of the chip bag.

"You sure you don't want it?" the bum asked pleadingly.

"Naw, you keep it." R.I.P. said, still in awe.

"I made it for you. You can put it to good use. Or, you can save it. You should always save money whenever possible."

"Ain't that the goddamn fucking truth!" R.I.P. laughed.

"You shouldn't take the Lord's name in vain, you know," the bum politely scolded. "Or, say that other word, either."

"My bad!" R.I.P. chuckled as an adult does at a child who does something precocious. Normally, holy talk in any form got his blood boiling.

He considered taking the dollar sign, but politely declined it one last time.

"Have a good night," R.I.P. said, turning his back to the bum.

"You, too," the bum said. "Thanks again. And God bless!"

R.I.P. couldn't stop smiling.

7

As R.I.P. made his way back toward his stolen car, he had one regret.

Why the fuck didn't I take his fucking dollar sign?

What harm would it have done? Sure, it was trash, but it was offered with good intentions, unlike the trash he was offered on the elementary school playground.

Why did he suddenly give a shit about a goddamn bum?

R.I.P. had a nagging feeling that perhaps he could have done more.

But what?

Provide financial assistance?

Nope.

Then what?

Nothing.

But there *was* something.

He could have taken the goddamn dollar sign.

But he didn't.

Maybe it wasn't too late.

He turned around, but the bum was gone.

He couldn't have gone too far, yet it was as though he had vanished without a trace.

He turned down an alley to take a piss. He looked up and spotted a message spray-painted on the wall:

"THOU HAST UTTERLY REJECTED US; THOU ART VERY WROTH
AGAINST US." LAMENTATIONS 5:22

Truer words had never been scrawled.

R.I.P. finished his business, then located his stolen car. It was time to refocus on the task at hand and leave emotion out of this. That was the last thing he needed right now.

He drove off and flipped through the presets on the car radio: lite rock, rock, and country.

Goddamn fucking cracker ass shit.

He scanned through the dial until he landed on some old school jams. 97.9 WJLB.

He cranked up the stereo until he approached his house, lowering the volume out of respect to his father. Even though he probably couldn't hear it, he would certainly feel the bass. He couldn't give two shits about the other few remaining neighbors on the block.

R.I.P headed inside, feeling only slightly better than he had a few hours earlier. As he sorted through the mail, one particular envelope caught his attention. He ripped it open.

A fucking foreclosure notice.

Certainly not the first one, but this one felt like a final warning.

He crumpled the letter up, tossed it onto the nearest trash heap, and found a way to resist the urge to punch another hole in the wall. Lately, he was really regretting his decision to give up weed—a strictly financial move. He would have to rely on deep breaths—or at least as deep as an overweight motherfucker with shortness of breath could get.

Of course, weed was only a short-term solution to a much bigger problem. What he really needed was therapy. However, he couldn't afford that. So he stole a bunch of self-help books from the library.

Hadn't put another hole in the wall since.

He took one more, deep breath, then headed into his father's room.

Maybe this time, he would be dead.

Then it could finally all be over with.

R.I.P. put his ear right up to his father's face and felt his warm, stale breath, which triggered a mixture of relief, disappointment, and guilt.

He cleared some trash off a chair next to the bed and sat down. His father awoke.

"Did you get it?" his father finally asked through a dry, hoarse voice.

Death encompassed him.

"Not yet. But I will."

"When? And how?"

"Don't worry about it, pops. I'll get it."

"I have every right to worry about how you getting it. How many times have I told you that I would rather die in peace, before you die in violence?"

R.I.P. looked at his father's nightstand and the pills he left earlier were still there.

"Why didn't you take your fucking pills?"

His father waved a dismissive hand.

"They supposed to control my nausea. But they only make me more nauseous."

"Goddamit! I'm busting my ass here tryin' to keep your ass alive."

"How many times do I have to tell you to stop taking the Lord's name in vain? And how many times do I have to tell you I'm not worth it."

"Bullshit!"

Goddamn, maybe I should stop taking the Lord's name in vain?

"Why don't you just go and take a chill pill?"

"Why don't *you* take your goddamn pills!"

"You gotta get on with your own life," his father implored. "Let me get on with what's left of mine."

"Not while I can still do something about it."

R.I.P. took a deep breath and made one final, calm plea.

"Look, pops, will you please just take your goddamn pills?"

"Are you going to stop taking the Lord's name in vain?"

R.I.P. and his father could not be any further apart on this issue.

"Yeah . . . sorry," R.I.P. said, holding out his father's pills.

His father finally relented and R.I.P. handed him his water.

"I didn't mean for any of this," his father began. "You know that, right?"

"I know it, pops."

"You have your *own* life to live."

"Yeah, well, ain't much of one," R.I.P. said as he looked up at the empty crucifix.

"But it can be. Without me."

"You're my father. I'm doin' what I'm supposed to."

"You sure about that?"

R.I.P. hesitated.

"You promised me. But even more importantly, you promised your mother."

R.I.P. felt himself tear up and looked away in shame. Perhaps his pops was right. Maybe they would both be better off if he just let his father go.

But could he live with the guilt?

And as much as he wanted to assure his father that he was keeping his promise to stay on the straight and narrow, it was a goddamn lie.

"No matter what you do, just keep on doin' what's right, son."

Damn, he's laying it on thick.

"I'm tryin', pops."

"Tryin' ain't good enough," his father said, trying to sit up. But he was too weak. R.I.P. offered him a hand.

"I can do it myself," his father insisted, waving his son away.

"Yeah, and I can help," R.I.P. replied.

He had inherited his stubbornness from his father, who finally relented and allowed R.I.P. to prop his pillows between the bed and the wall so he could get as comfortable as possible.

"Never thought I'd say this," R.I.P. began. "But lately, I been thinkin' that I'd like a family of my own someday. You know? A normal life. A day job. Maybe even live in the suburbs? Don't want to be another headline on the evening news, you know what I'm sayin'?"

His father smiled.

R.I.P. knew these were words his father had longed to hear.

"First off, did you get hit in the head or something?" his father asked, with what sounded like a painful chuckle. "And secondly, this is exactly why you gotta let me go!"

"I can't."

"Why not?"

"Look . . . I gotta get goin'," R.I.P. replied, changing the subject. "You want me to help you lay back down?"

His father nodded, then groaned in pain as R.I.P. tucked him into bed, just as his father had done for him years earlier—always followed by a lesson about bullies and perseverance. These talks were quite likely the difference between life and death. It wasn't until recently that R.I.P. fully understood this. Although he could never really imagine taking his own life, the thought had certainly crossed his mind from time to time.

Before he learned the coping strategy of simply not giving a fuck.

"You be careful, son. Promise me that you won't do something stupid once you leave this house."

He grabbed onto his son's hand and lifted himself up just enough to hold eye contact.

"Everything's gonna be fine, pops," R.I.P. replied, in a feeble attempt at reassurance.

"Yeah, well something's giving me a bad feeling."

"It's just the pills kicking in," R.I.P. responded. "It'll all work out. You get some rest, okay?"

R.I.P. reached into his pocket and felt something in there. He pulled out the pale man's pamphlet.

"Hey . . . I almost forgot," R.I.P. said, handing his father the pamphlet. "Got you some reading material."

His father looked it over with interest, before uttering, tongue-in-cheek, "old news."

R.I.P. stepped into the hallway. Halfway down, he heard his father's weak voice struggle to blurt something out. He poked his head back into the bedroom.

"You say something?"

"I love you, son."

Though he never doubted his father's love, he couldn't remember the last time he heard his father say that. Certainly not since he was a child.

"I love you, too, pops," R.I.P. replied, just barely managing to hold back tears as he headed out the door.

As he drove off into the night, his father's words echoed in his head:

I love you, son.

It felt finite. Complete. Like a closing statement.

I love you, son.

His father's voice continued to echo in his mind as he drove through endless rows of enormous, abandoned brick warehouses that resembled the set of a post-apocalyptic horror film.

The deafening hollowness of his surroundings slowly began to drown out his father's voice, until there was nothing. Nothing but neglect.

Rotting, empty window frames alternated with graffiti-strewn bricks.

A lost civilization, trying to scratch and crawl its way back, but failing miserably.

8

R.I.P. turned down a non-descript, mostly vacant residential street, checking the address scribbled on the napkin. As he drew near, he slowed down to a crawl and parked behind several cars already parked along the trash-strewn curb. It amazed him that so much trash could accumulate in such a low-populated neighborhood.

Steam rose from the streets as though smoke from the depths of hell.

He took a deep breath and got out of his car just as a black Cadillac reminiscent of a hearse passed him by. He approached the entrance of a run-down cinderblock house, which pulsated to a deep jungle beat. A strobe light jettisoned out of a cracked basement window, and danced in rhythm to the pounding bass.

R.I.P. headed up the steps leading to an enormous, dilapidated porch. A sign on the door simply read: "BACK."

As he made his way toward the back, an elderly black man dressed in a purple pin-striped suit passed him by, nodding at him with a cocky smile.

R.I.P. nodded back, but offered no smile

He finally reached the entrance, startled by the sight of the Grim Reaper—a shadow within the shadows of the doorway, who greeted him with a stone-faced nod of recognition, before issuing him a full pat down.

The Grim Reaper motioned for him to enter.

R.I.P. followed him inside the empty house.

The ground floor was *literally* empty.

Neither of them spoke a single word as they headed downstairs into the blinding strobe lights of a basement permeated with sweat, blood, and cum. In the middle of the basement floor was a single pool table, that was being used as a stage for two incredibly young-looking, naked girls. No way they were a day older than eighteen. R.I.P. wouldn't have been surprised if they were younger than that. He had been around too many places like this to think otherwise.

A handful of men watched the girls from metal folding chairs along the wall, smoking pot, sipping out of 40's and downing cheap liquor.

A stoned DJ spun bass and hardcore hip-hop in a corner; an equally stoned bartender worked behind a small, makeshift bar.

"Nice place," R.I.P. said, hoping it sounded more sincere than it came across.

"Thanks," the Grim Reaper said.

"Come on, motherfuckers," the DJ exclaimed. "Pot, pussy, and fifths are waitin' for ya! Show these bitches your love!"

Three completely nude girls walked past R.I.P.

"I have some loose ends to tie up before we head out, so feel free to play around," the Grim Reaper said, signaling for the bartender.

"This one's on the house."

R.I.P. hesitated, but then decided he needed the release.

Like a kid in a candy store.

He was certainly no stranger to strip clubs. In fact, he had frequented one regularly ever since he was twelve, when his uncle used to manage one. In exchange for washing dishes, he would occasionally receive "payment" in the form of hand jobs and blowjobs—the only attention he ever received from women. After his uncle died, however, he lost his free pussy pipeline and was both too cheap and too poor to pay out of his own pocket.

Though he appreciated the unexpected freebie, R.I.P. couldn't help but wonder just what kind of danger he was getting himself into to warrant such special treatment.

After he surveyed his options, he settled in on a very young looking piece of jailbait who stood against the bar in nothing but a thong. She bobbed her head along to the music, in what he assumed was a drug-fueled haze.

Despite his qualms, he couldn't help himself. He was a sucker for the young ones. She was also his type in the ass and tits department. He knew he was an anomaly, but he preferred them petite; tight ass and matching perky tits.

R.I.P. continued to ogle her, but she didn't seem to have noticed him yet—a welcome relief, since he had a tendency to grow sheepish when any woman paid any attention to him. This was precisely why when it came to the opposite sex, he was most comfortable with strippers and hookers: the attention wasn't *real*, even if his bashfulness was.

"Get you anything?" the bartender asked.

"Don't drink," R.I.P. replied.

"I don't think you were staring at my liquor bottles," the bartender responded. "She's yours if you want her."

"Alright."

The bartender nodded at the young girl. With drugged, seductive eyes, she put her delicate hand into R.I.P.'s meaty, sweaty palm and led him over to a sort of crawl space, illuminated in an eerie, dim blue light.

A basement within a basement.

Can't get more motherfucking underground than that.

Ghetto bass enveloped them, bouncing off walls.

The girl sat down on a torn couch against the back wall and motioned for him to join her. She lit a joint, took a hit, and offered it to him.

"Don't smoke," he said.

"Don't drink. Don't smoke. So what do you do, mister?"

"Elementary school teacher."

She appeared confused for a moment.

"What?"

He laughed.

She took a seductive hit off her joint, then got to work. She stood up and gyrated in front him, slowly removing her thong, while balancing her joint in her hand. He was amazed by how such a tiny swath of silk could yield such a prolonged removal.

As the next song started, she straddled R.I.P., bobbing and grinding into him in perfect synchronization with the music against the throbbing monstrosity in his pants. After a couple of minutes, she turned around, reverse cowgirl style. In the midst of a long dry spell, R.I.P. struggled not to shoot his load.

She did a sudden spin move, which ended with her shoving her little hand down his pants and seizing his massive cock with a graceful corkscrew motion.

He tensed up in surprise.

Once he got past the initial shock, he completely surrendered himself as she held his dick in one hand and her joint in the other. She handled him with gentle precision. Each stroke intensified, in perfect rhythm to the music. Before he knew it, he was being jacked off in a fury, as though her life depended on it—or at least her livelihood. It was as though she was channeling a lifetime of pain and aggression onto his cock.

R.I.P. winced, never having felt anything like it. She eased up and whispered into his ear.

"Too rough?"

"Naw, I'm good," R.I.P. said.

He tried to play it off, for fear of coming across as a coward. Considering how long it had been since somebody other than himself had touched his dick, he would take it any way he could get it.

The pain kept his urge to come in check.

The girl bit his neck with the fury of a venomous snake. He liked it, but didn't. Meanwhile, she continued working her way down his chest, stomach, and until she reached the bull's-eye, swallowing his cock with ease. He threw his head back in ecstasy as she sucked in rhythm to the music.

Just when he reached the point of no return, she climbed aboard, keeping his cock securely in her hand, as she guided it inside her in one smooth operation.

She rode his cock like hardcore hip-hop.

R.I.P. grunted in a mix of pleasure and pain as she continued to pound him. He grabbed onto her hips in an effort to assuage the pain, but she slapped his hands away.

His cock belonged to her now.

"I don't wanna fuck no bitch," she said to him.

"I ain't no bitch ... *bitch!*"

"Okay, then let me fuck you like a man," she replied, breathlessly.

What the fuck does that even mean?

She grabbed both of his hands and thrust them behind his head, then pinned him down, her face inches from his, her perky nipples tickling his chest. She began to fuck him even harder, and he found himself, once again, drifting back to his elementary playground.

The bully and the bullied.

We are who we are.

Five minutes passed, and showed no sign of letting up. The pain had become so intense, he had completely lost the urge to come. All he wanted now was for it to be over.

Who's the fucking customer here?

He wanted to physically slow her down with his hands, but her hold on his wrists was too tight to escape—at least, not without causing her injury. That was the last thing he wanted to do—not necessarily out of respect for her, but out of fear for himself.

He would have to somehow find a way to see past the pain.

And then he did, erupting in the most intense, equally pleasurable and painful orgasm of his life. It also appeared that she had joined him—or at least did a great job of faking it.

To his knowledge, he never made a stripper come before. And it felt pretty damn good.

Then again, it wasn't like he had much to do with the outcome. She did all the work. His cock was simply the conduit. He may as well have not even been attached to it. It certainly seemed as though she was trying everything in her power to remove it.

She dismounted him and reached for her joint, taking an extra long drag before offering it to R.I.P, still lulled by orgasmic paralysis. After a couple of minutes, he pulled up his pants, and headed toward the stairs.

"Have a good night."

"Da fuck?!" she exclaimed with daggers in her eyes.

"Excuse me?"

"I said 'What da fuck'?!"

"Yeah, I heard that. But what are you 'what da fucking'?"

"I got bills to pay."

R.I.P. thought about it for a moment.

"Yeah, me, too."

"Fucking asshole."

"I thought it was on the house?"

"Not the tip, you fuck!"

"Based on how much you seemed to be enjoying it, maybe you should be tipping me."

"Yeah, well I was faking it, *bitch*!"

As R.I.P. took a deep breath to suppress his rage, he noticed the hurt and desperation in her eyes—a look he knew all too well. He softened.

"How old are you?" R.I.P. asked.

She held up ten fingers, then added four more, stopping *at least* four short of what he was hoping for. Although he knew he wasn't entirely to blame, he should have known better. Then again, deep down, he already knew the answer.

So he reached into his pocket to offer the one thing he could offer. A $20 bill. Sure, he needed the money as much as she did—maybe even more so. But he sure as fuck didn't want to be at the mercy of the Grim Reaper.

With her job done, she headed back over to the bar, leaving him alone with his guilt. He was surprised that his guilt still lingered—for the second time that night. He also felt a tinge of paranoia that he had just fucked a minor. However, the thick skin he developed in early childhood was a coping mechanism that allowed him to quickly compartmentalize life's darkest moments.

It was the only way he had survived for this long.

The bartender nodded at him, but R.I.P. did not acknowledge him.

There was something about this girl, however, that gnawed him like wet rawhide.

Not only was she fourteen, but she was probably a slave. And because of the job he took tonight, he was pretty sure he was now aiding and abetting in the practice of child sex slavery. Yet, even with this realization, he knew that it was too late to walk away from the mess he was in all together. He knew all too well that desperation rarely subscribes to a moral code. The deeper the desperation, the more shades of gray the world becomes.

He was also fully aware that by turning down the job, somebody else would slide right into his place and nothing would change in the whole scheme of things—except for the fact that he wouldn't get the money. Somebody else would. Just like somebody else would be fucking that young girl. And others just like her. The bottom line was this: if he were to abandon his mission, he wouldn't be able to get the medication his father so desperately needed. So he would remain on course.

R.I.P. was just one cog in a massive wheel. A vicious cycle, where victims prey and feed upon victims in an endless loop.

As it has been and always shall be.

No matter how hard he tried, he couldn't stop thinking about that girl—and dozens of others just like her—runaways, orphans, and even kidnapped children plucked off the street.

Once upon a time, not so long ago, somebody's baby.

Now, somebody's slave.

As much of a victim life had made him out to be, this certainly put everything into perspective. In a world of victims, some had it far worse. And because of him, one young girl had now been even further victimized.

And in realizing this, he began to weep. An unexpected downpour of tears that he had accumulated ever since—well, ever since his mother's passing. In fact, he couldn't remember the last time he shed a single tear—

let alone a deluge such as this. He couldn't stop. In fact, the harder he tried, the more he cried. So he simply allowed himself to let go.

No point in trying to stop what couldn't be controlled. He already knew that much.

At that moment, his young "victim" appeared, saw him crying, and began to laugh hysterically.

"Da fuck, nigger! Seriously?" she said through tears of laughter.

"I'm sorry. I just . . ."

"What you crying 'bout?"

He tried to respond, but he was choking on his tears.

"I'm sorry. I'm . . ."

"Hey, I really don't give a fuck. But I do need you to get the fuck outta here. I got work to do, bitch."

R.I.P. finally got himself under control before anyone else could see him and began his slow ascent upstairs.

By the time he reached the top, he had experienced a perfect moment of moral clarity unlike anything he had ever felt. In his gut, he now felt an absolute sense of right and wrong and an understanding of which side he wanted to stand on.

The side he promised his mother he'd always stand on, despite always stepping down.

Why now?

Better late than never.

His mind was made up. He was getting the fuck out of there.

And never looking back.

He scanned the room, hoping to avoid detection by the Grim Reaper—but the Grim Reaper was nowhere in sight.

A clean getaway was within reach!

R.I.P. rushed out the back door and headed toward the front of the house. Just when he thought he was in the clear, he spotted the Grim Reaper, receiving an orange duffel bag from the slick-looking man he had spotted in the People Mover stairwell.

As the Grim Reaper opened the bag and inspected the contents, R.I.P. hid behind a ghetto palm on the abandoned property next door.

"You sure he'll fall for it?" the Grim Reaper asked.

"Have I ever let you down?"

"But can you trust him?"

"Like I said, have I ever let you down?"

R.I.P. saw this as an opportunity to escape. As he emerged from his hiding spot, the two men shook hands before the man from the stairwell hopped into his car and drove off into the night.

"So how was Candy?" the Grim Reaper asked, without looking up.

R.I.P. froze in his tracks.

And just like that, there was no turning back.

"Delicious," R.I.P. said, trying to appear calm and collected, despite the fear and disappointment building up inside him.

"Care for another?"

"Naw, man, I'm good."

Does he know I was trying to escape?

"So, you ready to roll?" the Grim Reaper didn't so much ask, as demand.

Say "no."

Tell him to go fuck himself.

But R.I.P. said neither of those things.

Not because he didn't want to.

But because there was only one *safe* answer.

"Yeah, let's roll."

9

"Head toward Jefferson," the Grim Reaper instructed as R.I.P. started the engine. "And watch your speed."

R.I.P. did as instructed, as the first raindrop landed on the windshield. Within seconds, they were driving through a steady rain.

The Grim Reaper pulled out his phone and hit the call button.

"We still on?"

Pause.

"See you at the docks."

He hung up, then turned his attention to the CD collection in the console.

"Michael Bolton. Michael McDonald. Celine Dion. Nigga, that's some real honky-ass shit."

"Keeps me relaxed," R.I.P. responded.

The Grim Reaper said nothing, but it was clear he wasn't buying it.

Dammit!

It was probably already too late. How could he *not* look suspicious at this point? No way this fucker was *that* naïve.

They passed the abandoned Packard Plant—a shelled-out behemoth spanning several blocks. To R.I.P., nothing symbolized the city's plight more than this building, which was built on the precipice of Detroit's industrial heyday. Like so much of the city, it was now a ghost of its former self.

It was only fitting that years before R.I.P. was born, his father worked there, until the day the plant shuttered its doors. He then headed to the blue oval, but was fired when he became mixed up in, and took the fall for, some stupid petty crime scheme. After that, he worked odd jobs as a handyman, barely making enough to make ends meet, leading directly to this current financial predicament.

"Hang a left," the Grim Reaper demanded as they approached Jefferson.

And then, throwing R.I.P. for a loop.

"You got kids?"

"No. Why?"

The Grim Reaper motioned toward the backseat.

Fuck! The toys! The carseat!

"Oh. My nephew. I babysit for my sis. Love that little fucker."

"And the doll is his, too?"

"Yeah, well, in this day and age . . ." R.I.P. began, cool as a cucumber. "My nephew, he's, well, he is who he is."

"You be one big, lyin' motherfucker," the Grim Reaper said with a sly smile.

R.I.P. put both his hands up in the air in surrender.

"Keep your fucking hands on the wheel!"

He did as he was told.

"You got me. It ain't my car. But you see, my pops . . . he's sick. And dyin'. And I need the money to—"

"Hey, nigga. Spare me the details. I don't give a shit. About you. And especially your pops. And it looks like neither of us has much of a choice right now, do we?"

R.I.P. nodded. He wasn't sure if he should feel relieved, or not. He still had the job.

But what about after the job?

R.I.P. knew well enough that when it came to motherfuckers like the Grim Reaper, consequences often came later.

When least expected.

Which meant living in a paranoia of *always* expecting it.

R.I.P. looked at the clock. 2:45 a.m.

Forty-five minutes.

Was there enough time?

"Got somewhere you gotta be?"

"Nope. I'm on your clock."

"Then why you keep staring at that clock?"

"I looked once."

"Bullshit! I saw you look at least twice."

"Nervous habit."

"Why you so nervous?"

"Just don't wanna fuck anything up."

"Then don't! Hang a right at the bridge. And keep your eyes on the road. And your hands on the wheel, goddamit!"

"Sorry, boss."

"For now." the Grim Reaper replied.

What the fuck does that mean?!

The bridge connecting the mainland to Belle Isle loomed ahead and R.I.P. couldn't help but feel like he was entering a trap.

He spotted a couple cuddling beneath a tree.

Why couldn't he have *that* life?

Maybe soon?

"Eyes on the road!"

This triggered the onset of a panic attack. Again, a problem typically remedied by weed, before all his money went toward his father's endless need for medication.

R.I.P. was increasingly concerned about the possibility of overlapping meetings.

When the fuck are things going to be on my time?

At least the meetings were in close proximity.

Unless . . .

Unless both meetings were the *same* meeting?

What were the motherfucking odds?

After all, Belle Isle was a common meeting place for any number of illicit activities at that time of night.

Yet, he couldn't seem to shake the feeling that he was about to be caught in the crosshairs. He couldn't bear to imagine the outcome.

Would he be able to hide the fact that he was connected to both parties?

"Hang a left and head to the docks," the Grim Reaper ordered.

They finally reached the parking lot of the Detroit Boat Club, where the dilapidated docks resembled the outstretched arms of rotting corpses, rising from the river.

"Kill the engine. Kill the lights."

R.I.P. did as instructed. They both stared in silence across the river at the sporadic blinking lights of downtown in the distance.

"So what now?" R.I.P. asked.

"We wait."

The vagueness of the instruction only amplified his anxiety.

"How long?"

R.I.P. understood perfectly well that when it came to these sort of man-for-hire gigs, the general rule of thumb was simple.

Don't ask questions.

Do as you're told.

Nothing else matters.

But R.I.P.'s nerves were getting the best of him.

"You got a problem?" the Grim Reaper asked.

"Naw, man."

The Grim Reaper offered him a stick of peppermint gum.

"Naw, man. I'm good. Thanks."

The Grim Reaper popped his gum as he stared out at the river.

"Okay, here's what it boils down to," the Grim Reaper finally said. "Something might be going down. And if it does, you need to be ready to get us the fuck out of here."

The Grim Reaper reached into his coat and handed R.I.P. a 9 mm.

"So your job is to have my back. That is your primary duty. You got that?"

R.I.P. nodded as he took the gun.

The Grim Reaper did a quick survey of his surroundings, exited the car, grabbed the orange duffel bag, and headed out to the end of one of the docks.

"I love you, son."

R.I.P.'s father's words still echoed in his mind.

Why does this man trust me?

Why would he be so sloppy?

And what happens to me when it's over?

There was only one answer.

Then it dawned on him.

He was completely disposable.

One and done.

Single serve.

Nothing he could do about it now.

Flee. I can fucking flee. Like I already tried to do before.

This was his second chance.

He thought about it, but found himself frozen in place.

The Grim Reaper finally reached the end of the dock, and set the duffel bag down at his feet.

A few minutes passed before a shadowy figure approached. R.I.P. squinted in an attempt at a clearer view, but the rain was making it difficult to determine if it was his guy, or not.

The two figures shook hands.

So far, so good.

After all, he said things *might* go down.

Not an absolute.

Probably just preparing for a worst case scenario.

Just in case.

A sliver of moonlight gave R.I.P. a fleeting glimpse of the man's face.

Suspicion confirmed.

The dealer.

His dealer . . . was the Grim Reaper's dealer.

Motherfucker!

Flee!

But he felt as though his legs were encased in concrete.

Just have to get through the night.

This night.

Maybe things would work out for him after all.

Nobody would get hurt.

And then he could finally get his clean break.

Everyone deserves a break, right?

But this was Detroit.

And he was working for the Grim Reaper.

The dealer stooped down to open the bag and examine its contents with a flashlight.

R.I.P. could tell from the dealer's body language that something wasn't right.

Paranoia, perhaps?

The dealer shouted something, but R.I.P. couldn't make out what was being said. But what he did understand was this: the Grim Reaper was now aiming a gun at his dealer's face.

And the dealer responded with a gun of his own.

Both men fired.

The Grim Reaper immediately hit the deck.

The dealer appeared unscathed.

Maybe things *were* turning out in his favor.

Is this a fucking movie?

He knew damn well this wasn't a fucking movie.

This was real life

His life.

Endless, looping, motherfucking life.

~Lacrimosa~

LEAF MAN: REQUIEM

"What's your name?"

Leaf Man's parting words to his muse echoed in his mind as he jogged back to Belle Isle in a steady drizzle, certain that they had fallen on deaf ears before the bus was swallowed whole by the night. At least she knew where to find him. He just wished he had a way to find her.

As much as he wanted to rely on fate, he knew better.

He had to take matters into his own hands.

Just have to get through the night.

Leaf Man looked at his watch and picked up his pace. He was cutting it much closer than he had expected. He just wanted to put these final deals behind him.

He threw his headphones on and played his mother's song, settling his nerves, then turned his thoughts back to his muse, pondering what would have happened had he shown up just a few minutes—*seconds*—later on the bridge. He regretted the harsh manner with which he initially treated her, even though he realized early on that toughness was the only way to reach her. His sincere hope was to keep her in his social orbit beyond this encounter. He prayed she felt the same.

At the very least, he took comfort in knowing that no matter what the future brought, he had made a difference in someone's life.

If even for one night.

And not just any difference—but *a life and death kind of difference.*

He realized that he hadn't felt quite this way in…well, years.

He was floating.

And this time, it had nothing to do with drugs.

The only thing that could deflate him would be never seeing her again. She represented the life he could soon have once tonight was over.

He did what he had to do.

There were no regrets.

The stage was finally set.

His phone rang. He didn't recognize the number, but knew exactly who it was.

"Yeah?"

"We still on?"

"Have I ever let you down?"

"See you at the docks."

Leaf Man finally reached the turn onto the MacArthur Bridge, running parallel to the massive, suspended Ambassador Bridge—the connecting tissue between Detroit and Canada.

His pipeline.

As he crossed the bridge, the rain grew steadier. Raw sewage seared his nostrils as a sudden whipping wind made every step a struggle. He looked down at the river below him. A bottomless tar pit.

When Leaf Man reached the island, he headed toward the dilapidated docks of the Detroit Boat Club—a rotting 1920s Mediterranean-style villa.

The bells from a distant church struck three, as he passed by rusted, vintage playground equipment and a carousel, waiting for children who no longer came, alongside an abandoned Olympic-sized swimming pool filled to capacity with filth and algae.

He scanned the grounds, but they appeared devoid of human life. But then he detected a cloaked figure at the end of the furthest dock, illuminated by a silver moon spying from behind the clouds.

Leaf Man approached with extreme caution, with one hand safely secured upon his firearm. He normally kept his cool in situations like this, but he didn't have a good feeling about this, especially when meeting with the Grim Reaper.

"After all of these years," the Grim Reaper began, "you still feel the need to put your finger on the trigger before we even say hello?"

Leaf Man knew that in all likelihood, the Grim Reaper did the same in return.

"You're the one dressed as death," Leaf Man said, pocketing his gun. "What do you expect?"

The Grim Reaper offered a cloaked hand. Leaf Man shook it and the Grim Reaper nodded toward an orange duffle bag beneath his feet.

Leaf Man stooped down and opened it.

Empty.

When he looked back up, he found himself gazing straight down the barrel of a 9 mm.

"What the fuck, man?!"

"You want out, then this is the out you get."

"It doesn't have to be this way," Leaf Man pleaded.

"Not according to my playbook."

Leaf Man weighed the probability of retrieving his gun in defense and concluded that he didn't stand a fucking chance.

Why the fuck did I put it away?

"Hey! I got a kid, man."

"So does every other goddamn nigger in this city."

Realizing he would probably die either way, he decided he would rather die trying. In a deft move, he snatched his gun and fired off a quick shot, propelling the Grim Reaper back, falling just short of the river. Somehow, the Grim Reaper managed to fire off two shots from the ground—both of which missed his target. He collapsed into a ball, clutching onto his shoulder and writhing in pain, somehow still finding the strength to shout out.

"You motherfucker . . ."

Leaf Man pondered his next move.

Shoot the fucker dead?

Or, flee?

He aimed the gun at the Grim Reaper's head, but relented when his target appeared dead.

And then . . .

BANG!

BANG!

BANG!

The cold river swallowed Leaf Man whole, as the rain continued to fall.

~Lacrimosa~

R.I.P.: REQUIEM

Fuck. This. Town.

R.I.P. couldn't believe his eyes.

But now sure as fuck wasn't the time to panic.

Through the windshield and wipers, he watched as the Grim Reaper, clearly in pain, grabbed both the duffel bag *and* the dealer's rolling suitcase, which had lodged itself into a piece of broken concrete. The Grim Reaper struggled to pry it loose as a steady rain fell.

Still not too late to get the fuck out.

Yet, he didn't.

The Reaper finally arrived, injured, but still in full command.

"Give me your gun."

R.I.P. did as instructed.

"Floor it."

R.I.P. remained frozen, unable to move a single muscle.

"Are you deaf? I said drive, motherfucker!" the Grim Reaper shouted, clearly agitated, aiming the gun at his temple. This did the trick.

"And watch the speed limit."

Under ordinary circumstances, when driving a stolen car filled with guns and drugs, the last thing one would want would be to get pulled over. But in this instance, it might be the only thing that could save his life.

But would prison really be an upgrade over death?

"You were supposed to have my back!" the Grim Reaper barked.

"I didn't have a chance—"

"Keep your eyes open and keep driving!" the Grim Reaper said, still aiming the gun at R.I.P.'s head.

The car hit a pothole, causing the tip of the barrel to jam into R.I.P.'s temple, which in turn caused him to swerve across several lanes on the wide avenue. Fortunately, no one else was around. Somehow, he regained control of the car, but then drove into a giant pothole that could easily be mistaken as a sinkhole.

"Watch the fucking potholes!" the Grim Reaper demanded.

Potholes were the least of his concerns.

"And slow down. You're about to turn into an alley."

R.I.P. slowed down.

"Okay, it's coming up. Turn. Now."

Shit! He overshot it. In his defense, R.I.P. was not expecting to turn down a goddamned alley.

"You missed it. How fucking hard is it to follow simple directions?"

"My bad."

Thanks for the late notice, fucker.

R.I.P. thought briefly about doing a U-turn, but instead opted to pull into the driveway of a boarded-up, burned-out church.

This time, he made sure to turn into a debris-strewn alley.

"Stop here. Kill the engine," the Grim Reaper demanded.

R.I.P. closed his eyes and began to pray.

"I did everything you asked," R.I.P. pleaded, his eyes closed.

"Which is exactly why you are going to shut the fuck up and continue to do what I ask," the Grim Reaper replied. "Now, give me your wallet."

R.I.P. hesitated.

"Are you deaf? Give me your fucking wallet!"

R.I.P. could feel his heart pounding like a bass drum as he struggled to remove his wallet from his pocket. He fumbled, dropping it onto the car floor. He struggled to locate it in the dark, trying not to panic, but failing miserably. He finally located it and handed it over, all the while struggling to catch his breath.

"Now, get outta the fucking car."

R.I.P. slowly climbed out of the car, his eyes still shut, as though doing so could block out reality. He stepped down on something soft.

A decaying cat holding the remains of a dead mouse in its mouth.

Victim and prey.

The bully and the bullied.

"Turn around," the Grim Reaper demanded. "Slowly."

R.I.P. closed his eyes again and, as he did, felt an unexpected sense of calm wash over him. An unfamiliar feeling.

Nothing else seemed to matter in that moment.

But the moment he began to turn away from the car, the Grim Reaper, and the cat and the mouse, he suddenly felt lightheaded and began to sweat profusely. Though sweating was nothing new for R.I.P., this felt different.

A cold sweat, followed by a sudden, stabbing pain in his chest. He clutched his chest, coughed, then turned back toward the Grim Reaper.

"Help . . . me!" he implored, reaching out.

He collapsed to the ground, face up, arm out.

A fuzzy image of the Grim Reaper slowly faded from view.

There was nothing left to negotiate.

~Lacrimosa~

NYC GIRL: REQUIEM

"What's your name?"

The DJ's words echoed in NYC Girl's mind, as she made a conscious decision to sit at the front of the bus. Even though she had blurted her name, she was pretty sure that the roar of the bus had drowned her out.

She felt a bittersweet pang in her heart that she could only describe as separation anxiety.

But seriously?!

She struggled to remember the last time she considered anybody a hero.

Especially a male.

On the surface, she had every reason to hate the fucker for interfering with her plans. But deep down, she felt nothing but tremendous gratitude for saving not just one life that night, but two.

She put a comforting hand over her future child, and, as she began to hum "You Are the Sunshine of My Life," she realized that she had finally been granted the clean slate she had so desperately craved. She could have redemption right here on earth. She knew sure as fuck that she wouldn't be getting it anywhere else.

All it took was for her to stand on the precipice of death to realize that she wanted *life*. She was going to keep her unborn child and return to her mother, who she now understood in ways she never before had: once upon a time, her mother had given her a chance at life and did the best she could under unbelievably difficult circumstances. Both were born into the same hell. Now, it was her chance to try to make things better.

To make things *right*.

As NYC Girl rubbed her swollen belly, staring at the raindrops accumulating on the bus window, she thought of her life's one singular mission, which had been born on this very night: to do everything in her power to give her unborn child the life she never had.

She now knew that having her baby would make her a better person. This time, things were going to go in her favor. She didn't escape from the clutches of death only to fail again. She felt it in her veins. Everything else existed solely as her route to this moment.

She knew better than to trust such unexpected clarity.

The DJ's words continued to echo in her mind:

It's never too late . . . until it's too late.

As her experience could attest, acts of heroism usually came attached to favors expected in return. If any night should give her reason not to trust *any* man, it would be tonight. But somehow, this felt different. In fact, it was unlike anything she had ever felt before.

It was simply too *real* to be a wolf in sheep's clothing.

Though she desperately craved rest, her newfound tranquility masked her exhaustion.

Every question had a concrete answer.

Every problem had a solution.

All doubts erased.

The time had come to make everything right, everything whole.

And the first thing she had to do was go back to her roots—her home —and make amends with everything that had been lost all those years before. It wasn't too late. *It's never too late.* She had reached a new layer of rock bottom tonight, but now, the time had come to reach greater heights than she ever imagined.

She no longer felt the need to forgive her mother.

Nor, the need to be forgiven.

She just wanted to thank her.

Not only for life, but also for the strength to navigate it.

And for the adversity that made her stronger than she otherwise ever would have become.

She toggled her thoughts between her mother and the DJ. She couldn't stop thinking about how he had *listened* to her. Every word. Every pause. Absorbing her into his consciousness.

She was surprised how easily her life story had poured out of her, stopping just short of her encounter with Elijah. That was too soon—too *raw.*

It felt so goddamn good to have someone *listen.*

Until that moment, she would have found his advice not only foolish, but naïve. And cheesy as fuck.

Now, it all made sense. For the first time in years, she felt in control, not only of her life—*but of the entire fucking universe.*

She looked forward to her date. She couldn't remember the last time she had a real date. Only time would tell where it would lead. Perhaps, minus the emotion of this particular night, everything would be anticlimactic?

She certainly hoped not.

NYC Girl reached her transfer stop. One more fucking bus to go.

She floated off the bus into a steady rain and headed across the street in front of an abandoned skyscraper on an abandoned street, but as far as she was concerned, the street bustled beneath an illuminated skyscraper that soared like a beacon of hope over the entire city.

In fact, the city had never felt more full of life.

NYC Girl heard a squeal of tires as a car came skidding around the corner. Next thing she knew, she was lying on her back, gazing up at the murky sky. There was no pain; just an unfamiliar feeling of complete tranquility.

She spotted a slight sliver of moon half-hidden behind a cloud, as a steady rain washed away her sin.

The rain came to a stop and for the first time in her life, she saw a sky full of stars.

And the moon seemed brighter than ever.

"So beautiful."

A wave of happiness, unlike anything she had ever experienced, washed over her.

She had never felt more calm, more relaxed.

As she began to close her eyes, a bright, vivid vision came into view. Her daughter, now grown up, pushing her own little girl on a playground swing.

NYC Girl felt full. An overwhelming sense of pride, of joy, and unconditional love. And in that moment, she knew that everything was going to be alright. The future is unwritten.

She felt herself slowly begin to drift into a deep, beautiful sleep.

Rest. Finally.

And then everything went black.

Before returning to light.

THE ZEALOT

Remember, O LORD, what is come upon us: consider,
and behold our reproach.

The smell of autumn over sunset
Of death.
And fire.
I see smoke in the distance.

And I'm reminded of my purpose
I pop my trunk and remove one of the crates.

It is cold.
But it awakens me.
Makes me feel alive.

I enter the dimly-lit cellar.
More like a crypt.
Fitting.
A single yellow bulb dangles on a string.
Blinking intermittently in a haze of stray smoke,
barely illuminating newspaper clippings,
showcasing acts of redemption.

Prostitutes.
Drug dealers.
Murderers.
Rapists.
Homeless.
Filth.

A new millennium
harking the arrival
of end times.

Death not by my hand,
but the hand of the Almighty Creator,
through whom all Judgment
and fire comes.
I am merely the conduit.
The spark.

Red crosses drawn over each article.
With blood.
My blood.
Unsolved case known by two beings:
GOD
And myself.
Nothing else matters.
A clandestine, holy covenant between
a mere mortal and the most high.
For the good of all His church and of all this city.
I carry my crate to my father's old workbench.
Rotting wood.
A cockroach runs out underfoot.
I am a living corpse inside my self-made tomb.
I snuff out its life with one swift stomp of my foot.
If only my other victims were disposed of so easily.

Sacrificial lambs.
I retrieve my other crates, then get to work.
I grab an old pair of rusty scissors—
my mother's scissors.
And cut six-by-six inch squares out of old rags.
Like Jesus turning water into wine.
Each cut reveals flashes of my angel in white.
And then she fades.

But the feeling remains.
It always remains.
It is my fuel.
I fill the empty bottles with kerosene
and stuff the rags into them.

I put four boxes in my trunk.
Each crate contains a dozen bottles.
Each bottle contains a message.
Each message an intended receiver.
A message of hope.
Salvation.
A cleaning solvent.
Fuel.
Holy water to purify.
To make this city chaste.
I am a sweeper of the streets.
Cleansing this ash-covered town.
One night at a time.
One abandoned house at a time.
Ashes to ashes.
Dust to dust.
Till death do us part.
Amen.

Our necks are under persecution: we labour, and have no rest.

I am almost ready.
But there is still work left to do.
I put Mozart's Ave *Verum Corpus* on my record player.
I step into the bathroom and regard my reflection.
Raw.
Desperate.
Covered by a rotting mask of sin.
My original sin.
I must first purge myself before I can purge this town.

I reach for my straight edge.
Feel its familiar ivory grip.
I feel its power.
And its ability to set me free.
I remove my shirt,
revealing a scar of my savior's cross.
Matching scars on my inner forearms.
My crown of thorns.
Blood that flows with sin.
The scars have now hardened,
sealing the poison inside me.
It is time for a fresh purge.
I recite the LORD's Prayer,
lining the razor up
at the apex of the scar cross on my chest,
gouging downward,
tracing the trail I blazed earlier.

Blinding white light surrounds me.
I hold back tears.
New blood emerges.
My own personal cross to bear.
In this pain is my salvation,
like CHRIST himself.
My razor, to HIS nails.
Blood drips, oozes, and runs
to the already blood-stained ground,
forming a fresh pool of liquid sin.

I grow faint.

I bleed out for a full minute,
and wait for the initial wave of pain to subside,
then bandage my wounds before pulling
a black, blood-stained shirt over my stigmatic torso.
I feel my blood continue to soak the cloth.
My very own shroud of Turin.

And finally, freed from my own demons,
I am ready to face the demons of the night.

One last ritual.
I enter the room that we once shared,
now risen from the ashes to become
a shrine to you.

To us.

To what we used to be,
and now an eternal vigil
for our unborn child
and any future child
the good LORD might have bestowed upon us.

To what we never had a chance to become.
A future snuffed out by the demons
I am fighting to put an end to.
A losing battle that I will never give up on.
Sparing lives by taking lives.
The world won't see it like that.
It's expecting too much.
But this world doesn't matter.
I don't work for this world.
I work against it.
I work to save it.

I light the votives.
Equaling your age.
When the world took you from me.
When the world:
beat you
stripped you
raped you
gutted you.

The lights flicker against our wedding portrait.
A fallen angel in light.
The peak of your beauty.
The peak of *us*.
An angel on earth.
Now a bird in paradise.
Bathed in heavenly light
and wrapped in eternal glory.
Hail Mary full of grace.

I reminisce about the day we met.
Good Friday.
That little café.
I was reading scripture.
You were writing poetry.
You smiled at me first.
(Even though you were convinced it was the other way around).
We fell in love.
Married.
Talked about kids.
Three months later,
you carried our child.

The needle reaches the end of the record.
Skipping.
Like a heartbeat.

Three months later,
Good Friday came again.
And on the third day ...
... there was no resurrection.
Nothing can bring you back.
Nothing.
Nothing.
Nothing.

Vengeance is mine; I will repay, saith the LORD.

It is not simply revenge I seek.
I aim to spare others from my fate.
I work as HIS immortal instrument.
To cleanse this city of mortal filth.
I kneel before my angel.
My anchor.
First in life …
… now in eternal life.
Like Jesus Himself.
Sacrificed for a higher, nobler cause.
And it is my duty to ensure you didn't die in vain.
Especially *this* most unholy night.

DEVIL'S NIGHT.

The flame's flickering light distorts my angel's visage.
An illusion of blood trickling down her face
and onto her white wedding dress,
as I wither in shadow.

I know it's not an illusion.
The time has come.
Amen.

Our inheritance is turned to strangers, our houses to aliens.

I shut off the turntable.
I depart the only home I have ever known.
South of the 8 Mile divide.
When my parents were granted eternal rest,
I lived here alone.
Until I was married.
Until my angel arrived.
Our plan was to begin a life here,
then eventually move out.
To raise a family in the suburbs.
Away from immoral filth and decay.
But it wasn't GOD'S will.

I'm still here.
And it is here where I shall stay.

I enter my black Crown Vic.
Our wedding carriage.
When life was beautiful.
And symphonies from heaven
smiled upon us.
Before the dissonant chords
of hell drowned them out.
It is now a hearse.
Serving as the vessel
in which GOD
sends me forth to carry out His
earthly mission.

A dangerous undertaking.
but I place myself in
HIS hands.
What I do is seen as wrong,
but wrong only in an earthly sense.
I know this path can only
end with my earthly demise.
But I must stay the course,
to thwart off future tragedies
such as the one I endured.
Otherwise, what else is there to live for?

I drive down desolate streets
toward my former shelter.
Five blocks.
Four blocks.
Three blocks.
I round the corner onto St. Aubin.
And I am nearer to thee.
My old parish.
I park a block away to avoid detection.

I approach the empty church and enter.
I kneel before the altar
of the old cathedral I knew as a child
and that has stood over a century
before my birth.
But I do not pray.
Cannot.
What does this mean?
Has prayer eluded me before?
If so, I have no memory of it.
I am surprised, but do not fret.
The LORD is telling me that
the time has come to complete my mission.

I stand up and turn toward the exit,
but am startled by the silhouette of a man
standing in the doorway.
Pastor Emmanuel.
My former mentor.
Now, a tormentor.
He guided me to the light,
But I, alone, found the only *true* path.

Pastor: "You don't have to break in, you know."
I nod without meaning.
Pastor: "You are always welcome here."

He thinks I broke in.
The lock was already broken.
I simply entered, hoping to avoid detection.

"It was open."
He *wants* to believe me.
But I'm not so certain.
I wish he hadn't seen me.
I prefer to hide in the shadows,
and sneak up on the demons living within them.

And remove shadow from the world with God's holy light.

I realize not everyone finds the light.
Some may think they have found it.
But that's fool's gold.
Like Pastor Emmanuel.
Satan in sheep's clothing.
I had to lose *everything* in order to find salvation.
It is my duty to put others on the same path.
By any means necessary.
If blood must be shed, it will be by *my* hand,
reaching out of the shadows to shine GOD'S light.
Freeing souls from earthly flesh.
To save them.
Not to punish.
But to cleanse the world:
Of filth.
Of temptation.
Of wickedness.
So that *good* may prevail.
Free from corruption.
To forever abolish
the stained spot of sin
that saturates this city.
I am salvation's solvent.
And the world needs me more than ever.
A lone lighthouse in a sea of darkness.

The man before me will never understand.
I am contrary to everything he knows to be true.
He avoids the darkness.
Hides from it.
Escapes it.
But I seek it and look it directly in the face.
And I crush it by seeking out those lost in the darkness,
that need most to reach the light.

It is time for the protégé to become the mentor.
He is a lost cause.
Too set in his ways.
Like most others who have yet to see the one true light.

Most are too sheltered from reality
to feel the need to alter it.
Heal it.
Deep down, he knows this.
Yet he refuses to do anything about it.
This is the worst kind of sin.

Pastor: "It's always nice to see you. It's been way too long."

Me: "Sometimes, I like to be reminded of what
things *used* to be like, before . . ."

My voice trails off.
Why did I even begin to bring it up?
It's easier when I don't.

He places a "concerned" hand on my shoulder.
It disgusts me.

Pastor: "Come back and visit anytime. Or, stay."

Me: "Perhaps, it's time for you to join me on *my* mission."

Maybe now, he will finally come around and see the light.

"Mission?"
"To purge this city."
"Of what?"
"Of everything that seeks to destroy it."
"Specifically *what*?"
"If you have to ask, then you're more misguided than I thought."
"I don't understand."
"Then you're no different than all the rest.
And as long as that is true,
you are no longer my mentor, and I am no longer your pupil.

You—and everyone like you—are now my enemy."

I am done hiding.
The line has been drawn.
Will he cross it?

Pastor: "We are on the same team. Together in CHRIST."

Me: "No! That's what you want to believe. But that is where
you're mistaken. You and your kind are the enablers of sin.
This is worse than a sinner, who so often knows not
what they do. Your lax urgency to punish sin only adds
fuel to the raging fires of hell."

He is visibly shaken, but tries to justify his ignoble stance:

"You got me wrong. I have little tolerance for sin, but I still
love the sinner. There is a difference. But that's up to God
to decide. Not us. We all misjudge sometimes. In fact, humans
have a tendency to be the worst judge of character."

Me: "Sin feeds upon the weak like the plague. Failure to act
is enabling the sinner. Words are *nothing* without *action*.
Tonight, I will use the spirit to go in God's name and wipe
the sin from the face of the world.
Those who refuse to comply must be extinguished.
If not by me, then by whom?"

Pastor: "This is not God's will."

Me: "*You* are not God's will. Your disingenuous nature
offends God. Your ineffectiveness angers God. I *understand*
His wrath. Therefore, it is my *duty* to clean up the mess your
cowardice and the cowardice of your ilk have left behind."

He tries to respond. But cannot.
Because he knows I'm right.
He can feel his soul slipping into the shadows.
Letting others off the hook alleviates his own guilt and shame.

I slip my black gloves on and head out the door
into a setting sun where the shadows await.

On the horizon,
I see a break in the clouds.
As though the sun wants
one last glimpse of the dying city,
before it turns in for the night.

But looking around at the density
of gray desert surrounding
the sun and the moon's sudden presence
creates an otherworldly presence
that defies all logic.
Is this real?
A physical sign from GOD?
More fool's gold?
Satan's gold?
And then I see it.
Formed from a swirl of red clouds.
Nain Rouge.

The devil vision fades
And I take comfort in the fact that
like the sun, I am also bursting through the clouds of sin and despair.
Reaching out from behind the shadow and delivering salvation
to those who accept it.
Amen.

*How lonely she is now, the once crowded city. Widowed is she who was
mistress over nations; The princess among the provinces has been made
a toiling slave.*

As I make my way toward my car, I am besieged by a cyclone
of torn plastic bags, newspapers, and assorted pieces of trash.

Steam billows from manholes.
The devil's breath.

Some don't even have covers.
Stolen by thieves.
Sold as scrap.
To feed their addiction.

This city.
This whore.
This rotting junkyard of human waste and decay.
Praying to be cleansed by the Grace of GOD.
It is my purpose.
My reason for being sent to this earth.

This is my mission.

Now, the prayers begin to flow.
The streets are my church.
My *altar*.

Reminding me of my purpose.
HIS purpose.

Dear GOD,
Please grant me the courage necessary to purge this spawn of hell
from all of its filth. Its whores and hookers. Its pushers and pimps.
Its vagrants and vagabonds. I am your servant. You are my master.
Therefore, I obey. I willingly obey. I am sent to redeem, to purify.
Through death, the city will be restored to its former glory.
Your glory. Thank you for appointing me the new millennium
Christ, seated at your right hand. Savior of a new world order.

I maneuver through this cesspool of human excrement.
Through a sea of souls so lost,
they seek not redemption,
but justification for their impurities—
forging their own path
into eternal damnation.
I am their knight in Christ's shining armor,
I am the King of Kingdom Come.

The Alpha and Omega apprentice.
Even though they don't know it *yet* …
… their savior is here.
Their souls are already rejoicing,
while their flesh toils in earthly rot and filth.

I am interrupted by a junkie degenerate in a hooded sweatshirt
proudly displaying the Olde English D.
Bastardizing the emblem of this once proud city.

Junkie: "Gimme your wallet, freak!"

He produces a switchblade two inches from my face.

In one swift motion I kick the knife out of his hand,
grab his arm, and slam him to the ground.
He screams in pain.
"Jesus Christ!" he cries out.
He takes the LORD'S name in vain.
But GOD is working through me.
As I keep his arm pinned down,
she reappears,
a ghost in a white gown
stained with blood.
My sacrificial lamb.

She boosts my strength,
as I crack the degenerate's wrist.
Vengeance will be mine.
Her ghost dissipates.

He writhes in pain on the ground,
as I continue to hold his wrist behind his back.
I release and he rolls over on his back.
He's too stunned to respond.

I remove a pocket Bible from my coat and toss it at my prey.
It lands just out of his reach.

Me: "Pick it up."

The degenerate appears confused.
I repeat: "Pick it up!"

He sees what I'm pointing at
and stretches his arm beyond its limit.
But still, it remains just out of reach.

"Try harder."
I kick him.
He strains, screaming in pain.
He picks up the Bible.
"Turn to Deuteronomy 5:7."
He is confused.
Lost in his pain.
In every conceivable sense.
My patience wears thin.
He is clearly not educated in the good WORD.
He knows not what he does.
But I do not forgive him.

Me: "Page 78."

He fumbles the foreign object in his hands.
Nearly drops it onto the poisoned ground.
He thumbs the pages backward and forward.

Me: "Now, I want you to recite it out loud."

The confused look reappears on his face.

"Can you read?"

He nods, staring in blank verse.

"I don't have all night. And neither does your soul."

He slogs through it.

Junkie: "These are the Ten Commandment things, right?"

Me: "Do you know them?"
Junkie "You joking?"
Me: "Do I look like a joker?"

He shakes his head.
I am reaching him.
He begins. Then stops.

"Keep reading."

He continues to read.
His voice shakes with the hesitation of sin.

"Read it like you believe it."
He makes an effort.

Progress.

"Verse 19. What does it say?"

"Thou shalt not steal."

"Get on your knees!"

He does.
A willing pupil.
He can still be saved.

"It's hard to stumble when you're already kneeling.
Do you know the Act of Contrition?"

He mumbles something indecipherable under his breath.

"Speak up!"
I kick him again.
He cries. Screams.

"GOD is listening."

"I said no, I don't know it!"

"Do you even know what contrition is?"

The degenerate shakes his head.

"It means to be sorry. GOD wants you to be sorry.
HE wants you to tell HIM that you're sorry."

"I'm s-s-s-sorry."
It barely registers.
"Sorry is not good enough! Repeat after me."

I give him one line at a time.
And he repeats.
Incoherent mumbles.
I make him repeat.

*"O my GOD, I am heartily sorry for having offended Thee and I detest
all my sins because of Thy just punishments, but most of all because
they offend thee, my GOD, who art all good and deserving of all my love.
I firmly resolve with the help of Thy grace, to sin no more and
to avoid the near occasions of sin."*

As the junkie repeats the last line,
I hear a bloodcurdling scream.
Her scream.
Before me, an image of *her* battered body,
an angel in white, bloodied and bruised.

I reach toward *her*.
I want to save *her*.
But then *she's* gone.
Why does *she* always leave?

My pupil watches me.
Confused.
Frightened.
But redeemed?

An old man also watches from a bus stop across the street.
In judgment or indifference?
Perhaps my lesson reached him, too.

At least he didn't try to stop me.
That counts for something.

Me: "Now, follow the path set before you…"

The junkie nods, then limps off into the night,
holding his mangled wrist.
His first steps toward salvation.
He will never forget me.
More importantly, neither will his soul.

The old man is still watching from a bench across the street—
the lone audience member of a one-act morality play.

Me: "He was lost."

The old man doesn't respond.
I do not expect him to.

It is time to move on.
I walk away, crossing myself.
I pick up his switchblade.
My journey is far from over.
I must keep moving forward.

I cannot save everyone.
I accept this.
It's about saving
whomever I can,
wherever I can,
whenever I can.
A losing battle.
But one I will not give up.
I do away with those who cannot be saved;
who choose not to be saved.
Despite every opportunity granted.
Only *I* have the power to stop them,
through the grace of GOD.
Amen.

We are orphans and fatherless, our mothers are as widows.

An empty bottle of sin lies in the gutter near my car.
Vodka.
Satan's serum.
I pick it up.
I open the trunk and slip the bottle into one of two crates,
filled with empty bottles.
Vodka. Gin. Tequila. Whiskey.
There's room for more, but this will suffice for tonight.
Rome wasn't built in a day.
Nor was it destroyed in one.
There will be other missions.
And no shortage of discarded bottles to aid me on future quests.
Disposed of by the future victims of my mission.
I laugh at the irony.
Bottles that contained the very poison that fuels sinners,
that will help to lead them to their Final Judgment.

As I close the trunk.
I see a homeless mother and her bastard children.
They each haul a torn garbage bag over their filthy shoulders.
I am usually disgusted.
Yet, in this specific instance my heart bleeds.
An unexpected twinge of sympathy.
Satan planting doubt in my mind.
But I can overcome the dark prince.

I watch the family disappear down the street.
Conflicted, I get into my car.
A pile of pamphlets proclaiming
GOD'S message beside me.
Where she used to sit.

This whole city must burn to the ground.
And begin anew.

I open my leather binder and remove a tattered street map.
It covers the entire city.
A comprehensive map of hell.
I trace an efficient route with my finger.
However, I could have just as easily closed my eyes
and dropped my finger anywhere.
Nowhere shall be immune.

I drive away.
And turn on the radio.
Gospel.
AM.
Static.
A lone island surrounded by airwaves of sin and depravity.

Steam rises from sewers like spirits from the depths of hell.

The cross hanging from my mirror sways back and forth.
A holy clock measuring time.
Tick tock.
Tick tock.
Amen.

We have drunken our water for money; our wood is sold unto us.

I drive through abandoned neighborhoods,
passing one derelict house after another,
as Mozart's *Requiem* plays. *Lacrimosa.*
One particular house catches my attention.
A litter of thugs gather around the porch.

They glare at me.
I glare back.
An unwritten, mutual agreement.

I slow down and pull over to the side of the road,
hoping to avoid detection.
Should I shut my headlights off?

I decide doing so will possibly draw more attention.
So far, nobody seems to notice.

Another man approaches the gathering.
A silent business transaction takes place.
I grab my black leather binder and a red pen.
I strain to locate an address
to add to my expanding list of future conquests.
Many addresses are already crossed off.
With many more to come.

I start a new page and make a careless error.
I rip it out and try again.
Good enough.
But *good enough* is not acceptable.
Good enough equals mediocrity.
Lowered standards.
Without perfection, there is nothing.
Which is why I can never give up.
Amen.

We have given the hand to the Egyptians, and to the Assyrians, to be satisfied with bread.

I often think about moving out of the filth.
North into the suburbs.
Where I can be among my own kind.
Away from those who took her from me.
And forever turn my back on this cesspool.

But I must remain steadfast.

Staying behind enemy lines—on hell's doorstep—
keeps me focused on my mission.
An infiltrator.
Being far removed from this filth,
would make it easier to ignore,

like my suburban brethren,
when they come in and out
for ballgames and concerts,
ignoring reality and turning a blind eye—
unless they find themselves walking alone down a dark street,
when nobody else is around.
When they are most vulnerable.

Some pass through the ruins.
Comment on them.
Some are just glad it's not them.
Some feel their hearts bleed.
And then they all head home.
Into the safe confines of suburbia.
Atop their ivory towers.
I don't blame them.
I wish I could do the same.
But, for me, this is not GOD'S will.

Our fathers have sinned; and we have borne their iniquities.

Clouds of smoke swirl amid the clouds.
Sulfur in the air.

Sometimes, I wonder if it will ever end?
If my mission will ever be complete?
I take solace in knowing that
no matter how many more are left to discover,
there will be less once the night is through,
as the gray sun rises again to soak
in the desolate wasteland,
where my yeoman's work smolders.

I pull up to my destination.
Roll down my window.
Nobody in sight.
Perfect silence.

Glowing embers in the window.
The glowing rectums of Satan's minions.

I exit my car.
Leave the engine running.
Open the trunk.
Remove a couple of bottles from their crate.
Strike a match.
The wind blows it out.
I strike another match.
Success.
I hold two flaming pillars.
One in each hand.
I toss the first.
It lands square in the middle of the porch.
A direct hit!
The second lands in some tall weeds outside the window.
Perfect kindling.
I jump back into my car and wait.

I hear commotion.
Screams.
My angel's eternal wail echoes through my mind and soul.
A reminder that my course is just.

Through my rearview mirror,
I watch as my victims are flushed
out of their homes, like rats.
GOD'S exterminator.
Poison is my holy water.
Boiled by my flames.
I wish for them to stay inside.
But GOD'S will be done.
One of the rats carries a baby.
I do not wish this on a child.
Then again, what future does it have?

The flames lick with intensity
bathing my car with orange light.
Despite my victory, I must remain humble.

I slam on the gas.
She appears before me.
Floating.
I slam on my brakes and stop just short of where she
stood before she dissipated into the white beam of my headlights.
In her place stands a filthy vagrant.

The cries from the flaming house of heathens are absorbed
into my angel's screams.
Echoes in my head, as shadows flicker from the flames,
producing demonic faces.
Shrieking and writhing in pain.
And then the shadows die.
And the faces fade.
And the screams turn to whispers.
And then there is only silence.
God's will be done.
Amen.

*Servants have ruled over us: there is none that doth deliver us out of
their hand.*

12th and Clairmount.
The site of devil riots that destroyed this once proud town.
A black plague.
I pull over to the side of the road
and reach for the stale bread on the dashboard.

I break off the hardened crust and devour its remains.
My first nourishment in over twelve hours.
Man cannot live on bread alone.
But better to have bread than nothing at all.
Devotion is my fuel.

I fear I am withering away.
I have lost weight;
grown more gaunt;
more pale.
For the sake of my mission, I must remain strong.
GOD has chosen me.
It is HIS will.

I open up my leather binder and cross off
my first address of the night.

I continue driving.
A radio evangelist preaches about the end of the world.
What does he know?

I drive a quarter mile to my next destination.
Another ramshackle house of sin.
GOD'S plan leaves no rest for the weary.
Nor the wicked.
But I am a steadfast soldier.

I pull up in front of yet another GOD-forsaken
property in a town festered with them.

I park across the street.
Two white males come out of the house.
Hurried.
Frantic.
Scared?
Suburban shoppers at an urban supermarket,
shopping for wholesale goods.
Compromising their safety for a quick fix.
Prostituting their brains with drugs, funded by wealthy parents.

They get into a beat up pick-up that struggles to start.
The passenger jumps out and gives it a good shove.
The truck rolls for several feet before it revs to life—
in need of life support.

He has to run to catch up.
Finally, he hops in and the truck sputters out of sight.

Now it's my turn.
I light a cocktail from my trunk and toss it toward the porch.
Another direct hit!
My aim is improving.
I am God's bullseye.
Practice makes perfect.
The house lights up like a Christmas tree
as I scramble back into my car.

In my mirror, I see three people dash out of the house.
One is covered in flames.
He rolls on the ground, screaming.

BANG!
Followed by a voice vomiting obscenities at me.
I close my eyes and pray.
Protect me, LORD.
I floor it.
A gunshot smashes my rear windshield.
I feel the bullet whiz past my head.
The cross on my mirror shatters as the bullet
exits the front windshield.
Am I hit?
No.
GOD is my shield.
The ripped out piece of notebook paper disappears into the night.
One more piece of trash on a giant trash heap of a city.
I panic.
Could it come back to haunt me?
Incriminate me?
I can't let it worry me.
It's in GOD'S hands now.

I turn the corner.
A third gunshot.
Then silence.
I sign myself.
Thank you LORD.
Thank you LORD.
Thank you LORD.
I must be more careful.
Lest GOD find a more worthy soldier.
I must not let HIM down.
Cannot.
Shall not.
Will not.
LORD, continue to be my rock.
Protect me from myself.
Protect me from those who work against you.
Lead me not into temptation.
And deliver me from evil.

I need to refocus.
I look at the clock.
9:45.
I check my planner:

10:00: Saint Andrew's Hall.

The epicenter of sin.
On Devil's Night in Detroit.
Someday, I will burn the place to the ground.
But not tonight.
GOD will speak to me.
HE will let me know when the time is right.
On the radio, a preacher proclaims
that he has been summoned by the LORD.
A false prophet.
The only logical explanation of our clear disconnect.
I've heard it all before.

Though, I agree with most of his message.
Naïve as he may be.
He's preaching to a one-man choir.
The people who most need to hear his message—*our message*—
don't even know what the AM dial is.
It's not so much the preacher's message that irks me.
It is his delivery.
This is why GOD must turn to *me*.
I take to the streets.
A holy street cleaner.
One block at a time.

The station is losing its signal.
Through the static comes a cacophony
of screams and demonic voices.
Indecipherable whispers speaking in tongues.
They are trying to tell me something.
To *sell* me something
Real estate on their wasteland.

I cover my ears and almost collide with an oncoming car.
I swerve.
The station returns to static.
Dear GOD,
Please, protect me from:
My own carelessness.
My ignorance.
My entire being.
My flesh and my soul.
I am not afraid to die.
But I am afraid to fail in my holy, sanctioned mission.

I flip the dial past one soulless station after another.
The voices go away.
New voices emerge.
I stumble upon the news.
Reporting on the world's trespasses.

Not judging as they should, but merely reporting.
This is condoned indifference to sin.
I come across a station: live from Saint Andrew's Hall.
My destination.
An omen.
Soon, my broadcast will be clear.
There will be no static.
I am an emcee of salvation.
Amen.

*We gat our bread with the peril of our lives because of the sword of
the wilderness.*

Downtown.
The Devil's domicile.
The epicenter of depravity.
I drive past my destination, seeking a place to park.
And then, she appears, again, in front of my car
My angel!
I slam on my brakes.
But it's not her.
It's a filthy vagrant.
He smiles and waves apologetically.
Before a violent cough.
Infecting the city with his festering sickness.
He walks away and I keep on driving.
Oh, to rid the earth of one more piece of human trash.
But there are too many witnesses.
My purging pilgrimmage would come to a premature end.
But then another part of me gives thanks to GOD that I didn't.
A part of me I haven't felt since before *her*.

I park in a lot, across the street from a former movie palace,
raped and gouged into submission.

No shortage of parking for an onslaught of sinners,
coming into town to commit assorted acts of debauchery.

I pull the junkie's switchblade out of my pocket
and place it in my glove box.
I grab a stash of pamphlets.
My ammo.
I lock the door and pray that my car will not
be stolen by wanton thieves.
So far, I have been fortunate.
It helps to have GOD on your side.

The club is a couple of blocks away.
I scan my surroundings and place my trust in GOD.
I am not afraid of death.
It is life I fear.
And the fear of not fulfilling my duty.
I am prepared for martyrdom.
A terrorist against sin.
Working *for* GOD, not against.
Sacrificing a few to save the masses.
As it was foretold.
Only, I don't work for history.
I work for GOD.
It is my holy obligation.
GOD'S will is not a choice.
It is a destiny.

Since I couldn't save my own beloved, I will save others,
by destroying heathens that have chosen a life beyond redemption.

Other than this mission, there is nothing to live for.

I look around.
No one in sight.
This puts me even more at risk.

I finally reach the club.
Unscathed.
Splattered on a wall, I read:

DON'T CRY FOR US, CRY FOR THEM

Bleeding heart propaganda.
Tears of white guilt, feeding the monster.

Heathens line up outside their pagan temple.
Rats and cockroaches in a rush to worship at Satan's altar.
But their savior has arrived.
It is time to lay witness.

I approach the line and distribute pamphlets.
I get the usual reaction.
Jeers.
Indifference.
Threats.
I've heard it all before.
Their taunts bounce off me like ticks on armor.
It means *nothing* to me.
And yet, it means *everything*.
I will not back down.
Some take my pamphlet.
Some glance at it,
then throw it down on the ground,
among the other discarded flyers promoting temptation,
smothering my cardstock offer of salvation,
trampled with blind negligence and stale indifference.
A heathen disguised as the devil rips one up
and throws the pieces back in my face.
His soul already condemned.
A small few stuff it in their pocket.
Too drugged out of their minds to recognize their actions.
Perhaps, it will reach them after they come down.
Other flyers are more eagerly taken than mine.
I expected this.
It is human nature.

A filthy vagrant reaches out for one.
I refuse to comply.
He can pick one up off the ground.

The voices return.
As does my blood-soaked angel in white.
I watch the knife pierce her dress.
Her flesh.
I cannot look away.
Frozen in time and space.
Blood onto snow.
Snow into blood.
I shriek in the man's face.
He backs off.
The voices retreat.
The blood dissipates.
The crowd fears me.
And in fear, an opportunity for salvation.

It is time to enter depravity's den.
A nest of sin.
I pray for my prey.
They don't realize that I'm the savior they so desperately need.
Whether they know it or not.
Whether they want it or not.
Needs and *wants* are distinctly separate.
The soul needs.
The body wants.
I am the final solution.
The *only* solution.

I approach the front of the line.
The charred gates of hell.
One of Satan's servants fights another,
each battling for their own place in hell.
Security attempts to break it up.
They resist until they have no choice but to submit.

Though tossed back onto the street, there are
no shortage of other caverns of sin for them to covet.

They have lost their chance to gain salvation through me.
At least, this is what I tell myself.
Do I really believe it?
I must.
Or else, I am *nothing*.
I reach the gate.
Satan's sentries pat me down.
A den of sin requires such precautions.
They pat me down.
Instruct me to empty my pockets.
Confiscate a small crucifix.
They tell me it could be used as a weapon.
They are right.
The most powerful weapon.
I don't need it.
It lives inside me.

Bouncer: "Cool costume, bro."
I don't respond.
He lets me in.
Who would have thought one had to pass through
so many hoops to enter hell?
I thought everyone was welcome.

Dear LORD,
I thrust myself in your hands.
Amen.

Our skin was black like an oven because of the terrible famine.

I enter.
I can smell the sin.
Taste it on my lips.
Feel it in my groin.
It penetrates my soul.

I dispense more pamphlets.
A massive orgy of bodies writhe in ecstasy,
as my angel writhes in pain.
The devil's symphony is drowned out by the demonic
voices in my head.
I cover my ears.
And the voices speak louder.
I head upstairs to the balcony.
Retreat into a dark corner, in the shadows.
I *am* a shadow.
I pray.
And the voices go away.
I look down below and feel a hardening of my flesh below.
I must suppress it.
But as I fixate on one particular whore, it continues to rise.
A flash of my angel's bloodied and bruised carcass.
And then I'm flaccid again.

I head downstairs.
Past the filth of humanity, who trample upon my
discarded leaflets with their writhing bodies.
How could such grime make my loins pulsate?
I head into a restroom, desecrated with the gospel of graffiti.
A heathen stands at the urinal.
I splash water on my face, to wash the sin from my eyes.
I must refocus.
There is too much at stake.
I must temper the beast within me.
My rod of sin.
I scrub my arms.
Let the warm water soak into my flesh.
Over my scars.
I look into the mirror.
Where is the light?
I am what I fight.

I recite the LORD'S Prayer.
It soothes me.
Reminds me of my purpose.
A toilet flushes.
A man emerges from the stall.
I know I will be judged.
But so be it.
I continue to cleanse, and pray under my breath.
I want the heathen to hear me.

The man flushes the toilet with his foot.
I make him wait for the sink.
I will not be rushed.
He grows impatient.
But I stay the course.

Man: "I think they're clean, bro."

Me: "But is your soul?"

I stare him straight in the eye.
I am not his "bro."
None of these heathens are my brothers.
He doesn't stand back.
Man: "Judge not lest thee be judged."
A weak attempt to rattle my nerves.

Me: "Who is judging who?"

Man: "Okay, look. I appreciate the Bible study, but you're not the
only one who wants clean hands, dawg. I got a job to do."

Me: "Like corrupting souls?"

Man: "Naw, man. Their souls are already corrupted.
I'm just tryin' to provide them with an escape for a few hours."

I begin to dry my hands on the filthy towel.
Why did I touch this filthy rag?

It is surely stained with STDs and sin.
It is too late.

As Satan's pawn washes his hands,
I remember that some stains never come out.
But I must at least try.

I lock eyes with him.
He stares back.
I look away and prop a pamphlet up against the soap dispenser.

Me: "Good luck getting out of this house of Sodom alive."

As I head out to join the masses, I wonder:
Did he even hear me? Does he care?
Somehow, his message strikes a chord with me.
Once again, Satan is attempting to penetrate my soul.
But I shove him out.

I need to clear my mind.
I head to the basement—
"The Shelter," as the heathens call it.
Shelter from the Gospel.
Shelter from the LORD.

I make my way down the stairs.
Costumed freaks stare me down.
Only, they see *me* as the freak.
These enemies of morality.
I am their enemy.
HE is their enemy.
And through HIM, I will defeat them.

I make my rounds downstairs.
Scatter flyers like Easter eggs.
Golden tickets to salvation.
A bouncer warns me to stop.
GOD is clearly not on this guest list.

Not when Satan is the V.I.P.
But I am GOD'S proxy.
GOD'S chosen one.

I ascend the stairwell.
Rounding the corner, I bump into a beast of a man.
My pamphlets fall to the ground.
Satan's watchdog stares me down.
I crouch down to pick up my pamphlets.
I take notice of his tattoo:
"R.I.P."
Wishful thinking.
I watch as the beast picks up a pamphlet
and walks away.

For some unexplained reason,
I find myself feeling sorry for him.
Another unexpected sign of *weakness*.
What is wrong with me?
What used to be crystal clear is now a murky swamp.
Is this the natural order of things?
Progress?
Evolution?
Regression?
In GOD's hands I place my soul.
There is no other way.
In a world of darkness, HE is the only light.
Without HIM, all light in the world would be gone.
And *everything* would cease to exist.
Everything.
Amen.

Princes are hanged by their hand: the faces of elders were not honoured.

I'm back upstairs, organizing my pamphlets.
Among them ... a prescription slip!

Presumably illegally obtained to feed an addiction.
I drop it.
This room is less crowded than the other floors.
The music is very odd.
Startling.
I detect a trace of gospel.
As though GOD was channeling HIMSELF through
the unmanned turntables.
Reminding me of my purpose.
Reassuring me.
Rejuvenated, I head to a corner armchair,
to pray,
to formulate a plan.
What exactly is my next move?

The heathen from the restroom enters
and steps behind the turntables.
The DJ!
Perhaps I read him wrong?
The gospel music is surely his doing.
But then he changes the album.
And GOD'S Word is no more.
Was it all in my head?
These days, it is becoming increasingly difficult to tell.

After I finish my prayer, I spot her.
A fallen angel.
Alone.
Awaiting salvation, despite the eventual condemnation
that surely will come.

Under my breath:
"They have seen her nakedness: yea, she sigheth,
and turneth backward. Her filthiness is in her skirts."

I know her type.
Loose.

Spread eagle on a cross of silk sheets.
Between her legs, a portal into sin, traversed by many.
She *smells* of sin.
I can smell it from across the room.
I have the nose of a bloodhound.

Regardless of my judgment, there's something about
her that makes me think of my *beloved*.
I can't quite put my finger on it.
Something in her steely, assured demeanor.

But what?

Her eyes tell me she is different than the rest.
She *wants* to be redeemed.
I can sense it.
I can't help but feel that it is my destiny.
To save her soul.

She looks at the DJ and smiles.
He smiles back.

She notices my gaze.
But does not smile.
With salvation so close at hand,
I must be careful not to frighten her.
I cannot let her off the hook, lest she suffer
the same fate as the one I loved.
Still love.

The dancefloor swells with heathens.
Glow sticks hypnotize drug-addled minds.
The girl looks out the window.
I stare at her lush, round bottom
and the stiff serpent returns;
the music a snake charmer.
I suppress it.
But the serpent strengthens.

I usually keep it under control.
But not tonight.
I have entered the Garden of Eden.
GOD is testing me.
And I am a willing pupil.
I refuse to succumb.

I certainly know temptation.
Have even succumbed to it.
But more often than not, I have triumphed over it.
In my younger years, before *her.*
And then again after, when I lost it all.
And contracted the Devil's virus.
A sign from GOD to change direction.
Haven't veered since.
And I'm certainly not going to allow myself to do so now.
But her eyes …
There was something just so …
different.
So pure.
So much like my angel.

Two depraved faggots—a cowboy and milkman—enter.
They approach my target.
Offer her a joint.
She takes one hit. Two hits.
The voices return.
Like nails on a chalkboard.
I can't understand them.
I don't want to understand them.
Yet, they remain.
Perhaps for good?

The men lead her to the dance floor.
The milkman rubs on her from the front.
The cowboy from behind.
They might as well all be procreating.

Like animals.
"Mating" would be too civilized a term.
There is hypocrisy in how quickly she has dismissed me.
She looks over at me in fear.

She would rather rub herself against the loins
of two condemned souls, than seek salvation through me.
The Satanic spell is that deep.

The pleasure of the flesh outweighs the need to be saved.
The devil's best move on the soul's chessboard.
It is why the LORD sends earthly redeemers like me.
A lone soldier in GOD'S vast army, sent into battle
against Satan's multiplying empire.

As the orgy continues on the dancefloor,
the two men continue exchanging lit venom with her.
Satan's grasp has my serpent fully engorged.
The rod of temptation.
And then my *angel* appears before me.
Bloodied more than ever.
Shame fills my soul.
I fear there is no turning back.
I am weak.
I am human.
I am human.
I am human.
The voices inside my head intensify,
but their message is muddled.
The men kiss her neck.
The serpent throbs inside my pants.
My *angel* appears again.
This time more vivid and iridescent.
I squeeze it.
Not for pleasure, but for pain.
To suppress my thoughts.
To make the voices go away.

But it doesn't work.

She releases herself from the clutches of the sinners
and returns to the couch.
Unable to quell my desire, I head downstairs.
Enter the restroom.
Hide myself in a stall.
Reach down into my pants, feeling the bumpy,
scarred flesh made by my own hand.
I try to fight it.
But I reach the point of no return.
I release the sin within me.
An accident.
Soaked in shame, I head back upstairs.
I wish to sever my serpent from my body.
Banish it.
Burn it.
At least now, I can refocus on my mission.
GOD'S will be done.
Amen.

They ravished the women in Zion, and the maids in the city of Judah.

She sits alone.
The perfect opportunity.
I join her.
She recoils.
An expected reaction.
She moves over.
At least she doesn't get up and leave.

She smells of sex and perfume.
The scarred serpent stirs, still stewing in its self-made baste.
Like her, it cannot be tamed.

Her sights appear set on the DJ.
He matches her gaze.

There is no doubt that she would spread her legs
for him in a heartbeat.
Women like her waste no time.
There is no courtship in Satan's kingdom.
Whores like her make it so damn easy.

A suave-looking black man
dressed in black approaches her.
He exudes sexuality.
I feel a hardening again.
More shameful than the others.
Not the first time.
But a glitch.
I've seen him before.
Each week, it's a different victim.
I must protect her from the devil on her left.
By being her angel on her right.

I listen to their conversation.
Is it flirtation? Or some sort of interview?
Or something in between?
A fine line.
I imagine there's only one way she will get the job.
Probably how she gets *most* jobs.
Her greatest asset.

The man in black heads downstairs.
She closes her eyes.
I move in closer.
I must not lose this battle.
She is inches from me, but doesn't know it.
I don't want to startle her.

The DJ is also honing in.
He seems concerned, but for reasons different than my own.
He wants her body as much as the man in black.
I cannot blame them.

But unlike me, they can't control their impulses.
As they fight for her body, I fight for her soul.

She looks up at the DJ.
I am losing ground.
But the game isn't over.
I watch her.
She metamorphoses into my *angel*.
Smiling through a face smeared with blood.
My *angel* is gone.
I need to get a grip.
I fell for her illusion again.

She closes her eyes.

Me: "Are you aware you're in danger?"

She looks up, her eyes glazed over.
"From what?"
"From sin."
"And you know this how?"
"Every week, it's someone different. And they never come back."
"The fuck you talking about?"
"I think you know the answer to that question."
"You do, huh?"
"Let me ask you something. Do you have God in your heart?"

She laughs.
Mocking me.

"Look, if you wanna help people find religion, this ain't the place."
She laughs again.

"You're right. Which is why if you fail to heed my word, you will
pay the price."
"Is that a threat?"
"It's a promise."
"Fuck off!"

"And that's precisely your problem?"
"I *said*, get the fuck outta my face, asshole!"
"So be it."
I stand up.
"In God's name, I go."

A man's voice: "You got a problem, nigga?"

I turn and face the man in black.
Two glasses of wine.
Are they drugged?

Me: "The problem is you . . . *nigger.*"

"Who the fuck you think you talking to, *freak*?"

I disregard the man and heed the whore one final warning:

"Remember, if you fail to take heed of my advice,
you face certain death. This I promise you."

Man: "You face certain death if you don't get
your sorry old cracker ass outta here,
you clown-faced motherfucker."
The man sets down his drinks.
He attempts to shove me.
But he's not trained as I am.
I block his amateur move and shove him instead.
He topples onto the couch, before ricocheting off it.

I dart toward the stairwell.
I assume that he is following.
Thank the LORD that I'm a swift-footed state champion.
First in the 440.

I reach the lobby.
Fresh cannabis fills my olfactory glands.
I sense the enemy on my heels.
I want to make him disappear into the smoke
and become one with the shadows.

I head toward the main floor and scramble up the
steps leading to the balcony.
I turn, hoping to have eluded him, but he is still
giving chase, pushing patrons aside.
I run around the entire balcony and head back down
the stairs on the opposite side from where I started.
The man signals for security.
"Get him out of here!"
He can't defeat me without help.
A victory for me in its own right.
Security nips at my heels from all possible directions.
I dodge and dart through the crowd.
But I'm outnumbered.
I'm cornered.
I submit.
Despite my lack of resistance, I am forcefully dragged
into the depths of The Shelter.
I am shoved out the back door of the Devil's rectum.
I recite the LORD'S Prayer at the top of my lungs.
My only defense.

Outside, two bouncers hold me up.
A third punches me.
Three times in the gut.
Once in the crotch.
JESUS fell.
I stay on my feet.

Blinding white light reveals my bloodied angel.
And then I hit pavement.
Amen.

They took the young men to grind, and the children fell under the wood.

I remain on the ground, gasping for air.
Alone again.

Yet, relieved to be out of the house of Gomorrah.

I put my hand to my mouth.
Blood.
Spilled in the name of my LORD JESUS CHRIST.

I hear commotion in the adjacent parking lot.
Another fight has broken out.
I begin to wonder if this city is truly beyond salvation.
Yet, I must keep on fighting.
I scramble to get up.
GOD help them all.
Help *us* all.

A heathen approaches, with a whore on his arm.
He flashes me the peace sign.
I glare, then zip into an alley to disappear into the shadows.
I catch my breath, look up, and read:

"THOU HAST UTTERLY REJECTED US; THOU ART
VERY WROTH AGAINST US." LAMENTATIONS 5:22

Only some of us are chosen.
I close my eyes in prayer.
Amen.

Our skin was black like an oven because of the terrible famine.

Church bells strike in the distance.
Midnight.
I open my eyes.
And there she is.
She struggles to walk.
Like a rag doll.
Aided by her executioner.
Yet, I'm the one who's punished.
She keeps looking back toward the club.

She seems to have forgotten something.
But he ignores her.
I follow.

Dear Lord,
Please guide me safely through my mission, protecting
all that is pure and holy and punishing all that brings
destruction, mayhem and pain into the world you created.
In your name, I go forth.
Amen.

I follow them to a parking garage.
Why so far?
I race a block down the street, until I reach my car.
I must act quickly.
I get to the garage just in time for them to pull out in a Lexus.

I follow at a safe distance.
I turn on gospel music and hum along.
I feel calm.
In control.
Confident that I will successfully carry out the LORD'S mission.

Feelings of *guilt* and *doubt* begin to race through my mind.
Storm clouds of ambiguous morality.
I am not used to this.

No sign of the Lexus, but I trust that GOD will guide me.
I am surrounded by a lonely wasteland.
I reach the next intersection.
I spot my target.
I turn and follow.
Led through a cesspool of abandoned mansions.
The former hedonistic palaces of auto barons, now
transformed into debauched crack houses of despair.

The Lexus parks in front of one of them.

I park a block away and turn off my headlights.
I pray that I am not noticed.

He helps her out of the car.
She is like a toddler learning to walk.
She flops to the ground.
Her dark knight comes to her aid.
A wolf in sheep's clothing.
And *I'm* the bad guy?

Though they both deserve to be two drops in hell's bucket,
I feel a need to save her.
But if I set the house ablaze, will it be too late?
Then again, though she may perish, there would still
be one less den for predators.
How many lives will be spared as a result?
This sudden lack of clarity frightens me.
I must continue to focus on the big picture.

He leads her up the sidewalk to the doorless mansion.
They disappear inside.
This is my cue.
I will wait ten minutes, and pray fervently.
I can't afford to jump the gun.
But I must also act in a timely manner.

I step out of the car and quietly open my trunk
to gather my ammunition.
A gas can and a Molotov cocktail made from
a discarded vodka bottle.

I approach the dilapidated mansion and proceed around the back.

The yard is littered with trash.
I cross myself, then get to work, baptizing
the mansion's perimeter with gasoline.

I move quickly.

Muffled words and screams,
Only I have the power to stop it.

And then — BANG!

Who is doing my bidding?

When the can is empty, I set it down and light the vodka bottle.
So beautifully lit, against the backdrop of night,
forming a holy ring of fire.

Soon, the whole city will be illuminated through my mission.
I toss the bottle toward the back porch.
It lands directly against the backdoor.
The shatter of glass
I rush back to the car to admire my handiwork from afar.
A blaze of glory.
Will they escape?
Or perish?

I recite a passage:

*"All her friends have dealt treacherously with her.
They have become her enemies."*

Smoke rises high above its earthly ruins, ascending to heaven.
And then the voices inside my head return.
Louder than before.
I cover my ears, but the voices continue.
I cannot stop them.
I watch as the smoke takes the form of my angel,
ascending high above the house.
I watch her disappear like an escaped balloon.

A figure emerges.
I duck and peer above the dashboard.
The man. He appears hurt.
But she is still in there.
Dead?

He gets into his car and speeds away.
He has abandoned her.
One is better than none.
But not as good as two.

The elders have ceased from the gate, the young men from their music.

I cross off another conquest.
Another mission complete.
But gone is the familiar and satisfying feeling of completion.
Instead, I feel the twinge of sadness and regret.
What am I becoming?
From where does this weakness appear?
I must shake these thoughts.
Maybe I'm just tired.
Or hungry.
I must eat.
I take a deep breath and recite more scripture:

"She weepeth sore in the night, and her tears are on her cheeks. Among all her lovers she hath none to comfort her."

I want to rescue her.
But it's too risky.
And more than likely too late.
And if I were to die, by my own hand, my mission
would be over, before it is accomplished.
My biggest fear.

She is better off.
And the world is better off with me on Earth
to carry forth HIS mission.

I start my engine and drive away,
I watch the flames in my rearview mirror and
feel pangs of guilt burning deep within my soul.
Amen.

The joy of our heart is ceased; our dance is turned into mourning.

As I head back downtown, waves of doubt
and guilt continue to override my soul.
That sense that something else could be done.
That there is another way. A better way.

Satan's heart is bleeding.
Infecting me with a guilt,
from which I was once wholly immune.

I turn on holy music.
It washes over my soul.
Soothes it.
But does not wipe away the lingering guilt.

I shut the music off.
I want silence.
Maybe HE will speak to me through the silence?
Maybe he will ignore me?
It is HIS will.

I keep driving.
There are no dead ends.
Only alternate routes.
I must seek them out.

Something glitters in the road ahead.
Something metallic.
I come to a stop.
I can't tell what it is.
I am compelled to find out.
I step out to retrieve it.
A broken crucifix.
A sign?
The two parts of the cross have been separated.
My LORD'S body lies in the street, trampled
by those who know not what they do.

I scoop up the three pieces and carefully place them in my pocket.
A broken holy trinity.
I will resurrect it later.
Make it part of my shrine.

I drive away.
Lost.
Confused.
I know that I must continue with my mission.
Yet, something seems off;
feels wrong.
Then I realize that dark forces are ambushing me; using me.
Steering me off my course.
I know that I must resist.
I reach into my pocket and grip the broken pieces of the crucifix.
And realize that GOD was sending me a message.
A holy omen.
I feel emboldened.
I see the light.
Epiphany.
Yet, I can't help but sense that it's a false flag.
Satan's trickery and treachery on Devil's Night.

I park outside an abandoned church
and approach its rotted-out doors.
I enter and bow at the steps of the rotting altar:

"Dear LORD.
I praise you for leading me without temptation
through the perils of this hell.
Continue to guide me in my quest for the purification of this city."

I stand up.
"Before GOD, I go."

I make the sign of the cross and drive away,
bearing the persistent pangs of hunger.
Maybe that is my problem?

Hunger can lead one astray.
Like alcohol and drugs.
Amen.

The crown is fallen from our head: woe unto us, that we have sinned!

I head back downtown in a cloud of guilt and hunger.
The sense that something else could be done.
That there is another way.
But why now?
And if so ... *how?*

I park on an empty street and exit the car.
I take in a full breath of the crisp, autumn air.
The smell of leaves and concrete.

I look around.
Nobody.
Not even a single vagrant.
Sign of progress?
Yet I can't help but think:
What is the point of redeeming a city when no one is left?

I arrive at Lafayette Coney Island.
The place my father would take me every Saturday.
Two thugs loiter outside the door, staring me down.
I usually don't back down.
I usually stand my ground.
But I hang my head low.
I enter.
A refuge.

I take my favorite booth by the window and begin to pray.
But my prayers feel like empty words.
My soul feels empty.
Just like my stomach.

I sit where we sat on our first date,

before the town's collective soul was lost.
Sold to the lowest bidder.

Unlike the outside world, nothing in here has changed.
A fixed orbit.
A reminder that some things never fade,
even though everything around it does,
through tragedy and empty promises.

The waitress looks up.
Recognizes me.
Tries to conceal her disgust.
I ignore her.
I am also her only customer.
I can handle the judgment.
I am used to it.
I am a regular here.
Yet, she treats me like a drifter.
She has no idea that I'm trying to rid the world
of something we equally abhor.
I am sickened by the fact that she probably views me
as no different than *them*.
I realize there's nothing I can do to change this perception.
It is the cross I must bear.

I head to the restroom.
I cleanse, free from judgment.
Another disgusting hand towel.
I use toilet paper to dry myself.
It tears to shreds.
Melts in my hands and becomes nothing.

I return to my booth and look out at the street.
Litter everywhere.
Not a soul in sight.

The waitress flashes me a phony half-smile.
Might as well have been an eye roll.

I wonder if she is loved.
And if so, then by whom?
In a different life, I could see myself with her.
Where are these thoughts coming from?
I could never do that to my beloved.

She brings me a menu.
It is filthy.
Like everything else in this city.
I dismiss it.
I know what I want.
Always the same.
Bowl of fruit.
Cottage cheese.
Water. No ice.
"We are out of our mixed fruit. Would you like an apple instead?"
"What kind?"
"Red. Or, green."
"Not the color. What *kind*? McIntosh? Granny Smith? Washington?"
"No idea. They're just apples.
"Any one will do."
"Coming right up."
"Thank you."
She judges me.
I realize my hypocrisy, but at least I judge on the *right* side of things.

I try to clear my mind of all thought.
But I fixate on the girl in the burning house.
Could I have saved her?
Should I have saved her?

Something catches my attention.
A figure outside the window.
The homeless man I almost hit.

He waves at me.
I ignore him.

He waves again.
I look up and flash him a disapproving look.
He walks away.
I am mistaken to think that he is gone for good.
He enters.
The one upside is that the waitress appears
even more disgusted by his presence than by mine.

He stands in the doorway, waddles back and forth.
A lost soul.
He heads downstairs to the restroom.
I'm glad I was there first.

The waitress brings me my sustenance.
I thank her. She doesn't respond.
A lot of nerve if she's expecting a tip.
I silently pray over my food.
The vagrant returns from the restroom
and takes a seat at the counter.
He waves at me.
I ignore him.
He waves again. I glare.
He smiles. He is relentless.
He attempts to order, but the waitress
isn't convinced that he can pay.
He shows her that he has just enough for hot chocolate.
She seems disappointed.
I don't blame her.
I wouldn't want to serve him, either.
But then, suddenly, out of nowhere,
I feel an overwhelming need to save him.

Amen.

~Rex Tremendae~

CAT MAN

1

Cat Man turned to his favorite passage in the Bible and readied himself to face his congregation, huddled inside a tattered, makeshift tent.

He could smell fire in the distance. More so than usual.

At least to the best his memory would allow.

He was dressed in everything he owned: a green, threadbare military jacket, gray sweatpants and Velcro-strapped black shoes, topped off with a knit cap that had more holes than fabric.

His loyal parishioners—a dozen or so cats—listened intently as their caretaker, their human Lord and savior, began to read:

"When I was a child, I talked like a child, I thought like a child, I reasoned like a child. When I became a man, I put the ways of childhood behind me. For now we see only a reflection as in a mirror; then we shall see face to face. Now I know in part; then I shall know fully, even as I am fully known. And now these three remain: faith, hope and love. But the greatest of these is love."

As he finished the passage, he broke into an uncontrollable cough—a worsening of the untreated asthma that had plagued him since childhood. The smoke in the air certainly didn't help.

But nothing could stop him from his daily devotion.

He used to go to a church on a regular basis, and, as far as he could remember, he had never missed a Sunday service.

Until it burned down.

Ashes to ashes, dust to dust.

Rather than seeking out a new sanctuary, an old, tattered Bible that he found in a shelter became his church. It was his most cherished possession. He never felt closer to God. Cat Man had come to realize that the less one has, the more one has God; the more one has, the less one needs God.

Cat Man gently closed his book and set it down adjacent to a pile of neatly arranged remnants that he had found on the streets of Detroit. He took great care in collecting and carefully curating other peoples' castoffs. He scooped up the latest addition to his family—a scruffy, malnourished kitten that he brought back from the dead—and placed it into the front pocket of his jacket. He emerged from his homemade tent, a living, breathing piece of performance art in the epicenter of the Heidelberg Project. Despite its deceptive name, the Heidelberg Project was not a low-income housing project. It was an urban art project designed to inject new life into a no man's land on the east side of the city.

The entire neighborhood *was* the canvas. Abandoned houses were adorned with colorful polka dots. The empty spaces where houses once stood now showcased displays of mannequins, old phone booths, and discarded stuffed animals—all strategically placed for a specific purpose.

A Salvador Dali junkyard.

Though considered art by many, city officials saw it as an eyesore drawing unwelcome attention, despite the irony that the whole purpose of the Project was to put a man-made bright spot on man-made blight. Despite recent efforts to erase it from existence, the Project continued to subsist through multiple arson attempts and city-sanctioned razes. In fact, a significant portion of it had been razed by city bulldozers just months earlier. But it refused to back down, standing its ground. It embodied the city's spirit like nothing else.

And Cat Man was its beating heart.

Armed with his newfound comrade, Cat Man was ready to take the town by storm. He was imbued with a great sense of optimism and had a feeling that there was something extra special about this day, although he did not know why. He knew that he could no longer rely on specific, long-term memory. He simply relied on feeling.

He grabbed his rusty shopping cart and went on his merry way, with a slight, but determined limp. He whistled improvised jazz—he couldn't remember any of the melodies to actual songs—accompanied by an unwelcome percussion in the form of the stubborn cough that often transformed into violent fits.

Despite his limitations and circumstances, Cat Man always remained upbeat. He feared nothing. Not even death—although lately he found himself thinking about death more frequently. Not in a doom and gloom sense, but with the hopeful paradise of an afterlife. Though he was in no rush to get there, he certainly didn't dread it.

Most of the time, he focused on the present. And he embraced it. It was the only thing he had any control over. His past was as unclear as his future.

The whole night lay in front of him. This meant the possibility of new friends. In Cat Man's mind, friendship was life's greatest nourishment—at times, even more so than a warm meal, though he certainly desired one of those, too. Friendship was better than any substance on earth. Then again, as far as substances were concerned, he had never experienced a single sip of alcohol in his entire life. He had been taught at an early age that drugs and alcohol ruined lives.

Cat Man made his way down the surreal, candy-colored confines of Heidelberg Street and headed to an equally desolate Gratiot, toward downtown.

Though there was no shortage of trash in the city, Cat Man didn't let a single piece slip by. He simply tossed it into his shopping cart.

Everything has a purpose.

Every last bit of trash.

Every last, unwanted kitten.

And certainly every single human being.

He was overcome with a sense of pride with each collected piece, like rare jewels plucked from the earth. He received no greater satisfaction than doing the *right* thing, which he had thrived on and strived for his entire life. He made it his mission to clean up the city he loved so much.

While so many saw the city as a dumping ground, Cat Man saw hidden opportunity. Where some saw danger lurking around every corner, Cat Man saw only hope. Sometimes, hope was only a block away. Sometimes, he had to search all across town. No matter what, he never stopped looking and marveled over the fact that no piece of trash was exactly the same.

Like snowflakes.

Of course, most people wouldn't even notice a random piece of trash to begin with. Or, they would simply choose to ignore it. Cat Man didn't just look on the surface of his accumulated treasures. He studied each piece from the inside out, mining it for its full potential. Take, for instance, a candy wrapper. Cat Man loved to examine its unique imprint of chocolate, dust, and dirt. Though he found beauty in it, he would trade finding trash for a world without trash any day.

Being homeless certainly didn't make Cat Man's life any easier. Not that he ever regarded himself as homeless. He regarded himself as an urban nomad and took great pride in the city he called home. When he picked up after others, he felt both a sense of duty and fulfillment and was hopeful that one day, others would follow suit.

Fueled with hope for what the rest of the night had to offer, Cat Man made his way through the streets, gathering trash and occasionally passing a fellow human being. Most, however, did not view him as such. Cat Man smiled at everyone he passed, but was mostly ignored. Even his fellow urban nomads ignored him. Like Jesus, he was friendly to the occasional Mary Magdalene, despite the fact that he disapproved of their line of work.

But even they ignored him.

They knew he had no money. This same principle kept him safe from thieves, too. To the general passerby, he was no more relevant than one of his collected pieces of trash.

But *he* knew he was better than that. And that's all that mattered.

As he crossed at an intersection, a beat-up van booming with bass whipped around the corner, narrowly missing him.

"Get the fuck outta the street, motherfucker!" the driver screamed, shattering the silence with his horn.

"So sorry! Sorry!" Cat Man responded, coughing uncontrollably as he continued on his merry way, pushing his cart.

The driver slammed on the gas, disappearing from view like a bat out of hell.

Cat Man recovered, then trudged onward, walking alongside some abandoned train tracks. Though he couldn't quite put his finger on it, the tracks always provided him a sense of comfort and security. On the horizon, he saw a tiny break in the clouds up ahead, as though the sun wanted one last glimpse of the dying city before it turned in for the night. Looking around at a gray desert, the sun and the moon's sudden presence created an otherworldly scene and seemed to defy all logic.

A vision of hope?

It was so beautiful and breathtaking, he wondered if it was even real at all. Hallucination, or not, only God had the power to create such beauty.

And it gave him hope. Whether real or imagined—the sight faded away much too quickly. One thing was clear: he would never forget it. Or he would certainly try his best not to. As to just what exactly it was, he had no clue.

But he took comfort in it nonetheless and was certain it was a sign of good things to come.

But then a red tinted cloud formation formed what, to him, looked like an elf. Or, perhaps a dwarf?

Something from his past. But what?

And then, like most of his memories, everything dissipated.

2

With the sun slipping into night, Cat Man searched in vain for human life. As he pushed his cart down one deserted block after another, he couldn't help but feel as though he were the last man on earth.

But then, finally, signs of life! A young couple with a toddler, approaching a previously abandoned warehouse that had recently been renovated into residential lofts.

Prior to the renovation, the building had been one of Cat Man's primary shelters. Though the memory had long slipped from his mind, the place felt familiar to him. And he felt drawn toward it.

Cat Man's eyes lit up at the prospect of making some new friends.

He parked his cart alongside the brick building and entered the lobby, where he spotted the family waiting for an elevator. He could sense their nervousness, but he also knew that anything he tried to do about it would only make it worse. He watched the woman whisper something into the man's ear. They then both looked away, but the little girl continued to stare at the stranger standing before them. Cat Man seized the opportunity.

"How you doin' tonight?"

The couple ignored him as they stared straight ahead at the elevator.

"How you doin' tonight?" Cat Man asked again, assuming they somehow didn't hear him the first time. They continued to ignore him.

Finally, the elevator doors screeched open and the couple scurried in. Cat Man ran toward them, but the doors bounced off of his body and reopened, before closing again. Somehow, he managed to squeeze himself in. The couple retreated kitty corner from Cat Man, shielding their daughter from him.

"Floor?" Cat Man asked.

"Four, please," the man said.

Cat Man beamed with pride and pushed four.

"Where you goin'?"

"Up," the man said, as the elevator started clinking and clunking its way to its destination.

"No, I mean, where you going after you go up?"

The couple ignored him.

"Do you live here?"

The man shakes his head.

"Just ignore him," the woman whispered—but still audible enough for Cat Man to hear.

"You mean you're riding the elevator, but you don't live here?"

Though the couple ignored him, the little girl continued to stare with fascination.

"You are so lucky to have parents to keep you safe, young lady. I'm so glad you're safe. Praise the Lord. Praise the Lord!"

The parents pulled their daughter closer into their orbit.

"Your parents best always keep you safe, you hear?"

They nodded, but it was clear they were very much concerned about their safety. Cat Man continued, building into a feverish pitch.

"You keep that little girl safe! Lord Almighty, please keep this little one safe!"

Cat Man realized that he was probably making them feel uncomfortable, but he knew just the trick to diffuse the nervous tension. He reached into his pocket and pulled out his kitten.

"Hey! You like cats?" he asked, holding out his kitten for them to see.

The couple showed no emotion, while their daughter's eyes lit up with glee. The kitten let out a tiny "mew."

"You can stroke her if you'd like," Cat Man said. "She won't bite."

Cat Man extended the kitten closer toward them, until it was just inches from their faces. They flinched, but he insisted.

How could they ignore such cuteness?

The little girl stepped forward and reached to pet it, but her mother quickly pulled her arm away.

"Honey, no. Don't touch."

The elevator doors opened and the family dashed off down the hallway.

Cat Man tucked his kitten back into his pocket, disheartened that yet another friendship opportunity had reached such an abrupt end. He considered following them, but their message was clear.

He wasn't wanted.

He was now so used to rejections, they bounced off him like rubber bullets. But, still, each one hurt a little more than the previous.

The elevator closed and Cat Man headed back down. By the time he reached the ground floor, he remembered that the night was still young. As he headed out of the building, he spotted assorted trash and rat droppings. He wished he had a broom so he could sweep it all away, but he knew that he would be trespassing. He gathered a few random pieces of trash, avoiding the ones in direct contact with rat feces, stuffed them into his pocket, and headed out.

Things were already looking up.

3

As he left the apartment building, Cat Man found himself completely alone. Knee-high grass and weeds surrounded the old brick tenement—the only standing structure on two-and-a-half acres of urban prairie.

He looked up into the night sky.

Where were all the stars? Were there ever any stars?

As he wandered down the street, he couldn't stop thinking about the little girl. There was *something* about her. He knew it was important. But he just couldn't quite figure out *why*.

Night had now fully taken over the city and the streets seemed even more desolate. It was time to head toward the bright lights of downtown, which beckoned like the Emerald City—one of the few childhood memories he did remember. This was where he was most likely to strike gold and find a friend. Even though it was all in the Lord's hands, it was up to him to do the walking.

He approached his favorite landmark: the giant Spirit of Detroit statue, the cross-legged-not-so-Jolly Green Giant of Detroit.

A symbol of hope.

"How you doing tonight?" Cat Man asked enthusiastically.

It wasn't that he was crazy. He knew that it was only a statue. But it was at least *someone . . . something.*

Cat Man made his way down Woodward Avenue, where there would surely be a steady flow of humanity. He nodded and said hello to everyone he passed, but nobody seemed interested in returning the favor. They were no more responsive than statues.

As Cat Man passed through Grand Circus Park, he climbed into an empty fountain. The physical exertion triggered another coughing attack. Once he had regained his breath, he gathered up several coins—mostly pennies—and placed them into the pocket of his tattered pants. Searching for discarded coins in a fountain was as close to begging as Cat Man allowed himself to get. Yet, most people seemed to naturally assume that he was begging for money. In fact, not only did he refuse to beg, he also refused to accept any money from a stranger if it was offered. He simply had too much pride for that. The way he saw it, at least the money in the fountain was freely discarded and up for grabs.

First come, first served.

The money certainly had more use in his pocket, than it did in the fountain. Besides, if he didn't take it, then some other nomad would, even though he didn't feel that he deserved it any more than they did.

Cat Man certainly went the extra mile for his keep. He knew how to find coins in every nook and cranny. Even though it usually meant getting dirty, he was usually rewarded for his efforts.

Short of breath, he gave the fountain one last excavation, which yielded him an additional quarter. As he bent over to retrieve it, he heard footsteps. Before he could even react, somebody grabbed him with both arms and attempted to pull him out of the fountain. Cat Man tried to resist, but he was too weak and was tossed to the ground, where he got a good look at the culprit—a fellow fountain walker. This one looked only vaguely familiar.

"Hey! That's my money!" the man barked.

"I'm sorry, but I found it first," Cat Man pleaded.

"You're on my turf."

Cat Man wasn't going to argue. He surrendered his quarter.

Certainly not worth getting hurt over. Or killed.

Let him have his turf. I have the rest of town.

The man snatched the coin from Cat Man's hand and hopped back into the fountain in search of more. Cat Man took a measure of glee in the fact that he had already drained it for all its worth, but then immediately felt awash in guilt for wishing such ill on another human being—particularly someone much like himself. He knew he had been wronged, but once again, he preferred to turn the other cheek, rather than to retaliate or wish someone ill. And he considered the possibility that the man needed that quarter more than he did.

Cat Man shook off the incident and then headed over to a bench to count his earnings. It amounted to just under a dollar, which was well below his usual intake.

Things could always be worse.

This was his life motto, no matter how dire the situation. But lately, following an unusually long string of bad luck, he had found himself occasionally wondering: maybe it *couldn't* get any worse? Maybe this *was* rock bottom? But whenever he had these thoughts, he would always refuse to give in to negativity. He had been raised to only see the bright side of life. This was one of the few things he could clearly remember from his past, which he saw through a kaleidoscope of fragments. Memories would often arrive from out of the blue, triggering tiny snippets of his former life, like sea flotsam.

Most of the time, it was less than a memory and more like a feeling associated with a memory that he couldn't quite grasp. But like most of these moments, the feeling was gone before he could reflect on it in any meaningful way. All that remained *temporarily* was a lingering *feeling* from the memory—a ghost of what once was. Like spotting a pebble on the shore, only to have it instantly washed away by a wave.

What Cat Man did gather during these rare moments of clarity was that once upon a time, he had a good life—at least, if the random, short-lived scattershot slivers of his past were any indication. The mere knowledge of this made him happy, since some people never got to experience a good life at all. Some were doomed from the start. Unfortunately, Cat Man could never grasp enough fragments at one time to piece together the entire puzzle.

A blessing and a curse.

The less he could remember, the less he could forget.

Each new experience and memory felt like a gift—until his mind faltered and they began, slowly but surely, to fade into oblivion, with no guarantee that they would ever return, even though he would try with all his might to grasp on to them and never let go. But no matter how hard he tried, they would all eventually disappear, leaving only an aching void.

His mother's embrace.

A childhood birthday party.

A friend.

A vacation.

A holiday gathering.

A fishing trip.

A game of hide and seek.

A first kiss.

And then—*nothing*.

Often times, the memories would be painful, and he considered himself fortunate that those particular memories did not linger.

He couldn't even remember why he couldn't remember.

And for that, he was sad—and he was grateful.

As he whistled more jazz, Cat Man placed his loose change back into his pocket before heading over to the People Mover station across from Grand Circus Park, picking up a few pieces of trash along the way: a candy wrapper, a snack-sized Better Made chip bag, and a broken pair of children's sunglasses. He examined each item like a jeweler examining rare gems, before tossing them into his cart. He lingered over the sunglasses, imagining the child who had once owned them, and felt a surge of nostalgia mixed with a strange sense of loss. He imagined that the child was missing her sunglasses and was probably sad. He wished there weren't so many sad people in the world.

He wanted *everyone* to be happy.

Like him.

He entered the deserted station, taking great care but still struggling to drag his cart up the steps to the platform. An earlier tumble in the same location had left him with a permanent limp.

When he finally reached the platform, he buckled over, out of breath, as he coughed up a storm, hacking up what sounded like a hairball.

When he had recovered from his coughing fit, he scraped together enough change for the coin slot and walked through the turnstile. Cat Man could count on just one hand the times he hopped over the turnstile without paying. He would prefer to walk than to steal. As long as he had enough money, he was going to pay—even if it meant going hungry. Worst case scenario, there was never a shortage of discarded food. There were a couple of instances when he had been short a couple of cents, but paid with what he had, so at least it was only *partially* stealing. And he always made sure to pay the rest back later, adding in extra coins.

He disliked owing the universe *anything*.

While Cat Man waited on the platform, he approached a bronze sculpture of a man reading a newspaper and struck up a conversation.

"How you doin' tonight? Is that the Bible you got there?"

Cat Man pointed up toward the sky.

"He watchin'. He sees all. Watchin' over his children."

The kitten meowed in response.

"All his children. Even you. You like cats?"

The train squealed into the station before coming to a screeching halt. The doors slid open and Cat Man entered the empty train with his shopping cart, but not before telling his bronze friend: "You take good care now. God bless."

He found his favorite corner spot and sat down, out of breath. The electronic bell of the train chimed, the doors slid shut, and the train took off into the night.

Cat Man gently removed the kitten from his pocket to pet it, as he glanced out of the window, hypnotized by the blur of lights and buildings.

After a few minutes, he tucked his kitten safely away. Before he knew it, the train had made almost two full loops and Cat Man wondered if he would ever see another human being. Just when he was about to lose all hope, another passenger entered: a pretty lady, with a sparkly medallion around her neck.

She seemed familiar to him, but then again, so did most people. And even if he had met her before, he would never really know—unless, he were told directly, in which case he would just have to take her word for it.

He flashed his warmest smile, but the lady did not appear to notice.

Or, maybe she did.

She headed to the opposite side of the car, sat down, and closed her eyes. When the train started with a jerk, her eyes opened, but she didn't look his way until he began to cough. It was that look of disgust that he knew all too well.

"How you doing tonight, ma'am?" Cat Man asked.

Despite endless rejection, he never stopped trying.

It was his greatest attribute. And perhaps his greatest flaw?

The lady closed her eyes again. He could sense that something was troubling her and he wanted to help, but he knew that she wouldn't want him to help, even if he tried. She looked so beautiful, yet so broken, and in that moment, there was nothing he wanted more than to cheer her up. He was confident he had just the cure.

He pulled some paper out of his cart and carefully began folding it in a very specific, methodical way. He took particular care not to tear any trash, no matter how tattered and torn it was. Halfway through the process, Cat Man realized that the lady had opened her eyes and appeared to be watching with some interest.

Curiosity didn't kill the cat. Curiosity saved the cat.

With his trash sculpture close to completion, he wasn't quite satisfied. He needed more red, so he began to dig around in his cart until he found exactly what he was looking for—a Kit-Kat wrapper. He proceeded to weave it together with the first piece.

As the train pulled up to the next station, he noticed that the girl was startled at the sight of the bronze statue reading a newspaper.

Cat Man chuckled.

"It's okay, ma'am. He scares me every now and then, too. But he's friendly."

The lady ignored him. As the train continued on its journey, Cat Man put the finishing touches to his sculpture, which he inspected with an equal measure of pride and wonderment. It was a perfectly formed rose, fully grown out of the trash of the city he loved.

Bursting with excitement, he stood up and made his way over to the lady, struggling to maintain his balance. She rolled her eyes, but it didn't faze him. He was used to it. In fact, he was used to far worse treatment.

"How you doin' tonight?" Cat Man asked her again, noticing her suitcase. The lady continued to ignore him, but he was determined to make her his friend—partly because of his need for companionship, but mostly because of what he assumed to be her need.

He plopped himself down next to her and pretended not to notice that she moved further away from him. Not that she was subtle about it. Despite this setback, he was confident that once she saw his exquisite work of art, she would melt.

He took a deep breath, and then presented it to her.

"I made this for you."

After he finally convinced her to take the rose, he reverted to his usual refrain: "You like cats?"

The lady looked at him as though he had just asked for a kiss. To appease her fear—and to avoid pepper spray in the face—he opened up the front pocket of his coat to reveal his kitten, which let out a small peep. He thought he saw the semblance of a smile on her face as she stared at the tiny kitten. Or, maybe it was just wishful thinking on his part. When she noticed that he was watching her, the lady averted her eyes and took a sip from a bottle of milk.

"May I have some milk, ma'am? For my cat?"

Reluctantly, she offered it to him. As he reached for it, he took good care not to touch her fingers, knowing full well that the last thing she would want was physical contact with a nomad like himself.

The train pulled up to another empty station.

"Would it be okay if I use the cap?"

She rolled her eyes.

"Whatever."

"You can say no."

"You deaf? I said *whatever*! I don't give a fuck!"

Satisfied with her response, Cat man removed the cap from the bottle and carefully poured some milk into it.

He set the cap down on the floor, then gently removed the kitten from his pocket and placed her down on the floor, where she immediately began lapping it up.

"That's my girl," Cat Man said, letting out a warm chuckle, which loosened phlegm in his throat, prompting another coughing fit. He hacked up a wad and swallowed it, realizing it was the polite thing to do.

"Excuse me," he said, embarrassed.

At the next stop, a man who looked as though he could well be from the future entered. The man struggled, with one hand, to pull his suitcase on board after the train doors had closed, trapping it. He held a coffee cup in his other hand. Cat Man failed to suppress a chuckle. He knew it was rude to laugh at someone. He certainly didn't like it when people laughed at him, even though he was used to it.

"Son of a bitch!" the man from the future muttered under his breath, as he pulled his suitcase onto the train.

As future man and the pretty lady made eye contact, Cat Man instantly felt himself sliding deeper into the void of irrelevance. Although he was happy to have *two* fellow passengers on board now, being ignored was worse than being alone.

So he decided to do something about it.

"How you doin' tonight?"

No response.

Cat Man turned his attention toward his kitten, who was finishing up her milk. When she was done, he scooped her up and placed her into his pocket. He removed a couple of pieces of trash from his cart and began to think of something to make for the new passenger. Women were easy. They always got a rose. As for men, he didn't want them to get the wrong idea about him.

Still flailing for an idea, Cat Man watched future man transfer some vials out of his coat pocket and into a small compartment of his suitcase. The main section of his case was filled with records. This triggered an idea. Cat Man immediately got to work. When he was done, he walked over to future man, beaming with pride and presented his latest creation: a perfectly formed treble clef.

Future man examined it with curiosity.

"Wow. Impressive," the man said, reaching into his pocket and producing a five-dollar bill. "Here ya go, my man!"

Cat Man refused to take it, and instead, revealed his kitten.

"You like cats?"

"Naw, man. Allergic."

This saddened Cat Man, as much as he tried to fight it.

"Yours is definitely cute, though," future man said.

"She sure is," Cat Man said. He smiled in agreement. "She sure is."

His sadness subsided.

Cat Man noticed future man's ring. It appeared to feature some sort of plant.

"Is that cat nip?"

Future man flashed him a befuddled glance.

"On your ring."

"Oh! Yeah. Kind of," future man said with a chuckle, before turning his attention to the lady.

Good luck, mister.

Cat Man stared out the window once again, hoping to reclaim the memory that he had lost earlier. But it was no use. Instead, he focused on his reflection, projected onto the facades of the abandoned buildings that passed by. He returned his focus back onto his new friends.

The lady appeared annoyed by future man and turned her focus to outside the window, before closing her eyes. Cat Man couldn't tell whether she was asleep or awake.

Cat Man wondered what else he had in common with future man, aside from their interest in the pretty lady. If only future man was willing to give him a chance. But he seemed more focused on the lady who still had her head turned toward the window.

"So, seriously, where you heading?" future man asked her.

"I'm going to heaven!" Cat Man interrupted.

Future man laughed.

Why is he laughing at me?

At least *she* wasn't laughing at him.

Instead, she was now shouting at future man.

"First, what makes it your business and, second, why do you give a shit?"

"Honestly, I don't. But there's no one else on this train to talk to, other than Picasso and his pussy over here."

Both passengers looked toward Cat Man and he beamed back at them. They both looked away, and laughed. Even though there was nothing he loved more than laughter, there was nothing that hurt him more than being laughed at. It hurt more than any insult; more than any physical abuse.

Meanwhile, Cat Man listened intently as his new friends continued their conversation. He wondered if future man could somehow help the lady. Cat Man wished that he could help her, but if not he just wanted her to be happy.

However, it appeared that future man wasn't having any luck reaching her, either. One thing seemed clear: he wasn't backing down—especially after the girl's purse slid off her lap and onto the ground, spilling its contents onto the floor of the train.

She shouted an obscenity as she scrambled to pick up her possessions. Future man rushed to help, but she made it clear that his help was not welcome. This lady was one tough cookie. Of course, Cat Man knew that if he tried to help, she would probably assume that he was trying to steal from her.

As the train approached the Greektown station, both of Cat Man's new friends stood up. He realized he was about to be alone again.

But the night was still young.

He thought about following them off the train, but then thought better of it. He didn't want to appear to be a nuisance—especially to the lady.

"You be careful now," Cat Man said, as the pretty lady and future man headed toward separate doors. "God bless."

"You too, dude," future man said with a wink.

Cat Man watched his friends leave, like a dog watching its master leave for work.

He noticed that future man had left his coffee cup behind.

"Your cup!" Cat Man shouted, hoping to seize a golden opportunity.

But it was too late. The door slammed shut.

"Lord, keep 'em safe."

As the train took off, Cat Man watched future man and the pretty lady head off in opposite directions.

He was alone again as the train to nowhere continued its long journey into the night.

4

Although he was now alone, Cat Man found a sliver of hope in the form of future man's discarded cup. He headed over to pick it up, lifted the lid to sniff the remnants of tea, then gently placed the cup into his cart as though it were made of fine China.

He sat back down to catch his breath and pondered his next move. He decided that unless somebody else boarded at the next stop, he would get off. Odds were, no one would come. Meanwhile, at least it was warm on board—and relatively safe.

There was *always* a silver lining.

Furthermore, walking was becoming increasingly difficult by the day. But he also preferred not to go around in circles if he could help it.

Next stop: the Renaissance Center. An angry-looking man boarded. He kicked a balled-up piece of paper, which landed at Cat Man's feet. Even though he knew that he would not illicit a friendly response, Cat Man decided to address the angry man.

"How you doin' tonight?" Cat Man asked as the man threw his heavy mass down into his seat.

No response. Cat Man picked up the balled-up paper, then asked: "Is this yours?"

One quick glare told Cat Man that this man was in no mood for conversation. Yet, this wasn't enough to deter him. Cat Man had nothing to fear. He turned his attention to trying to figure out what kind of trash sculpture to make for this angry man. Nothing came to mind.

He was usually able to get a quick sense of a person's interests, but this man wore his anger like a shield. He noticed the R.I.P. tattoo, which didn't exactly inspire any ideas.

Cat Man continued to study the man, who seemed too immersed in his own misery to notice. Whatever it ended up being, he hoped it would help cheer the man up.

But still nothing came to mind, so he decided to bring the man back his trash, banking on the hope that that man had not meant to discard it so irresponsibly.

Cat Man walked over to the angry man and waved the piece of paper in front of his face like a small flag. At first, the man ignored him, but with each wave, the angry man's breaths intensified until he finally exploded with intense rage:

"Get the fuck out of my face!"

Cat Man retreated to the safety of his own corner of the train, gently placing the trash into his cart for later use. He didn't even bother using his kitten as bait this time around. He had a feeling that the angry man might just very well rip its neck off. Even Cat Man knew when to leave well enough alone.

Like the lady, Cat Man got the distinct sense that this man was also in need of help. He wished there was something he could do to help him, but knew it was probably no use. The feeling of being *unable* to help was too much to bear at times. He wanted to believe that his art was *always* the necessary elixir, but knew all too well that it was a futile effort. Sometimes, he wished he didn't care at all, but he knew that God wouldn't want it that way.

At the next station, the angry man stormed out. As much as Cat Man wanted to make a friend, he was actually relieved to see him go.

As Cat Man stroked his kitten, he watched the angry man reach street level and was suddenly overcome with guilt. Not only did he fail to help the man, he couldn't even do the bare minimum of creating a piece of art to at least cheer him up. Perhaps it wasn't meant to be, but it bothered him nonetheless.

The kitten meowed. "It's okay," he assured his furry friend. "You're safe here. There will be others. There always are."

Cat Man realized he was growing restless. As the train passed through Greektown, he looked down on the busy streets below, which filled his heart with excitement. It was one of the few sections of the city with a pulse. And a place where he was most likely to make a friend.

As the People Mover approached Bricktown Station, Cat Man stood up, coughed, and then headed toward the door, using his shopping cart for balance. The train came to a stop and he knew that he had to pick up the pace if he were to exit in time. Though it was a struggle, he managed to get almost out until the doors slammed shut on his cart. Like future man before him, he had to put up a struggle, pushing with all his might to pull both himself and the cart through. He felt a sense of both karma and kinship. If only future man were here to laugh at him! The thought made him smile.

As Cat Man squeezed himself out of the train door, he lost his balance, flailing, and falling backwards onto the platform. He sat on the ground, struggling to catch his breath, amid a barrage of coughs. The coughing was getting worse. When the storm inside his lungs had passed, he used his cart for support to pull himself up, but not before collecting a few pieces of trash that were laying on the platform next to him: a burger, some candy, a condom wrapper, an empty Faygo Red Pop bottle, and a worn-out basketball shoe.

Every moment is an opportunity.

He placed the items in his cart, which he then carefully dragged down the steps. He wished the city cared enough to fix its broken elevators. That would at least be *one* way for the city to rise. He chuckled to himself.

Halfway down, the coughs returned and Cat Man almost lost his cart, but in a rare moment of nimble agility, he managed to catch hold just in time. He paused to regain his breath on the busy, neon-lit street. He lumbered down the street unnoticed by any of the passersby, before finally cutting through a parking lot across from Saint Andrew's Hall. There was a long line of people outside St. Andrew's.

Each person a potential friend!

Cat Man paused in front of a nearby building and read the spray-painted message on its wall:

DON'T CRY FOR US, CRY FOR THEM

At first, he was touched by its sincerity, but the longer he pondered the significance of this statement, the less sense it made.

Who is "us" and who is "them"?

Unable to decipher its meaning, Cat Man shifted his focus to the fact that this was yet even more graffiti in the city he loved so much.

Trash that couldn't be picked up.

One thing was certain: he didn't want anyone to cry for him. Though others in his position would blame their misfortunes on society, the government, or any other scapegoat, Cat Man was a rare exception. He blamed himself for his plight more than anyone—or anything—else. Rather than dwell on the things he didn't have, he focused on all the blessings he had.

Before crossing the street, Cat Man looked over toward Saint Andrew's Hall. And right there, in a second floor window, he spotted *her*.

The lady from the train!

He waved, but she did not respond.

Did she notice him?

He peeked into his pocket, where his kitten blinked at him.

"Folks keepin' together. Just like you and me."

The kitten peeped in response.

Cat Man pushed his cart into the street, making his way over toward St. Andrew's. He spotted a penny lying in the road and stooped down to pick it up.

"Find a penny, pick it up, all day long, you'll have good luck!"

Suddenly, he was startled by the sound of a car horn and squealing tires. A black car that resembled a hearse stopped less than a foot away from him.

God willing.

With the car at a standstill, Cat Man made momentary eye contact with the driver—a pale, white man with devilish eyes who glared at him with a look that suggested eternal damnation.

Cat Man offered a friendly, apologetic wave—as though it were somehow *his* fault. Cat Man didn't just simply turn the other cheek—he shouldered all the blame when he really deserved none.

"Sorry. So sorry!" Cat Man said, before he began to cough uncontrollably—still standing in front of the hearse. When he had recovered sufficiently, he continued on his merry way, pushing his cart across the road.

The pale man slammed on the gas and sped off out of sight.

Cat Man thanked God for saving him, but knew that if he wasn't more careful, he would be meeting God face-to-face sooner than expected.

In the meantime, there were friends to be made.

He approached the crowd. Though most didn't seem to notice him, the ones who did looked at him with disinterest. Cat Man tried to take it all in stride and waved as he approached them. He noticed that everyone seemed to be wearing costumes.

There *was* something special about this date.

But what?

Then he remembered.

He looked down at his cat.

"You know what tonight is, don't ya? It's the Devil's Night. Gotta keep you safe from the Devil. Gotta keep you safe. But I'm not afraid of him. You know why?"

He pointed upward toward the starless sky. The cat followed his gaze.

Cat Man continued to scan the crowd, eavesdropping on conversations, wanting so much to be a part of one. But he knew better. And then, he noticed someone attempting to pass out leaflets. He was largely being ignored. He could certainly relate. And then he realized. It was the same pale-faced man who had almost hit him with his car several minutes earlier.

The pale man caught Cat Man's gaze and glared back with black eyes that pierced his soul. This startled Cat Man, but he reminded himself not to judge even when being judged himself. Before long, the pale man disappeared inside St. Andrew's, but it was a while before Cat Man could shake the chills from the fear he felt from the pale man's steely gaze. He continued to scan the crowd for potential friends. Some pointed and laughed at him. Per usual, he tried not to let it get to him and, instead, bobbed his head to the pulsating rhythm of the music emanating from inside the club.

As long as there was music, there was joy.

Cat Man continued to attempt friendly conversation with anyone in earshot. Sometimes, he merely showed off his kitten to anyone willing to look or listen. His cat got only slightly more favorable attention than the pale man's flyers. He seemed to have better luck with women.

Two pretty young ladies in particular caught his attention: one was dressed as an angel; the other as the devil.

He now knew exactly where to begin.

"How you pretty ladies doin' tonight?"

"Fuck off. We don't have any money," said the girl in the angel costume.

"Aww, leave him alone," said the devil.

"Do you like cats?" Cat Man asked the devil, removing his kitten from his pocket.

"He's got a kitten! How cute!" said the devil.

"Which probably has fleas and rabies," the angel replied. "Ignore him. All he wants is money for booze."

A bouncer with enormous biceps approached and stood between Cat Man and the two girls. He reminded Cat Man of a cartoon character, but he couldn't remember which one.

"Stop flirting with the ladies and get lost!"

"I ain't flirting. I just want to show them my kitty."

"Yeah, well they sure as hell ain't gonna be showin' you theirs. Now get the fuck out of here!"

Cat Man pushed his cart, head bowed. Halfway down the block, he turned his cart around and headed back. He refused to give in—not so much out of defiance, but rather out of desperation for attention. He knew that this crowd represented his best shot.

He greeted everyone within earshot with his usual refrain: "How you doin' tonight?"

No response, Cat Man removed the kitten from his pocket and asked out loud: "Who likes cats?"

A man dressed like a cowboy shouted out.

"I hate cats. So fuck you and your little pussy, too."

The people around them erupted into laughter.

A man dressed as a milkman standing next to the cowboy threw a handful of pennies onto the ground in front of him.

"Here! Call someone who gives a fuck!"

Cat Man ignored the taunts and scrambled to pick up the pennies. Amid the pennies lay a single pamphlet with a recognizable face on it: his Lord and Savior, Jesus Christ.

He picked the leaflet up and opened it, only to be smacked in the head by a Styrofoam cup filled with coffee, the contents of which splashed all over his face and jacket. Fortunately, the coffee was already cooled to a tolerable level.

Always a silver lining.

Cat Man shoved the leaflet into his pocket and picked up the cup. He shook out the rest of the coffee and placed the cup in his cart, which was already close to overflowing.

He checked on his kitten, who had fallen asleep, then took the leaflet out of his pocket.

Damnation.

Sin.

Hellfire.

It certainly wasn't the religion *he* was accustomed to. In fact, it seemed like a whole other religion all together. But to each his own.

If he were to make a leaflet for people, the focus would be on:

Love.

Forgiveness.

Peace.

Nothing more. Nothing less.

It was the way Cat Man chose to live his life. If others chose this same path, there would be no need for leaflets like the one he held in his hand. And if he had the means to make a pamphlet, he was confident that his wouldn't end up discarded on the ground. But since he couldn't make a pamphlet of his own, he had to depend on himself to serve as a beacon of hope and joy in a world filled with anger, hatred, and indifference.

I practice what I preach.

Only problem was, nobody would listen. Just like the pale man's pamphlet, Cat Man, too, was discarded, trampled upon, and forgotten. It wasn't because of the message that he carried inside. It was because of the way the message was packaged—in the guise of a vagrant. After he finished reading the entire pamphlet, he closed it up and slid it into his pocket for safekeeping.

From the corner of his eye, he noticed something fall out of a man's pocket. It was a twenty dollar bill. As he stooped to pick it up, the owner slapped his hand away.

"Hey asshole! Hands off!"

"I just wanted to let you know that you dropped it."

"Bullshit. You were going to steal it."

"I never stole a thing in my life."

"Yeah. Sure."

Nothing Cat Man could say or do could convince the man otherwise, so he did the only thing he could think of: reveal his kitten.

"Do you like cats?" Cat Man asked.

"Hey, cat fucker!" boomed a second voice.

Cat Man looked up. It was the bouncer from earlier.

"When are you going to learn? *Nobody* cares about you and your goddamn cat. And nobody is going to give you any money. So get the fuck out of here!"

"I don't want money—"

Before he could finish his sentence, the bouncer grabbed a broom from a witch and lunged after Cat Man.

"What did I just tell you?" the man said, broom raised over his head. Cat Man cowered.

"Can I please just use the bathroom? I'll be fast."

"Unless you got ten bucks for cover, the answer's no."

"Please?" Cat Man begged.

Cat Man looked up and saw the lady from the train again, still in the second floor window. For a brief moment, they made eye contact, before the bouncer began prodding him with the broom, drawing wild applause from the crowd. Cat Man collapsed to the ground and curled up into a ball, more concerned about his kitten than himself. Though he wasn't afraid to face his own death, he certainly didn't want to be responsible for the death of a harmless kitten.

"Okay, okay. I'll go. I'll go." Cat Man surrendered. "Just, please, don't hurt my kitty."

"Keep your hands off his pussy, man!" someone shouted. This was greeted with more laughter.

The bouncer relented as Cat Man broke out into another coughing fit. As he lay there on the cold pavement, not a single person came to his aid. Once his cough was under control, Cat Man checked on his kitten. She meowed gently, as if to let him know she was okay.

"C'mon on! Move it!" the bouncer yelled. Using his cart for support, Cat Man pulled himself up. He looked up toward the window one last time, but the girl was gone. With his tail between his legs, Cat Man pushed his cart out into the street where he saw another coin, this time a nickel, lying in the road. He stooped down to seize it and placed it into his pocket, just as a car slammed on both its horn and its brakes, missing him by inches. Cat Man buckled over, illuminated by the car's headlights, coughing until he spit up phlegm.

Once his coughing fit had subsided, he looked up and noticed that he was staring face-to-face with the angry man from the train. Despite the circumstances, Cat Man's face lit up with glee and recognition.

"I'm sorry. So, so sorry," Cat Man repeated.

In response, the angry man lifted up a middle finger, which Cat Man took as his cue to walk away. He heard the laughter from across the street, but pretended it wasn't aimed at him.

Down the street, he spotted a recognizable fellow nomad with no legs in a broken wheelchair and was reminded about just how blessed he was. Despite this brief hint of hope, the thought then only served to make him feel guilty that he had considered another man's horrible plight to be a blessing.

Though Cat Man would have loved to be the man's friend, he knew from previous experience that this man spoke only gibberish, swore, and spat at every chance he got.

No, siree, thank you!

Instead, he set his sights on a nearby hot dog stand, run by a dreadlocked hot dog vendor who blasted funk music from an old-school boom box.

"How you doin' tonight?"

"Can I help you?"

Another customer lined up behind Cat Man.

"I would like a hot dog, please. How much?"

"$1.75."

Cat Man took out his change, struggling to add it up. Meanwhile, the other customer was not hiding his impatience.

"For Christ's sake, hurry it up!"

Cat Man turned around.

"Sorry to keep you waiting."

He continued counting his change.

"Oh, darn. I lost count. Gotta start over."

"You got to be fucking kidding me," the other customer said.

"Need help?" the vendor offered.

"No, no, I got it. Oh shoot. Have to start over again. So, so sorry!"

Third time was a charm.

"I have one dollar and two cents. What can I get for one dollar and two cents?"

The vendor extended an empty hand.

"You get this."

Cat Man noticed a container filled with pickle slices.

"Can I get a pickle?"

"No."

Cat Man revealed his kitten.

"But, my cat . . . she's hungry. See?"

The vendor gave in and gave Cat Man a pickle.

"Thank you, Sir. God bless."

He turned to the other customer: "And you, too! You all have yourselves a good night!"

No response.

Cat Man spotted a tip jar, removed a penny from his pocket and placed it into the jar.

"Keep the change," Cat Man said with a warm chuckle that morphed into a violent, phlegmy cough.

Once his coughing had subsided, Cat Man walked half a block, then sat down on the curb. He set the pickle down on the ground, removed his kitten from his pocket, and placed her in front of the pickle. She gave it a single lick, then turned away.

"C'mon, kitty," Cat Man said, putting the pickle up to her mouth. "You gotta eat."

The kitten still refused, making a sour face. Cat Man regretted putting it down on the ground in the first place, considering how hungry he was himself. He refused to let it go to waste, so he wiped it off on his shirt and proceeded to eat it. The kitten watched him. He felt guilty that he got to eat, but she had not.

If she has to starve, then why not me, too?

Since it could well be a while before she might get anything to eat—and despite being so hungry himself—Cat Man saved her a small chunk, just in case.

As he pondered his next move, he looked up and saw the angry man once again, tossing a wallet into an overflowing trash can located next to the hot dog vendor.

"How you doin'?" Cat Man asked, but the angry man simply hurried past him, then crossed the street, making a beeline toward St. Andrew's.

A man on a mission.

Cat Man pocketed his kitten and headed over to the trash can. He removed the wallet, which had a 100 Grand candy wrapper stuck to it. He placed the candy wrapper in his cart, then began to thumb through the wallet.

Why on earth would somebody throw away a perfectly good wallet?

It contained no cash, but was filled with family photos—none of which featured the angry man. The pictures triggered bittersweet nostalgia in Cat Man's mind—again, just a feeling, rather than any specific memories. He traced his finger over the faces of the family members and imagined them to be members of his own family. Abstract snapshots of his past sparked his memory like an engine revved to life for a split second before stalling and melting away into a void.

Cat Man didn't understand. Throwing money away was one thing, but *memories* like these were priceless. Surely it had to have been a mistake. He was overcome with a renewed sense of purpose. If there was anything he liked more than friendship, it was helping others.

He scanned the crowd for the angry man and spotted him as he approached the club's entrance. Somehow, he had managed to avoid the long line, which now stretched down the alley alongside the club and around the corner.

Cat Man figured anyone who could take cuts in a line like that must be someone important. This made him even more eager to be the angry man's friend, although this now probably meant that he had even less of a chance.

Perhaps the angry man would be turned away at the door since not having a wallet probably meant not having ID or money, either. This was Cat Man's chance to be the hero. But oddly enough, the bouncers let the angry man in, anyway.

Unfazed, Cat Man decided to wait outside the club until the man came back out. He would wait all night if he had to. It wasn't like he had any other plans. And how would the man *not* want to be friends after getting his wallet back? Maybe only then would he stop being so angry.

Cat Man smiled. Suddenly, everything was once again right with the world.

Even though he truly wanted to help the man, he was overcome with guilt for having an ulterior motive: making a friend. Then again, it would be even more selfish of him to not return the wallet at all. As he stared into the empty billfold, a piece of paper floated up, like a feather, in front of him. By instinct, he snatched it. He couldn't make out the writing, but he could tell that it was a prescription slip.

A light bulb went off in his head.

He struggled to stand up and grabbed onto his cart for support. After catching his breath, he retrieved the 100 Grand wrapper from his cart, sat back down on the curb, and weaved the candy wrapper and prescription slip together to forge a perfectly-formed dollar sign. When he was done, he secured it into the wallet, before checking on his kitten, which was sleeping peacefully in his pocket—perhaps the last vestige of peace on earth.

5

Forty-five minutes later, Cat Man was still waiting on the curb. Though he was primarily concerned with the angry man, this didn't stop him from smiling at every passerby in the hope of making other friends. Of course, he was mostly ignored, but it was a lot easier when he reminded himself what awaited him at the end of the rainbow. He wondered how much longer he would have to wait.

As long as it took.

Suddenly, three men approached.

"Look at this piece of shit!" one of the men proclaimed.

The time had come once again to turn the other cheek. It was not only his best defense, but it was the Christian thing to do.

"Get a fucking job, loser," said one of the others.

"Then again, who would hire trash like this?"

Cat Man continued to ignore him.

"So instead, we have to see his pathetic ass out here on the streets," said the third man.

"There's only one way to put an end to that," the first man said, then lifted Cat Man up by the collar and punched him square in the gut. The other two were upon him, shoving him back and forth. He considered dropping to the ground and curling up into a ball.

Maybe that way, he would disappear.

Maybe his time had finally come.

And then an angel in disguise . . .

The angry man!

Is he here to save me?

But as the men continued to shove Cat Man with increasing force, the angry man just stood there, watching.

And then, just as Cat Man had all but given up hope, he watched in amazement as the angry man sent each of the three men to the ground with three swift punches.

This man sure was strong.

Exhausted, Cat Man collapsed to the ground as his attackers scurried off.

The angry man—his guardian angel—reached out to help Cat Man get back on his feet.

"Thank you, sir! Thank you," Cat Man said, short of breath and coughing violently.

"You okay?" the angry man asked.

"I am now. Thanks to you, my friend. I have been waiting for you."

Cat Man held out the wallet.

"I believe this is yours."

The angry man's eyes widened.

"What the fuck makes you think I want that?"

"I found it in the trash."

"Exactly."

"I thought maybe it was an accident?"

For the first time, Cat Man saw the angry man crack a smile.

"You're one crazy ass motherfucker."

"Take it!"

"Naw, man. I'm good," the angry man said.

Cat Man opened up the wallet to reveal his artwork. He gushed with pride.

"It's money," Cat Man said.

The angry man looked at it, before backing away.

"Impressive."

"You sure you don't want it?"

"Nah, you keep it."

"I made it for you. You can put it to good use. Or, you can save it. You should always save money whenever possible."

"Ain't that the goddamn fucking truth," the angry man said.

"You shouldn't take the Lord's name in vain, you know."

"My bad," the man said with a chuckle. Suddenly, he didn't seem quite so scary anymore. And though Cat Man knew he was sort of being laughed at, he didn't mind.

"Have a good night," the angry man said.

"You, too. Thanks again. And God bless!" Cat Man replied, trying to sound joyful—despite being denied—as he watched the angry man disappear around the corner, past a wall upon which was written:

"THOU HAST UTTERLY REJECTED US; THOU ART VERY WROTH AGAINST US." LAMENTATIONS 5:22

Though saddened by the fact that angry man had rejected the wallet, Cat Man was more concerned about the fact that his new friendship had ended so quickly.

Or, was the angry man even a friend at all?

He stuffed the wallet into his pocket, and once again glanced over toward St. Andrew's, hoping to catch another glimpse of the lady in the window. All he could see was the swirl of club lights.

He sighed.

It was time to move on.

The past was behind him.

The future was ahead of him.

All he had was the present.

A block away from St. Andrew's, Cat Man came across a nickel on the ground.

There we go! Things were already looking up!

He stooped down to pick it up. This prompted more coughing. The coughing fits were getting worse. He wheezed, struggling to catch his breath. He carefully placed the nickel with his other change, which jangled in his pocket as he walked. He sang "Jingle Bells" in rhythm with the coins, managing to sync up the squeals of his cart—a one-man band playing for an audience of one. Of course, to the handful of passersby he encountered, he sounded like a crazy person—but he knew he wasn't. And that was all that mattered.

After a couple of blocks, Cat Man once again became short of breath and was forced to stop singing. He found himself in one of the countless areas of no man's land that existed between city hot spots.

The silence was deafening.

In fact, he was convinced that the only sound left on earth was the duet between his labored breaths and his squealing cart. Cat Man couldn't stand it. This was the language of loneliness.

A couple of blocks over, he came across a dime in the road. As he picked it up, making sure this time that traffic was clear, he heard the sound of a trumpet emanating from an unknown destination.

An acoustic mirage?

It was getting louder. And the emerging bass line and drumbeat confirmed that it was not his imagination. It was live jazz! The DNA of his soul. On rare occasions, his memory recalled brief snippets from his days as a saxophonist. He wondered if he could still play a tune.

He had held on to a memory of his playing days at the Soup Kitchen Saloon, which he had been saddened to discover had recently closed.

But where was *this* music coming from?

Once Cat Man figured out which direction the music was coming from, he became a moth drawn to light. After all, where there was music, there were people. And where there were people, there were friendships waiting to be made. He followed his ears down Gratiot Ave. until he reached the doorstep of a jazz club. Bo-Mac's Lounge. He had played here! Once or twice. Maybe more. He was sure of it.

Or, maybe, it was never at all?

6

An attractive couple sat at a table in front of the window. They seemed like nice people. Cat Man waved at them. At first, they didn't seem to notice. So he waved again. This time around, they clearly noticed him, but ignored him nevertheless.

A bouncer approached and Cat Man found himself once again wishing for a world without bouncers. They always assumed nobody wanted to talk to him, but he knew otherwise. He was interesting. He had a lot to say. And he was a great conversationalist. Of course, his memory problems could throw a wrench into any conversation, but nothing that couldn't be overcome.

"Sir, no loitering," the bouncer told him.

To be called "sir" was a pleasant surprise.

In Cat Man's experience, a polite bouncer was a rarity. He never understood why they had to be so rude to him. Didn't they understand that if they are polite to the universe, eventually the universe will be polite back? Every now and then, at least.

"I love jazz," Cat Man replied.

"It's for paying customers, sir."

"I got seventy-one cents."

"More like no sense. Sorry. But that ain't gonna cut it."

The polite bouncer was suddenly polite no more.

"If I had more, I'd pay."

"You don't, so you're going to have to leave."

"Can I please use your restroom? I really gotta go."

"Sorry, but not my problem. Now move on."

"Okay, okay," Cat Man surrendered. He grabbed his cart and headed down Gratiot Ave.

It dawned on him, however, that he was more fueled by his desire to urinate than to converse. He grabbed his crotch, hoping it would alleviate the urge. He had too much pride to relive himself in an alley. Any desire to protect any semblance of dignity outweighed his need to pee. He would rather go in his pants. But he was running out of time.

Another light bulb went on in his head, which prompted him to turn his cart around and head back to the jazz joint.

"Hey! What did I tell you?" the bouncer demanded to know as he approached.

In response, Cat Man revealed his golden ticket: his kitten.

"Do you like cats?"

"No. I don't like cats. I fucking hate cats. And I hate people who like cats, so I'm going to tell you for the last time . . ."

"Please, sir. I really gotta go. And I really love jazz. I won't be long. I promise."

"Look. I'm going to count to three. One . . . two . . ."

Cat Man surrendered.

"Alright, okay. You win. I won't bug you anymore."

Cat Man continued on his way. Every cough increased his urge to urinate. He reached the point where he couldn't take it anymore. He snuck into a nearby alley, made sure no one was looking, and hid behind a dumpster. Just as he began to unzip his pants, somebody passed by. Paranoid, he zipped his pants back up and headed out of the alley.

He pushed his cart down the empty street with one hand while holding his crotch with the other.

Steam rose from the sewer caps and open manholes down the empty street, like ghosts, surrounded by nothing but abandoned homes and desolate, empty, litter-strewn lots.

A haunting, screaming sound echoed from somewhere in the distance. It was a noise he recognized. And then he saw it.

A male peacock, walking across the street, until it disappeared into the brush covering the sidewalk.

Why did the peacock cross the road?

To get to the other side!

Cat Man cracked himself up into another coughing fit.

An occasional car passed by. He wasn't certain, but he was pretty sure that he saw a familiar face in a black Suburban. The lady from the train? As Cat Man trudged on, he pondered the significance of crossing paths with this same woman over and over again. She seemed so familiar to him, though he couldn't figure out why.

My guardian angel, perhaps?

This last thought gave him comfort. And made him forget about his need to relieve himself—if only for a brief moment.

Lost in thought, Cat Man was surprised to find himself wandering the empty sheds of Eastern Market. The wind whipped through the vendor sheds as he maneuvered his cart around rotting remnants of fruits and vegetables, broken booze bottles, and soggy cigarette butts.

Cat Man spotted a nickel lying in a rotting cabbage leaf and chuckled, before stooping down to pick it up. He wondered where that nickel had been; where the cabbage had been grown; and how the two had ended up together.

He pocketed the nickel, then tore off a piece of cabbage and gobbled it down.

Maybe this was his lucky day after all?

He saw it as a reminder not to give up on his quest for fortune and friendship. At a crosswalk, he paused to look both ways, before pushing his cart out into the street. Out of nowhere, an SUV zipped around the corner and slammed on its brakes, just narrowly missing him, but smashing into his cart. His collection of trash was propelled into the air, before coming to rest to litter the street. The impact caused Cat Man to fall to the ground, bruised and shaken, but otherwise okay. The car didn't bother to slow down, as though Cat Man were a mere squirrel.

Once the initial shock passed, Cat Man sat up, coughed violently, and looked around with exasperation at his treasure trove of trash, now scattered around him, littering the very streets he had worked so diligently to keep clean. He refused to be part of the problem and collected everything up, one piece at a time. He laid each piece gently into his bent and mangled cart.

Each time he bent over, Cat Man would begin to cough. Although he was short of breath, he refused to leave a single piece of trash behind. He took one last look to make sure he hadn't left anything behind. Sure enough, a speck of trash caught his eye several feet away. He wasn't sure if it was his, but it was certainly his duty to pick it up. He headed toward it and just as he stepped forward, a gust of wind picked it up and blew it away.

As Cat Man chased the paper down the street, he began to wheeze. The wheeze turned into a coughing fit so violent that he buckled at the waist. Far from being a mere nuisance, his cough had begun to hurt more and more. He made one more dash toward the piece of trash and trapped it with his foot before the wind could torture him any longer. He stooped over to pick it up. It was one of the pale man's pamphlets. He carefully placed it in his cart with the rest of his collection.

With his task complete, he took a deep, wheezy breath, checked on his kitten, who was somehow still asleep, then set forward. Miraculously, the cart still worked, albeit with a limp that now matched his own.

As he turned his cart onto Gratiot—there she was! Again! The lady from the train!

Impossible! Was his imagination running amok?

As she drew nearer, he realized it wasn't his imagination. She appeared more distraught than earlier and was walking with a limp. Like him!

He wondered if perhaps her night had gone even worse than his. Even though she rejected him earlier, she certainly looked like she could use a friend now. It was certainly worth a try, even if he knew deep down that he was probably the last person on earth she would want comfort from.

"Hey, ma'am! I remember you!"

He wasn't sure if she heard him or not, so he added:

"How you doin' ma'am?"

He wasn't certain, but he thought he caught a glimpse of a slight smile form on her lips, as she continued to limp away.

"You have yourself a good night!" Cat Man said, hoping his words would somehow cheer her up. "And sweet dreams!"

"You, too," the lady responded, with a blank stare that suggested she barely even registered him at all.

And then, once again, just like that, she was gone.

Cat Man jingled his change, certain only of where he was headed, his love of God, and his love of cats.

He moseyed on down another couple of empty, lifeless blocks before deciding that he was going to turn around and head back to Saint Andrew's Hall. At least he would be around people—even if they wouldn't want to be around him. This included broom-wielding bouncers. At least it was attention in *some* form. It sure beat being alone.

Perhaps, things would be different this time around: different crowd, different bouncer, different outcome.

When he finally arrived, the line no longer wrapped around the building. Everyone was inside, having a good time—except for his bouncer nemesis, who immediately flashed Cat Man a menacing glance.

Cat Man knew better than to stay put, so he headed down the block. Then he remembered: *Steve's Place.* He had not called in on Steve in some time. Like Cat Man, Steve made friends with anybody and everybody. Even if they didn't want to be friends with him, he did everything he could to win their hearts and minds. In his mind, Steve was the friendliest man on earth.

If only more people aspired to be like Steve.

One thing that Cat Man did remember fondly were his conversations with old Steve. The only problem was—he could never understand a single word that Steve was saying. One thing was certain, the man certainly loved to talk. And Cat Man loved to listen. In fact, he much preferred listening over talking if he had his druthers. He not only found listening more interesting, but he knew it was polite to listen. He wished that he could understand Steve more, but knew that as long as he nodded from time to time, Steve would keep the conversation going. Cat Man fully understood that sometimes, it feels good just to talk, even if nobody is around to hear you. Of course, it is even better when somebody is listening—or even pretending to listen.

Once in a while, Cat Man did actually understand something Steve said. This was his reward for his patience; the problem was understanding everything that became both *before* and *after* the understandable part. He always found what he could understand very interesting and felt saddened by how many great stories he was missing out on.

Cat Man greatly appreciated another of Steve's attributes, aside from the old man's gift of gab. He would always allow nomads like himself to take shelter inside his bar during the winter months. In fact, there were usually more homeless people on hand than customers. The booths—which hadn't been used by customers since the kitchen was shut down by the health department—became makeshift beds.

Cat Man had not been visiting Steve as much as he used to, for two reasons. One was on account of the fact that he didn't get along with one of the other nomads—or, rather, the other nomad didn't along with him. Cat Man always preferred to avoid trouble.

The second, and more important, reason, however, was that he didn't want to wear out his welcome. Though he knew he was always welcome, he liked to keep some measure of independence and living in the Heidelberg Project made him feel like he was a king.

But now that he had been feeling lonelier than ever, the time had come to make his return.

Through the window, he spotted an attractive middle-aged woman sitting by herself at a corner table. Her attention was focused on a blues musician. He couldn't remember the musician's name, but seemed to recall that they had stopped being friends after a dispute of some sort.

What he did know was the woman looked lonely and Cat Man figured she could also use the company. He waved through the window. She either didn't notice him, or, as was the way with most people, simply pretended not to notice.

He waved again, with more enthusiasm. This time, the lady noticed and waved back. Ecstatic, Cat Man made his way inside, leaving his cart unattended—something he rarely did.

"Well, look at what the cat dragged in!" Steve proclaimed, as Cat Man entered. "How are you my old friend?"

"How you doin', Steve?"

Cat Man waved and smiled enthusiastically, then took a look around his surroundings.

The blues musician seemed to take notice of Cat Man, but with cold indifference. The only other patron was an old man with a frame around his neck who appeared to be sad.

Though Cat Man would have preferred to approach the woman sitting by herself, the old man seemed to be in even more need of a friend than Cat Man himself. Once again, Cat Man was reminded that things could *always* be worse. But as long as he had happiness, then he had everything he really needed.

Cat Man approached.

"Good evening, mister!"

Not only did the man not respond. He acted as though Cat Man wasn't even there at all.

"Do you like cats?"

Still nothing.

Cat Man set his sights on the woman. She had shielded herself from view, but it was too late. He had already honed in on her. And in his mind, she was already his friend.

He walked right up to her and with more unbridled enthusiasm than ever:

"How you doin' tonight?"

She looked away as she took a sip of her drink.

Cat Man moved in closer. Perhaps she hadn't heard him the first time over the music.

"How you doin' ma'am?"

"Fine," she said with a half-smile. It seemed forced. Not sincere. Cat Man was already losing hope. He dug into his pockets, pulling out random pieces of trash, which he assembled into a bouquet. The woman watched with curiosity, but he sensed she was keeping him at a distance.

"Here. Look. I made this for you!"

"How sweet!" she said with what sounded like genuine affection, before she set it down on the table. As Cat Man opened up his pocket, the woman at first seemed taken aback until she saw Cat Man's kitten greet her with a soft "mew."

"You like cats?"

She smiled warmly.

"I do. I have three of them myself."

To Cat Man's surprise and delight, the woman reached out to stroke his kitten, which closed its eyes and purred. Both he and his kitten were finally getting what they had waited so long for.

"Would you like to hold her?"

"Sure! But what if the bartender notices?"

"That's why we have to make sure we keep it our little secret."

As he pulled the kitten out of his pocket, a burly man approached the table.

" —the fuck is this?!"

"He was just showing me his cat."

"Get the fuck out of here!" the man growled.

"She just wanted to pet my kitty."

The burly man shoved Cat Man, causing him to drop the kitten, which ran toward the door. Cat Man attempted to chase it, but the man grabbed him by his coat collar and lifted him off the ground before slamming him against the wall.

Cat Man looked for help, but the blues musician ignored him, intent on strumming his guitar. Steve stood helpless. He was too old and feeble to raise his voice, let alone take physical action against this unruly customer. He usually relied on his customers to police themselves.

"My cat!"

"Fuck your cat!"

"Stop," the woman pleaded. "He didn't do any–"

"Shut the fuck up!"

"Please, gentleman," Steve said, finally stepping in. "Nobody means any harm."

"Stay out of this, old man!" the burly man shouted at Steve, who retreated backwards a couple of steps. Meanwhile, Cat Man craned his neck in search of his kitten, but she was nowhere to be found. The burly man clasped Cat Man's chin and jaw in the palm of his meaty, callused hand.

"Now listen to me," the man threatened. "And listen to me good . . ."

"My cat. I gotta find my cat!"

The man shook Cat Man violently.

"Please! Stop it!" the woman protested.

"Shut the fuck up. You brought this on yourself. I'm just cleaning up your mess!"

"He was just showing me his kitten" the woman pleaded.

"Now listen here, cat fucker. If you ever talk to my woman again, or even as much as look at her, I'm gonna rip your fucking head off. Do I make myself clear?"

"Yes. I'm sorry, sir. So sorry. But my cat, you see. I gotta find her."

Getting a fresh grip on Cat Man's jacket, the man proceeded to drag him toward the door. The bluesman continued to watch with indifference from the sidelines.

"No, please. No!" Cat Man pleaded incessantly, before the burly man threw him through the door and out onto the sidewalk.

As Cat Man fell backwards, the back of his head cracked against the pavement, his loose change spraying out of his pocket in a shower of clinks and chimes.

Disoriented for a moment, Cat Man saw a vision. A house. On fire. Somehow, it felt familiar. A wave of sadness engulfed him.

And then—just as quickly as it had appeared, the vision was gone—and he was back in the moment, discarded on the sidewalk.

As he lay on the cold concrete, several people passed by, all ignoring him, stepping around him as though he were simply a piece of the very trash he collected.

Cat Man looked up and saw the woman lingering in the doorway long enough for him to see genuine concern and pity in her eyes before the door closed and the strum of blues resumed.

He gasped for breath, looking every which way for his kitten. Thankfully his cart was still right where he parked it. He thought for sure it would be gone. A couple of seconds later, the bar door opened back up and his trash bouquet was whipped directly into his face from an unseen hand.

Cat Man continued to look around for his kitten in a panic. She was too young to survive on her own. He regretted not giving her a name. All he could do was call out through his phlegm-coated voice: "Here kitty. Kitty, where are you? Where are you?!"

There was no response. He started to accept the reality that the kitten was probably gone. Overwhelmed, he began to cry; tears for his lost kitten; tears for *everything*.

Everything he lost.

Everything he would lose.

Everything he forgot.

And everything he would continue to forget.

"Dear God, please. Please find my kitten. That's all I ask. She needs me. And I need her. And if she's gone. please take my soul."

He thought once more about the vision. That burning house. He felt as though he knew that house. But where was it? Who lived there? For the life of him, he could not remember.

Cat Man had never prayed for the good Lord to take his life until that moment. Of course, he could never do it himself. So all he could do was to turn to God and beg. Cat Man wasn't afraid of death, but he was quickly becoming afraid of *life* for the first time since . . . since . . . *when*?

He just couldn't recall.

And then he spotted something that made his jaw drop, lying alongside the curb. A dead kitten. Though he couldn't be certain, it was too much of a coincidence for it *not* to be his little girl.

As painful as it was, he mustered the strength to stand up and approach the lifeless body. As he approached the kitten, he closed his eyes, signed, then forced himself to look. He was certain it was her.

But then, catching him completely off guard, he felt something brush up against his leg. He looked down and was greeted by a soft, recognizable "mew." He scooped the kitten into his arms and hugged her tightly, before screaming at the top of his lungs.

"WHY CAN'T THEY LIKE ME?!!"

The kitten purred in response, as though letting him know that it was going to be okay. She reminded him that there was still good in the world; there were still friends to be made. Together, they would find them. He had already come close. Had it not been for that burly man, the woman at the bar would have been his friend. Now he would probably never see her again. And if he did, he would have to pretend not to notice her.

Cradling his kitten, Cat Man was overcome with sadness for the dead kitten lying dead in the street. Though it wasn't *his* kitten, it was *a* kitten. And there was nothing he could do to save the poor thing.

Cat Man began to look around and noticed his coins spread out around him. Realizing that he had work to do, he placed the kitten safely back into his coat pocket and began picking up his lost treasure. For the second time that evening, he was forced to pick up the pieces of his life, piece-by-piece, cough after breathless cough.

He headed over to a nearby curb to count his current savings: $2.05. Yes! He pumped his fist in jubilation and looked up toward heaven. Things were looking up. If given enough time, they always did—even during the darkest of times. Cat Man knew this more than anyone.

A gust of wind blew a piece of paper into his lap. He looked at it: it was another one of the pale man's pamphlets. As he glanced over it, he felt his soul surge with hope.

Filled with energy, he sprang from the curb, grabbed his cart and set out on his merry way. He whistled a merry tune like a child without a care in the world. He was alive and in that very moment, that's all that mattered.

He whistled as he ambled down Monroe Street with a singular focus, accompanied by the jingling of his change. His quickened his pace, due to his hunger and his desire to urinate. He knew that it was only a matter of minutes before he could satisfy both needs. He was surprised he hadn't peed himself during the altercation at Steve's Place.

By the time he reached Michigan Avenue, the only thing that kept him from dropping to his knees from fatigue was the adrenaline rush of knowing that he was so close to his destination. Each step moved him further away from the incident at Steve's Place.

Having a short memory made forgiveness that much easier.

One hundred yards ahead, the welcoming glow of Lafayette Coney Island awaited. As Cat Man passed by one of the diner's large windows, he froze in his tracks. Sitting in the window was the pale man who had almost hit him with his car. He appeared to be praying.

Cat Man quickly passed by the window and found himself in a quandary.

Stay or go?

As much as he would have preferred being nowhere near this man, his bladder and his hunger had already made up his mind for him. He would simply have to avoid the pale man.

Or, maybe the pale man needed a friend as much as he did? He certainly looked lonely.

Who didn't?

Maybe I shouldn't be so judgmental.

Emboldened by these thoughts, Cat Man abandoned his cart for the second time that night and entered the diner, as a light rain began to fall.

~Benedictus~

CAT MAN & THE ZEALOT

"How you doin' tonight?" Cat Man asked the waitress, who was working on a cross-stitch.

She greeted him with silent scorn. The Zealot looked up and shook his head in disgust.

"You got any money this time?" the waitress demanded.

"Yes, ma'am. I got money," Cat Man assured her. "If I didn't, I wouldn't come in here, just like you always tell me."

Cat Man revealed his coins. She had no valid reason for throwing him out. He knew it and she knew it. The waitress sighed, and headed over to the Zealot's booth as Cat Man hurried toward the stairs, which led down to a dungeonesque basement area.

Tucked beneath the stairs was a small closet that housed a single toilet and sink. It could barely fit a medium-sized human. Cat Man couldn't hold it in for another second. Had it been occupied, he might well have been out of luck. When he finally reached his destination, he uttered a tremendous sigh of relief as he *finally, finally*—was able to let it flow, and flow, and flow.

When he was done, he turned around to face the sink, without having to take a single step forward.

He washed his hands thoroughly, and splashed water on his face. He turned to dry his hands and face, but realized that the cloth towel drooping out of a dispenser was filthy. He settled for some toilet paper instead. The moisture caused the paper to disintegrate in his hands, leaving small chunks of tissue in his beard. It reminded him of snow.

Cat Man exited the restroom, now feeling like a brand new man. He labored up the steps and sat himself down at the counter in full view of the Zealot. Before he could catch his breath, he coughed up phlegm, drawing glares from the only two other people in the diner.

"So sorry about that," Cat Man said. "So, so sorry. But I'm okay now. I'm okay."

"What can I get you?"

"A hot cocoa, please, ma'am?"

"$1.95. Do you have $1.95?"

"Yes, ma'am!" Cat Man beamed with pride, as he poured his loose change onto the counter.

"Last time, you thought the same thing. But you fell a few cents short. Fool me once . . ."

"I promise you, ma'am, *this time*, I ain't gonna fool you. You can count it for yourself. There's even enough for a tip!"

Cat Man beamed as the waitress counted every last penny. There was enough. She had no choice but to serve him.

As he waited, Cat Man pulled out the pamphlet and began once again to read it with keen interest.

Behind the counter, the waitress topped Cat Man's hot cocoa off with whipped cream.

Across the restaurant, the Zealot took a sip of water and a bite out of his apple, as the waitress put the hot cocoa down in front of Cat Man.

"Thank you, ma'am!" Cat Man beamed.

He swept the money off the table and handed it to her.

"You can wait 'til you leave," the waitress said.

"I want to pay now. Can I pay you now?"

The waitress hesitated, sighed, then dragged the money off the counter and into the palm of her hand. Some battles simply weren't worth the fight.

"Oh, and . . ."

Cat Man offered her the dollar sign that had been rejected by the angry man. She took it.

"And keep the change," Cat Man said with pride.

"Thanks," she said with more than a hint of sarcasm and an eye roll as she walked way.

Cat Man suddenly had an idea and removed several napkins from the dispenser, which he folded into one of his signature roses. He walked over to the counter and handed it to her.

"For you . . ."

"Thank you. It's lovely," the waitress replied, this time flashing a genuine smile.

"You can put it in your shirt pocket," Cat Man said.

And so she did.

"Looks perfect!" Cat Man said.

As he lifted the cup of cocoa to his mouth, his kitten mewed.

Cat Man knew that the discovery of the kitten was a surefire way to get kicked out before he could even have his first sip. In his attempt to stifle the kitten's mews, Cat Man pretended to cough. This in turn triggered a real coughing fit. As he attempted to cover his mouth, he inadvertantly knocked the cup onto the floor.

He was devastated. An entire night's worth of work, gone in a split second, reduced to *nothing*.

He glanced over at the waitress, who initially seemed annoyed.

However, the tears on Cat Man's face soon coaxed her into sympathy.

"So, sorry, ma'am. If you can get me a mop, I will clean it."

And then, to his surprise, the waitress replied:

"Now, don't you worry. It's no trouble. And I'll make you another."

"But I gave you my last cent," Cat Man said, his eyes brimming with tears.

"On the house," the waitress said.

"Thank you, ma'am."

The waitress headed back to the counter to make another cup. She brought it over to him.

"God bless you, ma'am," Cat Man said, taking a sip.

The waitress chuckled.

"What's so funny?"

The waitress touched the tip of her nose, but Cat Man didn't understand.

"Your nose."

"What about my nose?"

"You got cream on it."

Cat Man took a napkin and wiped his nose.

"Sorry about that!"

The waitress laughed again. "You don't owe me an apology."

"Well, I can't take it back now," Cat Man replied.

He scooped up some whipped cream with a spoon, and, making sure that the waitress wasn't looking, snuck some to his kitten, who lapped it up eagerly.

After a couple more scoops of cream, Cat Man took a full sip. It burned his tongue. From that point on, he made sure to drink the rest with the spoon, blowing on each sip for safe measure.

Cat Man looked over at the Zealot, whose eyes were shut, his hands clasped in prayer. Cat Man knew what it was like to get so lost in prayer that everything else ceased to exist. He wished he could get to that point more often and continued to read through the pamphlet, hoping to draw attention from the man who represented his last shot at friendship for the night. Sure, there was always the waitress, but she didn't really count. She was paid to be nice to him.

The Zealot completed his prayer and looked up at Cat Man, who was still leafing through the pamphlet.

Cat Man stood up. The Zealot tried to return to meditation, but seemed too distracted and out of sorts. If prayer couldn't make Cat Man disappear, then hopefully ignoring him would.

Meanwhile, Cat Man was accustomed to people pretending not to notice. But this didn't stop him from heading over to the Zealot, cocoa in hand.

"How you doin' tonight?"

The Zealot ignored him.

"I saw you praying," Cat Man exclaimed in jubilation.

The Zealot closed his eyes and clasped his hands in prayer.

"I pray, too, sir. And look, I got your little book here," Cat Man said, waving the pamphlet in front of the Zealot's face.

The waitress approached. Her initial demeanor had now returned.

"Please don't bother my customers."

"I just wanna . . ."

The glare from the waitress was enough for him to realize she meant business. Cat Man retreated back to the counter and sat down, defeated. He watched his new friend take a bite of his apple, which he washed down with a sip of water before returning to prayer. Meanwhile, the Zealot struggled to feel anything resembling prayer or meditation of any sort.

While Cat Man continued sipping on his cocoa, an idea popped into his mind. He picked up the pamphlet and folded it into the shape of a perfectly-formed cross. When he was finished, he looked at it proudly.

Yes!

This was his greatest creation. Cat Man returned to the pale man and held the cross sculpture up in front of his face. If this wouldn't get him to pay attention, then he didn't know what would.

"I made this for you!" Cat Man exclaimed.

The Zealot opened his eyes and studied the cross.

"Do I need to call the police?" the waitress threatened.

"I don't mean to cause no trouble, ma'am."

"Well, you are. This is your final warning. I mean it."

Realizing he had little choice, Cat Man laid his cross sculpture down on the Zealot's table before returning to the counter.

"He isn't bothering me, ma'am," the Zealot said "He may talk to me if he'd like."

Cat Man smiled and stood up, then remembered the waitress's warning. He looked toward her for approval.

"May I help you?" she asked.

"May I please speak to my friend?"

"Whatever," she said, returning her focus to her cross-stitch.

"Thank you, ma'am! Thank you so much!"

He raced back over to the Zealot, unaware that he had spilled some of his cocoa on the floor—otherwise, he would have stopped to clean it up. He was simply too excited to realize what he was doing. The waitress shook her head.

Cat Man offered the Zealot a hand. It might as well have been a piece of rotten meat.

"So what are you doing?" Cat Man asked.

"Working in the service of God."

"Eating apples?"

"Cleansing."

"Like I was saying, sir, I pray, too. I pray all the time. And I like to clean, too."

The Zealot took a sip of water. Cat Man took a sip of cocoa.

"From the looks of it," Cat Man continued. "It doesn't look like I pray as much as you. I gotta work on that."

"Tell me, my friend. What do you pray for? More booze? Crack?"

"No, siree! I don't drink no booze. And I don't ask God for nothin' when I pray."

"Then what do you pray for?"

"I just *thank* Him for things."

"What can *you* possibly have to be thankful for?"

"My cats."

Cat Man showed the Zealot his kitten.

"You like cats?"

"I can't stand the filthy vermin."

"Well, I love them. Two things I know: God. And my cats. They're all I have. And all I remember."

As the Zealot glared at the kitten, Cat Man continued:

"Devil's Night is tonight. But I like to call it Angels' Night."

"As far as I'm concerned, every night in this town is Devil's Night. But I'm working to change that."

"Yeah? Cat Man asked, curious. "Like City Hall?"

"Let's just say, they have their ways and I have mine."

"All I know to do is pray."

"Not much else we can do."

Cat Man removed the Zealot's pamphlet.

"I appreciate your devotion to my work," the Zealot said.

"May I sit down?" Cat Man asked through a thick wheeze.

"Be my guest," the Zealot replied, much to his own surprise.

As Cat Man struggled to regain his breath, he began to cough. The Zealot shielded his face in disgust.

"I read the Bible every day," Cat Man said. "Do you?"

"Without hesitation," The Zealot replied. "Do you know any passages?"

"You mean, like parts?"

"Yes, *parts.*"

"I know my share." Cat Man took out another piece of paper from his pocket, on which was written some of his favorite passages—mostly from the New Testament. Once upon a time, he had them memorized.

"Recite one," the Zealot challenged him.

Cat Man searched through his list until he found one he wanted to share: "Blessed are you poor, for yours is the kingdom of God. Blessed are you who hunger, for you shall be filled. Blessed are you who weep now, for you shall laugh."

Impressed, the Zealot fired back from memory: "All we like sheep have gone astray; We have turned to his own way. And the Lord has laid on him the iniquity of us all."

Cat Man was impressed. He wished he had the ability to memorize words that way.

The two men volleyed back and forth:

Old Testament vs. New Testament.

Fire and brimstone vs. love and compassion.

Cat Man: *Judge not, and you shall not be judged. Condemn not, and you shall not be condemned. Forgive, and you will be forgiven.*

Zealot: *Adversaries of the Lord shall be broken in pieces. From Heaven, he will thunder against them. The Lord will judge the ends of the earth.*

Cat Man: *He that is without sin among you, let him first cast a stone.*

Zealot: *Thus saith the Lord God of Israel, Put every man his sword by his side, and go in and out from gate to gate throughout the camp and slay every man his brother, and every man his companion, and every man his neighbor.*

Cat Man: *Thou shalt not kill.*

Zealot: *Upon the wicked he shall rain snares, fire, and brimstone, and a horrible tempest: this shall be the portion of their cup.*

Cat Man: *Whoever is born of God does not commit sin; for His seed remains in him: and he cannot sin, because he is born of God.*

Zealot: *And that the whole land thereof is brimstone, and salt, and burning, that it is not sown, nor beareth, nor any grass groweth therein, like the overthrow of Sodom, and Gomorrah, Admah, and Zeboim, which the LORD overthrew in his anger, and in his wrath.*

Cat Man had one last passage left:
Love is patient, love is kind. It does not envy, it does not boast, it is not proud. It does not dishonor others, it is not self-seeking, it is not easily angered, it keeps no record of wrongs. Love does not delight in evil but rejoices with the truth. It always protects, always trusts, always hopes, always perseveres.

Zealot: *Behold, ye have sinned against the Lord: and be sure your sin will find you out.*

Cat Man: *Love never fails.*

Zealot: *And I will plead against him with pestilence and with blood, an overflowing rain, and great hailstones, fire, and brimstone.*

Cat Man: *When I was a child, I talked like a child, I thought like a child, I reasoned like a child. When I became a man, I put the ways of childhood behind me. For now we see only a reflection as in a mirror; then we shall see face to face. Now I know in part; then I shall know fully, even as I am fully known.*

Zealot: *But the fearful, and unbelieving, and the abominable, and murderers, and whoremongers, and sorcerers, and idolaters, and all liars, shall have their part in the lake which burneth with fire and brimstone: which is the second death.*

Cat Man: *And now these three remain: faith, hope and love. But the greatest of these is love.*

Cat Man took his last sip of cocoa and waited for a response.

But the Zealot did not respond.

Above all, Cat Man was overjoyed that he had found someone who seemed to love the Bible as much as he did.

Both men sat in silence until Cat Man reached into his pocket and removed a bunch of random photographs, including some from the angry man's lost wallet.

"Hey! I got pictures. You wanna see?"

Before the Zealot could formulate a response, Cat Man had scattered the pictures across the table.

"These folks look real nice, don't you think?"

The Zealot looked at them with feigned curiosity.

"Who are they?"

"I can't quite remember," Cat Man said, before pointing to one of the photos. "This one's my favorite."

The tattered photo featured a young, attractive mother, flanked by two smiling boys around five and eight.

"Is this your family?" the Zealot asked.

"I don't really know. I think it might be. Or, maybe it isn't. But I sure like to pretend it is."

"Where are they now?" the Zealot asked, as Cat Man looked off in the distance.

Cat Man shrugged and studied the photograph, as though the answer he was seeking was buried somewhere in there.

Perhaps it was.

"They're dead. Aren't they?"

Cat Man diverted his eyes to the floor and the Zealot was suddenly overcome with an unexpected rush of sympathy, before returning his gaze to the photo. Even though he had stared at it numerous times, he never quite felt what he felt now. The longer he gazed at it, the more everything seemed to come into focus.

Everything once gained. And everything now lost.

As tears streamed down Cat Man's face, the Zealot put a comforting hand on his arm.

"I can remember that it was Devil's Night. And the flames. I can't remember their names. The way they sound or anything. I can't remember anything I said to them. But I know they are gone, waitin' for me in heaven. They sure look like they're good people, don't they?"

The Zealot nodded as he saw and felt the pain of every victim projected onto the tormented face of Cat Man.

"I can see it in their eyes," Cat Man continued. "They are good people. I just wish I could remember more. And remember longer. I get to worrying. If I can't remember them now, how will I know them when I get there?"

"Because they still live in you," the Zealot said, gently tapping his heart.

"He will lead me to them if I get lost, right?"

The Zealot nodded, then both men sat in silence until the Zealot spoke up:

"I lost someone, too."

"Who?"

"She was the love of my life. We had been friends since kindergarten. *Best* friends. And then later, high school sweethearts. And by the end of our freshman year of college, we were engaged. A year after that, married. I became a preacher. She was an elementary school teacher at the same church. We devoted most of our free time to helping out the needy, bringing food to the homeless."

He took a deep breath, then continued. "After a couple of years, we decided to try for a family. But it didn't seem to be part of God's plan. At least, not yet. Nothing worked. Methods. Prayers. Nothing. Five years passed. And then the Devil intervened. One night, we were coming back from a meal delivery. A stranger approached. A carjacker. I handed over the keys, but he wanted more . . ."

The Zealot paused, then taking another deep breath, forced himself to continue.

"He stabbed us both. Multiple times. As we lay on the ground, I crawled over to her. We held hands, awaiting our salvation. We were ready. At least we would be together. But, somehow, I survived. I did not let go of her hand until paramedics arrived. I prayed that I would die before they could save me. But my prayer was not answered."

Cat Man sat in silence as the Zealot continued. "And that wasn't even the worst part. She was two months pregnant. It had taken us more than four years. I was broken. And I knew I would never be the same again. But then God spoke to me."

Cat Man listened intently, filled with compassion.

"I have never told *anyone* about this. I have never talked about it before."

The Zealot trembled, fighting back tears that had been dammed up for years. He put the heels of palms against his eyes, but it was no use. Tears dripped down onto the table. Like raindrops.

Cat Man put his hand on the Zealot's arm.

"What did He tell you?" Cat Man asked.

"That I was spared so I could carry out His mission."

"Which mission is that?"

"I thought I knew, but, well, now, I'm not so sure."

After a prolonged silence, the Zealot asked Cat Man, "What's your name?"

Cat Man struggled in search of his name, but nothing came to mind. As much as his inability to remember his name saddened him, it delighted him that somebody had cared enough to ask. He was used to being called plenty of names that weren't his. He often wondered if somebody actually called him by his actual name, would he recognize it?

"Your name?" the Zealot repeated.

"Well, I, err . . . I can't exactly remember."

Cat Man's eyes welled with tears.

"You can't remember your own name?"

"I forget so many things."

"I'm sure it will come back to you."

"Only God knows."

Cat Man stared into the bottom of his empty mug, as though by some divine miracle, his name would appear there.

The two men once again sat in silence until Cat Man spoke up.

"Well, it's getting late. And I'm pretty tired."

"Go in peace and serve the Lord," the Zealot said.

"It's all I can do," Cat Man replied.

"All any of us can do," the Zealot said. This time, he offered his own hand.

Cat Man shook it and both men looked at each other square in the eyes.

"Thank you for being my friend," Cat Man said, not letting go of the Zealot's hand.

"Thank you. Thank you for listening," the Zealot said, before pulling his hand away.

Cat Man headed toward the door, then stopped to face the waitress.

"You have yourself a good night, ma'am!"

"You, too!" she replied, without looking up from her cross-stitch.

And then he was gone.

"God have mercy on his soul," the Zealot muttered as he watched Cat Man through the rain-splattered window. "And on mine."

Once outside, Cat Man glanced around frantically in the rain.

"It's gone! It's gone! It's gone!"

His cart was gone. Stolen.

He always knew there was a chance this could happen, but he always erred on the side of humanity. He wanted to believe more than anything that the world consisted of more good than bad. Though he didn't regret his decision to abandon his cart, he just wished he had been more careful. He knew he could find another one and that there would be no shortage of trash to replenish it with. But it hurt and angered him.

Perhaps the wind blew it away into a hidden corner?

He knew he wouldn't be so lucky.

He glanced across the road and saw his cart, being pushed by another nomad who was already close to the end of the block and about to turn the corner.

Meanwhile, the Zealot connected the dots and realized why Cat Man was shouting.

He darted out the door, unaware that he was dragging the dollar sign trash sculpture with him.

"My cart!" Cat Man exclaimed, pointing across the street.

Now was not the time to turn the other cheek. Nor, was it about greed. That cart was his *only* possession.

"Hey!" Cat Man screamed out. "That's mine! That's my cart!"

The thief quickened his pace.

Cat Man tried to keep up—his wheezy breath in synchronized unison with the cart's squeaky wheels until he keeled over coughing as the cart disappeared around the corner.

The Zealot darted after the thief.

A scream rang out into the night, followed, a few seconds later by a recognizable squeak. The Zealot appeared from around the corner, pushing Cat Man's cart.

"I believe this is yours," the Zealot said, rolling the cart over to Cat Man.

"Thank you, my dear friend! You are an angel."

"Hardly."

"You have yourself a good night!"

"You, too, my friend. You, too. May God bless your soul."

Cat Man held out his hand once again.

This time, the Zealot embraced him.

And with that, they parted.

THE ZEALOT: REQUIEM

After helping my new comrade in CHRIST,
I head back inside, finish my meager rations, and pay.
It is time to head home, to rest.
My judgment is so clouded, I no longer know myself.
Yet, there is so much clarity.
I can't help but feel like I'm finally headed in the right direction,
after going the wrong way down a one-way street for so long.
A dead end street.

And then I notice ... my car is gone.
Stolen from right under my nose.
The price I pay for my bleeding heart.
I consider calling the police, but am wise to avoid them.

I spot movement kitty-corner from me.
A hooker?
But I'm wrong.
It's *her*.
The one I left to perish.
Back from the dead.
Is she haunting me now, too?

She doesn't see me.
Now there is nothing I want more than to save her.
Like the man with the kitten.

But why now?
Why tonight?
Am I ill?
Have I lost my way?
Or, do I see the light?

I want to apologize.
I motion toward her.
She freezes, then stumbles out into the road.
Limping.
I see it coming before she does.
Does she have a death wish?
The only explanation.
The SUV slams into her, sending her flying into the air.
An angel without wings.
She lands with a heavy thud of broken bones onto broken concrete.
The SUV drives off as though nothing happened.
When *everything* happened.

Judgment awaits us all.

I rush to her aid.
She is motionless.
Maybe it's not too late?
Maybe she can still be saved?
She is motionless.

Like watching my *beloved* die all over again.

Her eyes are open.
But she is already gone.
I check her pulse.
She is with the angels now.
Awash in a serene calm.

I gently close her eyelids.
And pray for her soul.

"Thou wast slain, and has redeemed us to God by thy blood.

Come to me, all you who labor and are heavy laden, and
I will give you rest. Take My yoke upon you and learn
from Me, for I am gentle and lowly in heart, and you will
find rest for your souls."

I cannot leave her in the road.

Across the street is an abandoned church.
I cradle her in my arms and lift her light, lifeless body into my arms.
Like the sleeping child I never got to hold.
I set her gently down at the top of the crumbling steps
in front of the boarded-up entrance.
I fold her bloody hands over her bloodied clothes.
A body in repose.

Tears fall down my face, and suddenly,
through blurred vision,
I see two angels standing before me,
newborns cradled to their bosoms.

Sirens loom in the distance.
The image fades.
I must go.

I look at her one last time.
Something sticks out of her pocket.
A paper rose.
Could it have been made by my friend?
I place it gently into her clasped hands.
I head to a nearby station.

The station is empty.
I glance over toward the church and see the angel's body
lying on the church steps one last time.

"The young and the old lie on the ground in the streets: my virgins
and my young men are fallen by the sword; thou hast slain them
in the day of thine anger; thou hast killed, and not pitied."

The train arrives.
I enter and sit in the back.
I can still see her.
Now fading away into a mere speck as
the train rounds the corner.

I sit in silence.
Close my eyes.
And pray for her soul.
For my soul.
For the souls of this entire city.
Forgive HER.
Forgive me.
Forgive *them*.
Forgive *us*.

Remorse consumes my soul.
I open my eyes to escape from the darkness,
and gaze out of the window.
See the flames.
Smell the flames, started by my own hand.
Regret that can't be extinguished.

I begin to pray:

*"O my God, I am heartily sorry for having offended Thee, and I detest
all my sins because of Thy just punishments, but most of all because
they offend thee, my God, who art all good and deserving of all my love.
I firmly resolve with help of Thy grace, to sin no more and to avoid
near occasions of sin."*

The train pulls into the next station.
I open my eyes.
I am no longer alone.
A recognizable face.
The junkie who attempted to mug me
outside the church.
He doesn't sit down.

We make eye contact.
Recognition.
He appears nervous, agitated.
I don't want to judge, but he makes *me* nervous.
Still standing, he almost topples over when the train moves.
Why doesn't he sit down?
I remove my — *his* — switchblade from my pocket.
Before I know it, he's upon me.
We wrestle.
A fair fight.
But now the switchblade is back in his posession.
Cold pain pierces through my stomach.
And then again. And again.
And then my chest.
I am on the floor.
The assault continues, but I don't resist.
Each thrust gives me a glimpse of my *angel*.
Only this time, she is not bloody.
She is pure again.
And I'm ready to join her.
I thank my assailant as he rifles through my pockets.
The three pieces of broken crucifix fall out.
He rips up my pamphlets.
Tears apart the cross sculpture.
Takes my wallet.

At the next stop, he is gone.
Returning into the dark.

Everything slows down.
Even the raindrops on the windows.
I spread my arms out.
I struggle to breathe.
Choking on my own blood, as I await new life.
I am ready to go home, to, once again, embrace my beloved,
the only thing that ever really mattered.

If GOD can forgive me.
Forgive me.
Forgive me.
Forgive me.

I close my eyes.
Instead of black, I see only light.
And my angel waiting for me
upon the altar of our holy matrimony.

Soaring on wings singed with sin,
I am surrounded by the glory of eternal light.

I am free.
We are free.
I am at peace.
I am at peace.
I am at peace.
I am love.
Light.
Confutatis.
Domine Jesu.

Amen.

~Lacrimosa~

CAT MAN: REQUIEM

Relieved to have his cart back—but, more importantly, elated to have finally made a true friend—Cat Man watched the pale man retreat back to the diner. Though sad to see him go, he was certain that he would see his friend again soon.

Content with how his night turned out, he pointed his cart east, toward home. It was late and he was tired. Tomorrow was another day and the promise of making even more friends gave him the energy he needed to make his way back.

He traversed one empty block after another in a steady rain, high on life. He replayed his conversation with the pale man over and over in his mind, cherishing the memory, but painfully aware of the fact it would only be a matter of time before it faded away into the great abyss of his mind.

He was most impressed by his friend's knowledge of the Bible. He never would have guessed that they had so much in common. And although they disagreed on many things, Cat Man took solace in the notion that their disagreements were stemming from the same source. And that counted for something.

He continued his journey home, completely lost in thought. He reached the outskirts of downtown, surprised that he had already made it this far. However, every step now seemed to become a greater struggle, measured with endless, excruciating bouts of coughing that grew in length and frequency. He felt something wet on his hand.

Blood.

He coughed again.

More blood.

He walked alongside the same train tracks as he had when his night first began, once again comforted by their predictable, linear order.

The rain suddenly ceased. He gazed up to the sky. A full moon was making an appearance from behind the clouds, lighting his way one step at a time, reflecting on the puddles surrounding him.

As he made his way under the full moon, the rain returned. His labored breathing and coughing was now becoming almost too much to bear. He began to wonder if he even had the stamina to make it all the way home. He trudged onward, despite every ache and pain in his body.

He finally stumbled into the Heidelberg Project.

Home sweet home.

He parked his overflowing, mangled cart alongside his makeshift tent, barely managing to crawl inside. His cats eagerly greeted him with soft purrs, rubbing against his legs like children greeting their father at the door.

Cat Man removed the kitten from his pocket and placed her in front of her eager mother. The kitten nuzzled against Cat Man's leg for a moment, before she began to nurse.

""Don't you worry, mama. She was a good little girl tonight," Cat Man told his kitten's mother.

His cats climbed all over him, purring with affections, as he proceeded to tell them everything he could remember about his night while he still remembered: his *almost* friends, his hot cocoa, and especially all about the pale man who loved the Bible.

As they shared his adventures, he began to transform his found trash into a higher purpose. Each piece represented a different, abstract scene from his evening. They would serve as reminders once his actual memories had dissolved into oblivion. Just maybe, they would help spark a memory—if only a partial one. He placed each piece into its rightful place in the space surrounding his tent and adjusted each piece's position just so. He took a step back to admire his work.

Loud explosions boomed and echoed in the distance, illuminating the darkness.

Cat Man cowered behind a disfigured mannequin; a friend he often imagined watching over him as he slept.

More explosions of color.

He coughed. Streaks of blood burst out of him like fireworks, coating his arm and jacket.

Cat Man looked up to see a sky aglow with fireworks and his fear morphed into childlike joy. His artwork was aglow with a majestic beauty he had never seen before, illuminated by a world on fire. He wished more than anything that he could share this moment with his new friend.

Once the fireworks were done, Cat Man reflected on how blessed he felt for the life he had been given. Sure, others may have had it better than him in many ways, but he couldn't have felt more content with his life.

He nestled himself beneath his blankets and curled up into a ball. His cats congregated around him as he drifted off to sleep.

Minutes later, he was jolted awake by a sudden, vivid memory:

Christmas morning.

Cat Man is sitting with his wife and young daughter around a brightly-lit, fully decorated Christmas tree. He's still in his work clothes, just home from the midnight shift at the stamping plant. He surveys the pile of presents under the tree that his labor made possible, all wrapped in colorful paper. He smiles at his wife, as they eagerly watch a young girl open up a box. Inside the box is a tiny kitten, which lets out a little mew.

The girl runs over to Cat Man and gives him the biggest hug he has ever received in his life.

"Daddy! Daddy!" the girl squeals in delight. "You remembered!"

A smile lights up her face.

"Thank you! Thank you so much! I love it!"

She reaches for something beneath the tree.

"Here, Daddy! I made this for you!"

A red and white origami heart.

He gave his daughter an enormous hug, barely able to hold back tears of joy.

It was the happiest moment of his life.

Holding tight onto this memory, Cat Man drifted off into a deep and contented sleep, as he entered the very void where his memories are locked away.

They were finally his. Forever.

Even in death, a warm smile covered Cat Man's face.

The last light in the city.

~Sanctus~

On the other side of town, the prescription slip-turned dollar sign sculpture tumbles past the immaculate yard and broken mailbox of Mrs. Harris, who has passed away, peacefully, in her arm chair. Static blares from the TV. A framed photo of NYC Girl watches from above.

The prescription continues to drift past the only other inhabited house on the block where a woman watches the dancing paper from her front window. It reminds her of a little girl who used to dance there once upon a time. A cockroach runs across the floor, before disappearing beneath a floorboard in the deepest recess of the room.

Across town at the Wayne County Medical Examiner building, a medical examiner's assistant closes up five body bags, each containing an unidentified body.

One by one, they are placed into cold storage.

Waiting to be claimed . . .

. . . but too late to make any difference.

Waiting.

Waiting.

Waiting.

~Agnus Dei~

November 1, 1999
All Saints' Day

Wayne County Medical Examiner's Office: Detroit, MI

Jane Doe: "NYC Girl." A badly bruised and bloodied female. Late-20's. Pregnant. "I Love NYC" medallion. Severe head trauma. Multiple fractures. Laceration on left hand.

John Doe #1: "Leaf Man." Bloated. Mid-20's male with a gunshot wound to the chest. Marijuana leaf ring on right ring finger.

John Doe #2: "R.I.P." Late-30's male. Obese. Barely decipherable "R.I.P." tattoo etched on left bicep.

John Doe #3: "Zealot." A mid-40's male. Thin. Pale. Multiple stab wounds to the chest. A cross-shaped scar across his torso.

John Doe #4: "Cat Man." Late-50's male. Scraggly, peppered beard. No obvious sign of physical trauma. Smile etched onto face.

~Lux Aeterna~

"Speramus Meliora: Resurget Cineribus."
"We Hope for Better Days: It Shall Rise from Its Ashes"

— City of Detroit motto, created after a fire destroyed
most of the city on June 11, 1805.

R.J. FOX is the author of "Love & Vodka: My Surreal Adventures in Ukraine," published by Fish Out of Water Books in 2015. He is also an award-winning writer of short stories, plays, poems, and screenplays. Two of his screenplays have been optioned and his work has been published in numerous journals and magazines.

Fox is the writer/director/editor of several award-winning short films. His stage directing debut led to an Audience Choice Award at the Canton One-Acts Festival in Canton, MI. Fox graduated from the University of Michigan with a B.A. in English and a minor in Communications and received a Masters of Arts in Teaching from Wayne State University in Detroit, MI.

In addition to moonlighting as a writer, independent filmmaker and saxophonist, Fox teaches English and video production in the Ann Arbor Public Schools, where he uses his own dreams of writing and film making to inspire his students to follow their own dreams. He has also worked in public relations at Ford Motor Company and as a newspaper reporter.

He resides in Ann Arbor, MI.

Visit http://www.foxplots.com or follow him on Twitter @foxwriter7.

Acknowledgments

It all started with an article I came across in the *Detroit Free Press* in 1999 by Patricia Montemurri. I wish we lived in a world where this type of story was only fiction.

Also, this book wouldn't exist without my original writing partners Joshua St. John and Louis P. Kerman. It all began with you guys, but in screenplay form. The movie *will* happen.

Thank you to Jon and Laurie Wilson of Fish Out of Water Books who took a chance on me with my first book. And now a second. You are dream makers.

Thanks to my editor Alice Peck who took my book to where it had to go.

And to Anne Gautreau . . . every word I write is because of you. Thank you once again for believing in me—before I believed in myself. You inspire my teaching as much as my writing.

Special thanks to my parents, siblings, my Godmother Jo-Jo, Aleesa Aronoff, Tiffany Borrebard, Herb Boyd, Mike Clark, Valerie Culip, Dominic Daniel, Sean Deason, Karen Dybis, Alison Eberts, Aaron Foley, Kelly Fordon, Heidi Greggo, Stephen Holowicki, Jennifer Hopson, Keith Jefferies, Scott Lasser, M. L. Liebler, Frank Morelli, Susan Murphy (Pages Bookshop), Camille Pagán, Michelle Ratering, John G. Rodwan, Jr., Kara Roquemore, Robin Runyan, Ann Marie Rydesky, Miriam Silverstein, Ian Thorton, Carrie Treece, Kenyatta Tucker, Lori Tucker-Sullivan, Lauren Warren, and Marni Webb.

Additional thanks to my late-night muses: Starbucks, Sweetwaters, Corner Brewery, The Ravens Club, 327 Braun Ct., The Habitat Lounge, and Cultivate Coffee & Tap House.

Last, but not least, thank you to Ellen, Lillian, and Bobby for reminding me that there is way more to life than writing.

CPSIA information can be obtained
at www.ICGtesting.com
Printed in the USA
BVHW03s0921110518
515915BV00014B/57/P